# ANTIETAM ASSASSINS

# ANTIETAM ASSASSINS

## Michael Kilian

This first world edition published in Great Britain 2005 by
SEVERN HOUSE PUBLISHERS LTD of
9–15 High Street, Sutton, Surrey SM1 1DF.
This first world edition published in the USA 2005 by
SEVERN HOUSE PUBLISHERS INC of
595 Madison Avenue, New York, N.Y. 10022.

British Library Cataloguing in Publication Data

Kilian,  Michael,  1939 -
     Antietam assassins  :  an American Civil War novel
     1.   Raines, Harrison  (Fictitious character) - Fiction
     2.   Antietam,  Battle of, Md., 1862 - Fiction
     3.   Murder - Investigation - Virginia - Fiction
     4.   United States - History - Civil War, 1861-1865 - Fiction
     5.   Detective and mystery stories
     I.   Title
     813.5'4 [F]

     ISBN-10 :  0-7278-6272-3  (cased)
                     0-7278-9150-2  (paper)

Typeset by Palimpsest Book Production Ltd.,
Polmont, Stirlingshire, Scotland.
Printed and bound in Great Britain by
MPG Books Ltd., Bodmin, Cornwall.

*For my ancestors,*
*William and Oliver Showers,*
*who were there.*

# One

It was August of 1862, and Harrison Raines had decided that, for him, the war between the states was over. He had spent much of his Federal service in the West and was now heading straight for home as fast as the Baltimore and Ohio Railroad could take him, his spirits uplifted by the familiarity and beauty of the Appalachian Mountains they were now at long last passing through after endless miles of flat, hot plains.

He had grown up on a plantation on the James River down in the Tidewater region of Virginia and had lived as a young man in Richmond and Washington City. But home now was a horse farm he had inherited from his mother on the Potomac River near Shepherdstown in Virginia's mountainous western counties and he was more than content to have it so.

The railroad train he and his companions were riding was bound for Baltimore and Washington, but it stopped near Shepherdstown beforehand. They had just come through the hot springs town of Spa, where George Washington had frequently taken the waters, and would be at Shepherdstown within two hours—Confederate raiders permitting.

Not yet thirty, Harry was a fellow of agreeable countenance. He wore his sandy hair long and sported a cavalier's moustache, though women tended to find him more amiable than dashing. Near of sight, he was too vain to wear his spectacles in their company. Skilled with horses, like his hero, General Washington, he was also an excellent shot—when he was wearing his eyeglasses and could see his target. Before the war, Harry had supported himself for a time as a horse trader and gambler. He would settle now just to be a simple farmer.

1

He hoped never to raise a firearm against a fellow human being again.

Shepherdstown had long been divided on the question of slavery but most of the mountain counties were opposed to it and in favor of Abraham Lincoln and union. This was one of the more compelling reasons he now considered the farm home.

Harry despised slavery, though he was the son of a wealthy planter who now commanded a Rebel cavalry regiment in General James Longstreet's corps. He had broken with his father over the issue. His belief that Lincoln was unreservedly committed to abolition had prompted Harry to serve the Union cause—not in uniform, but as an army "scout" in the employ of the famous detective Allan Pinkerton, now Lincoln's chief spymaster.

In his year and four months of service, Harry had survived the battles of Bull Run and Ball's Bluff, undertaken an espionage mission to Richmond, and been involved in bloody engagements in New Mexico, Tennessee, and Mississippi.

He'd been wounded, several times jailed, and barely escaped a hangman's noose. He'd killed people—among them, inadvertently, a woman. He had had enough.

There were several thousand dollars in his saddle bags that he was obliged to return to Mister Pinkerton. Along with that sum, he would submit his resignation.

He was traveling home with two improbable companions—a half-breed Canadian Metis Indian who was wanted for murder in British Columbia, and a beautiful but maimed Louisiana-born actress who was likely a Confederate spy but made a point of working for both sides.

He had encountered the Metis in the New Mexico desert, when the half-breed—who went by the name Jacques Tantou—had saved his life by killing three Apache renegades hot after taking it. A scout for the Union Army as well, Tantou had decided to decamp with Harry when word of the Canadian murder warrant with his name on it reached the Federal command in Santa Fe.

Long-haired, the Metis still dressed as though in the West—

yellow leather jacket, homespun shirt, Mexican belt, cavalry trooper's trousers, soft brown leather boots, and wide-brimmed hat. He carried a Bowie knife, a .44 caliber dragoon pistol, and a long Buffalo rifle, which he'd placed under the seat.

Tantou did not like trains—they occasioned the only sign of fear Harry had ever noted in the man. Taller even than Harry's six feet, he sat very stiffly in the seat opposite Harry, flinching at every lurch of the passenger car or belch of spark-laden smoke from the locomotive blowing by the open window.

Seated next to Harry, using his shoulder for a pillow as she attempted sleep, Louise Devereux was still recovering from two wounds she had suffered when caught in the midst of fighting at Corinth, Mississippi, that spring. She had had a finger shot off and had taken a round through the side that had nearly killed her, as wounds of that seriousness had killed so many men in uniform.

Harry had known Louise before the war when she was performing Shakespeare on stages in Washington, Baltimore, and, earlier, Richmond. She had occasionally been his lover, though that was perhaps an exaggerated term for a woman who had enjoyed the company of a wide variety of gentlemen, including generals in both armies and a number of Washington politicians.

Sleep eluded her. She opened her eyes and sat straighter. "How long before we're there?" she asked.

Harry looked to the window. The Baltimore and Ohio ran straight but, with the numerous loops and turns of the Potomac, crossed in and out of Maryland and Virginia several times. They were crossing the river again, near a long lake that reached to the approaches of Fort Frederick, Maryland. It had served as a fortress in the French and Indian and Revolutionary Wars and now housed Confederate prisoners of war.

"Not long. A little more than an hour."

"I shall be so grateful to arrive. I hurt most everywhere."

He lifted her gloved hand and kissed it, only to have her pull it away. He had taken the hand missing the central digit—cotton wadded into the finger of the glove doing in its stead.

3

"Sorry."

She said nothing, and closed her eyes again.

Tantou said something in French. Louise replied in the same tongue. They conversed briefly, back and forth—Harry's name spoken in the flow of foreign words. Like many a wealthy planter's son, Harry was ill-educated in some respects, and this was one of them. It irritated him a little that they could have these exchanges without including him. He realized he must be falling in love with Louise.

But that had happened before.

The train chuffed into Martinsburg in late afternoon. Amazed to find a trap for hire during a war that was devouring vehicles and horseflesh at a Biblical rate, he quickly secured it, helping Louise aboard. Tantou leapt onto the rear. The driver was a young man Harry only vaguely recognized—the son of German immigrants from across the river named Lemuel Krause.

"I'm Harry Raines," Harry said. "I own a horse farm in Shepherdstown, two miles up the river road. Do you know it?"

"Yessir." He was an inordinately handsome fellow, with hair as blond as Harry's sister.

"Well, that's where we're going."

Lemuel cracked the reins. "Yessir."

They proceeded the eight miles to Shepherdstown, then turned upriver, the horse plodding up the long hill.

"Is this trap always available at the depot?"

"Don't know, Mister Raines. It belongs to Mister Harding. I just work for him sometimes."

John Harding was probably the richest man in Shepherdstown.

"Were you waiting for someone?"

"Guess I was waiting for you."

Harry didn't quite fathom that, and said nothing. He put his arm around Louise, steadying her against what he knew would be a bumpy if not overlong ride.

"Is everything all right in town?" Harry asked.

"Nossir."

4

"Why not?"
"The war, Mister Raines."

As the trap turned up the lane that led to his farmhouse, Harry at once decided he would postpone his confrontation with Pinkerton in Washington, some seventy-five miles down the Potomac, and linger in this happiest of places a few days longer than he had intended. And then, after dealing with Pinkerton, he'd waste no time returning.

His actress friend's disposition toward his plans was hard to tell. There was no predicting anything about Louise Devereux, who'd been born an aristocrat much given to her own way. On the journey here from the West, she had repeatedly expressed an ardent desire to visit the Federal City again. But for all he knew, she might decamp to Richmond.

He yearned for her to take refuge here with him. She ought by now to have wearied of her dangerous wartime adventures. For the moment, he doubted she was up to a single evening of performing Shakespeare.

Harry was equally unsure about his friend Tantou, who was still worried about the warrant that had been issued for his arrest, now that it had gained currency in the Federal army. Harry seriously doubted any such document would ever reach the Eastern Theater of the war. In the odd event it did, Harry had dozens of places in which to hide the Metis, including most especially the Killiansburg Caves directly across the Potomac from his farm.

There were five Africans on Harry's place, all free. Four of them—a groom, two field hands, and his housekeeper, Estelle—were paid good wages. The fifth, named Caesar Augustus, was Harry's partner in his horse business. He had grown up on Harry's father's plantation as one of more than a hundred slaves held in bondage there. Because Caesar Augustus had been Harry's constant companion and best friend in childhood, Harry's father had made a present of him to Harry on his twenty-first birthday. Harry had promptly taken his friend to Richmond and filled out manumission papers, setting him free. Harry's rupture with his father had stemmed from that moment.

It had been many months since Harry had last seen Caesar Augustus and he looked forward to a reunion now. Estelle was by way of being the black man's common law wife and Harry presumed he'd been content to abide here with her.

Harry's house was large, and sat upon a rise high enough to catch whatever breeze came along the Potomac Valley and provide him with a view of a turn of the river from his long front porch. As the trap came up the lane, several people gathered on the porch; among them a little girl.

Her name was Evangeline. She was the daughter of Arabella Mills, a childhood sweetheart of Harry's in Richmond who had committed suicide in a moment of despairing madness, as much a victim of the war as any fallen soldier. Arabella's husband, an old rival of Harry's, had abandoned the girl in the belief that Evangeline had been illegitimately fathered by Caesar Augustus. The girl had a dusky hue, but blue eyes and copper-colored hair.

For his part, Caesar Augustus had protested to Harry that he was incapable of fathering children, and had argued that Harry himself might be a more likely candidate, for he had lain with Arabella before he had left Tidewater. As Caesar Augustus had rudely reminded him, Harry had a dark-skinned, part-Indian, witchy woman from the mountains among his great-grandmothers.

But Harry was of very fair coloration. His sister was blonde and had blue eyes, and very fair as well. Evangeline had the complexion of coffee and cream.

Harry had not pursued the matter further. He'd vowed to provide a home for the girl until she reached adulthood, and had left the question of her fatherhood a mystery.

She ran down the steps of his long front porch to greet him. He'd expected that, in his long absence, she would have forgotten him. He had not known her long. Perhaps it was just the excitement of their return.

He lifted her up, holding her at face level.

"Mister Raines, you have come home," she said.

6

"Yes, I have."

"Are you going away again?"

"Not any time soon. I'm going to stay right here where it's peaceful and quiet."

"There was shooting. Down by the river. I was afraid."

"Maybe that will now stop."

Louise observed him with some amusement as he lowered Evangeline to the ground.

Caesar Augustus came down the porch steps hesitantly. "You're a long time getting back, Marse Harry."

"No 'Marse,' please, Caesar Augustus. Never again, and especially not here."

"I have done something without asking you."

Harry looked about the pasture. "You sold some stock. Quite a few."

"Yes, Marse Harry."

"Well, we agreed you were to run the place as you thought the best."

Caesar Augustus shrugged. "The Federal army took 'em. They paid fair money. But they took 'em. Had some Rebels nosing around what was left but I told them your father was a friend of General Lee's, and that they'd best leave your holdings unmolested."

"You would seem to have been persuasive."

"I told them I was your slave. I do not like to do that, Marse Harry."

"I know that. I thank you."

Louise had preceded them all going inside. She might have been a duchess entering her castle.

Soldiery from both sides of the war had heavily foraged all over this Potomac River country in recent weeks but they managed to dine excellently that night nevertheless, with a meal prepared by Estelle that included fried chicken, roast pork, fish from the river, yams, sweet corn, and two bottles of Harry's best wine.

Afterwards, they sat in his parlor—all of them—the men drinking whiskey and smoking cigars while Louise played his

7

spinet piano—as best she could given her infirmity. Her most serious injury still caused pain—and weakness—but she became quite animated by her effort and the music it produced.

Flush with whiskey, Harry became rapturous, especially when Louise played his favorite song, "Barbara Allen." He sat with Evangeline on his knee but his eyes fully upon Louise while she played, fixed on her dark hair, bare shoulders, and still incandescent beauty. He even put on his spectacles to enjoy her loveliness more fully.

She had become his Barbara Allen. Louise had the same wild, raven hair, fair skin, perfect features, flashing spirit, and slender grace of the girl he envisioned in the song. If life could be this way for the rest of his days he should count himself the luckiest man in America. He felt almost giddy in this new happiness—and the great freedom that would be his now that he had decided to part company with Pinkerton.

When Louise was finished, he set down Evangeline and went over to the actress, putting his arm around her shoulders and kissing the top of her head, a little intoxicated by the scent of her French perfume.

"I cannot tell you how much you have cheered my heart," he said.

She reached to touch his hand with her injured one, and then—to his stunned surprise—turned and pressed herself against him and burst into uncontrollable sobbing. It went on and on unendurably. He sat down on the bench beside her and held her tightly, but still her sobs and sorrow continued.

Harry looked to Caesar Augustus.

"It's the war, Marse Harry," the black man said. "She's not like you. She knows it ain't over. Not anywhere near."

Harry ignored this. When at last her misery showed signs of subsiding, he rose and fetched her a brandy. When she had drunk it, he escorted her to her bed chamber, then quickly returned.

"It will get better," he said, re-entering the parlor. "When she's recovered some, I'll take her on a picnic."

"I told you, Marse Harry," said Caesar Augustus. "There've been soldiers here."

"I'll go across the river into Maryland," Harry said. "I know a place. A beautiful place. A peaceful place."

"Where's that?"

"Up along Antietam Creek."

# Two

Harry had no buggy, trap, or carriage on the farm, but there was a serviceable wagon. It was not elegant nor very comfortable, but the distance was not far. He crossed the Potomac south of Shepherdstown at Packhorse Ford, and then proceeded the short two miles uphill on the Saw Mill Road and then down the following slope to Antietam Creek and his favored picnic place near an old stone bridge.

There were Union soldiers posted along the Chesapeake and Ohio Canal, but they let Harry and his pretty passenger pass without bother. The traffic between the two sides of the river was frequent, even in wartime.

Louise had finally recovered her spirits, but still appeared weak, the rigors of their long journey from the West lingering in their effect upon her. Swinging her down from the wagon, Harry took note of how disturbingly light she was, but was gladdened to see her smile again.

When he'd spread out the ground cloth—a Union Army blanket he'd brought back from Shiloh—she reclined upon it gently. "'True is it that we have seen better days,'" she recited, almost idly. She lay back, gazing at the sky. There were few clouds, and it was cooler.

"*The Tempest*," Harry said.

"*As You Like It*," she corrected. "Clod."

He had brought a book of verse to read to her from—Tennyson—but he left it in the wagon, preferring her face to the printed page. "Would you like some wine?" he asked.

"Thank you, no. Not just yet." A frown came over her face as a small cloud might pass across the sun. "You are certain it is safe here?"

10

Harry gestured at the peaceful setting. Birds were flitting in the trees. The sun was sparkling on the waters of the swift, wide creek. "I can think of no place safer—not in the Potomac Valley."

"Caesar Augustus said Confederate soldiers have been in these parts—that there was shooting."

"I talked to him after you retired for the evening. General Jackson was trying to cut the railroad and canal. But that was months ago. He moved on down to the Shenandoah Valley, and then joined up with General Lee outside Richmond. It's quiet here now."

"Those soldiers along the canal . . ."

"Our protection, ma'am. They're one of the reasons it's quiet."

"Very well. Come lie by me."

He did so, taking her hand and sharing her view of the sky. "Have I told you how happy I am to have you here?"

"I am happy to be here, and grateful to you, but I could be happier. I want to go to Washington with you. I was born a lady of New Orleans, Harry. I've lived in Richmond, Washington, Philadelphia, New York. Never on a farm."

"Give it some time."

Her left hand, which he held, was bare. Her right, absent the middle finger, was encased in a white glove. She held it before her eyes. "When do you intend to go see Allan Pinkerton?"

"Not as soon as he would like."

"Is that wise? You could be charged with desertion."

"We in Mister Pinkerton's organization are not under Army orders or regulations. But as I told you, I mean to resign. My reluctance to make the journey to the Federal City just now has to do with you. I fear for your safety there."

She sat up. "*Tu es fou.*" He possessed enough French to know she was calling him "crazy." He was flattered that she had used the familiar. But then, they had been very familiar.

"Louise, they may have let you go but you still stand accused of the murder of a Union officer. They had you in the Old Capitol Prison. It was only through the intercession

11

of President Lincoln that you were allowed to go to Richmond, where he has sent many of the Confederate ladies of Washington."

"Not all of them, sir. John Wilkes Booth's mistresses alone make for a sizable contingent."

"Please, Louise. Be sensible. Caesar Augustus told me that Colonel Lafayette Baker is now in charge of the War Department's intelligence service. He is the very worst man I know of in Washington. If he does not hang you or clap you in irons, he will ask things of you that would be horrible for a lady of your refinement to contemplate. I know this man. He had me locked up for a time. He's utterly ruthless and I think corrupt."

"I am not afraid. Not of him."

Harry raised himself on his elbow. "I'm not doubting your courage, Louise. Only your wisdom."

"I have survived thus far on my wits."

"With some losses. Please. Let us wait awhile."

"I have a pass from General Grant. He can vouch for me." She had in fact been a spy for the general.

"General Grant is in Tennessee. Colonel Baker is here."

She closed her eyes. "Harry, I mean to be back on the stage. It is my life."

He lay there quietly for several minutes. His bliss had fled as though into the stream. "All right, I will take you with me. Allow me a day or two longer. I have some further business to attend to here."

"I will go to Washington, Harry, with or without you—if I have to steal one of your horses."

He raised her to him and took her in his arms, pressing his cheek against hers. "You will not need to do that." She kissed him back—on the lips.

Then Louise sat back, her eyes seeking his as she recited yet again. "'Take, O take those lips away, that so sweetly were foresworn; and those eyes, the break of day, lights that do mislead the morn. But my kisses bring again, bring again, seals of love, but sealed in vain, sealed in vain.'"

He knew the play—*Measure for Measure*—but not her

12

meaning. Knowing not how to ask it, he reached for the wicker picnic basket, and the food Estelle had prepared.

They left by a different route, following the creek upstream past Snavely's Ford to a bumpy lane that led to Harper's Ferry Road. It went straight down a long slope to the canal, not far from the river crossing at Packhorse Ford. As they approached the steepest part of the grade, near a large, twisted tree that grew at an angle out over the road, Harry pulled back sharply on the team's reins and then the wagon's brake.

Hanging from a branch, twisting slowly, with head hanging over, was the body of a very large, handsome, bearded man, eyes bulging as he looked down at his own feet.

Harry knew him well.

# Three

Cautiously moving the team forward again, inching down the incline, Harry proceeded until he was nearly under the dead man. The deceased was dressed in a blue work shirt, overalls, and muddy boots, which struck Harry as extremely odd. Normally, he had gone about in frock coat and waistcoat, when not in his pastor's stock.

Louise had taken one look at the corpse, then turned away, shuddering, though she'd certainly seen enough dead men since the war had begun. Her attention now was fixed on Harry. "Are you ill?" she asked. "You look very strange."

"I know this man."

She kept her eyes averted from the body, though the man's boots were not three feet from her face.

"Who is he?" she asked.

"The minister of my mother's old church—a Presbyterian church in Shepherdstown." Harry watched as the body slowly twisted to face him. The rope was thick and the knot large, but the man might not have died from hanging. There was a knife in his chest, near the heart. Pinned beneath it was a large piece of paper, bearing just one word: "Lincolnite!"

"Harry?"

"I don't understand. This is the Reverend Ashby. He was a Douglas man. A Democrat. He opposed abolition. I've heard him speak out against Lincoln from the pulpit. Yet his killer sticks a note to his chest proclaiming him a Lincoln supporter."

"I do not feel well, Harry."

Harry moved the team and wagon a few feet further, then pulled on the brake again and handed the reins to Louise. "Keep the horses quiet, love. I'm going to cut him down."

14

He stepped up on the seat and reached for the rope, using the sheath knife he always kept in his boot. Ashby dropped into the wagon bed with a loud thump, his outflung arm upsetting the picnic basket. His eyes were wild and staring. His fate must have come upon him of a sudden.

"What are we to do?" she asked.

"We'll take him to the military down by the canal. Perhaps I can find an officer."

The nearest thing to that proved to be a sleepy young Federal lieutenant who'd headquartered himself in a barn overlooking Packhorse Ford. Bits of straw still sticking to his uniform when he emerged testified to his method of command.

He became very wide awake upon seeing the cargo in the back of Harry's wagon. "Where'd he come from?"

"We found him hanging from a tree on the Harper's Ferry Road. He's a minister, the Reverend Horace Ashby. Has a church in Shepherdstown."

The lieutenant's eyes lingered on Louise for a long moment, then returned to Harry. "What do you expect me to do with him?"

"You're the local military authority."

"No sir, I am not. I command a platoon of pickets on this section of the canal. You will be wanting the provost guard. There is an office in Sharpsburg."

This man would be of little help. "You have troops in Shepherdstown. Is there a provost guard there?"

"Don't know. Maybe."

"He's from there. I should take him back. I'll report to an officer there."

The lieutenant had brightened at the prospect of being so readily relieved of the matter, but remained uncertain. "Maybe I should take you to my captain."

Harry pointed to the church steeples visible above the trees up the Potomac. "There should be captains aplenty in Shepherdstown," he said. "It's just across the river. If we are to discover what happened to this man, the answer will be found there, not here."

The young officer twisted his mouth as he wrestled with his indecision. "Who are you?" he asked, finally.

"Harrison Grenville Raines. I have a horse farm upriver on the Virginia side."

"You're a Virginian."

"So is General Winfield Scott."

"Do you have a pass?" He looked to Louise as well.

Harry's was signed by "A. Lincoln;" Louise's by "Maj. Gen. U.S. Grant." Harry handed over them both.

The lieutenant studied them as though they might be rare gems. "These are genuine?"

"You asked for our passes, sir," Harry said. "Now you see them. If you find it necessary to question military passes, there is no point to having them."

More doubt.

"I will report first to the highest-ranking Union officer I can find in Shepherdstown," Harry said. "I shall report all that has transpired, including this interview."

At that, the lieutenant handed back their papers, then took one more look at the corpse. "If you found him hanging from a tree on the Harper's Ferry Road, then he must have been killed here in Maryland."

"That's a question still to be answered," Harry said. "Thank you, sir, for your courtesy." He snapped the horses' reins and they jolted forward.

They passed several Federal officers in Shepherdstown, but Harry continued past them, heading first for Doctor Ricketts' establishment halfway up the hill on German Street. The physician was on the premises, examining a farmer with an injured foot. Upon hearing whose remains lay in Harry's wagon, he abandoned his patient and accompanied Harry outside.

A crowd had already begun to gather. Ricketts asked two young men to carry the body inside, and then to stand at the entrance to prevent those out in the street from entering.

As the farmer was occupying Ricketts' examining table, they had put the Reverend on the parlor sofa. Ashby had long since stopped bleeding.

The doctor removed the knife and then pulled open the dead man's shirt, and began busily probing about the chest. Then he loosened the rope and examined the flesh of the neck. Finally, he rolled Ashby over, making a thorough study of his back. At length, the doctor returned the body to a more seemly position, folding the arms across the chest and closing the wild, staring eyes.

"The good Reverend is definitely dead," he said. Harry knew the doctor only slightly, but enough to be familiar with his mordant sense of humor.

"Yes, but how?" Harry asked. "And why?"

"The Reverend Ashby was killed by a gunshot," Ricketts said, standing back. "The ball is still in his back."

"But the rope, the . . ."

"The neck does not show what would be typical signs of strangulation. And there is only marginal bleeding about the knife wound. I would say that was an afterthought."

"It was a well considered thought. You note the message on that paper."

The doctor nodded. "Passing strange, as the bard would say. Ashby was a slavery man."

"He owned none," Harry said.

"No. He did not. But few do here—even the Secesh." The doctor returned to his examining room, beckoning to Harry to follow. Opening a cabinet, Ricketts took out a decanter of whiskey. "Would you have a dram, Captain Raines?"

"Captain?"

"Your services to the Republic as a 'scout' have been no great secret hereabouts, Harry. Isn't that right, Emil?"

The farmer, whose German family had been in the Shepherdstown area as long as Harry could remember, sat up on the table. "Ja. Good it would be to have more here like you."

The doctor poured three glasses and handed theirs to Harry and the farmer. They drank, to the Union.

"The war has come here," the doctor said. "Tempers are high, Harry."

"How high?"

17

"When General Jackson removed his force from here and the Federals came back in," Ricketts said, "the Singleton family got real stubborn. One of the boys—Samuel Singleton it was—fired shots at a Union patrol coming up the road."

"There was no reason for this," the farmer said. "Nichts."

"They shot the boy when he tried to run," the doctor continued. "I did what I could but there was no saving him. Under the general order, they had to fire the house. They dragged out the family, piled the furniture in the yard, and put torches to the place." He paused to pour the glasses full again. "But they didn't bother with the piano. Too heavy. They left it inside. The house was half ablaze when Peggy Singleton ran back in and started playing 'Dixie.' Playing it and singing it at the top of her young lungs. The burning ceiling damn near came down on her. Three Federal soldiers got bad burns getting her out of there before it collapsed. Can you imagine such defiance? Burning yourself to death to play a song?"

"A year ago I wouldn't have believed it," Harry said. "Now, nothing surprises me." He remembered Louise. "I should go."

"Have you informed the authorities of this?" Ricketts asked.

Harry shook his head. "I came straight here."

"I'll send for the sheriff in Charles Town—and let the Army know. Where will you be?"

"On my farm. For some time."

The crowd outside had grown larger, though there was nothing now for them to see. Louise sat stone-like on the seat of the wagon, enduring more than waiting, accumulating barely controled anger.

A few in the crowd recognized Harry.

"They killed Preacher Ashby?" said a woman.

"Was it the Yankees?" said a man.

"What happened?" said the woman.

"I don't know," Harry said. "I found him across the river. I brought him here. That's all I know."

He climbed onto the wagon seat, putting his arm around

18

Louise but finding her hard and unyielding. Before he could loosen the reins he felt a tug on his coat.

It was James O'Malley, the town blacksmith and a friend of Harry's for years.

"Stop by my place on your way out of town," he said. "I'll be along presently."

"Your shop is not on my way, James. It's on the way to Charles Town."

"Today it should be on your way."

"Very well." He flicked the reins. The team seemed as happy to get away as Louise.

"I'm sorry," Harry said to her. "I neglected you."

"What were you doing in there?" They were moving down German Street at a trot.

"I was discussing this lamentable occurrence with the doctor. He was a friend of my mother's."

"Did she not raise you to be a gentleman? It was most ungentlemanly of you to leave me out on the street. That rabble pestered me with questions."

"They're not all rabble. Some are friends and neighbors."

"I wish to leave. Is this the correct route?"

"Actually, it's a slight digression. As you heard, I am proceeding to the establishment owned by the man I was just talking to. He is a very good friend and a stalwart in the Union cause."

"So you mean to keep us in this town longer?" Her eyes were full of unhappiness.

"If you would indulge me, Louise, I would be most appreciative. Mister O'Malley is not a frivolous man. I believe he has something of import to tell me—about the Reverend."

"I do not wish to become involved in a murder. I have had enough of such dreadful matters, Harry. So have you."

"Only a few minutes. Nothing more."

"I will endure this if you will make me a promise. If not, I will run screaming through this town, accusing you of everything vile."

"A promise of what?"

"To take me to Washington tomorrow."

He turned the team onto the Charles Town Road. "Very well. I have no wish to make you unhappy, Louise."

"But you have so done. You truly have."

Harry pulled up the team to the side of O'Malley's yard. A curl of smoke was rising from the glowing forge. Stepping over a large, sleeping black dog, he entered the yard. A comely young lady was straightening the wood pile.

"I was to meet James here," he said.

"Not back yet."

"I see. May I wait?"

"Of course."

O'Malley came in at something of a rush. Taking Harry by the arm and tugging him away from the street.

"The woman in the wagon?" O'Malley asked.

"A friend. She's an actress. If you spent more time in Washington, you'd know of her."

"To be trusted?"

"Oh yes." Harry was more confident in uttering this statement than believing in it.

"They're saying there was a note pinned to the Reverend's chest with a knife. It proclaimed him a Lincolnite."

"Yes."

"Harry. It is true. He's been a great help to us. Passed on information about the Rebs. We moved on his word."

O'Malley was a conductor on the Underground Railroad. The cellar beneath this big room was used to house fugitive Negroes until a propitious moment arrived for a crossing of the Potomac.

"The Reverend Ashby helped you with escaped Negroes?"

"For six years now, Harry."

Harry sighed. "I must go," he said. "The lady."

"We cannot let this pass," O'Malley said.

"No."

"So what shall we do?"

"Let us think upon that."

# Four

They dined early at the house. To Harry's relief, Louise decided to retire immediately afterward, leaving him free to pursue his new problem. Saddling his favorite horse, Rocket, a large, powerful animal whom he had much missed, he set off on the road back to Shepherdstown in the last light of day. He hadn't progressed a mile when he heard a rapid clip of hoofbeats behind him. Pulling out his Navy Colt, he turned his horse quickly, then returned the weapon to his belt.

Jack Tantou was on a fine bay horse Harry had told the Metis he could borrow.

"Where are you going, Jack?"

"With you, Harry Raines."

"But you don't know where I'm going."

"Wherever it is, it will be of more interest than the walls of your house."

The sun was turning red in the haze above the western ridge of mountains. "I thought you wanted to come back East with me."

"I want to go back to Canada, but I cannot do that now. Until I can, I am very happy to be with you, but I am unused to sitting in houses doing nothing."

"I'm only going into Shepherdstown."

"You want to know more about this murder."

"I knew the man, Jack. He was a good man, I think. His manner of death is a puzzlement."

"Murders are more interesting than farms."

It was nearly dark when they came trotting down German Street. Harry stopped first at Doctor Ricketts' office. It was

21

closed but his house was nearby, only a block to the rear. The doctor came out onto the side porch before Harry could dismount and knock at the door. Ricketts had been in the midst of dinner and was holding a chicken leg.

"Saw you through the window," he said, taking another bite of the meat. "You like to join us?"

"No thank you," Harry said. "We've had our supper. Stopped by your office. Where's the Reverend?"

"His widow Martha came for him. Took him to the undertaker's. The sheriff won't be out until the morning. Maybe the afternoon. Don't know much more."

"This looks to be a lynching, Doctor. We can't allow that to take root here. There'll be gun fights in the streets."

"There are two companies of Federal troops here and more across the river to prevent that. Don't understand how this could have happened with so much soldiery under foot, but I don't think they'll let this get out of hand."

"I hope not. Remember Kansas."

"We're not about to become Kansas, Harrison. This is Union ground. There's talk the western counties of Virginia may form our own state—and soon."

More than thirty thousand men from the western counties had volunteered for Federal service in the war—an accounting in whose numbering he supposed he should count himself.

But more than twenty thousand had joined up with the Confederacy.

"I hope you're right. Doctor. Good night to you."

There was a saloon where the two main streets of the town intersected, just up from the river landing. In a different time, Harry would have taken Jack Tantou inside the establishment with little qualm. These were his neighbors. Most would respect his wishes. What he feared was the reaction of the Union soldiery, who had been keeping the local dramshops very busy. Except for his broad, flat cheekbones, Tantou had very French features. But his skin was dark, almost the color of teak.

There were many Union men fighting to free the slaves,

especially from New England. But the ranks of the Federal force included others who had volunteered only to keep the Union intact, not to liberate the black man. Many were as racialist as any on the Rebel side. If they took Tantou for something akin to black, there might be as much trouble here in civilized Shepherdstown as they'd encountered in the saloons and cantinas of unruly Texas.

Harry's main reason for joining Pinkerton's group was the hope of ending slavery. He might leave Pinkerton, but he wouldn't back away from the cause. "Come on, Jack. I'll buy you a whiskey."

There were only five soldiers in the establishment—all sergeants and corporals and all seated at the same corner table, playing cards. Harry went to the end of the bar furthest from them. Tantou followed warily, looking behind him before he stepped up beside his friend.

As Harry feared, the bartender motioned him aside. The heavy-bellied, baggy-eyed man's name was Hugo Klostermann—a good and often merry fellow, but a cautious one.

"Who's your friend, Harry?" he asked.

"His name is Jack Tantou. He's French Canadian, but he is presently a U.S. Army scout. We were out West together."

Klostermann lowered his voice to a whisper. "Is he colored?"

"No."

"Is he Indian?"

"Partly. So was President John Tyler. Pocahantas was one of his ancestors."

"Tyler was president. Your friend ain't."

"No, but he's my friend. Two whiskeys, please. If you have Old Overholt, I should like some."

"I don't." Klostermann glanced about the room. "But I've got whiskey." He poured two tumblers full, and then lingered. "You heard about Belle?"

Belle Boyd, who lived in Martinsburg, was Harry's distant cousin through another relative's marriage. She was also an incorrigible Confederate operative, lately in the service of

23

General Jackson. She had killed a Yankee sergeant the previous summer. The man had entered the house of her mother and had been abusive and Belle had gunned him down in the hallway—on the Fourth of July. She was absolved of that crime, but was later arrested and locked up in the Old Capitol Prison on espionage charges.

"She is not hurt? Not ill?"

"No, Harry. They let her go. 'Insufficient evidence.'"

Harry frowned. "Is she coming back here?" That would complicate his life here. Belle would be after Louise like a cat with a mouse.

"Don't think so. I heard she's heading for her aunt's in Front Royal—out of the way of the Federal army. But if Jackson comes back this way, I'm afraid she'll just start all over again."

"If she comes anywhere near here, would you let me know?"

"Sure that I will, Harry. Now you tell me something. Who do you think killed the Reverend Ashby?"

"Hugo, I came here to ask you that."

The bartender gave the matter a moment of thought. "Pretty near everybody liked him—aside from the politics."

"Politics seems to have been involved."

"Can't figure that. He was no Lincoln man."

"Maybe he was, but wasn't telling."

"Ain't many in this town hold back on speaking their mind. Especially him. He sermonized every day."

Tantou finished his whiskey. Harry did the same. Klostermann hesitated, then refilled their glasses after Harry gave him a hard look.

They sipped as what sounded like a troop of cavalry galloped by. Harry wondered at their urgency.

"You cut Ashby down from a tree?" Klostermann said. "He was a big man, the Reverend. Surely no woman hauled him up there."

"Woman? Why would you say that?"

The bartender leaned close. "If there was anything to put the good Reverend in the way of trouble, it would be the ladies."

"I never heard that."

24

"You aren't around here that much, Harry."

"I'm changing that."

When his mother was alive, and came here in the summer to avoid the heat of Tidewater, Harry recalled her spending part of almost every day in some sort of church work. "Which ladies?"

Klostermann shrugged again. "Don't know any names. But there's been gossip about him."

"You think his wife could be responsible for this? She's barely five feet tall."

"That's what I was saying, Harry. A woman like that couldn't have strung him up on that tree."

Tantou turned to face the door. A moment later, more horsemen came pounding down the street. Then came a man running. He flung open the door.

"Calamity! Calamity!" he shouted. He looked around the room. Two of the card playing soldiers were on their feet. "A disaster at Centreville! General Pope is defeated!"

The man came up to the bar, where Klostermann quickly poured him a whiskey. He drank it down in a gulp.

"John Pope?" Harry asked. The general had recently been placed in command of a large Union force in Northern Virginia, though General George McClellan, Harry's ostensible superior, still led the main Federal army headquartered in Washington.

"The wires are hot with the news," said the man, pushing forward his empty glass. "Pope got outfoxed by Jackson and General Lee, on the same ground where we was whupped last year."

"Bull Run?" Harry asked.

"Aye."

Harry had been there for the first battle. He remembered well the pell-mell flight of General Irwin McDowell's entire army—a rout that continued until the troops had crossed the Potomac and reached the muddy streets of Washington.

"Where's Pope's army now?"

"Don't know for sure. But it was at Centreville an hour ago. An orderly retreat, they say. Not like last time."

"And the railroad? It's still open?"

"Must be. The telegraph's still working."

Harry paid for the drinks. "Thank you, Hugo. I'd best be back to my farm."

Tantou was already going out the door.

He was surprised to find Louise awake, out of bed, fully dressed, and sitting on his front porch. As he drew nearer, he saw that she was smoking one of his small cigars and sipping brandy.

"I could not sleep," she said.

Tantou had taken the horses. Harry slumped wearily into the chair beside her. "There is terrible news. Pope's army was badly defeated outside Centreville. General Lee is free of Richmond and in the field in northern Virginia." He took her hand, fearing she would be fretful. "I think we will be safe here," he said. "Lee will be angling for Washington. Maybe cutting around behind it."

"Are the trains running?" she asked, removing her hand.

"I believe they are—for now."

"Good. I mean to be on one to Washington tomorrow."

"Louise. You can't. Not now."

"You have to go there. I will as well." She gestured to a carpet bag beside her that he had not noticed. "I have prepared for the journey. You'd best, too. I mean to be on the first train departing."

"I don't know when that will be."

"Then we'd best rise very early, for I do indeed intend to be on it."

# Five

There were Union pickets and cavalry patrols all along the railroad right of way until they reached Monocacy Junction south of Frederick, Maryland. The Federal presence was at once both reassuring and alarming. Whatever Lee had in mind to do, he'd not yet started doing it. Otherwise there'd be a greater sense of urgency with these idling fellows. But they were numerous along this line. The Union commanders were clearly worried.

They bumped and rattled southeastward in silence; the railway coach windows were open to relieve the heat but admitted dust and the occasional hot cinder. Louise was somber, almost sullen, sitting very close to Harry, but stiffly. He sensed she'd been making a summation of all that had happened to her in the year that had passed since she'd been run out of the Federal City. The ledger's balance, apparently, did not please her. He guessed she was bent on settling accounts more to her favor.

Tantou had insisted on coming along and sat just as stiffly upright on the opposite seat, facing Louise but staring at the passing countryside out the open window. He did not speak much, either, but then, he seldom did while riding on trains.

For his part, Harry passed much of the journey in quiet worry about how soon and even whether he might return to Shepherdstown. This fearsome doubt stuck to his mind like gum arabic.

Though he despised the cause in which General Lee had enlisted, Harry had long admired the man, who was a friend of his father's. Lee was decent and kind and the epitome of what people intended with the phrase "the Virginia chivalry"— a term sometimes applied to Harry himself with less occasion.

But now Harry was furious with the general—close to hatred—for his bringing the war into the northern and western counties again. Why could he not just sit and protect Richmond? The North had no general capable of prying him from that place. Harry's section of Virginia wanted no part of secession or confederacy. It was not fond of slavery and served no part of Richmond's cause. Lee had thrown his hand in with the South. He should stay here.

With sulfurous smoke spilling every which way, they chuffed into the Baltimore and Ohio Station on Washington's New Jersey Avenue in early afternoon—an hour late. As they stood outside the depot waiting on the wooden walkway for a trap to take them to the hotel, Tantou suddenly announced he was going off on his own.

"Going where, Jack?"

"To find work."

"Here?"

"Goodbye, Miss Devereux. Goodbye, Harry Raines. I will find you again soon." The tall Metis flung his saddlebag over his shoulder and walked off toward Pennsylvania Avenue.

"Do you know where you're going?" Harry called after.

"*Comme toujours*, Harry Raines."

Harry preferred Willard's, but Louise insisted on staying at the National Hotel. In Andrew Jackson's day, when it had been called Gadsby's, it had been a center of Democratic Party political life. Now it was abode of the Southerners and Southern sympathizers still resident in the capital. They were surprisingly many.

"You know that John Wilkes Booth keeps rooms there," Harry said, as their trap clattered across the low wooden bridge that carried Pennsylvania Avenue over a branch of Tiber Creek.

"I have no interest in him. Your concern in that regard should be for Caitlin Howard."

That marvelous English actress, proclaimed by the local newspapers as the finest Shakespearean heroine ever to appear

28

on the Washington stage, had for several years before the war been the love of Harry's life. But that was in an altogether different life. She had responded with a certain fondness for Harry, but she was besotted with Wilkes Booth, and had gone off the previous fall with him on a tour of theaters in the North.

Booth was addicted to the women who constantly threw themselves his way, but not individually. The only woman he truly loved was the nineteen-year-old sister of a brothel madam whose house of easy virtue was situated southwest of the President's House near the hellish neighborhood called Murder Bay. Caitlin, Harry suspected, was at times treated as little more than baggage. Still, she hung on.

No matter. In his sweep through the South, Harry's attentions had become fully taken up with Louise. In her time in Washington, the capital papers had declared her the most beautiful of Shakespearean actresses. And, like so many of the swaggering Washington swells, he had become madly infatuated with her.

Now she seemed a stranger. There had been so many rumors surrounding her—that she was in truth a Confederate agent, that her mother had been a mulatto, that she was a murderess. Harry had discounted all of them. Now, he was sure of nothing. Perhaps this ambiguity was a trait of all actresses. Even so, he could not imagine life without these two ladies of the stage. He preferred their company to that of any of the belles of Tidewater—with the exception of his sister, Elizabeth.

Louise was well known and popular at the National and the desk clerk raised neither objection nor brow at Harry's request for two adjoining rooms. The porter who carried their baggage lingered in the corridor, however, obviously waiting to see which of them went where.

He was wasting his time. Louise said she would join Harry for supper, then hurried inside her chamber.

Harry did not linger long in his.

The Union spy chief kept rooms in the Willard, but Harry expected Pinkerton might more likely be found at the War

Department on 17th Street or General McClellan's headquarters on H Street at the northeast corner of LaFayette Park. As he was carrying the not-inconsiderable burden of Mister Pinkerton's gold, Harry elected to stop first at the latter, where he would be better known.

The diminutive general had taken over the large yellow mansion that had previously been the residence of President James Madison's widow, Dolley, until her death thirteen years before. It was easily the grandest headquarters in the Union Army, and astir with activity, though Harry could not fathom why. From all reports, "little Mac" and his army had not stirred a foot from Washington since their return from his monumentally unsuccessful attempt to capture Richmond by means of a slow march up the York Peninsula. In seven days of fighting, Lee had sent McClellan reeling back to the Chesapeake.

Harry was challenged at the gate of the wrought-iron fence that surrounded Mrs. Madison's house, but his Lincoln-signed pass secured him entry without hesitation or comment.

Happily, Pinkerton was indeed on the premises. Harry was escorted to an upstairs office whose lone small window gave a view of the President's House across the park. The great detective showed no surprise whatsoever at Harry's sudden appearance.

"Raines. You're back. Which way did you come? And why has it taken you so long?"

"By way of Ohio—by train. I acquired some companions. One was badly injured and I was compelled to wait until recovery was certain." He thumped the leather pouch containing the gold on Pinkerton's small desk. "Here is your money back. Some is missing."

The detective gestured for Harry to take a chair. "You were authorized expenditures. As your enterprise was a success, no one will quarrel with it."

Harry lighted one of his small cigars. "You don't understand, sir. Most of it is missing. But it was turned over to General Grant in Tennessee. I have a receipt."

"You gave it to General Grant?"

30

"No, sir. Not exactly. One of his agents took it from me and deposited it with Grant after passing through Confederate lines in Mississippi after Shiloh."

"And what agent was that?"

Harry puffed on his cigar, wishing the conversation had not carried this far. "Louise Devereux. She is the injured companion I just mentioned."

Pinkerton came forward in his chair. His fringe of beard and chin whiskers gave his countenance an impish aspect, as though he were in a perpetual state of amusement. But he was decidedly not now.

"That woman was deported to the Confederacy as an act of leniency by the President. You yourself took her into Virginia. She murdered a Federal officer and carried secrets to the enemy."

"I think both counts are now open to question," Harry said. "At all events, she seems to have served General Grant very usefully. And, as I've just told you, she was badly wounded in the effort."

"But she lives?"

"Yes."

"And she's with Grant?"

"No. She's with me. We're staying at the National Hotel."

Pinkerton's face flushed. He was a Scot and professed high moral principles. "You abide together?"

"No, sir. But in proximity. Because of her injuries, I have taken her into my household on my farm upriver. She wished to visit Washington with me, but I expect her to return. We are well chaperoned."

"Harry. This woman was banished. She was denounced in the Republican newspapers as one of the enemy."

"Well, they had best correct their error. She has proved herself otherwise. And, at all events, Mister Pinkerton, she won't be a nuisance to you much longer. I intend to have her stay at my farm until she has completely recovered, and where she will be under my protection."

"Protection? What of your service to the Army?"

Harry had thought this would be easier. He puffed some

more. "It's my intention to resign from the service, Mister Pinkerton."

The detective abruptly stood up, fidgeted, then went to the window and flung up the sash. The room had been filling with Harry's cigar smoke. "You cannot do that, Captain Raines."

"I didn't enlist in the Army, Mister Pinkerton. I signed up as 'scout.' That was more than a year ago. In the intervening time, I have been several times imprisoned, innumerable times shot at, beaten, pursued by vigilantes, hunted by wild Indians, nearly drowned, and almost hanged. Thanks to my father, who now despises me, my loyalties are well known to General Lee and Jefferson Davis himself. I truly can be of no further use to you."

Pinkerton turned around, assertively folding his arms across his chest. "Every man is of use to us now, Raines. After this second disaster at Bull Run . . ." his arms came free as he made a gesture of frustration, "some in the press are blaming us, you know—blaming General McClellan. They say Pope would have prevailed if we had sent reinforcements from our force here as he requested. That damned fool was wandering about that country out there like some lost child. He'd no idea where Jackson's troops had gone—nor Longstreet's. Then he was flanked by both."

"He must have had poor reconnaissance."

Pinkerton pounced on this. "Poor? Dreadful! That's why we need you. And every experienced man. Lee is out there. We know not where. Except that it's in country you know well."

"But McClellan's army is here in Washington, where it will likely stay, Mister Pinkerton. He can find Willard's and the War Department without my assistance."

"That's an impertinence, Raines."

Harry stared at the floor, then looked to the Scotsman and slowly rose. "I am sorry, but my mind is made up. I have killed people—one of them a woman."

"She was a rebel assassin. You had no choice. And as I recall, it was an inadvertance."

"Nevertheless, sir, I want no more of it. Maybe in a while

my mind will change, but right now, I desire only my porch. If General Lee comes my way, I will send word to you." He took a step toward the door.

"I could have you arrested for misappropriation of the gold I entrusted to you."

"But that would be calumny, sir." Harry resumed his departure.

"Wait, Raines. I think the President would be pleased to see you—to hear about the West first hand. Indulge me, please, in that at least."

Harry could not walk away from such an invitation. "Of course, Mister Pinkerton."

It had been many months since Harry had last visited with Lincoln and he was shocked to see how wearied, worried, and older the President now looked—his face incredibly creased and weathered and sad. The second defeat at Bull Run must have been terrible for him.

The President shook Harry's hand—his grip still iron-strong despite his seeming frailty—and then Pinkerton's, asking the two of them to seat themselves. Settling his long frame back into his own chair, he put his hands together before his chin, as though in prayer.

"Have you new reports?" he asked Pinkerton.

"Lee is moving north," the detective said.

"We knew that this morning," Lincoln said. "We presumed that. Your people are plowin' the same furrow."

"The telegraph wires are today unreliable," Pinkerton said. "We expect he's at least to Leesburg. He had Longstreet's corps with him. Don't know where Jackson is."

"Hardly anyone ever does," Lincoln said. "Going by the dispatches I've read, John Pope didn't either."

"He should have made better use of his scouts, Mister President."

"Pope can fret over that at his leisure. I'm throwing his army into McClellan's. Pope will presently have nothing to command."

This was information for which the enemy would pay

dearly, and Harry was surprised the President had shared it with Pinkerton in Harry's presence. But then, were anyone to deliver this important intelligence to Robert E. Lee, the Southern general would doubtless not worry overmuch. Lee had doubtless learned a great deal about McClellan during the Peninsula Campaign. He'd know that it wouldn't matter much if you put three or four other Union armies into McClellan's command. He'd just sit there, in Dolley Madison's house, asking for more.

But Lincoln had other ideas.

"In exchange for replenishing McClellan's force with Pope's troops, I'm ordering him into the field again. Giving him no choice—move or make way for another who will. He's had all summer to refit. Lee's just been through a big battle. We have an advantage that this time I'm not going to let our 'little Napoleon' squander."

"Which way are you sending him, sir?" Pinkerton said.

"Depends on where Lee is going, and I expect your people to provide the answer to that." He looked to Harry. "Pinkerton tells me you know that country along the upper Potomac well, Raines."

"Yes, sir. I spent all my summers there growing up. I have a farm there."

"Then we shall once again rely on you."

Harry wanted no one to rely on him—except Louise. He said nothing.

"Mr. President," said Pinkerton. "Raines here is just now back from the West. He got as far as New Mexico Territory."

Lincoln was interested. "You were at the Battle of Glorieta Pass?"

"No, sir. Got there too late. But I can tell you it cost the Rebels plenty. All their supplies were burned and they had no choice but to abandon the territory and crawl back to Texas. They left the corpses of men and horses all along the Rio Grande. I don't think they'll be coming back any time soon."

"That scrap saved the Far West for us," Lincoln said.

"Might have lost California for us, had it gone the other way," Pinkerton said.

"We could not get the newspapers interested in it," the President said. "All they want to know about is the defeats."

"Raines was also in New Orleans—and with Grant in Tennessee," Pinkerton said.

A sort of warmth came into Lincoln's eyes. "Tell me about Shiloh. Were you there?"

"Again, I arrived too late, Mister President," Harry said. "But I surely learned about it. The first day was a slaughter, and pretty near a defeat. But the Rebel commander, General Johnston, had no real strategy. He just threw his men into the attack as viciously and aggressively as possible. Grant was able to pull together enough troops and position them to hold the ground. The next day, Johnston was dead and Grant was easily able to out-general Johnston's successor. It might have been a rout of the Confederates, sir. It should have been. But after Grant's victory, General Halleck took over and everything stopped. We were only thirty miles from Corinth, but it took Halleck fully thirty days to move the army to the town, even though the Rebels before him were a shambles of an army. When we finally got there, they'd abandoned the place and burned everything militarily useful they couldn't carry. General Halleck called it a great victory."

Harry's account did not much please the President.

"I read his dispatches. I would not dispute what you say, Captain Raines. But General Halleck is now here, where his organizational skills are most useful. Grant is back in the field. What do you make of him?"

"He fights, sir, and I believe him to be very smart."

Lincoln's brow furrowed. "Was he drunk at Shiloh? There are rumors."

"Never that I saw, sir. Never saw him drink a drop."

The President nodded. "You think we have a chance for more victories out there? They're after me to dismiss the general because of the terrible losses at Shiloh."

"I think you'll find the war in the West going better than here."

Lincoln sighed. "We've got to catch up with General Lee. At the very least, divine what he intends. You will no doubt

35

be very helpful to us, Raines. It's a great gift to have Virginians like you remain so loyal to the Union. If only General Lee had shown the same example."

"Yes, sir." Harry was not sure what he had agreed to.

The President's attention turned to the large pile of dispatches and correspondence on the desk before him. "Good to see you well, Raines. Help us to find Lee."

Pinkerton led Harry out of the White House to the walk along Pennsylvania Avenue.

"I've business to attend to, Raines," he said. "I don't know what your plans are, but I would appreciate it if you could stop by my office before you depart the capital."

"Very well." Harry wondered where Louise was, and how soon they might leave.

"Maybe I can arrange an audience for you with General McClellan."

Harry supposed that would be considered a high honor. "If there's time, sir."

Pinkerton grinned. "Oh, there'll be time." He clapped Harry on the shoulder. "Later then. I trust you will stay away from the abodes of crime you used to frequent."

"I may look up old friends."

"We are also your old friends, Harry. Don't forget that."

With that, Pinkerton walked away, moving quickly back toward Dolley Madison's house, hunched over slightly, as though in deep thought.

Louise had left her room at the National, leaving no message for him as to her destination or time of return. Expecting that she would be back at least for supper, Harry wandered back down Pennsylvania Avenue, stopping first at his friend Matthew Brady's photographic studio just up Seventh Street.

Mounting the stairs, he found several soldiers seated on chairs in the anteroom of the establishment, and then another in the studio proper, posed holding a drawn revolver. He was a young officer, and Harry guessed he had not yet experienced combat. His beardless face appeared too blithe and innocent, despite the bravado of his pose.

"Hello, Brady," Harry said. "Can I buy you a drink?"

The photographer, who'd been busy at the rear of his large camera, glanced back at Harry over his shoulder. "Raines! They'd told me you were killed."

"Not yet. Would you like to stop at Willard's?"

"I cannot. My trade is brisk these days. I have this gentleman, and the others, and when I finish with them there will be still more. There are every day."

"I'm looking for Louise Devereux."

"She fled to the Confederacy."

"No, she has returned as well."

"There's hardly room in this city for either of you," Brady said, putting his head beneath the camera cloth. "The population has near to tripled. Try Grover's Theater—or the new one, Ford's, up Tenth Street. The actors will know where she is. If you find her, tell her it's been a year since I've photographed her. I would be appreciative of another appointment."

"I will." Harry noted some of the daguerreotype plates Brady had set upon a table. There were actors and actresses, a number of politicians, and a row of pictures taken of dead Union soldiers. He wondered if the young officer had taken a look at them. "Any news?" Harry said.

Brady did not reply. He opened his camera lens for the exposure, waited several seconds, then replaced the cap. "John Wilkes Booth is back, though not performing," he said, removing the photographic plate. "There's talk of conscription, now that the Rebels have resorted to it. And everyone fears that General Lee will attack the city."

"But General McClellan and his army are here."

"Precisely so," said Brady. "Returned from his great victory on the Peninsula. If it was such a victory, why is he here instead of Richmond?"

Harry went to the door. "Fear not, Brady. We'll survive both Lee and McClellan. I'll look for you at Willard's."

\*     \*     \*

Hungry, Harry stopped in at Harvey's Oyster Saloon across the Avenue for a whiskey and a dozen Chesapeakes, then proceeded to Ford's. It was closed, with none but a watchman on the premises. Moving on to Grover's on Rum Row, he found a number of actors there—some rehearsing, others simply hanging about. None had been aware that Louise had returned, though the news seemed to animate several of the male performers.

Avoiding a wandering pig, Harry set off again, but with no clear destination. The Avenue was thick with traffic—military vehicles, farmers' wagons, horse cars, and a few grand carriages. The dust they kicked up quickly accumulated on Harry's clothes, turning his brown frock coat a dun color. Had it been raining, his boots and trousers would have acquired a similar hue from the mud. Hard cold winter was the only time of year to stroll the Avenue unmolested by its dirt and muck. Harry was fond of the Federal City, but it woefully lacked the elements of civilization enjoyed by Philadelphia, New York, and Boston—including most particularly paved streets.

When he'd been in Richmond the previous winter, he'd been stunned by the outrageous prices charged for the most basic foodstuffs and staples—and by the plethora of saloons, gambling parlors, and whore houses that had sprung up along what had been the most respectable commercial streets in the city.

The same condition was now evident in Washington. When he'd last been in town, the brothels had been well-regulated and confined to an area south of the Avenue near the river end of the canal. Now they and other vice dens plying the soldier trade had spread north and east to the Avenue itself. One could stand on the steps of the National Hotel and watch brazen daughters of Venus plucking at the sleeves of passersby in bright daylight on the opposite side of the street. Harry could only wonder when they'd cross the unofficial boundary and invade the more respectable side of the thoroughfare.

One fixture from the old days was still in place—the Palace of Fortune. Dodging a cantering rider and more pigs, Harry crossed to the south side of Pennsylvania again and headed for the gambling hall, where he was no stranger.

He bought a tumbler of Old Overholt at the bar and then looked for an available game. Big Jim Coates, a one-time mountain man from the West and a good friend of Harry's, was at one table. Taking note of Harry as he lowered his hand, he cheerfully motioned him to a chair.

The other players raised no objection. At the table with Coates were a Union Army captain; John Russell, the war correspondent of the *Times* of London; a professional gambler named Oral Simms; and another civilian not of Harry's acquaintance.

"Didn't expect to ever see you again," Coates said. "Where've you been?

"In the West," said Harry.

"Any news?" Russell asked.

"Union victories. If the Federals can take Vicksburg, they'll have the entire Mississippi. They have a good general out there in Mister Grant."

"The drunken butcher of Shiloh," muttered Simms, a hatchet-faced man Harry did not like and suspected of being a cheat.

"I never saw him drunk," Harry said. "And Shiloh was a victory. If Halleck hadn't intervened, Grant might have captured an entire Rebel army."

"Grant's had weak opponents," said the army captain. "Here in the East, Little Mac is up against Robert Lee. Licked 'em good on the Peninsula, though."

"Any more such victories and General Lee will be joining us here in Washington," Harry said.

The captain pushed back his chair. "Sir, if you impugn General McClellan with another word, I shall have you detained for agitating against the Federal authority. I am with the provost marshal's office."

Harry was about to respond that he worked for General McClellan, but reminded himself that he had just resigned. He hoped he had made that clear to Allan Pinkerton—though he had avoided making that declaration to President Lincoln.

"Gentlemen," said Coates, who had just won the pot. "We are here to play cards." He shuffled the deck, passed it to Harry to cut, then dealt the first two cards of five card stud.

Harry had a ten face up and a jack as a hole card. He saw a bet and two raises. His next card was a deuce. That was followed by a four of clubs. His last was a useless ace.

By the time the deal came to Simms, Harry was down nearly twenty dollars. When he had first come to Washington before the war, he had supported himself for a time as a gambler. With this sort of luck, he'd soon be destitute.

After another whiskey and three more hands, his losses exceeded thirty-five dollars. It was time to leave. He reminded himself of his original purpose in coming to the Palace of Fortune.

"Is it true Wilkes Booth has returned to Washington?" he asked.

"Heard that," Coates said. "He's not been in here, though."

"And Caitlin Howard?"

"Marvelous actress," Russell said.

"Has she come back?"

Russell shrugged. "I've not noted her name in any theatrical advertisement."

Harry played one more hand, and lost. "If you'll excuse me, gentlemen. I must attend to some business."

It wasn't far to Mrs. Fitzgerald's boarding house just north of the Avenue, an establishment he had haunted for the better part of a year when Caitlin was in residence there. It had been nearly that long a time since he had last visited the tall brick house, which had originally been the home of a U.S. Senator.

Mrs. Fitzgerald, a large, friendly, and understanding woman who'd lost her husband in the war with Mexico, answered the door. She squinted at Harry before recognizing him.

"Mister Raines," she said. "Tis a surprise to be seeing you again."

"I've come calling on Miss Howard."

"I'm sorry, but she no longer resides here."

"I know. She left Washington—with Mister Booth. But I was told she has returned. I know that he has."

"Yes, she has returned. But I'm full up. I believe she took a room south of the Avenue in Marble Alley. A Mrs. Bannerman's place."

Harry frowned. Marble Alley had been one of the most notorious sections of the city. It could not have improved much in respectability since.

"Thank you, Mrs. Fitzgerald. I shall go there." He tipped his wide-brimmed hat and turned to leave.

"Mister Raines, there's something you should know."

Harry stopped, wondering what dreadful news about Caitlin she was about to impart. "Yes?"

Mrs. Fitzgerald was smiling. "She didn't come back with Wilkes Booth."

Harry stood there, uncertain.

"Mr. Raines," she said. "Do you not ken my meaning? She came back on her own before he did. She is on her own now."

He bowed to her and then departed, moving much more quickly now.

Reluctant to go farther, Harry paused on the corner outside the Bannerman house, watching as an army officer and a plump young woman entered through the front door. They eloquently confirmed his suspicion that the establishment might be little better than a brothel.

He decided to wait a while, in hopes he might encounter Caitlin on the street and thus avoid having to enter the building. He could not bear speaking with her again in such a setting.

No one remotely resembling her came by. Caitlin was a remarkably handsome woman, and unusually tall—five feet and nine inches. She had wide, gray-green eyes that put one in mind of the sea, aristocratic English features, and light brown hair she had customarily worn with side curls.

As Louise had a smoldering, sensual quality, Caitlin was known for her regal bearing and repose. When Louise came on stage, she prompted a low buzz of gossip and appreciative comment. Caitlin's entrances usually brought a hush.

41

Harry had seen her otherwise—delirious, thrashing in her bedclothes, and dripping in sweat from excessive doses of laudanum. Booth had provoked at least two of these incidents in the past. If he'd broken with her yet again, it would be no surprise if she were to turn to the drug again. It could be had at any apothecary in Washington.

Taking out his watch, and noting the advance of the sunset, Harry took a deep breath, then started toward the house.

No one responded to his knock. Pushing open the door, he heard laughter and the sound of bare feet running upstairs. In a sitting room to the side, an older woman was seated on a sofa, knitting. She looked up. "May I be of assistance, sir?"

"I'm looking for Miss Caitlin Howard. I'm a friend." As if to say, I am not a customer.

"Yes. Miss Howard. I'm afraid she's not here, sir. She's at the hospital."

# Six

The hospital to which Harry was directed lay on the other side of the canal. There was a narrow bridge over it just down from the Colonization Society building, but he elected instead to take the Maryland Avenue span several blocks to the east, which was wide and well illuminated with street lamps. The smell was all the same, however. The canal served as a sewer and a dumping place for garbage and dead animals. It swarmed so with flies and mosquitoes that their noise could be heard a hundred yards away.

Reaching the other side, he passed the gas works to the right and, further along, the lights of the capital penitentiary to the left. Ahead was what seemed more army barracks than hospital. There were several of them, laid out in rows. They'd not been there when Harry had left the city. It seemed a strange place to be attending to the ills of a lady.

As he came near, he was stopped by a sentry. Showing the youth his pass, along with the explanation that he was visiting a patient, he was allowed to proceed. At the entrance of the first building was another soldier standing with a musket, but he paid Harry no mind. Just inside, a sergeant sat behind a desk. He wore the uniform of the medical corps.

"Yes?" he asked.

"I'm looking for a patient—a Miss Caitlin Howard."

"This is a military hospital, sir. No female patients."

"You're certain? Caitlin Howard. She's an actress. I was told I could find her here."

"Wait a minute." The man pulled open a drawer, and took from it a thin sheaf of paper. Running his finger down a column of what looked to be names, he turned a page, then stopped.

43

"Go to Building Three. It's to your left as you go out. Two buildings down."

"Thank you."

Mystified, Harry hurried along. There were other sounds now more dreadful than those of the gorging canal insects—groans and moans, and then, as he came to the end of the next building, a scream. It was repeated, then became a sort of gurgle, then ceased.

The door to the third building stood open. There was no one in the small vestibule, but, stepping inside, Harry heard a rattling sound in the corridor beyond. Advancing forward, he encountered an orderly pushing a cart along the hallway. It was filled with dismembered limbs.

"Excuse me," Harry said. The man glanced up. He seemed weary, and little interested in Harry or whatever Harry wanted.

"I'm looking for someone. A woman. Her name is Caitlin Howard."

The orderly wiped his brow and stood erect, blinking. Then he nodded, as though to himself. "End of the hall. The big ward at the end."

Harry thanked him and set off where directed. There was the strong smell of lye and soap in the hall. At the doorway to the ward, it mingled with something worse. He stepped inside.

There were perhaps twenty men lying on beds in the room, which was illuminated by a single lantern. They seemed ghostly apparitions in the faint light. Few of them moved. Strangely, none of them made a sound. Pulling on his spectacles, Harry took note of a woman kneeling at the side of a bed in the far corner. She had a basin at her side and was dipping into it with a cloth. As Harry came nearer, he saw that she was bathing a badly injured soldier. Her hair was pulled back tight and gathered in a netted bun at the back of her head. He recognized her by her long, lovely neck.

"Caitlin?" he said, softly.

She failed to notice him, or did not wish to. She was quietly singing a little song.

Her dress was drab and looked cheap. Gently, he put his hand on her shoulder, and spoke again. "Caitlin. It's Harry."

She ceased her singing, slowly turning her head. "Harry? Harry Raines?"

"I've come back. I was out West. Louise has come back with me."

Caitlin did not rise. Her lovely eyes were very sad, and she did not smile. "I am very pleased to see you, Harry. With this war . . ."

"Are you with Mister Booth?" He'd blurted that.

She looked back to her patient, who was as still and quiet as the others in the room. Harry envied him her tender ministrations. "I must attend to my duties, Harry. Wait for me outside until the hour's done."

He sat on the steps, smoking a small cigar and sipping from his whiskey flask, still bewildered by this lady's extraordinary transformation. He judged it borne out of some black mood or bleak sadness—with Booth to blame. He'd come close to thrashing the actor on two occasions. He wished now for a third opportunity to accomplish the task.

The appointed hour came, and then went. It was another twenty minutes after that before she appeared at the door. Harry rose, but she bade him seat himself again and settled herself beside him on the step.

He put his arm around her. She did not resist, but she did not respond.

"I'm sorry to keep you waiting," she said. "The poor boy died."

"I'm sorry." He took her hand.

"Four of them died today."

"They're from Manassas?"

"Yes. Another senseless slaughter."

"Senseless, but not pointless. The Union cause is advancing. In the West, it is, at all events."

"There was talk of an emancipation—to be imposed upon the Rebel states. But nothing has come of it."

Harry did not want their words to become mired in politics. He lifted her hand. "Louise has lost a finger. This one here, but on the other hand."

45

"Dear God. How did that happen?"

"We got into a gunfight with some pursuing Confederate agents. The finger was not her most serious wound, but she has mostly recovered. She wears a glove now constantly."

"Was it you who took her into harm's way?"

"Quite the other way around. She's an intrepid lady."

"Where is she?"

"Here in Washington. My hope is that she will return with me to my farm in western Virginia, but I fear she wants to return to the theater."

Caitlin removed her hand. "They will arrest her."

"No. She has performed valued service for the Union—out West."

Caitlin leaned forward, elbows on her knees and face pressed against her hands. She sat that way for a very long time, then wiped at her eyes and came up straight once more.

"And you?" he asked. "Are you now back on stage? I asked, but . . ."

"I did not come back to do that, Harry. I came back to do this."

"I suppose it would be uncomfortable, with Booth about."

"It has nothing to do with Wilkes," she said. "You misapprehend. I left him this summer. We were in Chicago, in a fine hotel. Fine breakfasts, fine dinners. Shopping and promenades. A lovely life, I used to think. But every morning came the *Chicago Daily Tribune*. It has the most reliable war coverage in that city, they say. It relayed an endless succession of horrors. There is no tragedy in Shakespeare to rival what passed before my eyes on its pages. With breakfast. Every morning. I could not go on with a life like that. One day while he was in rehearsal, I packed my belongings and took a train east."

"And Booth?"

"I love him, Harry. But he has wed not me but the Southern cause. And slavery."

"I warned you about that."

Now she leaned close. "You're a dear friend, Harry."

"Join me for supper. At the Willard. We'll have a gay and

46

glittering time, as in the old days." He put his hand to her waist. "You could use some sustenance."

"I cannot, Harry. I am on duty tonight. I will take my supper with Miss Barton."

"Yes, I know her. She is a friend of my friend Colonel Gregg, the Army surgeon at the Georgetown hospital."

"Then join us. It will be simple fare."

It was, indeed. A barley soup. Some rough bread. A bit of fish and a bit of cheese. Clara Barton, a tiny but ebullient woman, was intent upon news of the West. "This Grant, is he the butcher they say?"

"He was taken by surprise at Shiloh and the Rebels fought viciously and recklessly. He had the damnedest time rooting them out of there. But he did not wantonly sacrifice his men. On the contrary, he saved them from being slaughtered at the river's edge. I saw such a thing at Ball's Bluff. He avoided that."

Caitlin seemed very pale, even in the warm glow of the lantern light.

"The hospitals must have been filled to overflowing," Miss Barton said.

"It's wild country," Harry said. "They used steamboats. The wounded were brought as far upriver as Cairo, Illinois."

"And he advances?" Miss Barton asked.

"Into Mississippi. I believe his goal is Vicksburg. A fortress of a town on the river."

The older woman shook her head sadly, as though she had had some vision of the arithmetic of death to come. "And General Lee. Shall we soon find him at the gates of Washington?"

"No. He is west of here. I think he is trying to draw the Union Army out of the capital."

"Which means more slaughter. We are full up here, Mister Raines."

"Yes, ma'am. But I fear you will be fuller."

They finished their meal without speaking further. Harry could hear the moaning and groaning again. When they were done, he bid Miss Barton a good night. Caitlin accompanied him to the door.

"Let me walk you home," he said. "I'll be happy to wait."

"I will sleep here tonight, Harry. I often do."

"And in the morning?"

"I shall be attending to my duties."

"How are you supporting yourself?"

"I have some savings. We get a small stipend from the Sanitation Commission. The meals are free."

"Caitlin . . ." He drew her into the light, searching her face for signs of illness. Instead, he perceived a kind of radiance. He judged it to be from the hanging, overhead lamp. "You are well, Kate?"

"Oh yes, Harry. Very well."

He pulled her close, but she averted her head instead of raising it to meet his lips. She held him tightly, though, and was pleased when he kissed her hand.

"May I see you again?" he asked.

"Of course, Harry. You are my friend. But I fear you will soon be taken up with other matters."

"No. I think I'm going to resign from the Federal service."

"Well, I am sorry to hear that."

"I've given them a year. It's not been easy."

"You must do what you think best." She stepped back. "Good night, Harry. It's so good to see you again."

And then she was gone, returned to her labors—and miseries.

Harry walked slowly back to the National, his mind full of confusion. A stop at the hotel's bar helped little. Upstairs, he rapped on Louise's door, but received no answer. He half hoped she might be waiting for him in his own chamber, but it proved to be as empty as he had left it.

# Seven

Harry was awakened by a loud and insistent knocking on his door. He thought, or at least hoped, that it was Louise, but there was too much muscle behind the raps. A fugitive might expect to hear such a pounding from lawmen whose next move would be to break down the door.

But then, they might not be representatives of the law. This was a Southern hotel and in many ways still a Southern city. Washington was full of Confederate agents, agitators, and sympathizers.

As a gambler who had encountered too many angry and unhappy losers in his time, Harry always traveled armed. He'd come into Washington with a two-shot Derringer pocket pistol and his beloved .32 caliber Navy Colt revolver, which he'd set upon the dresser.

Throwing back the covers, he flung himself across the bed and snatched up that weapon, turning to face the door just as it swung open, its lock picked. There stood not an enemy but a friend, Pinkerton agent Joseph "Boston" Leahy, who had been with him for a time in the West.

"A good morning to you, Laddybuck. Where are your clothes? Have you a woman in here?"

"No. It was a hot night. If you would be so kind as to close the door."

Leahy grinned and complied with the request. "Mister Pinkerton wants to see you. With your clothes on."

"I saw him yesterday. He knows my mind. I'm going back to my farm."

"I think he will tell you the situation has changed."

"Is Lee moving on Washington?"

49

"Get dressed, Harry. Let's not keep him waiting."

"I will take the time to clean my teeth and shave. We are not in the wilds any longer, Joseph."

In the hall, Harry turned to Louise's door, but Leahy stayed his hand. "She is not there," he said.

"How would you know?"

"Please, Harry. We are late. Let's not keep the Scotsman waiting."

The meeting place was not McClellan's headquarters, as Harry had expected, but the Willard, where Pinkerton kept rooms. Unfortunately, as the heat of the morning was upon the city, he kept the drapes closed against enemy spies and eavesdroppers. It was no wonder the spy chief wanted this interview over with early.

"Sit down, Raines," Pinkerton said. He was peering through an opening in the curtains, keeping his back to his visitors.

Harry did so. Pinkerton finally abandoned the window post and took a chair opposite. "This Indian of yours . . ."

"He's not an Indian," said Harry. "He's a Metis—a French Canadian."

"I don't care if he's a Patagonian. Is he a good man?"

"He's the best. I owe my life to him several times."

"Is he a good scout?"

"The best."

"Maybe in the West," said Leahy. "But he knows nothing about Virginia—or Maryland."

"He would be a good scout dropped into the middle of China."

"Good," said Pinkerton. "We have signed him up for the General. He's already been dispatched to Poolesville to look for Lee." The detective sat down in a chair opposite. "Now, as for you . . ."

"We settled that matter yesterday, Mister Pinkerton."

"No, we did not. You spoke your mind. I listened. That was all."

"I'm going back to my farm."

"Harry, I have no good scout who knows that country as well as you. No one who knows who is loyal and who is the enemy in those towns. There will be a battle and it could decide the war. Good God, man. How could you sit this out? Abraham Lincoln himself has requested your assistance."

Harry had no wish to reargue his case. He stared down at the carpet. "It may be that I will rejoin you sometime in the future. Maybe soon. But not now. I need to be away from all this death and misery. I need to look after my own."

Leahy still stood, his arms folded across his barrel chest. "There's not a man in the Union Army who doesn't hold the same sentiments, Harry. But there they stand."

"They'd be shot if they didn't. I signed no enlistment papers. All I'm asking for is a little time."

"Damn it, Harry," Leahy said, his face gone red. "There is no time!"

"General McClellan marches Saturday," Pinkerton said. "This game has commenced."

"But he knows not where he goes. Part of his army is south of the city at Aquia Creek. And he marches with the swiftness of the tortoise."

A sudden silence fell, each man contemplating his own thoughts. Finally, Pinkerton spoke.

"Very well, Harry. You leave me no choice."

"What do you mean?"

Pinkerton rose, walking toward his curtains again. "We have your woman. That actress. The Devereux woman."

"What do you mean, 'have?'"

"She is in the Old Capitol Prison."

"You can't do that! Under what law?"

"The President has the constitutional right to suspend habeas corpus in this emergency. But even had he not, this woman shot and killed a Union officer."

"My cousin Belle Boyd killed a Union sergeant, and she was let go. You just let her go again, though her loyalty to the Rebel side is well known. Louise carries a letter of recommendation from General Grant!"

Pinkerton put his hands behind his back, and began to pace.

51

"The President gave her what amounted to an unofficial pardon, Raines. The Federal government does not want to hang a woman. We do not want to make a martyr of Miss Devereux the way we did Rose Greenhow when we had her in prison."

"So why is she in jail?"

Leahy cleared his throat. "I think we'd better explain matters fully, Mister Pinkerton."

Pinkerton came back to his chair, leaned forward, and spoke softly, as if all of Washington might be listening. "It's as simple as this, Harry. If you agree to serve the General in this campaign—just give me your word—she shall be freed. I'll have the President write her a pass himself. If you refuse, I will have no choice but to turn her over to the tender mercies of Colonel Baker."

"Lafayette Baker?"

"He is now the authority in Washington City."

Harry leaned back and commenced the arduous mental process of deciding what to do, but quickly realized this would be a pointless endeavor. The choice had already been made for him.

"A pass for her from Lincoln?"

"My word on that."

"Two, in case something strange happens to the other."

Pinkerton nodded. He was sweating as much as Harry and Leahy.

Harry sighed. "Very well. I'll do it. I would spare even Jeff Davis himself from Colonel Baker's tender mercies."

"Dangerous talk, Harry," said Leahy.

Harry rose. "I said I'll do it. All I ask is that I be allowed to stop by my farm to see to my people. I'll stay only a day. I promise. I'll ride back toward McClellan down the Potomac. Whatever I learn, I'll bring it to the General directly."

Leahy and Pinkerton exchanged a glance.

"Go back on your word, Harry," Pinkerton said, "and you'll find yourself a guest of Colonel Baker's, too."

# Eight

Harry had wanted to be at the prison when Louise was released—in part to confirm that she was being freed but also in the hope that she might journey with him back to Shepherdstown. But Pinkerton was adamant that he depart as soon as possible so that he might avoid Lee's army and join up with McClellan all the sooner. Reluctantly, Harry caught the next train, transferring at Relay, south of Baltimore, to the westbound line.

There were more troops along the right-of-way now, especially west of Frederick. Sizable forces had been deployed to hold Harper's Ferry and Martinsburg, though they were not large enough to contend with Lee's entire army, or even one of his corps. There'd been some nearby cavalry skirmishes, but there was no sign yet that the Southern commander was moving that way. The most recent reports had him still down around Leesburg.

Harry reached Shepherdstown just after dark, stopping first at Klostermann's tavern for refreshment—and news.

"The Secesh element in this town is getting pretty lively," the bartender said. "One fellow was in here talking about the coming liberation from the Yankee yoke."

"What's coming is another big fight somewhere," said Harry. "I hope not here."

"You weren't long in Washington."

"My business was concluded early."

"You bring that pretty lady back with you?"

"I'm afraid not. Travel's a bit dangerous these days, with Lee in the field."

"More dangerous when Stonewall Jackson was around."

Two large men in rough clothes entered, moving to the other end of the bar. Klostermann went to attend to them, greeting them with some deference.

"The Singleton boys," he said quietly to Harry when he returned. "Don't want to rile them—if the Rebs take over here again."

"Poor Shepherdstown. A civil war within a civil war."

"Like that all over this end of Virginia. You back for good now?"

"Probably not. What's being said about the Reverend Ashby?"

"They're burying him tomorrow—in the cemetery behind his church."

"What time?"

"Eleven o'clock in the morning. Will you be attending?"

Pinkerton would want him on the road. "I don't know." Harry drank the rest of his whiskey. He was hungry, but preferred Estelle's cooking to Klostermann's fare, which ran to old ham, cold beans and boiled eggs in brine. "Is there no talk about the Reverend?"

"Half of it lies. No telling which half."

Harry stood up. "I believe I will attend the services. A good night to you, Hugo."

Instead of heading up German Street and the road to his farm, Harry went around the corner and crossed the center of town, turning down the wide dirt lane that led to Jim O'Malley's blacksmith shop.

The proprietor was busy at his forge. At Harry's entrance, he set down his tongs. "Didn't expect you to be coming by so soon. The war chase you back from Washington?"

"In a manner of speaking. I'm leaving again tomorrow." He hesitated. "I must beg a favor."

O'Malley invited Harry to a chair, then seated himself on a nearby bench. "Discretion, sir," he said.

"They could come this way," Harry said. "The Rebel army."

"I half expect it. They could cut the railroad, the canal, draw the Federal army out of Washington. Make plenty of mischief."

"If they do, Jim, I fear for my people. There's no white person on my farm, except for the little girl. The others could be seized as contraband, especially Estelle."

"You told me Caesar Augustus has manumission papers."

"Estelle doesn't. She's a runaway."

O'Malley lighted his pipe. "You're wondering if the Underground Railroad is still running."

"Yes, I am."

"No. I've had to shut down for a while. Some of the wrong-minded locals were beginning to take an interest in it."

"What about the hiding places here?"

"Still have a few."

"I'd like to send my people to you."

"You don't even have to ask, Harry."

"There could be trouble for you—if you're found out."

O'Malley shrugged. "Nothing new about that. What about the little girl? As you say, she's white. You want me to hide her with the Negroes?"

White enough, Harry thought. "My nearest kin are in Front Royal," he said. "Can't send her there. Full of Rebels."

The blacksmith thought for a moment. "There's Sally Thompson—the widow in the big brick house up on the hill? She has a good heart. And the right politics. I'll talk to her."

"You are a true friend, sir." Harry took out his whiskey flask and offered it to the man.

"No, thanks," said O'Malley. "Not while I'm working."

"I'm going to the Reverend Ashby's service tomorrow."

"I will see you there."


Federal soldiers loitered on both sides of German Street as Harry ascended the hill, ignoring him but not a young lady of the town as she traipsed by. Her name was Lucinda Weverton and Harry knew her father to be a Union man. She was inviting a change in family loyalties with such reckless behavior. Had he not been in such haste now, Harry might have paused to warn her of the risk, but he doubted she would have paid him much mind.

Turning north on the Grade Road, he descended the hill

again, quickly passing the last of the town buildings. The fields and woods beyond were only dimly illuminated by starlight. His spectacles were in his pocket. But he knew this two-mile stretch of road as well as he did the rooms of his own house, and he was able to move along easily, stumbling only once when failing to notice a rut in the dirt.

He rubbed his ankle, then froze. The night was full of the usual sounds of the country—frogs in the low ground, the call of an owl in the trees, insects everywhere. But there was something else. A human voice, some small distance behind him.

A curve lay ahead that rounded a high, fenced bank rising at the right. Ignoring the slight pain that now accompanied his step, Harry moved on quickly. When fully screened by the bank, he climbed up it, pulling his traveling bag behind him. At the top, he lay still on the ground, keeping a low silhouette, carefully pulling on his eyeglasses.

There were two of them, large men. He wasn't quite certain, but he took them to be the Singleton brothers from the tavern. Their house had been in the other direction, up the Martinsburg Road. As it had been fired by the Federals, they might have moved elsewhere in town. But he'd heard nothing about their settling out his way. The farms along his road were large and prosperous. The Singletons were poor—poorer now without their residence and the better part of their belongings.

Harry had no choice but to presume they were following him. He could only wonder why, beyond their political sensibilities as Confederate sympathizers. How much could they know about him? He supposed it mattered little. What mattered was what they thought they knew.

There was a more direct way to his farm, skirting the foot of a low hill, crossing a rambling stream, and then cutting through a fold of woods unfortunately thick with brambles. But the travail would be worth it. He wanted to be at his place before the pair came near it.

His "family" as such, was in the kitchen—Estelle busying with the dinner, Caesar Augustus and the two hired hands at the table, Evangeline playing on the floor. Harry greeted them all in turn, running his hand through Evangeline's copper-colored curls, then motioned to Caesar Augustus to follow him out of the room.

They stopped in Harry's study to pick up a double-barreled shotgun he kept there, then went out onto the front porch, where they would have a wide view of the road and anyone leaving it to approach the house. Harry gave Caesar Augustus the shotgun and put his finger to his lips. They took adjoining chairs.

The Singletons never showed themselves—not, at least, in any way Harry or Caesar Augustus could detect. Finally, Harry broke the silence.

"I'm leaving again in the morning," he said. "I find myself compelled to work for the army."

"Scout?"

"Genuine scout, this time. Not spy."

"When're you coming back?"

"Don't know. There's going to be a big battle—soon as McClellan finds Lee. Or maybe the other way around."

"Where'll that be?"

"That's what I'm supposed to help find out. My fear is it could be near here."

Caesar Augustus set the shotgun down on the wooden floor, using great care. "Wouldn't Lee be aiming for Washington?"

Harry thought upon this. "I don't think he's strong enough to try to take the capital. He ran McClellan back down the York peninsula with maneuver and lightning attacks. He's not a general for the siege. At all events, he hasn't gone anywhere near the Federal City. He's somewhere up the Potomac Valley. Which is why I'm a bit fearful."

"I can't defend this farm against Lee's army."

"No. I want you all to leave. At the first sign of the Rebs."

"And go where?"

"To Jim O'Malley's."

"The blacksmith?"

Harry lowered his voice. "He's a conductor on the Underground Railroad. He has many hiding places. He'll put

57

Evangeline with a widow woman in town named Sally Thompson. It's Estelle I'm mostly worried about. You and the hired hands are freedmen. She's a runaway. It wasn't so long ago they used to burn runaways at the stake—even females. They still flog them."

"You trust O'Malley?"

"With my life."

"And ours, now."

Harry grinned. "There's something else I'd like you to do. I want you to sell what's left of the stock. Keep the wagon team and a couple of saddle horses. Turn them over to O'Malley for safe keeping. But sell the rest to the Union Army. I'll take Rocket with me."

"Like I said, they don't pay much."

"Better Yankee dollars than Confederate paper—and that's what you'll get if the Rebs take them. You'd be lucky to get even that."

"Where should I sell them?"

"There's a brigade or more of Federals in Martinsburg. That'd be the easiest."

"Anything else?"

"See if you can get word to my cousin Belle Boyd. I believe she's with kin in Front Royal. Tell her we've abandoned this house for the time being and she's welcome to use it if she's in the vicinity. She'll understand. General Jackson is beholden to her. Perhaps he'll provide us some protection."

"Not likely."

"He's a complicated man. He loves to kill Yankees, but he's opposed to slavery."

Something rustled in the bushes off to the left. They halted their conversation, listening like cats. Then there was a vague blur of movement across the yard.

"Rabbit," said Caesar Augustus. Harry hadn't been sure.

"I smell chicken."

"Fried chicken. That's our supper."

"We'd best be at it."

They rose.

"Marse Harry?"

"I've asked you some ten thousand times not to call me that."

"Just tell me. This damned war going to end soon?"

Harry took a deep breath. "No."

# Nine

Harry packed his saddlebags carefully, filling them with socks, linens, and clean shirts, and then adding a bottle of Old Overholt, two small tins of shortbread, a box of his small cigars, and three boxes of cartridges. Like a soldier in uniform, Harry was embarking on this enterprise with just one suit of clothes: a dark-brown coat and light-brown trousers, a wide-brimmed hat, white cotton shirt, farmer's boots, and no cravat. His usual fancy dress, however much it impressed his table mates in the gambling palaces, would do him little favor if he got captured. He had to look like a local man, wherever he traveled.

He was not going to leave poorly armed, however. He put a new breech-loading Sharps rifle he had acquired out West in his saddle scabbard, his .32 caliber Navy Colt in his belt, and a two-barrel Derringer in his pocket. He had a sheath knife in his boot and a Bowie knife on his belt besides. If he was captured, that would not be the end of it.

The rest of the people gathered at the Presbyterian burying ground wore black. Harry stayed to the rear of the still gathering crowd, unnoticed by most but able to watch everyone else. The graveside services were performed by a preacher from Kearneysville whom Harry did not know. The clergyman portrayed Ashby as a Godly man, mistakenly murdered by parties unknown who had failed to understand that Ashby was as stalwart a believer in the Confederate cause as any man in Virginia.

Harry looked around. There were two Union soldiers lounging by the church. The Kearneysville preacher was a daring fellow. If Harry had been provost marshal here, he would have put the preacher in irons. Using his emergency powers to suspend the right of habeas corpus, Lincoln had put a congressman and several newspaper editors in jail. If he wasn't more judicious, this clergyman could end up spending the rest of the war in Fort McHenry or the Point Lookout military prison.

The Singletons were present—the two brothers and a pretty girl Harry recognized as Peggy Singleton, the defiant, piano-playing Rebel who'd so indelibly established "Dixie" as a Southern song.

Harry's eye was led to the many other women in the group. Ashby's widow Martha, a noble-looking lady of unusually small stature, stood at the head of the open grave, supported by a slender young man Harry recognized as Lemuel Krause. He might have been her son. She and the Reverend Ashby had been without children.

Circling a bit to the right better to see faces, Harry took note of Lucinda Weverton, as brazenly unchaperoned as she'd been the evening before. Ann Harding, one of Shepherdstown's more fetching belles, was also present, though with her mother. Selma Keedy, Rachel Fairbrother, and Susan Hodges were there as well. Ashby's mourners included the very prettiest ladies of the town.

Harry moved farther to the right, curious as to mood and expression. He was surprised to see Ann and Selma actually crying, sadder even than the Reverend's widow. If not tearful, Rachel and Susan were certainly somber. Lucinda, however, seemed close to smiling. Peggy Singleton, in contrast, was almost sullen. Harry had the sense that she might explode into anger like a flame from smolder if intruded upon.

One of her brothers noticed Harry and nudged the other. They both commenced staring at him with bold and threatening directness.

It was a useful provocation. He was late, and needed to be on the road. He turned to leave. Jim O'Malley was on the other side of the gathering. Harry nodded to him, but did not go near. It was known in town that they were friends, but he didn't want to do anything that might indicate they were involved in some current business together. He certainly didn't want the Singletons thinking any such thing while Caesar Augustus and Estelle were in the blacksmith's care.

He walked over to German Street, not looking back until he reached it. He'd not been followed. The Singletons, apparently, were satisfied with having occasioned his departure.

Rocket seemed happy to be away, moving into a brisk trot without urging. Harry turned south, breaking into a canter on the road to Harper's Ferry.

He had thought of taking a route through Maryland on his way east, hoping to encounter McClellan somewhere the other side of South Mountain or the Cactoctin ridge. But, as Lincoln had said, the general had "the slows." He would likely have waited until he had his entire army gathered from its encampments around the capital before moving a single trooper. Harry doubted he was yet halfway from Washington to Frederick.

So Harry decided to take a more direct route, from Harper's Ferry across Loudon County all the way east to Leesburg— hard by the Potomac and near the scene of the slaughter at Ball's Bluff the year before to which Harry had so unfortunately been a witness.

Lee was more likely on the Virginia side of the river than the Maryland. In any case, it would be vital now to know. His job was scout. He'd best be at it.

He found Harper's Ferry full of Union troops under the command of a General D.S. Miles. If Lee was marching this way, he'd not yet given sign of it. Miles had put some guns atop the cliff on Maryland Heights, a huge, steep hill just across the Potomac from the town. But he was so complacent that he'd failed to establish defenses on Loudon Heights, the ridge that loomed over Harper's Ferry on the opposite side of the Shenandoah River just where it flowed into the Potomac. Were the Rebels to get cannon up there, Miles would have to retreat or surrender.

Harry paused at a tavern near the Harper's Ferry armory for a meal and a tankard of beer. There was less talk about

General Lee than there was about the western counties of Virginia forming their own state. The townspeople here were largely in favor of this bold and necessary action, but the manager of the armory was a Democrat and a Douglas man, and apparently was employing various forms of intimidation to forestall the separation—at least as concerned the voters of Jefferson County.

This was news that Harry would need to get to Washington—after he had done his service for General "Slows."

The Shenandoah had fallen in the dry heat of late summer and Harry found an easy ford just upriver from the town. Reaching the other side, he headed south, skirting the ridge known as Short Hill and then crossing the Blue Ridge at Snicker's Gap, following the hard-baked dusty roads to Purcellville and then Hamilton.

It was in this town he saw his first Confederate—an enlisted soldier lounging on the steps of the general store and post office. He had a long beard and no shoes. Harry could feel the man's eyes on his boots as he trotted by, but there was no attempt to halt him.

Just ahead, in a field a few yards beyond the town, he took note of a number of supply wagons, and a company-sized contingent of cavalry in gray and butternut milling about among them. He turned into a side street and followed it north out into the open countryside. There was a stretch of woods perhaps a mile along. He breathed easier when he was in among the trees.

As day neared night, he stayed off the roads nearly all the way to the river. Ball's Bluff was just ahead—Leesburg two or three miles to the right. On the Maryland side of the river, across the ford, was a good road leading to Poolesville, and beyond that, the Rockville Pike leading northwest to Frederick and southeast to Washington. But there was the smoke of campfires ahead as well—too many of them. Harry decided to pass the night in the sheltering trees. He'd move on at first light.

\*　　　\*　　　\*

It was an eerie feeling returning to Ball's Bluff. That prominence overlooking a narrow stretch of the Potomac and Harrison's Island beyond had been fought over as viciously as the ground at Manassas or Shiloh or any of the other major engagements. The badly led Union force had broken and fled to the bottom of the bluff, where there were too few boats to take them back to the Maryland side. Confederate fire from the top cut them down where they stood. Bodies had floated downstream to Washington for days afterward.

Now this patch of heavily forested high ground was utterly deserted—useless to either side and forgotten. Keeping a gentle hand to Rocket's reins, Harry picked his way over the treacherous terrain, remembering exactly where bodies had lain, where the commanding general had been dropped by a sharpshooter as he attempted to train a cannon on the Rebels.

The general's body had been taken to the other side of the river. There was no telling what final resting place the common soldiers found.

Harry headed south along the river, sticking to the top of the bluffs though that meant following a more meandering trail. At length, the ridge diminished in size and sloped down to a draw with a narrow road running through it.

Harry knew this ground. Staying within the trees, he proceeded east, moving parallel to the road. Within a few minutes, he came in view of the Potomac. It was very wide here, but shallow. Even in the early morning light, he could see the bottom. This was Edwards Ford.

There were Rebel wagons moving across it, eight or nine, with cavalry as outriders, all bound for the Maryland side and the good roads there.

He glimpsed a gray uniform just below him, and then another nearby. The ford was well guarded.

Slipping back into the brushy overgrowth, he ascended the ridge again and continued on back toward the north. A few miles up was another ford near White's Ferry—a more difficult crossing that the Confederates might have ignored.

But this proved to be guarded as well—and in use. More

wagons were moving through the water. Parties of horsemen were using the ferry.

Wagons and cavalry spoke of supply lines—not of an army deploying itself for battle. Clearly Lee had moved on from Leesburg. He'd not come west toward Harper's Ferry and Shepherdstown. That much was plain. If he'd gone directly east, he'd be colliding shortly with McClellan's huge but creeping force. Unless he'd returned to Richmond, which Harry doubted very much, Lee could have gone nowhere else but north.

That meant Frederick, and the main east-west line of the Baltimore and Ohio Railroad. The Union was being intruded upon in a very major way.

Harry returned to Ball's Bluff and dismounted, leading Rocket with gingerly tread down the steep path to the river. The current cut deep on this side and he'd have to swim his mount part of the way. But he knew where the shoals were.

Dripping wet, he was on Harrison's Island within a quarter hour. Once in cover, he replaced the cartridges in his weapons.

A long cloud of hanging dust marked the pike that ran northwest to Frederick. The army Harry could see distantly upon it was too thinly spread and moving too fast to be McClellan. He could only wonder how many days back the Federal force was. For all he knew, McClellan was moving toward Baltimore. More likely, he might have stopped and gone into camp, begging Washington for reinforcements. According to the newspapers, that's how he'd conducted much of his Peninsula Campaign down in Tidewater.

Harry had to decide whether to try to find McClellan and inform him of what he had thus far discovered, or turn and shadow Lee's advancing column to discover more. Once Lee reached the important crossroads that was Frederick, he'd have to show his hand, revealing his intended direction. It seemed to Harry he'd best be there to see.

Doubling back, he found a rough old road that took him to the Monocacy River, a deep stream that fed into the Potomac. Crossing it, he trotted and cantered Rocket north over open farmland to the village of Buckeystown. Emboldened by the fact that he'd traveled all this way unmolested, he decided to ride into the town. This would be that rare occasion where he could actually tell the truth. As Pinkerton liked to say, the best lie was the truth. He was a farmer from upriver. His only falsehood would be his reason for going to Frederick. He contrived one about a search for a runaway fiancée. He and Louise were hardly betrothed, but they had most definitely had an intimate relationship, and she could be said to have run away.

"All right, Rocket, my friend," he said, patting his horse's neck. "Let us go adventuring."

He entered the town at a walk. There were some Rebel soldiers in the street, gathered by a grocery. Others were inside. Harry guessed they were doing some shopping—coffee, sugar, and whiskey—paying for their purchases with Confederate banknotes in a state that relied on the Yankee dollar.

Harry nodded to a fat sergeant who'd been watching his approach with too much curiosity, keeping Rocket to his ambling pace. He'd proceeded perhaps twenty yards past the soldiery when the sergeant called out: "You there!"

He gave a gentle yank to Rocket's reins and turned him, facing the sergeant but not coming near.

"Good morning, sir," Harry said. "How may I help you?"

"You live here?"

"No, sir. Across the Potomac, in Virginia."

"Why're you here?"

"Personal business."

The fat man was carrying a dragoon pistol. "And what business is that?"

Now Harry prodded Rocket closer. "I'm looking for a woman." He took Louise's *carte de visite* from a coat pocket and showed it to the sergeant. "Have you seen her?"

The other examined the cardboard-mounted photograph carefully—perhaps too carefully. Then he grinned. "No, but I wouldn't mind if I did." He handed the picture back. "Where'd you cross the river?"

"Over by Leesburg."

"See any Yankees?"

Harry shook his head. "Just gentlemen like yourself."

"What's your trade?"

"I have a farm upriver."

"You don't have a farmer's hands."

"This is Virginia, sir. My darkies do the work."

The sergeant spat. He looked to be a man far too poor to be owning slaves, and was doubtless somewhat resentful of those who did. "Get off with you then."

Harry touched the brim of his hat, then turned the horse into the direction he was bound and trotted off down the street. Rounding a corner at the center of town, he pulled up before a remembered tavern.

There were no soldiers inside. The barroom was fairly crowded, the patrons, perhaps, not wishing to be where there were soldiers. Harry had hoped to find a card game. As Pinkerton thought runaway slaves his best source of intelligence, Harry had found loquacious gamblers far more informative and reliable—especially those in enemy uniform. Unlike Caesar Augustus, who with the help of Harry and Caitlin Howard had become one of the better educated men Harry knew, the "John Henrys," as the runaway slaves were called, had little military knowledge. Harry had encountered one such man out West who'd described a cavalry squadron as an entire Rebel army.

He went to the bar, thinking he'd wait a while until someone started a game. The whiskey was local—and not good. He made do.

The man to his left was a farmer type, who smelled as though he'd missed a month's worth of baths. To his right was a better dressed fellow—almost a gentleman—his expensive clothes covered with trail dust and a bit of horse sweat about his trousers and boots.

"You've been riding far," Harry said.

The man, who had a wisp of chin whisker and a thin moustache, glanced at Harry. Twice. "You, too."

"I've come down river," Harry said, "from up Harper's Ferry way."

"Yankees up there."

67

"For now." Harry signaled to the bartender to bring two whiskeys. "Looks like our liberation has arrived."

The man, whom he judged to be probably ten years older than himself, squinted as he examined Harry again. "Harper's Ferry's been liberated more'n once. But you folks keep welcoming back the Federals."

Harry took a sip. "Actually, I'm from Shepherdstown— eight miles up the river from Harper's Ferry. Got a farm there. We haven't been so welcoming."

Chin whiskers nodded his thanks for the drink, then lifted the glass to his lips, wiping them afterwards with the back of his hand. "What brings you to Buckeystown?"

"I'm just stopping by on my way to Frederick."

"Frederick?"

"Just up the road."

"So's General Lee's army. Why you want to get mixed up with that?"

"I'm looking for someone."

"In Lee's army?"

"No. A woman." Harry produced Louise's *carte de visite*.

"That's Louise Devereux," said the other. "I saw her on stage in Richmond. Just last year."

"That's who I'm looking for." He returned the picture to his pocket.

"What's a farmer from Shepherdstown got to do with Louise Devereux?"

Harry finished his drink. "My respects, sir. But that's a private matter."

The malodorous fellow to his left indulged in an enormous belch.

"I think I'd best be on my way," Harry said.

He cantered Rocket on the road north until he came in view of the Rebel military column again, and pulled off into some convenient woods. The Baltimore and Ohio tracks lay just ahead and, a few miles east, there was a spur that ran into Frederick. Harry decided he'd avoid the roads by following the railroad right-of-way instead.

He had almost reached the spur when he heard riders behind him. Looking over his shoulder, he recognized the nearest of them as his barroom friend from Buckeystown, and guessed the large man on too small a horse just behind as the sergeant at the grocery. Two other soldiers, as ill-mounted, clattered behind. He couldn't imagine how they had found him and kept up with him. Perhaps they'd been just behind him all this time.

Rocket hadn't the greatest speed of any animal Harry had owned, but he was an athlete of a horse and could hold a pace far longer than most. Harry spurred him to his utmost, pounding past the spur and its switching house. Ahead, he knew, was a trestle carrying the railway over the Monocacy once again, as the line led east to Relay and Baltimore.

Thankful that the water was low, he slid Rocket down the embankment, rushing to tie the horse to a wooden support beam. Then he snatched up his Sharps rifle and a handful of additional cartridges, ducking under the trestle and moving upriver to a point yards away from where he'd left his horse.

He was taking a risk, and perhaps had made a dumb mistake. If they found Rocket, all they'd need do was take him in hand and then hunt Harry down at their leisure. But they appeared to be acting in as much haste as he was.

After pulling on his spectacles, and rechecking the load of his rifle, he crawled to the top of the rise and peered over it. The man from the bar had reached the trestle and stopped his horse, waiting for the others to come up.

It was an easy shot to kill him. But that prospect seemed too much like murder. He lowered his sights slightly, aiming for the man's leg. Unfortunately, the man's horse turned as he fired and the round struck the animal, dropping him by the forelegs and making Harry very sad. But he had no time to wallow in this regret.

Quickly sliding another cartridge into the breech as his intended target extricated himself from his wounded mount, Harry got off another shot, hitting the man in the foot. Cursing, the fellow pointed frantically in Harry's direction as the fat sergeant came bouncing up. Harry aimed high this time, just above the sergeant's head. Ignoring the curses and angry instructions of the civilian, the fat one yanked his horse around and sprinted back down the track—his two companions abruptly following.

The civilian fell silent, looking now to Harry. He seemed scared.

"I'll let you live," Harry said. "But you must leave me be."

The man swore, but remained where he was.

Rocket got him easily across the narrow river. Once on the opposite shore, Harry headed southeast, hoping he'd find McClellan soon.

# Ten

The cavalry troop that was the first Union Army unit Harry encountered promptly placed him under arrest, ignoring his protests and even the pass signed by the President. The captain in charge amicably explained that he couldn't spare a man or the time to send Harry back down the Rockville Pike to his brigade headquarters. His orders were to proceed to the outskirts of Frederick with all dispatch, taking prisoners as necessary. Heavily armed civilians bearing suspicious passes qualified as necessary under his orders, so he had no choice but to bring Harry along.

For his part, Harry was just as pleased. He could unburden himself to this fellow, rather than trying to penetrate McClellan's staff, which was the largest in the army.

So he related his findings to the captain, a ruddy-faced New Yorker named Karl Gross. They'd been riding alongside one another ever since Harry's "capture."

"You're damn well certain that Lee's in Frederick?" Gross asked.

"No, sir, I'm not. But I think that's where he must be, as he's crossed the Potomac and sent no troops this way."

"He could be bound for Baltimore. That would surely fry our fish."

Harry shook his head. "East of the railway and the Monocacy, I didn't encounter a single gray uniform."

"So what's in Frederick that Lee would come all this way for?"

"Not much. Maybe he's going on to Pennsylvania. His army needs shoes. It's an amazement, the number of his men without shoes."

*Michael Kilian*

"He could send a couple of cavalry brigades and wagons to accomplish that."

"I'm only speculating. My fear is he's headed over the mountains to retake Harper's Ferry and Martinsburg—cutting the railroad to the west."

"Why 'fear?'"

"I have a farm with people on it midway between those places."

"You're a Virginian?"

"President Lincoln, sir, was born in Kentucky."

"You don't sound like his kind of southerner."

Harry caught his meaning. "I haven't split rails, but I pay the people on my farm well above the normal wage to do that—and they are all African and all free. My father and brother are with Longstreet's cavalry, yet I fight them."

"You do?"

"That's why I'm here. I despise the institution of slavery."

"Well, sir. I hope you get the chance to do that some more."

Sagging in their saddles from the overpowering heat, Captain Gross's cavalry troop eventually reached a long ridge overlooking the wide valley where, in the hazy distance, lay the city of Frederick. The dust of a military column was visible proceeding from it west toward Cactoctin Mountain.

Gross observed the panorama through his field glasses, then handed them to Harry. Though Harry remained technically under arrest, they had become friendly.

"That Lee's army?" Gross asked.

"A big part of it, anyway."

"Heading west."

"Maybe," said Harry, squinting through the binoculars. "Once he gets over that ridge, he'll be screened from us. He could go into Pennsylvania and we'd not know it."

Gross sat his horse with folded arms, thinking. Then he took the field glasses back again, re-examining the situation. "I'll send a dispatch rider to McClellan. In the meantime, we'll camp here." He studied Harry a moment. "I can send you with

72

him, if you like. Your Mister Pinkerton can straighten things out for you."

Harry had come to trust this man. "I'll stay with you people. Maybe I can be of some assistance."

"Suit yourself. If Lee sends troops this way, we're not much of a match."

A day passed with no word from McClellan or sign of his army. Harry quickly grew tired of idling in camp. There were card games, but Harry had no desire to take money from ill-paid ordinary soldiers, and avoided them. There was whiskey, but he'd been consuming too much of that in this war. It had amazed him how massed soldiery in battle could advance shoulder to shoulder against packed rows of enemy muskets and cannon. Equally amazing was how they bore the long, dreary periods of camp life in between the battles.

Finally, he suggested that he be allowed to reconnoiter the town.

"Still Rebs in Frederick," said Captain Gross. "Seem to be, anyway."

"That's what I thought would be useful to find out."

"Maybe I should send someone with you."

"A Federal uniform might suggest something to them."

Gross allowed a little grin to come and go. "Raines, are you a Reb?"

"No, sir. I've told you that."

"If I let you go down there, can you promise me there won't be a squadron of Secesh cavalry coming up here to take us directly after?"

"My word, sir, as a gentleman and a captain in Mister Pinkerton's service."

"Very well, then. If you can recruit some coffee down there, I'd be obliged."

"Yes, sir."

"And leave that Sharps rifle with me. The Rebs see you with that and you're a dead man. Only a Union man would be carrying that fine a weapon."

Harry handed it over with some regret, feeling a little

vulnerable without it, and not knowing when he might see it again if Gross suddenly received orders to move out.

At the foot of the ridge on which Gross and his men were camped, Harry turned right, skirting the farmland in the valley before him so that he might come at Frederick from the east and thus lessen suspicion that he could be some harbinger of McClellan's army. Reaching the Baltimore Pike, he turned left onto it, holding Rocket to a trot, and then slowing to a walk when the first Confederate soldiers came into view.

They were pickets, strung out across the road. Several were clumped together in the yard of a small stone house on his right. One rose, aiming a musket at him. Another strode into the middle of the road. A corporal.

"Where're you goin', Mister?"

"Home."

"You live here?"

Harry thought upon this. He knew the town well enough. "Yes, sir. West end of Patrick Street."

"Where're you comin' from?"

"Ellicott City."

"What were you doin' there?"

"Visiting a woman. Would you like to see her *carte de visite*?"

The man shook his head. Harry noticed that the other pickets in this position were still looking east. It occurred to him they were posted there not to watch for the likes of him but for the dust of McClellan's army.

"You got a pass?"

"Why should I have a pass?" Harry asked. "I live here. When I left, wasn't any army here except a few Yankee teamsters."

The corporal looked over Harry's saddlebags. He had stuck his Navy Colt in his belt at the back beneath his linen coat.

"All right. Go on. Just stay out of our way."

Harry proceeded into the town, turning off into a side street as soon as the pickets were out of view. He waited for some civilian traffic, which turned up a few minutes later in the form of a bearded man driving an empty farm wagon. Harry supposed all the farm wagons hereabouts were empty now, with so many thousands of Rebs at forage.

As the conveyance passed, Harry returned to the main road, following just behind, hoping his nearness to the wagon might enhance his pose as a local.

Two blocks later, a buggy with a well-dressed man and woman aboard swung in behind him. He began to relax a little.

Nearing the large, pillared bank that marked the central intersection of Frederick, he encountered a small body of horsemen in gray he feared was a cavalry patrol, but as they passed before him he saw that they were the staff of a high-ranking officer. He was not aware of how great the rank until he noticed the gray-bearded, splendidly uniformed figure of General Lee in their midst.

Harry sat his stopped horse, fearfully assessing his chances of breaking and running from the town. Lee was indeed a longtime friend of his father, who had been in the Mexican War with the general. Harry had known Lee in childhood, had dined with him, and had had two interviews with him in his Richmond office earlier that year, having convinced Lee that he was a supporter of the Confederate cause. He'd even persuaded Lee to write him a letter of recommendation for the Rebel navy, which Harry had used thereafter in lieu of an official Confederate pass. If Lee saw him there now, there might be the worst kind of hell to pay, if only because Harry had failed to join the navy.

Discreetly pulling down the wide brim of his hat, Harry waited for the small procession to pass by, interested that they were heading toward the National Road, the hard-bed Federal pike that led over the mountains to Hagerstown and points west. Lee, happily, was absorbed with his own thoughts, and kept his eyes on the road ahead.

When they were gone and the jangle of spurs and swords could no longer be heard, Harry turned around and went up the next side street he came to, proceeding to a remembered livery where he thought he might put up his horse. Its stable doors were hanging wide open. Urging Rocket within, he found every stall empty and the place bereft of straw, hay, and grain. Paying in Confederate scrip, the Rebels had no doubt helped themselves to everything, even tack.

Pulling shut the big doors, Harry led Rocket into a stall, bolted its door, and then ascended the ladder to the hayloft, opening the shuttered window at the far end. It faced west, and had a view of much of the town and the high ridge that was Cactoctin Mountain just beyond. Putting on his spectacles, he could not discern Lee's little parade, but there were many Rebel troops still in the city—some on the move, too many just loitering.

He seated himself on the wooden flooring, leaning against the wall beside the window to increase the scope of his view so that he might be able to see the approach of any intruder. Despite the respite of a day in Gross's camp, he was very tired. He had just begun to drowse off when he felt the cold touch of hard metal against his neck.

Realizing it must be a gun, he made no effort to turn. "Who are you?" he managed to say, amazed that the visitor had come upon him so quietly.

"A friend, Harry Raines."

The gun came away. Harry turned and looked into the far-seeing eyes of Jack Tantou.

The Metis wore the yellow leather jacket and weather-beaten brown boots that had been his principal clothes in the West, but had replaced the yellow-striped Union cavalry britches with trousers of a more civilian hue. He was also wearing a remarkably clean white cotton shirt. He had pistols in his belt and a long knife hanging from it. His long black hair had been pulled back and tied. His hard, creased, deeply tanned face was as expressionless as ever.

"What in blazes are you doing here?" Harry asked.

"I am a scout for McClellan's army."

"And just where is that fine body of men?"

Tantou lowered himself onto the flooring, again making no sound. "I do not know, Harry Raines. They asked me to find the Rebel soldiers, not McClellan's."

"Well, so you have done."

"You, too, Harry Raines."

"How in hell did you know I was up here?"

"I was in an empty house on the main street. Many empty houses here now. I saw you ride in. I followed."

"Where's your horse?"

"In the cellar of the empty house."

Harry turned fully away from the window, relaxing. He took out two of his small cigars, but the Indian declined. He did, however, accept a swallow of whiskey from Harry's flask.

"Why are you here, Harry Raines?"

"I went to Shepherdstown to make arrangements for my stock and people. I was on my way back to report to McClellan when I ran into one of his cavalry patrols south of here. They put me under arrest and took me with them, but their captain is a nice fellow and let me come into Frederick to see what's what."

"You should have waited for the Rebel army to leave. Part of it has already." The Metis was sitting cross-legged, as though by a campfire in the West. His eyes were fixed on something in the distance out the window.

"Yes. We saw their dust."

"A man told me it was a General John Walker leading that column."

"Don't know of him."

"They are heading for the Potomac and Harper's Ferry."

Harry thought upon that prospect, and shuddered. "You're sure?"

"That's what I was told. They asked for shortest way to Point of Rocks. It is very easy to be a scout here. The distances are small. Many civilians, and they all talk."

"Just be careful, Jack. Some of them are Rebs."

"I am always careful, Harry Raines. That is why I am still alive—and why you are still alive."

He accepted another sip of Harry's whiskey. Harry took a couple more himself, then corked the flask and returned it to his pocket.

"We should get this news to McClellan," Harry said.

"I traveled for a while with the general and his army. He may not get here until next year. And there is more news to get."

"I just saw General Lee pass by. He was heading toward the National Pike. It runs east and west."

"I know, Harry Raines. I have looked at the map."

"But he could be going almost anywhere."

Tantou nodded, still looking out the window.

"How large a force did this General Walker have?"

"I was a scout in California and New Mexico Territory, where no one has a large force. This one was big, but only a small part of General Lee's army."

"It's odd that Lee would break up his people like that—so deep in Union territory."

"He has only McClellan to worry about."

"Lee got a good measure of the man outside Richmond. McClellan may be our worst general."

Finally, Tantou shifted his gaze to Harry. "Why are you scouting for him, Harry Raines? You said you were going to stay upriver there and be a farmer."

"They locked Louise up in the Old Capitol Prison. Pinkerton said he wouldn't release her unless I agreed to work for McClellan."

"They make you fight this war even if you don't want to?"

"That will soon be the law. Conscription is coming. They already have it in the South."

"Conscription?"

"They make you a soldier whether you want to be or no. They take you."

"Where is Louise Devereux?" Tantou had become greatly devoted to her.

"I do believe they have released her. Pinkerton is not a deceitful man—spy that he may be."

"Maybe then I should go back to Washington City and find out."

"No, Jack. I can see it now. We are needed here."

After nightfall, Harry went out to find a grocery, returning with two one-pound bags of coffee, cornbread, a few slices of smoked ham, and a half dozen apples. They consumed everything but the coffee and passed the night in the stable loft. Toward dawn, they heard numerous commotions over the way of Patrick Street, and then for a long time the sound of marching feet. At first light, they crept forth, finding their neighborhood deserted. Fetching their horses, they trotted west a few blocks, encountering only some tardy teamsters and, at the edge of town, some medical orderlies struggling with a military ambulance that had lost a wheel.

Turning back, they made their way back into the cover of the buildings.

"I would say Lee has gone," said Harry.

"As he is not here, that would be true, Harry Raines."

"We could follow him, and see where he is headed. Or we could go back and tell the army what we've learned. It might spur McClellan along."

"Or one of us could follow Lee and the other go back."

"Yes."

Tantou turned his horse in the direction the Rebel army appeared to have gone. "I will see you again, Harry Raines."

And then he vanished.


As Harry had feared, Gross's troop had moved, but, after a few inquiries among soldiers in the Union cavalry brigade that had come up, he was able to find them—camped now in a farmer's field near the B & O tracks below the ridge.

Gross was near his tethered horse, polishing his boots. If McClellan did arrive that day, such matters would assume supreme importance.

"I have news," Harry said, standing before him. "Lee's left Frederick—I think heading west."

Gross looked up, squinting against the morning sun. "Why d'you think that?"

"He split off part of his army—a division maybe—under a General Walker. They're bound for Harper's Ferry. The rest took to the National Pike. It goes west to Hagerstown."

"You find all this out yourself?"

Harry shook his head. "Ran into another Union scout. Name's Jack Tantou, originally French Canadian. He told me

*Michael Kilian*

about Walker. Tantou's still out there, shadowing Lee's main force."

Gross ceased his labor for a moment, screwing up his face as he pondered the grassy ground. "The both of you—this Frenchman—are sure about this?" Gross asked.

"I saw Walker's troops. We followed Lee's army to the outskirts of town."

The captain gave his boot another lick with the brush, then rose, hopping a bit as he pulled on the boot. "Very well, Raines. I'll ride on up to the colonel commanding the brigade and pass this on. Why don't you get yourself some breakfast and wait for me?"

"Happy to. Uh, captain. My Sharps rifle?"

"Color Sergeant's got it. He's around here somewhere." Gross mounted his horse. "Thanks for this. Hope you're right."

"You want Lee to go west?"

"Not in any particular. I just want what I tell the colonel to be what's true. He gets mighty disagreeable when it's not."

Harry went to his saddlebag, removing the coffee. "As you requested, sir."

"Why, thank you." He moved off at a trot.

Harry got some food, not liking it much, then went back to Rocket and unsaddled him, using that object as a pillow as he bedded down for a little sleep.

He awoke after only a short while, his neck hurting, the rising heat and the flies a pernicious bother. He sat up, slapping at the insects. At a snake-rail fence not fifty feet away a Union soldier was exclaiming in joyful spirit: "Cigars! I found me three good Reb cigars!"

Harry paid him little mind, except to consider how wonderful a good Southern cigar would be just then. He waited for a whiff of the smoke that would follow the soldier's lighting one.

But the man did not. He stood there, reading the paper that Harry gathered had been wrapped around the cigars. He seemed puzzled.

"What you got there?" Harry asked.

"Not sure. Some kind of order."

80

Harry rose, stretching, then ambled over.

"You a scout?" the soldier asked.

"That I am." Harry took the paper, pulling out his spectacles. At the top of the paper was the heading: "General Order No. 191." Harry read on with amazement. The order was from Lee, and set forth his army's order of battle. There was amazement more. Lee had not only broken off one part of his force; he was cutting his army into four parts!

General Walker was indeed bound for Harper's Ferry—to occupy the high ridge known as Loudon Heights that overlooked the town from the opposite side of the Shenandoah River. An even larger force under Confederate Major General Lafayette McLaws was to take the road from Frederick to Burkittsville, cross South Mountain, and descend on Harper's Ferry from the northeast, occuping Maryland Heights just across the Potomac. Stonewall Jackson was to quick march up to Williamsport, cross the Potomac and take Martinsburg, and then proceed toward Harper's Ferry from the west. In the meantime, Lee and Longstreet's corps would move on to Hagerstown.

If McClellan were made aware of this, he might for once hurry. With his far superior numbers, he could take on Lee's army piece by piece, destroying each in turn. He could end the war.

"What's it mean?" the soldier asked.

The man should have full credit for his discovery, even though it had bewildered him. Harry handed back the paper. "Hold this safe and come with me."

"Where're we going?"

"To find as high-ranking an officer as we can and see if we can get this to General McClellan."

"It's that important?"

"Sir, at this moment you are the most valuable soldier in the Army of the Potomac."

Harry went to saddle Rocket, realizing with sudden great sadness that, riding with Longstreet somewhere near the ridge that was South Mountain, was his father, a Rebel colonel, and his brother Robert, a captain.

81

# Eleven

The details of Lee's General Order No. 191 were sent to McClellan by dispatch rider and also by telegraph, yet it was two more days before the lead elements of his main body reached Frederick.

It was another day still before the great general himself arrived, with a staff so numerous they came into camp in a grand parade.

Gross shook his head. "My troop should be miles and miles ahead of the general commanding," he said. "I've been asking for orders for three days but they told me there would be no new orders until the general arrives."

They were at a fence rail, watching McClellan as he sat in the saddle in the pasture beyond, receiving the obsequious homage of the unit commanders who had reached this place before him.

"You are led by the wrong man," Harry said.

"You know one better?"

"Two. Out West. Grant and Sherman."

"The hero of Fort Donelson."

"The victor, at all events."

"General McClellan has friends in Congress." Gross spat. "I'll take a sip of your whiskey, if you'd oblige me, sir."

"Certainly," said Harry, handing the officer his flask.

Gross, Harry had discovered, was a chess player. If not of the caliber of Harry's army surgeon friend, Colonel Phineas Gregg, the cavalryman was a more than decent player. While McClellan continued conferring with his commanders, they sat on the grass and played several games, using a small folding board Gross carried in his pack. Harry beat him, two games to one, but by the time they'd completed five, Gross had three victories to Harry's two.

"Let us leave it at that," Harry said. He rose. "I wonder if McClellan plays chess." Two tents now had been erected for the general's use, and others were going up around it.

"He doubtless does," said Gross, putting away the board. "But I expect he takes an hour a move."

There were so many troops about now they seemed to fill the valley all the way to Frederick's outskirts. And all sitting on their asses.

Pinkerton arrived in the company of a column of supply wagons. Harry went to him immediately, disappointed that Boston Leahy was not there as well.

"Where is Joseph?" he asked.

"Arresting Rebel agents who continue to contaminate our capital," said Pinkerton, dismounting. "Good to see you, Raines. I feared you would not be with us."

"A Virginia gentleman keeps his word, Mister Pinkerton. May I inquire whether you have abided by yours?"

"In what regard?"

"In regard to Miss Louise Devereux."

Pinkerton removed his bowler hat and mopped his balding crown with a handkerchief. "Yes, yes. She is at liberty. Of course. Now tell me, was it you who found Lee's orders?"

Harry shook his head. "It was an ordinary soldier. He showed them to me, but it was he who first took note of their importance."

"Well, it was a discovery of great moment. You could see the Divine hand in it."

"It would be of greater moment if General McClellan would act upon it."

"He has, Raines, he has. He is here. When he makes his plan, we will be off against Lee."

"This situation needs no plan of his devise," Harry said. "We have Lee's plan. McClellan should be going hell for leather to get across the mountains. He could catch Lee between the Potomac and the ridges. If he'd move fast, he could do it before the other parts of Lee's army come back to him."

"One cannot advance a great army without plans," Pinkerton said, eyeing Harry as though he'd just said something lunatic. "There must be plans, organization, orders."

"*'L'audace. Toujours l'audace.'*"

"What?"

"Something Frederick the Great said, I think, or one of Napoleon's marshals. It well applies in the present circumstance. The general likes to think of himself as the Napoleon of our time. It's time he acted like one."

"Mind your tongue, Harry. That's impertinence. In war time, worse."

Harry actually liked Lincoln's master spy, and the Scotsman had been nothing if not hospitable to him. He regretted this conversation was taking such an acrimonious turn.

"At the very least, Mister Pinkerton, he should advance some troops to take and hold the mountain passes," Harry said. "If he doesn't seize them now he may have to fight for them later."

"I'll mention that to him." Pinkerton took a step forward and clapped Harry on the shoulder. "In the meantime, you should get yourself into that country. That's where we need you."

"Happily, Mister Pinkerton."

"If you can find Lee's army, send word back to us. Or come back yourself if necessary. But find that damned Rebel."

Harry held his tongue. He had already found Lee, but nothing had come of it.

"I want you to scout to the top of the Cactoctin ridge," Pinkerton said.

That wasn't ten miles distant. "I will go beyond if I can," said Harry. "If the passes are clear, I'll get word to you. They may be. Lee probably doesn't know that we know where he's bound."

"Good, good. Your Indian, he is performing well?"

"He's a better man than I am at this. He is doubtless in those mountains as we stand here."

"Then you will be wanting to join him."

Harry started toward Rocket, whom he had saddled. "There's an opportunity here, Mister Pinkerton."

"I know that, Raines. I know it. Don't worry. Lee will be sorry he ever decided to come north into Maryland."

Mounting and taking up Rocket's reins, Harry looked west to the ridge and then down at Pinkerton. "Celerity is the key here, Mister Pinkerton. You don't need a scout to tell you that."

"Go do your job, Harry."

The Cactoctin ridge ascended steeply in height as it ran north, but was fairly low immediately to the west of Frederick. Harry proceeded toward it cautiously, as wary of being shot by a nervous Union picket as by a Confederate. He kept off the main western road, crossing farmer's fields and jumping the fences. He reached the summit in an easy climb, pleased to find the draw unoccupied by soldiers.

Deciding to use the road, he held Rocket still for a moment as he surveyed the narrow valley beyond, wearing his spectacles and using field glasses loaned him by the army.

Directly below lay the town of Middletown, looking generally peaceful and unmolested by the enemy. Cactoctin Creek ran in a wavering pencil line just the other side of the place. Past it, depending on the state of harvest, was green, yellow, and brown farmland, and then the steeply rising and far more formidable ridge that was South Mountain. From where he sat his horse, Harry could see three of the passes that led through it—Crampton's gap, immediately before him, where the road went to Harper's Ferry; the smaller Fox's Gap, and the road to Sharpsburg; and Turner's Gap, slightly to the north, through which a road ran to Hagerstown.

McClellan should have dispatched a brigade of cavalry to each the instant he'd received the copy of General Order 191. Harry was going to make a poor substitute. He could only wonder as to which of the passes Tantou had gone—if any of them.

Harry was about to return his field glasses to their case

when a glint of something up the valley gave him pause. Turning the glasses in that direction, he felt a clammy chill upon his back despite the day's heat.

It was more than one glint. There was a turning of the north-bound valley road at that point. Horsemen were upon it, and as they came around the curve their sabers were struck by the light of the sun, which had just emerged from behind a cloud.

They kept coming. This was a brigade—possibly an entire division. Harry guessed it might be the glory hound J.E.B. Stuart, who the previous spring had famously ridden around McClellan's entire army down on the York Peninsula. Here he was attending to more serious business, providing a cavalry screen for Lee. When McClellan came up, he'd likely move his people back up into the passes.

No danger of that happening any time soon.

Sighting no rebels in Middletown, Harry rode down into it, pausing at a tavern on the town's broad main street. He took a seat at a long table, as there was no bar as such—only a grocery counter. He was served by a barefoot, slovenly, but pretty young woman, who looked at him speculatively. Likely she viewed every new customer as someone who might possibly extricate her from her circumstance.

Harry ordered beefsteak, a yam, and fresh carrots, and with that cornbread and butter and beer. Refilling his flask with the local whiskey, he returned the girl's flirtatious smile, somewhat abashed that he'd failed to remove his spectacles, as he always did when in the company of pretty ladies.

"Travelin' far, mister?" she said, leaning near. It had been a while since she'd bathed.

"As far as I can get without running into southern soldiers."

"Where you bound?"

"Shepherdstown," he said, sipping the good, cool beer. "I have a farm there."

"Well, they were headed that way, so you'd best linger a while. Two days they been gone from here—except for the horsemen who keep poundin' up and down the valley. You're a lucky man to have stopped in this house and be havin' such fine vittles. We hid everything from them soldiers. Folks who weren't so wise are goin' to be hungry for a while. The Rebels took whatever they could find on hoof and in sacks. If they hadn't been moving so fast, they'd have likely taken everything that weren't nailed down. Never seen such a miserable lookin' collection of men. I mean, some of 'em was marchin' barefoot."

Harry glanced down at her own grimy feet, but that only produced another smile.

"I wear shoes. I just don't like to wear 'em inside."

"They kept on west—Lee's men—on the Boonsboro Road?"

"Seems that they have. That's what my daddy said."

"Did they bother the townspeople much—aside from foraging?"

"Just to ask questions—like you're doing."

"What about those Confederate horsemen. Have they been back?"

"Just once through here. They've been lookin' for Yankees."

The use of the term troubled Harry a bit. "Are you 'Yankees' here?"

"We're a Union house, mister. I was just speakin' the way they were askin'. We were glad to see 'em go."

It occurred to Harry she might not have been glad to see all of them go. "Let us hope we can be glad that they don't come back."

She lingered, though someone was calling for her from the kitchen. "What about you?" she asked. "You a 'Yankee'?"

"I'm a farmer from upriver. I don't soldier for either side."

"What about the Union Army? Is it comin'?"

"Bound to be, I suppose. If they don't get lost." He smiled.

The summons from the kitchen became more insistent. She gave Harry a wink and hurried off, her bare feet moving like a dancer's.

Harry finished his meal quickly. She was a talkative lady, and he would surely be among the topics of her next conversation.

He took the Hagerstown road out of town. It led northwest. The Rebel cavalry had been heading south. Harry figured if he swung this way he might well miss them. He needed to get up onto South Mountain. What he needed to see was on the other side.

Reaching Cactoctin Creek, he turned Rocket into it, keeping the horse in the shallow water for a half mile or so before reaching a country lane that went west.

He'd devised a sort of plan, if the Confederates would let him carry it out. There was a trail that ran along the top of South Mountain from the Potomac River all the way to Pennsylvania. North of Turner's Gap, there was a stone tower erected to the memory of George Washington. Harry had visited it frequently as a child. From its top, one could see all the way west across the Cumberland Valley to Hancock, Maryland, a stretch of some fifty miles. If there was no sign of Lee in that wide swath of open country, Harry would take the trail south again down to Crampton's and look for dust on the road to Harper's Ferry.

Maybe, along the way, he might find a Rebel willing to engage in conversation—whether induced by whiskey or knife point.

He had removed his spectacles in the tavern. He put them back on and headed straight for the ridge.

There were Rebel pickets at Turner's—loud-mouthed fellows who announced their presence by sound before Harry had them in sight. He avoided them by detouring into the trees and crossing the road out of their view. Reaching the summit, he completed the short distance to the tower, pulling off into the trees.

He observed the scene for a moment. Nothing moved but a few birds. The tower had no clear view to the east, from which direction McClellan would be coming, so it was not much use to the Rebels at this point as a lookout station. With luck, it might be deserted.

Tying Rocket to a laurel bush, he crept to the edge of the trees and then darted across the small clearing to the tower's stone wall, flattening himself against it. Waiting a few minutes, he then edged forward, coming at last to the doorway. Within the cool, dark interior were stone stairs ascending in circular fashion to the open parapet on top. Harry moved up them quietly.

The sunlight came upon him brilliantly. Pausing a moment to catch his breath, he went to the edge of the stone wall and surveyed the territory he'd come to see.

There would be no need to scout further. To the north, a long curtain of dust marked a column heading for Hagerstown. To the west, reaching all the way to what looked to be Antietam Creek, was another, its baggage train still on the outskirts of Boonsboro directly below. Harry figured Lee himself must be with this body—the two columns together constituting half his army.

McClellan easily had twice as many men—four times, perhaps, or more. If he had his troops on this ridge now, Lee would be done for, however great his genius.

But McClellan was not here. Sighing, Harry took a sip of whiskey and leaned forward on his elbows. He wondered if Lee had ever visited this tower, honoring as it did the husband of Lee's wife's grandmother, Martha Custis Washington.

The sharp report off to the right was followed quickly by the sing of a bullet. Harry dropped beneath the parapet wall. He'd stupidly left his Sharps in his saddle and was armed only with his Navy Colt and Derringer. There was only the one way out of the tower. He had trapped himself in as tight a spot as a man could be. He thought how much Jack Tantou would laugh, but then, the Metis never did that.

# Twelve

One choice was surrender, but the consequences of that were clear. Harry would be assumed to be a spy and shot or hanged directly.

The shot had come from north of the tower. Rocket was in the woods to the south. If there was only one shooter, Harry might be able to run for it now, taking his chances with the enemy's marksmanship. He could wait until darkness to attempt the same thing, but the shooter might by then have a dozen reinforcements—possibly hundreds, if J.E.B. Stuart were to pull back to South Mountain.

Harry needed more information about his disagreeable situation, and there was unfortunately only one way to obtain it.

On hands and knees, he moved a short ways along the parapet, then sprung to his feet, his head rising above the wall just long enough to see the flash of the next shot, which missed him by a scant foot. He learned nothing new from this. A man with a gun was trying to kill him, and coming closer to accomplishing that task. The fellow was in the woods but had a clear view of the tower.

This observation gave Harry a more practical idea. Risky as it was, it seemed his only opportunity to escape the tower alive and at liberty.

Moving to the spot where he had originally stood up, he rose again, more slowly now. As he dropped at the sound of the next shot, Harry let out a powerful scream, tossing his hat over the side—acting of which Caitlin and Louise might be proud. Or at the least, amused.

He hurried now down the stone steps in the tower's darkness, trying desperately to avoid making noise. Nearing the

90

bottom, he dramatically failed in the latter task, slipping on a step and tumbling down those remaining. The wrenching cry he gave out upon hitting the floor was genuine. He could only hope it would add to the effectiveness of his charade.

Crouching then against the wall beside the doorway, rubbing his horribly bruised shin and knee with one hand while he held his Navy Colt at the ready with the other, he calmed himself as best he could and tried to ease his rapid breathing.

He was surprised to find himself near to shaking with fear. Charging the enemy in battle was one thing. The danger was fully known. One was on the attack, one of many attackers, carried forward by a mixture of anger, excitement, and—strangely—exultation. Here, though, he was simply prey, facing the unknown, as powerless as a possum up a tree.

His only hope was that his adversary was as incautious as he had been. Everything depended on the shooter's boldness and confidence in his abilities. Hunters liked to believe in kills, not misses.

Minutes passed. Harry fought to keep his mind from his pain, listening and watching for the slightest change in light or sound that might signal the approach of the predator.

It proved to be a sound. The ridge summit was stony, and the footfall of his adversary clicked one rock against another, and did so very near. Next came a shadow momentarily flickering across the opposite wall. Then came a boot upon the step.

Entering, the intruder proved small and slender, and wore civilian clothes—black farmer's boots, tan homespun trousers, dark gray jacket, and black hat, with long, straw-colored hair falling to his shoulders. He carried an outsized, long-barreled revolver, held to the fore, hammer cocked. His eyes were on the stairs.

Harry could now kill the pesky son of a bitch with a single shot to the back. It was war, he'd been fired on, and the bastard would kill him given a second's chance. But he now found that an impossibility. The finger muscle would not move. He'd come back home with an ardor to leave this war and this was the reason why.

91

He would wait for the shooter to act first. This was of course very stupid, but there were times when it was important to be stupid.

He was stupider than he thought. He had failed to cock the hammer of his Colt. He would have to do that now before he could fire. As quietly as he could, he pulled it back.

But the click might as well have been an exploding shell. The intruder whirled around so fast his pistol went off without aim, the round striking the wall just beside Harry's ear and ricocheting twice in the confining space of the tower. It was an amazement that neither of them was hit.

Harry still did not fire, his trigger finger stayed by another surprise. The face that went with that long, straw-colored hair was that of a woman.

It was a pretty, well-boned face, though one as homespun as her clothing. In a time when a lady's social class was in part determined by the lightness of her complexion, the girl's skin was tanned and a little weathered, a contrast to the bright blue of her eyes. He took her to be about his own age, though possibly younger. She was holding her big revolver in a practiced way. Something about her suggested the hunter. He wondered if, like him, she was employed as a scout. Many women on both sides risked their lives as spies and couriers, working the dangerous territory that lay between armies—or behind the enemy's lines.

Harry gently released the hammer of his Colt. "I am not going to shoot you," he said.

She hesitated, then lowered her own weapon. "I expected you'd be in uniform. Looked like butternut from below."

"You expected I'd be dead." He extended his painful leg, easing back against the wall. "Just why did that strike you as so desirable?"

"Just told you. Thought you was one of them. Are you?"

"Them?"

"The invaders. Hell's own hordes, trampling over the free soil of the Cumberland Valley yonder."

He rubbed his shin again, which seemed to worsen its ills.

"You're Union, then?" Her own broad but gentle accent was rich with the mountains, with a touch of the Scots her likely forebears must have brought with them.

She nodded. "That I am. But what be you, sir?" she asked, her pistol still firmly in hand.

"I'm a farmer from across the river, near Shepherdstown. Own a horse farm, though I've had to sell all my stock to the army."

"You don't sound like you're from over that way. You sound fancy, like plantation folk below the Rappahannock. I've lived up the valley from Boonsboro all my years and I never heard no one with house and ground hereabouts talk like you. Just the occasional 'Southern gentleman,' passin' through."

"I've lived both places," Harry said. "I live only here now."

"This ain't Shepherdstown. Miles away and on the wrong side of the river. What're you doin' up on this ridge?"

"You are with the Union, ma'am?"

"Free soil, free men, free labor. And may God damn to hell every slave-holdin' Rebel. I ain't partial to darkies. I ain't partial to most folks. But they're people. They got a right to their own lives."

"Why were you shooting at me?" Harry asked.

"I come up here to make sure the Rebels was gone, so I could bring my stock and valuables out of hiding. I was comin' south along the mountain trail when I seen you up here with your spy glasses—a Rebel scout if I ever saw one."

"Did it not occur to you that I was looking to the west, where General Lee has two columns kicking up miles of dust?"

"What's your meanin'?"

"My meaning is that you're half right. I am a scout, but for Mister Lincoln's side. I came here to find Lee's army, and have discovered a big part of it. It's news I'd like to share with the Federal army, which is over by Frederick, but instead I've nearly had my head shot off by an injudicious and impulsive young lady. What were you trying to do?"

"Kill me a Rebel before they was all gone." She grinned, sitting down on one of the stone steps, apparently satisfied with the placement of Harry's loyalties.

93

"Why such animus?"

She took off her hat. "Huh?"

"You hate them so much you'd shoot one on sight? You're not even a soldier."

"They fired three houses on the Funkstown Road for holding beef back from 'em. Killed a man and wife. Killed my husband, too—last year, at Romney." Her eyebrows twisted. "Why're you smilin'?"

"I'm not really. Just reflecting. General Lee was running the Rebel show out by Romney then," Harry said. "General McClellan had the Federals. Now here they are again—if McClellan would ever get here." He thought he saw tears gathering in her eyes. "I meant no offense to your husband's memory, ma'am."

"What's your name, Mister?"

"Harrison Raines."

"Don't call me ma'am. He's been gone more'n a year. I ain't old enough to be looked upon like I'm some wrinkly old widow woman."

"Yes, uh, Miss. May I ask your name?"

"It's Alice. Alice Robertson. That was my husband's name—Robertson. I was born McNair. My friends call me Allie." She holstered her weapon, and then stuck out her hand. "Happy to meet you, Mister Raines. Hope you're all you say."

Harry leaned forward to complete the handshake. Her hand was hard and strong, and as tanned as her face. Putting his own revolver away, he got clumsily to his feet. "I am, though not quite as fit as I was before I climbed this tower."

"Did I hit you?" She seemed genuinely concerned.

"No, Miss. I took a tumble descending the stairs."

"I guess that's my doin'—shootin' at you like I was."

"You needn't feel guilty. I was making haste in hopes of shooting you."

"Coulda put a ball through my back. Why didn't you?"

"I've been through two big fights in this war and quite a few little ones. I'm tired of the work of bullets—especially my own."

"You've killed men?"

He decided not to mention the Baltimore woman who'd accidentally died at his hand—as she was trying to shoot him. "Yes, ma'am—Miss. And you?"

"No, sir. But I'm fixin' to—like I told you."

"Then you'll be a busy lady. There are thousands of Rebels on both sides of this mountain."

"Don't you worry. I'll have my justice."

"You ought to throw in with us."

"Us?"

"The Army of the Potomac. McClellan will be up sometime. He'd appreciate some information about what to expect on your side of South Mountain."

"Then whyn't he send out more scouts? You're only the second I know of come out this way."

"Who's the other one you know about?"

"There was talk of some Indian working for the Federals. They say he killed three Confederate soldiers outside Burkittsville."

"An Indian? Hasn't been an Indian in these parts for half a century." It was troubling that Tantou was making such a name for himself.

"There 'pears to be one now," Alice said.

Harry was imagining the lady in a dress, but in that image she had a gun in her hand. "Why didn't you use a rifle?" he asked. "Why that horse pistol?"

"If I'd used a rifle, you'd be a dead man now. The horse pistol is all I had with me."

"Let us hope there will be no further occasion for using it today."

"Who are the Rebs on the east side of the mountain?"

"I saw General Stuart's cavalry down between here and Middletown. Pretty much all his people. I got around them coming up here, but I'm not sure it will be so easy now. Stuart's got to hold these passes and he'll be pushed back up into them when McClellan comes up. Hard for anyone to get through his troopers even now."

"You fixin' to go back? Thought you were goin' on to your farm?"

95

"That's going to have to wait. Lee's people are on the Sharpsburg Road."

"Saw some on the Hagerstown Road, too," she said.

"If you have stock in hiding, you'd best keep them there."

"I'd best be checking on 'em." She rose, nimbly, and went to the doorway, peering out. "Whyn't you come back through Boonsboro with me? You can wait there until your General McClellan arrives."

"It was my hope that what I have to tell him will hasten that event."

"Well, we won't hasten a damn thing lingerin' here. Can you walk?"

He took a step. "Mostly."

They retrieved their horses—hers a huge beast even larger than Rocket—and returned to the trail, riding single file, Allie in the lead. Her animal looked no stranger to the plow.

"It's gettin' late," she said. "You sure you want to try to get through all that Rebel cavalry right now?"

"If I'm to do my job, I have no choice."

She looked back at him. "Yes, you do. You can hole up at my place for the night and then work your way north in the morning to cross the mountain where those Rebels ain't."

"I'd probably lose a day getting to McClellan."

"Hell you will. You said he's comin' this way. He'll be coming to you. Anyways, you'll lose more'n a day if Jeb Stuart's horse soldiers grab you."

She stopped, waiting while he considered the matter. There was an appeal to her logic, especially since it included the promise of a decent meal and a bed. But if the way to McClellan was still clear . . .

"If there's a chance to get through, I should take it."

"You're to leave me then?"

She had struck him as a resourceful lady, but maybe that was more the boldness of her talk.

"I should be most unhappy to do that, since you've been

96

so kind as to miss me three times shooting. But I feel obliged to the army. A favor was done me by them. Perhaps you could come with me."

Allie shook her head, her blond hair swirling as she did so. "I got to get back to my place. I left it in the care of the hired man, an' he's about as bright as a dead toad."

Harry was irritating himself with his continuing indecision. "We'll ride to the gap. If the road's clear, I'll go east and you can take it west to Boonsboro."

"And if it ain't clear?"

He shrugged. "We must be resourceful."

"Does that mean go to my place?"

"I suppose it does."

She pointed to behind him. "Where this ridge trail reaches Pine Knob up there? It forks. The main trail goes up to the top of the knob, and then along the ridge to Black Rock. The other branch goes left, and works its way down the slope into the valley. Comes out not far from my house."

"Not so easy in the dark."

"No."

"Then on to the gap."

She backed her horse off to the side. "After you, sir. Since you're the one so bent on an encounter with General Jeb, you ought go first."

Overcoming his vanity, he put on his spectacles. With Allie dutifully following, he guided Rocket down the twisting trail to a small outcropping that overlooked the road at a point just below the summit. He wished he'd been more judicious. There was a whole company of gray-clad cavalry there, dismounted and digging in.

If any one of these people were to look up, Harry and Mrs. Robertson would instantly become prisoners—or worse.

Raising his hand to make the woman halt, Harry slowly turned Rocket and began walking him away. Allie had already begun the same thing.

"You'll be grateful it worked out this way," she said, once they were clear of the Rebels.

\*　　　\*　　　\*

97

The sun was lowering as they picked their way down Allie's trail. She had taken the lead, and moved slowly, reins loose, giving her big horse its head. She sang a song he had never heard before, a lilting air with a thread of sadness running through it.

"That's lovely," he said.

"It's a lament."

"Maybe the best songs are."

"It's a time for 'em, sure enough."

When they reached the valley floor, he pulled up beside her. "How large a place have you?"

"Three hundred forty acres of good bottom land."

"You're a wealthy woman."

"Can't bank dirt."

"You have only the one hired man?"

"Got my husband's sister, too. She's useful. Hire more help when I need them. I'm too pretty for plowin'."

"What do you farm?"

"Corn, wheat, dairy cattle, pigs, apples, and a table garden. The Rebels took the pigs, but I got my cows into a draw they ain't yet discovered. I was glad to see that General Lee go but now you got me worried about General Jeb."

"We're doing the same to them."

"Not enough. What do you farm?"

"Just horses, and garden greens. My mother's people used to grow grapes and make wine and brandy, but that's been neglected of late."

"Virginia wine? What a notion."

"If you ever come my way, I'll present you with a bottle."

She just shook her head, as though he was talking nonsense.

"Do you ever come my way?" he asked. "Do you come to Shepherdstown?"

"Been there, sure enough. Pretty little town. But too many Secesh."

"Ever hear of a Reverend Ashby?"

"Heard he was murdered. Heard him preach once."

In the gathering dusk, the vista of farm fields and foothills before them was taking on a soft and languorous beauty.

This was one of the loveliest valleys in the Appalachians, so much more agreeable than the swamps, cotton fields, and tobacco fields in the Tidewater where Virginia's gentry was concentrated.

"There was a note pinned to his body declaring him a Lincolnite, but he was a slavery man in the pulpit."

"For a preacher, the pulpit's what counts," she said.

"He was married, but had a wandering eye. It would have rested a long time on you."

"Don't fancy preachers," she said, and clicked heels to her horse's flanks, urging him into a lumbering trot.

There was a light in the near distance, coming from a tall stone house with several sizable outbuildings to either side.

"That's my place," she said.

The hired hand, whose name was Bannister, was not on the premises. The sister-in-law, a scrawny, dark-haired woman named Elspeth, was in the kitchen, already busy with the supper, her back to them as she fussed by the stove. "Where you been, Allie?" she asked, irritably. "Had me fearful. You said you were just going to check on the stock."

"I was up on the mountain. I was hopin' to find the countryside free of Rebels but now there's more comin'."

"None of our concern, Allie."

"Your brother was killed by 'em. Don't know what could be more a concern. Anyway, we got a guest."

Elspeth whipped her head around. "Who be you?"

"This is Harrison Raines," Allie said. "He's a scout for the Union, but I almost killed him, thinkin' he was workin' for the other side."

Harry wished the lady would be more circumspect. "How do you do, ma'am." He removed his hat, which he should have done upon entering the house, and made a small bow.

"Don't mind his fuss," Allie said. "He's a gentleman—a *Southern* gentleman. Where's Bannister?"

"Out lookin' for stray stock. Said he might stop in Boonsboro on the way home."

"That ain't on the way home." Allie went up to the stove,

looking into a large pot. "That's a fine-lookin' stew, Elspeth. Smells good, too."

"I tries. We got cornbread and berries, too."

"And wine. I think it's a night to open a bottle." She turned to Harry. "Meantime, you want some whiskey? Got some good sour mash."

He did want some, and he wanted to sit down and enjoy it, and pretend, at least for a little while, that there was nothing outside this house but peaceful countryside. "Yes, ma'am. Miss."

"Well, you go on back into the parlor and I'll pour you enough to keep you happy awhile."

"Thank you." He went back down the hall and turned to a big room on the right, seating himself on a large horsehair sofa. Two oil lamps were aglow, casting a pleasant light. He thought of lighting a cigar, but had no idea as to her disposition toward the habit. He decided to wait until he was out on his own again—wondering when that would be.

She was gone the longest time. So much time elapsed that he began to worry that she had wandered off and gotten picked up by some Secesh patrol. He was about to go back into the kitchen and ask after her whereabouts, when she appeared in the doorway holding a stone jug.

Harry stared. She had changed into a dress, a black and somewhat fancy frock. It was a garment suitable for Sunday church, but she was plainly wearing no corset or hoop, and she left the top few buttons undone.

"Here's your whiskey," she said, placing the jug on the table, along with two tumblers. Then she sat down beside him, putting pretty and happily clean bare feet up on the table in front of them.

"Thank you," Harry said. It was excellent whiskey, though probably home brew.

She rested her head on the back of the sofa. She'd washed, combed her hair, and applied perfume. It wasn't from Paris, Harry was sure, but it did.

He just then took note of three books on the table, one of them Victor Hugo's *Les Misérables*.

She caught his stare, and grinned. "Didn't you think I could read?" she asked. "Think I'm some ignorant farm girl?"

"No, I . . ."

"I've been to school through eight grades. I bet that's pretty near what you been, plantation man."

Actually, though Harry had received an excellent education from his very learned mother, Allie was not far off the mark.

"That's a splendid novel."

She leaned back, sipping from her own glass of whiskey. "Ain't you glad now you're not up on that mountain, or out in the pastures tryin' to hide from Jeb Stuart?"

"I suppose I am."

"Well, I must tell you, Mister Harrison Raines, I'm glad I was up there long enough to meet you, and I do beg your forgiveness for tryin' to shoot you."

"That's forgotten." It was an enormous lie.

She patted his hand. "After supper, let's sit out on the porch awhile."

Harry had two helpings of the stew, and probably a little too much more of the whiskey, which Allie generously kept offering him, and he kept happily drinking. Elspeth attended to the cleaning up, which gave Harry an idea of her status in the household.

"Your husband left everything to you?" he asked, when he and Allie were seated on her porch swing. The view, such as there was at that dark hour, was of South Mountain, but angled, slightly, toward the river.

She said nothing. His question was an intrusion. "I'm sorry," he said. "That is surely none of my business."

"No, that's all right. I just don't like to think upon such things so much anymore. I've done my mournin', though there's still a sadness." She swung her legs a moment, staring up at the sharp line of the mountain against the starry sky. "Anyways, he did leave me all he had. Every stick and field mouse on these acres, plus some property in Boonsboro besides. Elspeth was livin' with us then and she lives with me still. A good woman. Should have found herself another good

101

man, but they's in short supply. Goin' to be in shorter by the time this war's done."

"You're not worried about your hired man? He's not back yet."

"He'll come draggin' in 'round sunup, and still give me a day's work. I just hope he don't run afoul of the Rebels, if they's still lingerin' hereabouts."

Here and there were pinpoints of light along the ridge above. "They seem to be lingering up there," he said.

"Maybe they'll be gone by mornin'," she said. She moved a little closer, and put her hand on his. "Do you like me, Mister Raines? Maybe a little?"

"In truth, I like you a lot."

Now she took up his hand in both of hers, resting them in her lap. "Well, I've a notion, Mister Raines. I think there's a better way of spendin' this sweet night."

Harry took a deep breath. "It is a sweet night."

"Do you ken my meanin,' sir?"

Her perfume was making him as giddy as the whiskey had. "I do indeed."

She took her hands away, but left his in her lap. "I ain't a sinful woman, Mister Raines. I ain't lain with a man since the night before my husband left for Romney. But that was a truly long time ago."

"I understand."

"I have taken a liking to you. You seem a decent man, and a gentle one, even though you're doin' war work. I do like to look upon your face. And you seem most obliging."

"Happily so."

"Well, then, oblige me."

She rose, leading him up the stairs to a large corner bedroom with open windows admitting a cool night breeze. She had been wearing only the dress. The coolness vanished quickly.

Harry was awakened from his contented sleep by a sudden pounding on the door below. Allie stirred as well. He couldn't tell the hour, but it was still very dark.

He threw back the sheet, rushing to the window. But it was

too late. There came the sound of heavy, hurried footsteps on the stairs. A door across the hall banged open, and then did theirs.

A Confederate officer in cavalry uniform, backed by two troopers, entered the room.

"You own that chestnut with a Sharps rifle on the saddle?" he said to Harry.

# Thirteen

Since joining Mister Pinkerton's service the year before, Harry had been locked up in a wide assortment of dreadful places of confinement: Lafayette Baker's windowless private jail in the Treasury Building basement, a stinking barn full of Union prisoners in Leesburg, a drafty, vermin-infested secret prison behind a grocery used by Richmond's "plug uglies" secret police; an adobe-walled jail in the wilds of Texas, and a courthouse holding cell in Corinth, Mississippi, where he had awaited what was to have been his hanging.

He doubted what awaited him now would be much improvement. His chief regret was that Allie would have to share the experience. He had tried to persuade the cavalry officer to leave her behind, but the man—a major who said he was on General Stuart's staff—was adamant. The two of them had been sighted on the ridge, she firing a weapon and he spying on Confederate columns.

"You were carrying a U.S. Army-issue Sharps rifle, a pair of field glasses, and a map of the Maryland roads," the major had said when Harry had protested he was a mere farmer. "You're going to have to explain this and she's going to have to explain why she was in your company."

"Explain to who?"

"Mister Raines, if you don't want to be blindfolded and gagged, I suggest you concentrate on answers and abandon questions."

Their captors at least let them ride side by side, flanking them with outriders and keeping two troopers close behind them. The major rode ahead, but within earshot.

"I'm so sorry," Harry said to Allie. He had said this several times now.

"I invited you into my house," she said. "Needn't be so fretful. I'm sure not sorry."

"Let us hope you won't have reason to be."

"I'm just worried about Elspeth. All these Southern soldiers around. Them that carry guns with a government's blessing can take it into their minds to do as they will. I told you about the three houses they fired—and the couple they killed."

"Such conduct is expressly forbidden in General Lee's army," said the major, over his shoulder.

It occurred to Harry that they were being allowed the liberty of this companionship and conversation in the hope they might say something revealing.

"It's to General Lee I intend to make my complaint," said Harry, lowering his voice.

"How you goin' to do that?" she asked. "These ruffians are likely to hang us from a tree like that Reverend Ashby in Shepherdstown."

"They'll regret it if they do," said Harry, more loudly. "General Lee is a friend of my father, who is the colonel of a Virginia cavalry regiment in General Longstreet's corps. My brother Robert is his adjutant. I have been acquainted with General Lee since I was a child. There will be hell to pay if we are harmed."

Allie stared at him silently. The major slowed his horse somewhat, but said nothing.

Perhaps because of his remarks about General Lee, they were taken directly to Stuart. He had made a temporary headquarters for the night in a house on the Mousetown Road, a long way back up the mountain. The major had to awaken his commander. The young general came into the small parlor where Harry and Allie were being held without his boots and with his shirt buttons undone. He had a full bushy beard and moustache, which Harry had been told masked a severely receding chin.

Stuart rubbed his eyes and blinked. "What's this about, Major? I haven't had but an hour's sleep."

"We saw these two up on the ridge, spying on our movements. We captured them at her house, outside of Boonsboro. The man says he's the son of a Colonel Raines with General Longstreet, and knows General Lee."

"General Lee?" Stuart blinked some more, then stifled a yawn. Rubbing his eyes, he looked hard at Harry. "Do I know you?"

"You may know my father, and my brother Robert. He is with Longstreet as well."

"Colonel Raines. From the Belle Haven plantation?"

"Yes, sir. That's where I grew up." Allie's eyes were hard upon Harry. She reminded him of a hundred gamblers who'd discovered they'd been cheated at cards. But he had to persist in this. It was their only chance of survival.

"What're you doing here?" the cavalry general asked.

"I have a farm near Shepherdstown, sir. I was trying to stay out of the way of the war."

Stuart frowned at this. Harry's was one of the "First Families" of Virginia. It was considered an obligation for men at this level of gentry to join the fight. Failure to do so was betrayal of one's class.

The general sat down in a wicker rocker. He motioned Harry and Allie to the horsehair sofa. She stubbornly stood, until Harry pulled her down beside him.

"Just why aren't you in the army, too, Mister Raines?"

"I have people and property to look after. The Yankees have been all over the place."

"Maybe not for long," said Stuart. "You know the roads in this area?"

"I surely do. Spent summers up here nearly every year of my life."

"That could be a help to us. What do you know of McClellan's position?"

"Last I looked, he was in camp outside of Frederick."

"Moving this way?"

"Probably his intention, but he wasn't stirring when I passed through. He's not much for moving—except in parades."

"How'd you get through his lines?"

"Frederick's a big town. A lot of civilian traffic moving through McClellan's position."

Stuart scratched himself, then rubbed his eyes again. "My scouts have seen Yankee troops approaching South Mountain."

"The full army?"

"Don't know yet. Cavalry, anyway." The general studied Harry a moment, then turned to Allie and smiled. Then he looked to the major. "How'd you capture 'em?"

"Easiest way imaginable, General."

Stuart grinned. "Billy Sherman's wrong."

"Sir?"

"War ain't always hell." He stood up, and pulled out a glittering gold pocket watch. "Get them something to eat and then send them on to General Lee's headquarters under guard. I have to send a dispatch for the general anyway. I'll include a letter of introduction for them." He treated Allie to a slight bow. "We'll let the general decide if there's any need of hangin'."

The major saluted, then motioned to Harry and Allie to rise. As they filed out of the little room, Stuart bade Harry to wait a moment.

"I do know you," he said. "You were in attendance at a cotillion in Richmond before the war. I recall a beautiful young lady—Arabella . . ."

"She married a Confederate naval officer," Harry said. "Name of Mills. Unfortunately, she has died. Her daughter, Evangeline, is now in my care—on my farm near Shepherdstown."

"How so?"

Harry had gone up the wrong conversational street, but there was a quick way to conclude the matter. "The short of it is that she is my daughter as well. Mister Mills more or less abandoned her."

Stuart came wide awake, then grinned once more. "If your father will vouch for you, as I'm sure he will, I doubt you will be much longer inconvenienced. But for now I have no choice. A good day to you, sir."

As they went out into the night, Harry put his hand on

Allie's shoulder. She flung it away. "You are a goddamn Rebel," she hissed. "I shoulda shot you."

She said nothing further to him all the way back into Boonsboro and along the Sharpsburg Road. She was still silent as they approached the long ridge on the outskirts of the latter town. Lee's army was there, encamped, stretching a mile or more in each direction. Allie rode hunched in the saddle, eyes to the road.

Harry feared they'd be separated once they arrived at Lee's headquarters. Nudging his horse closer to hers, he leaned near her, hoping she wouldn't pull away.

She didn't, but she was not receptive. "I told you, Raines. I'd gladly shoot you."

"Damn it, Allie, I'm trying to save our necks."

"I don't believe you. You're a plantation man. A slaver. And sounds like you're a Rebel shirker to boot."

"You don't have to believe me. Just mind your words until I've got this figured out."

"How's it hurtin' you, my denouncin' you as a goddamn Rebel?"

He lowered his voice now to near a whisper. "It's not hurting me. It's putting yourself in danger. They do hang women spies now."

She leaned back in her saddle, still more sullen than contrite. "If I ever get free of these marauders, Harrison Raines, I am going to report you to General McClellan personally."

After their mounts were taken away from them, they were kept waiting, seated on the ground, guarded by a nervous private. The long, low hill they were on was called Sharpsburg Ridge and there were Confederate troops seemingly everywhere on it. Lee was fixing to have his fight here.

Harry had never had much interest in the military arts, but had learned a few things in the last year, having watched Union disasters at First Bull Run and Ball's Bluff, and been with General Grant after Shiloh.

Lee had picked good ground, country Harry had hiked and

ridden over growing up. The Potomac made two great turns west of Sharpsburg, its bends providing anchors for the Confederates' flanks. The long ridge gave Lee the advantage of high ground, and there was further protection provided by Antietam Creek, mostly deep though fordable in several locations. The general was disposed to invite Union attack, and disposed to make it costly for the Federals. There were stone walls, sunken roads, woods, and cornfields—among other cover and natural fortification along the ridge.

Lee was a commander for the offensive, as he had amply demonstrated in the Seven Days battles outside Richmond and this summer at Second Manassas. This was defensive warfare, in which his audacity and cunning could have little play. He seemed to have recovered part of his army, but even if he was able to pull it all together before McClellan came up, he'd still be terribly outnumbered.

But the Rebel commander had a tremendous advantage. He'd be fighting McClellan.

"Well, good God damn, it is you."

Harry looked up to see a Confederate general standing over him—a brigadier, slightly unkempt, his uniform coat unbuttoned, the smell of whiskey not a little in evidence.

"Colonel Evans?" Harry got clumsily to his feet. He had last seen Nathan "Shanks" Evans in the aftermath of the fight at Ball's Bluff. Harry had been his prisoner. "You've been promoted."

"And you are still not in uniform," Evans said.

"What're you doing here?"

"I command the brigade that holds this section of the line." He stepped back, eyeing Harry as he might a mule for sale. "When last we met, Raines, I gave you your liberty because the Union prisoners I had were about to kill you and I took you at your word for what you said you were—a man disposed to our side of this quarrel. Now why in hell are you our captive again?"

"It's a mistake. Stuart's people took us while I was on my way home to my farm at Shepherdstown. Presumed we were spies. I'm waiting to see General Lee."

109

"Well, you'll wait a while. He's kinda busy at the moment." Evans nodded toward Allie, who was seated facing away. "That your woman?"

"A friend. From Boonsboro."

Evans gave him a wink. "As you say, sir." He pulled forward a flask of whiskey, took a sip, then offered it to Harry, who accepted.

"Thank you, general." Harry returned the flask.

"Wish you luck, Raines. Though we don't got much to spare." He strode off, somewhat unsteadily.

Harry seated himself on the ground next to Allie, but she turned away. When he spoke to her, she did not reply. He put his hand on her shoulder. She let it remain there a moment, then flung it off, moving a few feet from him and putting head down, as though in deep thought—or sadness.

The private guarding them laughed.

They remained there more than an hour. A corporal came around and gave them water. Allie whispered something to the man and was escorted a short distance to a farm house privy. She was brought back by a young captain, who lingered a moment, engaging her in quiet conversation before walking off.

"What did you say to him?" Harry asked.

"None of your damned business."

Finally, a young and extremely well-uniformed lieutenant strode up and stood at attention before Harry, who rose, stiffly.

"You are Harrison Raines?"

"Yes, I am."

"General Lee would appreciate your attendance upon him."

The general was seated in a camp chair set beneath a tent fly that sheltered him from the sun's heat. A small folding table was at his side, stacked with papers. He was wearing spectacles, but not reading anything, staring at the ground. Harry had not seen a man so taken up with thought in all his life. He'd sustained some injury. Both his hands were bandaged.

A brilliantly uniformed Confederate major standing just

110

behind Lee came forward to greet Harry. "You are Mister Raines?" he asked.

Harry nodded, but there was no need for him to be announced. Lee's attention turned to him as it might to an intruding stray dog.

"Harrison Raines," the general said. "I had thought, sir, that our encounters were at an end."

"My presence here was not of my choosing, General."

"We last spoke in Richmond, as I recall. You sought the return of a slave—and I believe I gave you a letter of recommendation for the Confederate Navy. As you are not in uniform, I must presume it was of little use to you, sir."

It seemed a poor time to remind Lee that Caesar Augustus was not a slave but a freedman. "I was briefly aboard the *Virginia*, sir, bringing powder to the gun crews. But I went overboard during the fight with the *Monitor*, and was captured by the Yankees."

"Yet here you stand."

"I got away from them, knowing Tidewater much better than they did. I would have returned to Richmond, but the Federal presence on the peninsula prevented me. At all events, General, the Navy now seems to have far more sailors than berths for them."

Lee shook his head sadly. His extreme weariness was showing as much as his melancholy and mental exertion. "We are overwhelmed with the work of the day here, Harrison. How is it that I might be of help to you?"

The well-polished major handed the general a piece of note paper, which Harry presumed to be from General Stuart.

"This says you were seen atop South Mountain, observing the movements of this army," Lee said.

"That's correct, General. I am trying to get home to my farm at Shepherdstown, as I have tried to explain to your officers several times. It's the property I inherited from my late mother." Lee had been very well disposed toward Harry's mother, a woman of much higher social rank and gentility than Harry's father. "I wanted to see if the roads were clear to avoid just this sort of incident. No one is trusted by armies any more."

111

Lee glanced again at the note. "Do you always travel with a pair of Federal-issue field glasses?" he asked.

"I won them off a Union officer in a poker game in Frederick." Harry hated lying to this man, who, aside from the deceit employed in military tactics, had probably never told a lie once in his life. He had not received a single demerit in his time at West Point.

"And the Sharps rifle—a military weapon much esteemed but in short supply?"

"That I took off a wandering horse I found just east of Cactoctin Mountain. I assumed the animal to be the mount of a cavalry trooper who may have been otherwise engaged when his horse got loose. A prize of war, if you will."

Lee frowned, altering his expression very little. "And this woman who was with you?"

The polished major intervened. "She told Captain Morton that she is his wife, sir."

Harry was stunned. Lee's frown became a scowl. "Is this true, Harrison? You have taken a Maryland country woman into your family?"

"In a manner of speaking, sir. In a common law manner of speaking."

Lee simply stared at him, his eyes as hard as cannons. Then he took out his watch, which Harry took to be a prelude to concluding the interview.

"What can you tell me of General McClellan's movements? You must be acquainted with them, having come through Frederick."

Harry had no choice but to give at least the appearance of being informative. "Last I saw, which was from Cactoctin Mountain, he had his entire army camped outside Frederick. From what I know of his dread of haste, it was remarkable indeed that he had advanced that far."

Lee's eyes widened. "But General Stuart informs me that large bodies of Federal troops are now advancing on the South Mountain passes. General McClellan would seem for once to be moving with celerity. Why do you suppose that is?"

For an anguishing moment, Harry fought an impulse to tell

this old family friend about the discovery of his marching orders. If this prompted Lee to retreat, perhaps to rejoin the two sections of his army he had sent to Harper's Ferry, battle might be averted and thousands of lives saved.

But, as he had learned in the West from General Grant, averting battles and saving lives would only mean prolonging the war. The South would never surrender unless brutally crushed, as Pierre Beauregard's force at Shiloh eventually was. There needed to be a battle here.

At all events, making such a disclosure would likely get Harry hanged as a Yankee spy. The Confederates would not long wonder how he had come by such valuable knowledge belonging surely only to McClellan and his staff.

Besides, Lee was no retreater—never before a battle, certainly.

"General Stuart has been up on that ridge a lot longer than I was," Harry said. "I passed the night at the lady's house near Boonsboro, and then we were arrested and brought here. I've not had a look at McClellan's army in more than a day, sir."

"What is his strength?"

Harry shrugged. "I'm not a military man, sir. I couldn't tell you how many corps. But his numbers are far more than yours. Many more."

Lee sighed, wearily. "I've no more time for this matter, Harrison. I am going to leave your disposition up to your father, who will be joining us directly with General Longstreet's corps. I will send word that you are here at Sharpsburg, and under what circumstance." He removed his spectacles, keeping them in his hand. "I should warn you, Harrison, your father is not feeling kindly toward you."

"I'm aware of that, General. He told me when last we met that he would not speak to me until he saw me in Confederate uniform."

Lee returned to his work. "A good day to you, sir." The sudden coldness of his words would have frozen the Potomac that very hot day.

*     *     *

113

Harry and Allie were taken to a house on the main street of Sharpsburg, and made to walk the distance to it, as no one seemed to know what had happened to their horses.

Harry doubted their removal to these quarters was intended for their comfort. Lee or his staff likely wanted the two of them out of the way of the increasing military activity, or simply removed from view.

The general's hostility was in some respects puzzling. He and Harry's father had been friends for all the years Harry could remember, but Harry's father was a devoted slaver, as committed to the "peculiar institution"—which Harry styled the "evil institution"—as any man in the South.

Lee was a manumission man. He was opposed to slavery. He had raised his sword against the United States he had served in uniform for so long wholly in what he regarded as the defense of Virginia—his "country" as he called it.

Perhaps he viewed Harry less as an anti-slavery man like himself and more a traitor to his "country."

A soldier had been stationed out front, but they were free to move about the house as they pleased. It was a tiny dwelling, of only four rooms including the kitchen. Allie had gone directly to the small bedroom at the rear and shut the door without further word to him. He went there now, opening the door quietly.

She was on the narrow bed, curled up with her back to him—her long blond hair falling over the counterpane. He presumed she was the only woman in Sharpsburg wearing trousers.

"I didn't invite you in here, mister," she said, without moving.

He sat down on the edge of the bed, as there was no chair in the room, nor much room for one.

"There is something for us to discuss," Harry said. "You told that captain you were my wife and that message was given General Lee. He is a friend of my family. There was some consternation. My father is coming here to decide my fate—our fate. This will not improve his mood."

She sat up, still facing away from him. "I did that because

I did not wish to be left to the tender mercies of Rebel soldiers—because they ain't got any. Since you know all these high and mighty worthies like Bobby Lee himself, I figured I'm owed a share of whatever protection you got comin'.''

"I'm not sure protection is what's in order."

"Your own pap?"

"There are fathers, sons, and brothers fighting each other all over the country in this war."

"That's fightin', not hanging." She dabbed at her eyes, then turned at last to look at him.

"What I'm asking," he said, "is do you mean to persist in this charade of marriage. I tell you, my father will press me on it. We must agree upon a truth."

"Agree upon a lie, you mean."

"Lie or truth, we must agree upon it. For any variance, we could pay dear. Give them one lie and they'll presume others."

"What did you tell them?" She rubbed her nose.

"That ours was a common law arrangement."

"What's that mean?"

"A marriage without a wedding. Some law courts recognize it as concerns inheritance and the like."

"Damn all," she said. "You think no better of me than that?"

"I think immensely more of you than that. I spoke thoughtlessly, trying to think of what would upset the general least."

"Why would it 'upset' him that you and I be man and wife?"

"It's complicated. A matter of families. Tidewater's strange."

"You're strange, Mister Raines."

"Allie." He put his hand on her shoulder, but she shrugged it off. A moment later, there was a click of the latch and the bedroom door swung open.

There stood his brother Robert, his otherwise splendid uniform covered with dust, his plumed hat held in hand.

Neither brother said a word. Allie gave Robert a quick, unfriendly glance, then looked away.

"Come with me," Robert said. "Just you, Harry—not her."

They went out onto the narrow front porch. Whatever chairs had been upon it were gone, doubtless confiscated, but there

115

was a crude bench against the wall just large enough for two. Robert bade the soldier guarding the house to move off the porch, then followed Harry to the seat.

"Father will not come to you—or have you brought to him," Robert said. "He will not intervene in this matter in any way."

"General Lee said he would leave our fate to be decided by him. Isn't that by way of being an order?"

Robert was watching a file of troops coming up the street. "Father has decided. He will not intervene. He wants nothing more to do with you. I am reluctant to tell you this, but he has forbidden me to speak your name in his presence."

Harry studied his brother's handsome young face. It had been more than a year since they had last been together. "He told me he would speak to me if I would appear before him in Confederate uniform."

"That could be easily arranged, Harry, once we've settled some questions as to your loyalty."

The notion of enlisting there on the spot and converting back to the Union cause later crossed his mind—but that could get him hanged by either side.

"You know my feelings on the question of slavery," Harry said.

Robert nodded. "You and our sister. But this war is not about that, Harry. We're fighting for our rights. This is the second American Revolution. General Lee is our General Washington."

"The only right the South has ever been willing to go to war over is slavery."

His brother brought his fist down hard on the wood of the bench, which must have caused great pain. "Damn it, Harry. We have had this argument. Too many times. You're in trouble here—damn bad trouble. Try to be cooperative."

"I'll be happy to, Robert. All I'm trying to do is get back to my farm. If you will vouch for me, that is what I will do."

The file of troops had passed but a much larger body was approaching—heading east toward Lee's line and the Federals.

"Those are Jackson's men?" Harry asked.

"If you are a spy, you're a poor one. Jackson's at Harper's

116

Ferry, I trust in the process of taking the Yankee commander's surrender. These are McLaws' people."

"Heading up to South Mountain?"

"That is none of your concern."

"As I think upon it, Robert, this is a poor place to fight. Lee's got the Potomac to his back and only one ford to get all of you across it. McClellan must outnumber you two to one. If your line breaks and you have to fall back, you could be trapped."

"I prefer to take my military counsel from General Lee, Harry, not from the likes of you."

"Do you think he might be induced to retreat before McClellan gets here?"

Robert stood up. "I cannot vouch for you, Harry, for truthfully, I do not know what there is to vouch for. You turn up in the wrongest places. You were in Richmond, though you're living in Washington City. You got yourself aboard the *Virginia* somehow. You were out West mixed up in some kind of trouble. You've been riding between the two main armies here with Federal field glasses and a Sharps rifle. And now you pester me with questions about Lee's plans. None of that sounds like peaceful farming to me."

Harry hung down his head, taking note of his boots. They were in need of repair. "Very well, Robert, you do what you must. But spare the lady. She is innocent. They only took her because she was with me. She's no spy. She just lives here."

Robert stepped to the edge of the porch, looking down the street, and up it. "Regrettably, there is little I can do. Father's refusal to stand up for you will be taken as a signal for them to proceed as they will. But I'm your brother. Our sister Elizabeth would never speak to me again were I to abandon you." He surveyed the street again. "What I am going to do is engage that soldier charged with guarding you in further conversation. I'll stand the other side of him so that he must turn away from this house. I don't know how long I can hold his attention, but, however long, that will be your only chance. Take your woman and flee the house. You know this country. Find yourself a place to hide. There's a big battle coming, and whatever the result, the armies will be leaving this place afterwards. You can go back to Mother's farm." He turned and offered his hand. Harry, quickly rising, shook it. "Go now," Robert concluded. "Get the woman and git."

Harry did not hesitate. He was back in the house and into the small bedroom as quickly as his weary legs could move. Allie looked up at him as if he were Death himself.

"We have been given a chance to escape. The opportunity may only last seconds. Come."

When she continued to just sit there, staring, he grabbed her hand and pulled her to her feet, half dragging her through the house. He paused at the door. "Tuck that pretty blond hair of yours up into your hat," he said.

She did so. Perhaps she was at last going to cooperate with him in this.

He opened the door wide enough to see that the small porch was now deserted. Robert was down the street, talking to the soldier as promised. The passing troops seemed preoccupied with their march, a fierceness in their step.

Harry let go of Allie's hand. "Just follow me."

Rather than going over the porch's side railing, which someone would have marked as suspicious, Harry went down the front steps and walked up the street to the next corner, not looking back until he had turned it.

She was right behind him, head down, hat pulled low.

"Just keep with me," he said.

He followed the street to the end of the block, then turned north, proceeding to where the road bore again to the right. Before them loomed woods, with a small white church to the right. Glancing back to make certain no provost guard or sentry was following their movements, Harry and Allie slipped into the trees, the gathering darkness near complete in their shelter. The gunfire up on South Mountain, strangely, seemed louder here.

"You live in Boonsboro," he said. "Do you have friends here?"

"I have kin. I have an aunt who lives up the Funkstown Road."

118

"I will take you there. Then I must leave you. Don't worry. When this is over, I will see to it that all you have lost on my account—horse and gun—will be restored to you or replaced. But now you must see to your life."

"Where're you going?"

"I know pretty much everything now. Longstreet is up. Those soldiers marching by the house were some of McLaws', but Jackson's will be along as soon as they've taken Harper's Ferry, which he has done handily before. Lee will soon have all his people here. McClellan must be informed of this."

"But how you goin' to tell him? Lee's soldiers are sittin' on Sharpsburg Ridge from one end to the other, and now the mountain passes are blocked with the fighting. Why don't you just head on back to Shepherdstown? That way is still open."

"I think if I can get to the south of town and work my way over Elk Ridge, I can do it. I need to steal a horse, but that should not be difficult. Armies carry confusion around with them like they do munitions and provender."

"You are a crazy man, Mister Raines. You better go now, before there's even more of 'em against you."

"I'm worried about you."

"Then you don't know me well. Long as I can pass myself off as a man till I get to my aunt's, I should be all right. I know my way to my auntie's. I can get there without you—probably faster."

"Still, I'm abandoning you—a woman alone, with an army about."

"Forget that gallant plantation talk, Harrison Raines. We're in Western Maryland, where folks is far more sensible."

Standing on tiptoes, she kissed him—not for long but for long enough. Then she was moving on deeper into the woods, making little sound.

# Fourteen

The horse Harry stole was a civilian's that had been tied saddled to the porch rail of a small house on the western outskirts of the town. Harry marked the house well in his mind, intent on returning the mount or compensating the owner for it upon his return.

He felt confident he would return. The more he thought upon it, the more he realized that not even McClellan could fail to prevail here. If he showed no more generalship than simply ordering all his troops to advance, his superior force ought ultimately to crush everything before it.

But one could never be certain with George B. McClellan.

Harry was well clear of the house, but kept his horse to a walk so as to avoid raising any suspicion. The Rebels had taken all his arms from him but his hidden Derringer, a weapon largely useless at any range greater than the width of a poker table. Opportunities did present themselves in wartime to steal weapons, but usually only when their owners were deceased. He would have to travel defenseless among his enemies.

He kept his head down, his hat pulled forward, as he moved among the teamsters, sutlers and such like. The townspeople were mostly remaining indoors, whatever their loyalties. In full-scale open warfare, with .55 caliber minié balls and shell and shot flying every which way, a frame dwelling afforded poor protection. But they would have to learn that the hard way, as the residents of Winchester and Harper's Ferry certainly had.

Heading south, Harry passed one well-lit house where a young woman was standing in the yard, as if waiting for someone. He did not know her, but the sight of her tore at him, putting him fully in mind of Allie, moving all alone through the dark north woods. He tried to ease his guilt by reminding himself that she was a woman unlike the citified Louise Devereux and Caitlin Howard, formidable ladies in their own way but not much for hard climbs and brambles.

Allie had been atop South Mountain on her lonesome, fearing nothing. He could only hope she would now keep clear of the slightest sign of soldiery.

Harry was hoping to do the same. Moving on south and cantering onto an open meadow when the street played out, he glanced from time to time at South Mountain's rolling ridge, hearing the gunfire and occasionally seeing flashes of it, despite the distance. When these seemed well enough to the rear, he cut east, jumping two snake-rail farm fences in the slim light of the partial moon, and then following a trail that led to a remembered reach of Antietam Creek. There was an easy ford in this place, but no one was guarding it.

Sloshing his stolen horse across, he paused on the other side to listen to what presence the night and surroundings might hold. Hearing none but owls, insects, and frogs, he moved on, slowly, steering the animal toward the foot of the mountain. For a moment, he thought he heard something in the water behind him, but, pausing again, detected nothing untoward. Crossing a rutted dirt road and entering a patch of woods, he stopped again at what sounded like the snap of a branch. Had he one, he would have pulled a pistol out at this point, but again, the noise was not repeated.

Reaching the mountain at last, he halted his horse, looking straight up the steep slope. If there was a crossing over the ridge here, it was not visible in the darkness.

Harry tried ascending at an angle to the right, but the horse would have none of it, and almost fell. Moving to the left, he came to what looked like a slight defile and urged the animal up it. But this caused only a cascade of small rocks, which made the horse slide down again. Retreating to level ground, Harry sat his saddle, pondering the matter in some frustration.

Then, behind him, he heard a familiar voice.

"There is no trail here, Harry Raines."

Harry wheeled his horse. The Metis was mounted, his horse standing in the shadows of a large, thick tree.

"Tantou. How did you know I was here?"

"I followed you from the town. I saw them bring you and a woman there. I have been watching you ever since."

"From where?"

"From beside the porch of a house across the street."

Harry prodded his horse toward his friend, entering the shadows beside him. "I don't understand. How did you get into Sharpsburg?"

"Your Mister Pinkerton is paying me to be a scout. My job is to follow the Rebel army and see where it goes. It went into Sharpsburg, and so did I, Harry Raines."

"And no one stopped you?"

It was eerie conversing with Tantou's dark form, the eyes obscured.

"One soldier tried but he is now dead. Another did in the town but I told them I was a teamster with a wagon train and had lost my way. They told me where to go to find it and I did. I spent most of the day unloading wagons—until I saw you and yellow-hair come in. She is *très jolie, mais Louise Devereux est la mieux.*"

As Louise might observe herself. "So you've followed me. What now?"

"Now we should both do what you were trying to do, Harry Raines. Get over the mountain and go back to Mister Pinkerton."

"The mountain seems the hard part."

"No. We go to Crampton Gap."

"But there's fighting up there."

"Where there is fighting, there is the Union Army." Without a further word, he turned his horse and proceeded deeper into the darkness. Harry followed, a role in their relationship to which he was becoming much accustomed.

By the time they reached Crampton's Gap, it was firmly in the hands of soldiers commanded by Union General William Franklin. When they were taken before him at his command post in Rohresville, he seemed a little incredulous at the notion that Harry and Tantou had come from Sharpsburg, but happily passed them on to McClellan's headquarters. To Harry's surprise, that had been moved to Boonsboro. If he and Allie had been allowed to remain at her house unmolested, she might now be safe.

It was daylight by the time they reached Pinkerton, a densely foggy morning revealing little of their surroundings or of the large Federal army presumed to be here. The Scotsman pronounced himself delighted to see them, though an orderly had had to rustle him out of his camp bed for the occasion. Harry guessed that none of the intelligence chief's other operatives had reported in as yet.

Pinkerton expressed no doubt that Harry and Tantou had been in Sharpsburg, but was a little alarmed at Harry's revelation that he had been granted an interview with General Lee himself.

"Do not be telling that to General McClellan, Raines. If he were to believe you, he'd believe worse of you. That you were in Sharpsburg will suffice. Now, what is the size of Lee's force?"

"I couldn't say exactly," Harry said. "But not many. Longstreet has rejoined him. If General McClellan gets the rest of his army up and moving, he can overwhelm him."

"No, Raines, no. That would be incautious. And absent any exact figures . . ."

Tantou had been watching the various kinds of soldiery moving about the street they were standing beside. He turned his hard eyes to Pinkerton. "Mister Lee has maybe eighteen thousand, twenty thousand, on the ridge in front of Sharpsburg. When we left, Longstreet's men were coming into the town on the north road, from Hagerstown. General Jackson, the one they call Stonehead . . ."

"'Stonewall,'" corrected Harry.

"Some soldiers were calling him 'Stonehead,'" Tantou responded. "He is not there. He is at Harper's Ferry. Lee was getting ready to go there, too. To retreat."

"How in blazes would you know that?" Pinkerton interjected.

123

"I worked the afternoon unloading supply wagons for them. Before I left, the order came to reload them again, and prepare to move west across the river."

"The Potomac?"

"Yes. That is the river there at Sharpsburg."

"Harper's Ferry is under attack," Pinkerton said. "If it falls . . ."

"Then Lee will have Jackson, too," Harry said.

"A significant reinforcement," Pinkerton said. "You'd best come with me. General McClellan should hear this himself."

Pinkerton had received them in shirtsleeves and stocking feet, much as General Stuart had, but the Scotsman quickly attended to his haberdashery and, with his bowler hat firm upon his head, led the way down the street to the house McClellan had commandeered.

The general, dressed as though for the parade ground, readily received them in the house's front parlor, now a busy office. Several inches shorter than Harry's six feet—and towered over by the Metis—he quickly bade them both sit down and ordered that coffee be brought.

Harry and Tantou gave their reports in turn. McClellan appeared to mull over each word. "Interesting. Interesting. That sounds about right. Colonel Miles at Harper's Ferry reported he was under artillery fire from Maryland Heights and that Jackson had cut off all the roads out of the town. His position is untenable, alas. The town will fall and Jackson will reinforce Lee. We will be facing a formidable force."

The coffee came. McClellan added brown sugar to his and sipped, contemplatively.

"Very good work, men," he said. "Commendable." He smiled at Pinkerton, who grinned back. "You are to be commended as well, Mister Pinkerton. You have organized an excellent intelligence service. There can be none better in any army." His attention returned to Harry and Tantou. "But I fear you have greatly underestimated the enemy strength, gentlemen."

Harry took a swallow of the excellent coffee. "But sir, I

was at Lee's headquarters. Near there, anyway. He has placed his people on only two or three miles of that ridge line."

McClellan smiled, indulgently. "You could not have been at Lee's headquarters. No scout of ours has done that. It must have been some other general's. And it's hard to count troops when they're quartered in a town. No, sir. If your estimate is correct, Lee would have no more than thirty-five thousand or forty thousand at his disposal. He would not be preparing to do battle with so small a force. I have nearly twice that number. He would not be so rash as to fight me. No, I think he has made a great mistake in choosing this ground for a fight. And I intend to thrash him. But his numbers must be as great as mine, if not more. We are short of supplies. Some of our troops are in dreadful want. I have wired urgently for replenishment."

"I think, sir," Pinkerton interjected, "that, upon reflection, my scouts here now see the sense of that. Don't you, Captain Raines?"

This caught Harry by surprise, and he knew not what to say. The words he found were clumsy. "Of course, Mister Pinkerton. I wasn't actually counting the enemy."

"Thank you, gentlemen," McClellan said, returning to his coffee and a dispatch he was writing.

"The Rebels took my horse and weapons," Harry said, as Pinkerton led them away. "I cannot be much further use to you."

"You came in on a mount."

"One I stole from a U.S. citizen in Sharpsburg without compensation."

"I'll get you a remount—and a weapon. You had a Colt revolver?"

"And a Sharps rifle."

"Do you better than that, Raines. We have some Spencer repeating rifles. You'll never have to fear capture again."

"I am hungry," said Tantou. "Very hungry."

"Yes, Tantou," Pinkerton replied. "Let us attend to that. Then I must leave you. Some Negroes have come into our lines and I must interrogate them. You two have done excellent work, but our best source of intelligence remains the darkie."

They ate from brimming mess tins sitting against the wheel of a large wagon. The tins contained a beef hash, eggs, cornbread, and fruit.

"This is what the general calls 'short of supplies?'" Tantou asked. "When this army is fully supplied, it must carry oysters and wine."

"He likes to travel well," Harry said.

"Such an army can be defeated by hungry men."

"Lee has no shortage of those, I'll wager."

Tantou took note of the soldiers busying themselves about the place, and leaned close. "Harry Raines. This McClellan is a fool."

"Yes," said Harry. "But he's the fool Lincoln is depending on."

"I think maybe I leave his service soon."

"I would take it as a great personal favor if you would remain until the fight here is resolved. I have much at stake here."

"Your farm. The little girl."

"Yes."

"And the pretty yellow hair."

Harry thought upon this. "Yes." Having emptied his mess tin, he rose and went over to an area of grass more distant from the road. "I am going to sleep now, Jack." He lay down and did just that—in an instant.

Harry slept most of the day on the hard ground. He would have slept longer, had he not been awakened by cannon fire. Looking about, he saw Tantou standing, shielding his eyes from the bright sunlight that had replaced the fog.

"What's afoot?" Harry asked.

"McClellan has moved most of the army up near the Confederates," said the Metis. "It does not look like Lee is going to retreat."

Harry rubbed his eyes. "Has the battle commenced? Have I slept too long?"

"No battle, Harry Raines. Only cannons. They shoot at each other even though there is no battle yet. I do not understand."

There were four quick, sharp reports in succession, their echoes resounding along the ridge behind them. Harry stood up, brushing off his trousers. "Parrott guns," he said. "Long range. I don't think the Rebels have any."

"Then they will wish they did." Tantou pointed to a saddled horse that had been tethered to a small nearby tree. "Mister Pinkerton sends you this *cadeau*—this gift. This horse. There is a rifle and two saddle pistols. I do not understand how the rifle works. There is no ramrod."

"It's called a Spencer repeating rifle. I am not sure how it operates, either."

"The pistols are Army Colts."

"Good."

"There is ammunition, too, but not much."

"You seem to have examined my gift thoroughly."

"There is a note. It asks you to report to him when convenient." Tantou handed him a folded piece of paper.

The commencement of another round of artillery fire caused Harry's hand to shake momentarily as he read it. Pinkerton wanted him to scout to the south, down by the stone bridge where he and Louise had picnicked.

"Did he give you instructions as well?" Harry asked.

"He asks me to go north, up the Hagerstown Pike. He wants to know if the Confederate left flank goes farther than McClellan's right flank. I think the general is afraid that if he goes forward now, these Rebels will come in behind him."

Harry reread his own instructions. They were much the same, only directing him to the south, "when convenient."

"I don't understand what that means," Tantou said. "Nothing they ask me to do is convenient. It is the job."

"It means there's no great hurry. Otherwise, Pinkerton would not have let me sleep. It means McClellan will probably not move beyond his present position today."

"Now you are awake. I will go." The tall Indian started toward his own horse.

"Wait," said Harry. "I would trade with you."

"Trade what? Your strange new rifle?"

"No. Your mission. I would like to scout to the north."

Tantou thought for perhaps three seconds, then nodded. He resumed his walk toward his horse. "Yellow Hair," he said.

"What of it?"

"Nothing of it, Harry Raines. I will trade. I hope you find the Confederate left flank, and that it is not where you find Yellow Hair."

Harry tried to find Pinkerton, but could not. McClellan's headquarters was now a swarming beehive of milling officers and men, but no one in civilian dress was present. Harry did not perceive how a further interview with the general would be helpful—either to him or to the Union cause. He left a message for Pinkerton with an idle major, saying that he was embarking on his scouting duties, only proceeding to the north.

He had taken time to eat, wash, shave, and clean his teeth, as well as change his shirt. The soldiers who had observed these ablutions must have thought him strange. Why go to such bother on the eve of a fight? Unless one was overly concerned about how he might appear upon meeting his Maker.

McClellan's army had drawn up along the near side of Antietam Creek. In the north, however, the Union line crossed the creek and continued on just to the east of the Hagerstown Pike. Harry kept to the rear of the soldiers—stock end of muskets being preferable to barrels—nodding or saluting whenever he came upon a man who looked like he might want to impede Harry's progress.

Finally reaching the north end of the Federal line, he encountered a large body of cavalry, and was taken to the colonel commanding.

The officer, younger even than Harry, examined the note from Pinkerton. "It says 'south,'" he said. "Some scout you are, getting your directions mixed up like this."

"I traded with another scout. He goes south. I go north."

The colonel handed back the note, accepting it as bonafide. "Easier up this way. Not as many Rebs."

"I'll do my job, sir."


The horse he'd been provided was a good one—a roan mare with strong legs and an easy gait. Fearing no Confederates with the Federals so far advanced, he kept to the main road out of Boonsboro, reaching Allie's farm quickly.

It seemed much the same as when they had left it, though there was no livestock in evidence.

The front door opened almost the instant Harry stepped on the porch. The frightened face of Elspeth appeared in the opening. He feared for a moment that she was armed, but she presented no weapon.

"Mister Raines?"

"Yes." He took a step closer. "Is Alice here?"

She darted outside, carefully closing the door behind her, and came up to him in tiny steps. "She ain't come back since y'all left, but he's here."

"He?"

"Bannister. The hired man. In the kitchen, halfway drunk and maybe more. He's the one that told the Rebels where to find you. He told me so himself. Now he's moved in and is fixin' to set himself up in the place, dependin' on who wins the battle."

Harry looked to the door. "Is he armed?"

"Yes, sir. Got Miss Alice's shotgun."

"Very well. You stay out here. Stay away from the door."

He took out one of his new Army Colts and cocked the hammer, then pushed the door open with his other hand, stepping inside and moving quietly along the wall. Bannister coughed. Harry tried to imagine what the man would be doing. He'd be sitting, surely, whiskey bottle nearby. Where the shotgun lay was the question of the moment.

Harry halted, took a deep breath, and then continued forward, listening for the creak of wood. There was none. He kept moving down the short hall toward the sounds of the man's raspy breathing.

Another spell of coughing. Harry took advantage of it, reaching the doorway of the kitchen.

The shotgun was on the table, on the other side of the whiskey jug from Bannister, a lean, stringy man wearing a brown-striped cotton shirt underneath a pair of overalls. Greasy long black hair fell over a raw-boned, long-nosed face, the eyes vague and downcast. This might actually be easy.

Harry was to the table in two quick strides, his kick upending it and sending the shotgun and whiskey jug flying. The shotgun discharged into the ceiling with a roar and the whiskey jug shattered. Bannister went for the weapon, but another kick, aimed at his hip, sent him in the other direction.

Now he tried for the back door. Harry caught up with him, hauled him up by his shirt with one hand, and, with the other, shoved open the door.

"You want to leave this house?" he said. He gave the man another kick, sending him down the wooden stairs. When the wretch sat up, there was blood on his forehead.

The injury had imparted no wisdom. Though Harry was standing there with a loaded revolver, Bannister of a sudden lunged forward, as though to strangle Harry with his bare hands.

Harry sidestepped him, hitting him hard on the back of his skull with his pistol barrel when he came within range. Bannister rolled back onto the grass.

Elspeth was standing at the door. "Is there a bucket of water handy, Miss Elspeth?" Harry asked.

"Yes, sir."

"If you would fetch it, I would be obliged."

When she had done so, he poured the contents over Bannister's face. The man came to slowly, but eventually completely. Harry sat down on the step, holding the Colt aimed at the other's head.

"Do you know where Alice is?"

Bannister raised his eyes, glowering, then shook his head. "The Rebs took her prisoner. Don't know where she be. Who're you?"

"My name is of no consequence. What I have to tell you is, I'm a Federal scout. This whole valley is now full of Union troops—the entire Army of the Potomac. The commanding general has made Boonsboro his headquarters. I'm going back there, and I'm going to report you as a Rebel spy and informant. There are cavalry patrols out all the time and they'll be looking for you."

"You're the one the Rebels took with her. You passed a night here with her."

Harry stood up and extended the arm with the pistol. "I'm giving you this one chance, Bannister. You get off this property now and you never come back. I live just across the Potomac and if I hear you've returned I will hunt you down like a possum. Do you understand?"

"You're a Union scout?"

Harry brought the pistol closer. "You get yourself up and running now or I will shoot you for wounding and take you back to Boonsboro as my prisoner. Do you not believe me?"

Finally, the man did. His was a hobbling sort of run, but it carried him across the pasture fast enough. When he was out of range, Harry holstered the pistol.

Elspeth was already cleaning up. When she was done, she gave him a drink from a fresh whiskey jug and made him up some food for traveling. Harry reloaded the shotgun and set it back on the table after he'd righted it.

"He won't be back, Elspeth. Not now that he knows Allie and I are no longer guests of the Confederacy. But you keep this squirrel gun handy. Just don't turn it on any Federal troops."

"Yes, sir."

"This battle won't last but a few days, if that. Then things will return to normal. Now, if you please, I need directions to the house where Allie's aunt lives—the one on the Funkstown Road."

She readily provided them. Harry lingered not a moment longer.

\*　　　\*　　　\*

Harry crossed Antietam Creek well to the north of either army, evading pickets and cavalry patrols. Nearing the Funkstown Road, he became quite cautious, pausing in the woods to the east of the pike and listening attentively before proceeding. It was a wise precaution. A rumbling sound in the distance manifested itself as a large body of Confederate cavalry hurrying toward Sharpsburg. In its train, moving almost as fast, were a dozen or more ambulances. He would have to avoid the road, which meant more brambles and fences to jump. The roan mare seemed to sense the difficulties ahead, and became balky. Harry tried talking to her sweetly. After awhile, this began to work, and the animal calmed. But her progress remained slow.

It was nearly dark when he came upon the house he'd been directed to. Tying up the roan on a pasture fence, Harry decided to forego all formalities and courtesies. Allie would be taking no chances. Knocking on the door might produce gunfire instead of a warm welcome. Harry chose simply to enter.

But the door was firmly latched. He went around to the back and found the same condition there. Returning to the front, he knocked loudly but politely. When there was no response, he called out.

"Allie! It's Harrison. Come to the door, please!"

Nothing happened.

"Allie! Please! It's Harrison Raines."

"Raise your hands!"

The voice came from behind him. Harry did as bidden, turning to see a very small woman holding a very long rifle aimed in the general vicinity of his belly.

"Are you Allie's aunt?"

"I am. What do you know of Allie?"

"I'm a friend. A recent friend, but a friend. We were taken by Rebel cavalry but got away from them. She said she was coming here, and now I've come to take her to safety."

The woman lowered the rifle slightly. "She ain't been here, mister."

"Are you certain? We left each other just north of Sharpsburg. She said she was coming directly here."

"Well, she never got here."

"Are you quite sure?"

"How sure do you have to be? She never came. I wish to hell she had. It's a fearful trouble we're in with these Rebel soldiers marchin' everywhere they please. I'm all alone here."

"She sent no word to you? You've no idea where she went?"

"Now how would I if I ain't seen or heard from her since the Fourth of July?"

Harry dropped his hands to his side, shaking his head. "This is sorely worrisome."

"Everything in this damned war is worrisome, mister. You with the Yankees?"

"Yes, I am. A scout."

"Well, Allie got her strong opinions, but I got none except I want to be left alone."

Harry bowed to her. "I will do that now, madam. If Mrs. Robertson does call upon you, I would be pleased if you would tell her that Harrison Raines came looking for her and that I will return for her."

He took the road south back toward Sharpsburg, thinking he could not now be overtaken by any enemy on the pike and confident he could detect any force ahead before they could do him harm.

When he figured he was getting close to the battle lines, he pulled off and dismounted, walking the roan to the forested height of a small hill. Tying her to a low branch, wishing he had oats to give her, he unsaddled her and rolled himself in the horse blanket on hard ground. Something was irritating his eyes. He rubbed at them and discovered it was tears.

Exhausted, he tried to go to sleep, but remained wakeful as he lay listening to the sound of distant cannon fire. If he remained here, he could be captured again, and this time his treatment would not be so lenient. He was at all events being derelict in his duty. He'd been told to scout the enemy's left flank. He'd done so, finding it anchored near the Potomac but no farther north than the woods where he'd last seen Allie. This could be useful intelligence.

Wearily, he got to his feet and resaddled the mare in the dark. With luck, Allie may have gone back to Boonsboro after all.

McClellan had moved his headquarters—and, of all things, forward—to a bend of Antietam Creek just off the Boonsboro Pike. He was conferring with his corps and division commanders, but an aide took down Harry's information.

"We'll have three, maybe four divisions up there in the morning," the aide said. "They won't be in those woods for long."

"Is Pinkerton around?"

"Retired for the evening."

"May I camp here?"

"Anywhere you like."

Harry led the roan down to where a large campfire had been lit in the trees near the creek bank. He was unsaddling the horse again when he noticed that the men around the fire were getting to their feet and looking to where a road passed near their bivouac. A wagon was approaching, side lanterns swinging with the jolts as it turned off and bumped up into the encampment. The wagon driver called out, asking if General McClellan's headquarters was nearby.

What had attracted everyone's attention was that the wagon driver was a woman—a very small woman. Harry put on his spectacles and moved nearer. There were two women on the seat. Holding the reins was Clara Barton. Seated next to her, looking drawn and tired, was Caitlin Howard.

Harry stood motionless a moment, the joy he felt quickly diminished by a certain dread. He knew Miss Barton well. She had come to take part in this battle and had brought Caitlin to share her duties and her fate. Harry had seen men mown down in ranks as they stood, had seen farmhouses leveled and farm animals slaughtered by shell fire. One could bet on the survival of these women here and get hard odds.

He rushed to the side of the wagon, choosing to speak to his old love first. "Caitlin, you should not be here."

Miss Barton intervened. "It is a pleasure to see you again, Captain Raines. But do not fret for Miss Howard. She is here of her own free will and I am most grateful." She looked about, peering past the firelight. "I am looking for General McClellan. I have brought medical supplies. In this wagon, and others."

"His headquarters is back up the road at Pry House," Harry said. He turned, seeking an officer, and spotting one smoking a pipe by a tree. "Sir!" Harry called out. "Where can we find the chief surgeon?"

"I do not know, sir. But by morning I'm sure you'll know right enough. Just follow the wounded."

"There are wounded from here to South Mountain," Miss Barton said. "Has the battle not begun?"

"McClellan's advance guard had to fight its way through the South Mountain passes. It pushed Lee back behind this creek, but with losses."

"No doubt," the little woman replied. She looked to her driver. "We need to find a surgeon. I think anyone will do."

"A moment, Miss Barton," Harry said, reaching to take Caitlin's hand. "Do you need Miss Howard?"

Miss Barton smiled. "Not for this task. What I need is for her to sleep. A night's undisturbed sleep, Captain Raines."

"I understand, ma'am."

Caitlin gave him a curious look, but allowed him to take her by the waist and swing her down onto the ground. "Are there quarters here, Harry?"

"No, but if you stay with me I will see to it that you are not molested."

"Ever the cavalier. Find us a comfortable spot and I will put my trust in you."

"I would ask no more."

Miss Barton's driver snapped the reins and the team began a reluctant trudge, turning the wagon back to the road, where two others of Miss Barton's apparent jurisdiction had drawn up.

"Take great care, Miss Barton," Harry called after her.

135

"You as well, Captain Raines, and bring Miss Howard safe to me in the morning."

Harry brought Caitlin to the fireside at a place where two Union officers were sitting on a gum blanket and smoking, also passing a flask back and forth. At the sudden and amazing sight of a woman in their midst—and a remarkably beautiful one at that—they got to their feet and turned and bowed, saying, "Evening, ma'am."

"This is Miss Caitlin Howard," Harry said. "She is here to assist Miss Clara Barton with attending to the wounded."

"We are all obliged to you, ma'am," said the nearest officer. He looked to his mate, then to Harry. He and his comrade moved on, doubtless to continue the fortification of their nerves with the contents of their flask. They left the gum blanket where it was. "You may be needing that," said the other.

Harry moved the blanket to beneath a tree and then motioned Caitlin to it. She was wearing a cloak, and removed it before sitting.

"I'd no word of you," she said. "I'd feared the worst."

"That's safe to do for every man in the Federal service," he said. "Except, perhaps, General McClellan."

"He is here, ready to do battle, Harry. Do not speak ill of him." Her native English accent was decidedly pronounced this night, though she was present for this most American of events.

"You should not have come, Caitlin. There'll be the Devil to pay here tomorrow. Lee drove McClellan off the Peninsula. He means to do something of the same here."

"Your government allows women little enough to do in this war. This is the very least I could do."

"You're in thrall to Miss Barton."

"And who could not be? She is an angel."

"She could get you killed."

"Please, Harry." As if intending a gesture to silence him, or change this line of conversation, she reclined, pulling her cloak over her and turning away. "I'm sorry, but I'm dreadfully weary. We have been long upon the road."

"Where?"

"We tried to go to Harper's Ferry, but were turned back by Union cavalry, who said the Rebels had taken it."

"That's true. But if they're beaten here tomorrow, they'll leave. I can go home."

"To your farm in Shepherdstown."

"Yes."

"What is your service here?"

"I'm a scout for McClellan. I've just come back from behind the Rebel left flank."

She turned back again. He could barely see her eyes in the shadows. "You've always been brave, if often foolish."

"Thank you."

"There's something I should tell you. Louise has gone off."

"Yes. They freed her from prison."

"She was not in prison."

"Yes, she was. In the Old Capitol Prison. Allan Pinkerton put her there."

"No, Harry. That is not true. Wilkes found her at the National Hotel. She went off with him."

"Wilkes? John Wilkes Booth?"

"Yes. They have been lovers in the past, as surely you must know."

What woman in Washington had not been guest in the actor's bed? "She told me nothing."

Caitlin rolled over again. "I thought you should know."

Harry lay down, resting his head on his saddle. He looked at the back of Caitlin's head, auburn curls glinting in the firelight. He put his hand on her shoulder.

"I did not mean that revelation as invitation, Harrison."

"Yes, ma'am."

"We shall both be very busy tomorrow. We needs must sleep." She reached and patted his hand, then lifted it from her shoulder. "Good night, Harry. I am pleased that you are here."

He was chill in the clamminess of the moist night air, but kept his body a distance from hers, rolling up in his saddle blanket. He wondered where Allie was sleeping, wishing mightily it was a safe and pleasant place.

The clamminess of the air of a sudden turned to drizzle. He turned toward Caitlin and pulled her toward him, covering her fully with the gum blanket. This time she moved quite close. His coat quickly became soaked, but he ignored that. Thousands of men in these fields and woods were sleeping much less comfortably.

She put her head against his chest, her hair touching his neck and cheek. It was a wonderment, how they all had come to be where they were.

# Fifteen

Harry awakened suddenly to a long crackle of gunfire, followed by the thud and thump of cannon. It was some distance away. He assumed it was where the Confederates had taken a position in the woods on their far left flank.

Caitlin had gone. Harry sat up, rubbing the moisture off his face. The drizzle had stopped, but the early-morning light was dim in the heavy mist.

Soldiers were running by. Harry called to one to stop. He didn't but the next one paused, uncertain as to who Harry was.

"Do you know what happened to the woman who was here?" Harry asked, pointing to the ground beside him.

"Ain't no woman there."

"Yes, but there was. Do you . . . ?"

The soldier was on his way again.

Caitlin had taken the gum blanket, doubtless as a foraged medical supply. He guessed he'd likely find her with Miss Barton, who might well be at headquarters. He had to go there anyway.

Pinkerton was seated on the porch of Pry House, out of the way of the military bustle but at hand in case McClellan needed him. Again he seemed pleased to see Harry.

"Fine work last night, Raines," he said, rising from his chair. "The enemy were right where you said."

"Thank you, Mister Pinkerton. Actually, what I found out was where the enemy weren't."

"Which meant they were where they are. We've been hitting them since first light. Joe Hooker's got two divisions plus reinforced brigades across the creek and up by those woods you told us about. Maybe twelve thousand men. We should be rolling up that flank presently."

Harry listened a moment. All of the gunfire was to the north and northwest.

"What about the rest of the army?" he asked. "Why aren't they attacking?"

"The general's waiting to see how Hooker succeeds. When he breaks that Rebel flank, then we'll advance along the line."

Harry had never once read a manual on military tactics, but he knew the Confederates' commander.

"Mister Pinkerton, General Lee is a man of quick maneuver. He'll reinforce that flank with everything he's got handy. If you'd press him now along the entire line, you'd pin him in place and overwhelm him with numbers. I don't think he has forty thousand men. You must have twice that."

Pinkerton's voice took on a serious tone. "Raines, the general has reviewed all the intelligence reports—including yours. He is persuaded that General Lee is opposing him with a hundred thousand men or more. We will prevail, but much depends on turning their flank first."

Harry frowned, looking down at the much scuffed porch floor.

"Dispense with your doubts, Harrison," Pinkerton said, sternly. "A brilliant victory is at hand."

Harry went to the porch railing, watching as a general and his escort thundered up toward the house. The mist was thinning. He could almost see the shadows of the horsemen. "Mister Pinkerton, I have a small quarrel with you."

"This is a poor time for it."

"You told me you were holding Miss Devereux in prison— an inducement for me to provide service for this army. Yet I now am informed that she was at liberty from the first moment she set foot in Washington City."

Pinkerton joined him at the railing. "Her imprisonment was seriously considered, Harrison. She has much to answer for. But I decided not to subject her to that inconvenience because I know you well to be a loyal Union man and was certain you would not shirk your duty at such a crucial hour."

The general thumped up onto the porch, gave Pinkerton and Harry a curious glance, then entered the house, trailing lesser ranks.

"Mister Pinkerton," said Harry. "You know that I intend to return to my farm when this fight is over—presuming as we must that Lee is driven back south."

"We will discuss that later, Raines."

Harry stepped back from the railing. "What would you like me to do now? What are your orders?"

"You know the ground here. Ride to Hooker and tell him what you know."

The sounds of battle were increasing in volume. "Mister Pinkerton, he seems to be fully engaged. He by now knows the ground he's fighting for far better than I."

"Well, you've an eye for battle now. Ride up there and then come back here and tell me how things are going. The truth often gets bent when it comes up through generals."

"Bent" truth was that which contradicted McClellan's notions. "Yes, sir." Harry hesitated. "Could you tell me where my friend Jack Tantou might be found?"

"He's down with Burnside, scouting the Rebels' right flank. Contrary to original orders, I might add."

"That was my idea, sir. I knew the territory at the other end of the line better."

"We'll discuss that later also."

"And Miss Barton?"

"I observed a colonel on the General's staff order her off the battlefield, but I do not believe she obeyed him."

"Thank you, Mister Pinkerton. I will ride back north."

He crossed Antietam Creek at Pry's Mill Ford and rode cross-country to a long sweep of trees bordering the Smoketown Road, passing what looked to be two full Union divisions poised for combat. The men had fixed bayonets and were standing or leaning on their muskets, every eye looking west to where a veil of smoke hung over what Harry remembered was a cornfield.

Steering the roan clear of this vast, blue assemblage, Harry continued on to the trees, finding them generally clear of soldiery of either hue. Emerging from these woods on the other side, he had a clearer view of the fighting—and of the result. Wounded men were stumbling by.

Keeping off the road to let them pass, he proceeded south, tying the roan to a small tree and moving ahead on foot until he had a complete view of the field before him. The thwack of a bullet against a nearby branch compelled him to drop to the ground.

There was a ditch a few yards forward, paralleling a branch of the road where it turned due south. Moving on hands and knees, he rolled into it, then crawled forward, wishing it had not rained during the night.

The musket fire in the field ahead was a continuous rattle, but distant. It began to grow louder, and not simply because Harry was edging toward it. Reaching a hump of ground where the ditch made an angle, he lifted his head, reaching for the field glasses Pinkerton had given him. Adjusting the focus, he scanned the ground slowly, making his surveillance from left to right and back again until he was looking at the tree line that served as a horizon.

He was stunned. This had been a cornfield when he had last passed by, but seemingly every stalk and shock had been cut down as though by a scythe. But this was not the only harvest. Lying in rows all across the field were the bodies of soldiers—a few in blue but most in gray and butternut—cut down where they had stood in ranks. He guessed it was the work not of muskets but of cannons, firing canister. It had been brutally efficient. Harry felt fortunate not to have witnessed this horrific slaughter as it had taken its massive toll, though its aftermath was gruesome enough.

The victors, if that they were, could be seen at the far end of the now denuded cornfield, moving in fits and starts along the line toward the trees and a small white building that Harry recalled was a church, belonging to some strange sect. The Confederates were in retreat. Harry could not believe he was with McClellan's army. He was watching a victory in the making.

But no. Such a turn of events was of course too much to hope for at this unfortunate turn in the history of this embattled republic. The blue line wavered and stopped—and then began to fall back.

The rearward rush was inexorable, but the movement oblique. The men in the shattered ranks were heading toward the nearest shelter—another patch of woods that lay just to the south and east. The Rebels came shrieking and bellowing after them. Their ranks were massed so closely, Harry judged them to be reserve or reinforcements come fresh to the battlefield. The ferocity of their counter-attack was unlike anything he had experienced in this war before. He wondered if these could be Stonewall Jackson's troops, poorly rested from their march up from Harper's Ferry but still full of push and bloodlust for the Yankees.

Using his field glasses again, he made a disturbing discovery. Some of this gray line was coming his way, the shrieking yell as frightening as the bullets that now sang overhead in ever increasing volume.

Harry pressed himself against the earth, peering now around the side of the little mound. His immobility and indecision, the product of an all-consuming fear of remaining in this position, met with the fear of getting shot in the back if he got up and ran.

A young soldier dropped into the ditch beside him, the dust and mud on his uniform almost masking his sergeant's stripes.

"You on our side?" the youth asked.

"Yes, I am. Can't you tell by the way I'm faced?"

"Most of our boys I've seen the last few minutes are faced the other way, and moving toward it."

The Confederates were still coming, though more slowly now. Harry would have turned and run had not the sergeant joined him.

"I'm a scout for General McClellan," he said.

"Reporting to his headquarters?"

"Yes."

"Well, I'm a scout for General Mansfield, but I'm not reporting to his headquarters."

143

"Why not?"

"For one thing, I just got here. For another, he's a comin'."
The sergeant jerked his thumb over his shoulder.

Harry looked back. There was a wisp of blue in the distance,
across the road and extending to either side. The soldiers were
too far away to measure their movement, but they definitely
were advancing. Turning again toward the enemy, Harry
watched as they reached the edge of the cornfield and halted,
the most forward of them kneeling.

"Looks like we picked a bad place to be," Harry said.

"I'd prefer to be sucking oysters at the Marshall House in
Alexandria," the sergeant said. "But there are worse places to
be than this—one of them being that cornfield."

Harry glanced back again. The line of blue was coming on
fast—apparently at the double quick. "Or on that road."

In the way of punctuation, a bullet struck the top of the
mound, showering the both of them with dirt.

"Time to put scouting aside and take up surviving," the
sergeant said, getting closer to the ground. "What we need
most is for the Rebels to keep shooting so they stay where
they are."

"I'd prefer they'd go back where they came from."

"No, sir. You want them right there in the cornfield."

"Why is that?"

"Because we've been promised some excellent artillery
support of this attack."

"From where?"

"The ridge on the other side of Antietam Creek."

Harry studied the young man's face. He could not have
been twenty-five, but a sergeant. If he survived this battle,
he'd likely find himself an officer. Harry had heard of full
colonels not much older.

"Harrison Raines," Harry said, extending his hand as
another bullet clipped off a clod of earth to his right. "Belle
Haven Plantation, Charles City County, Virginia."

"Christopher Knapp," said the sergeant, shaking Harry's
hand. "Westchester County, New York."

Before they could further advance their acquaintance, they

were assaulted by a fury of sound as the Confederate ranks opened fire. There was a veritable rain of bullets passing overhead. Knapp raised his cap just over the top of the mound and a ball sang right through it before he pulled it down.

"If I kept it out there a moment more I might have filled it with bullets," he said.

Harry could scarcely hear him. All at once, he could hear nothing but explosions of gunpowder as the artillery fire Knapp had predicted made itself manifest in a continuous roar to the left.

Mindless now of danger, his fear swept away in the sudden, mad flood of excitement, Harry looked around the side of the mound—and quickly wished he hadn't.

It was all the same as having a front row seat at the Roman Colosseum during a major combat of gladiators or slaughter of Christians—times a thousand. Positioned on the flank of the advancing Rebels, the Federal artillery fire cut through their ranks lengthwise—solid shot removing heads and limbs and twisting bodies grotesquely; explosive shells finding victims in every direction. Men fell by the half dozen in rows or clumps. Those who survived looked all about them, waiting for orders to retreat or edging backward without them.

In a moment, they needed no orders. The forward elements of General Mansfield's XII Corps came charging past Harry's little mound, followed by a seeming endless stream of others. They spread out as they double-quicked onto the field, causing the Union artillery fire to abruptly cease. The white-bearded general led from the fore, exhorting his men to keep on as the Rebels hastily absented the field.

It was a journey Mansfield would not complete. A Confederate bullet struck him and spun him around. He fell crumpled to the ground. Knapp half rose, but remained where he was when he saw several soldiers go to Mansfield and carry him back to the road.

At the same time, like a theatrical understudy rushing on stage, another general ran forward and took the commander's place.

What followed was also theatrical—an epic scene of mass,

hellish madness. One of Mansfield's divisions remained on the road, charging the Confederates in the west woods but doing so in small groups. Protected by the trees and rocks, the Rebels cut them down. As more groups came up, Confederate artillery near the woods added to the slaughter.

The rest of the corps lunged on across the bloody cornfield, sweeping the remaining enemy back toward the little white church. Using his field glasses, Harry tried to make sense of the fighting when it reached that spot, but could make out only smoke and confusion.

There was no further movement, only combat, then of a sudden the Rebel line broke and fell back beyond the church. Union troops poured into the gap. Here was the success McClellan's plan had promised.

But it was the Devil's tease. The firing fell off. The brave men who had made the charge needed support now to exploit the advantage by pushing the Rebels aside and devouring their flank.

No such aid was forthcoming. Hooker's shattered division could not help. Some reserves were sent across the cornfield to shore up the Union hold on the area by the church, but they were inadequate for an advance.

A truce of sorts seemed to come over the two armies, as though they were two boxers pausing between rounds. It was a tense time, in which the commanders would be rearranging their ranks and calling for reinforcements and resupply. Harry could see movement in the woods near the white church. The Confederates were getting the troops up they needed. But they did not attack. They were waiting for the Federals to do that. Harry wondered who the Rebel commander there might be. Longstreet was an able defensive fighter, but this seemed more than that. It seemed a trap. Indeed, it was not long before the movement ceased. However many men were in those trees, they had taken cover.

At long last, the Union side made its next move. A column of fresh troops at least a division in strength entered upon the field from the east. With colors and banners flying in a freshening breeze, the now bright morning sunlight flashing on bayonets and swords, they seemed bound more for a parade ground than bloody struggle.

Knapp had a spy glass of his own. He stood up now, surveying the units. Harry joined him, feeling foolish and not a little cowardly for having spent most of this battle huddled behind a pile of dirt.

"It's General Sedgwick's division, which makes it Sumner's corps. General Mansfield was expecting him on the field more than an hour ago. His boys were up at dawn."

"They seem willing," Harry said.

"That they do." Knapp lowered his glass, squinting against the sunlight, then raised it to his eye again. "I think I see Sedgwick. Yes, yes I do. And there's Sumner."

The great procession moved on, the orderly ranks buckling in places as the men stepped over the fallen soldiery sprawled all over the field. Drummer boys, impossibly young, marched along at the rear, their beat and cadence stirring even Harry's war-weary blood.

Behind them came batteries of artillery, which set up in the cornfield, cannon barrels aimed at both church and adjoining woods.

When the last of Sumner's column was well across the field, Knapp suddenly turned to the left, aiming his spy glass toward the empty meadow along Antietam Creek.

"Something's wrong," he said.

"Seems peaceful enough to me," Harry said.

"That's what's wrong," Knapp said. "Sumner's corps has two divisions. There's the one. Where's the other?"

"Maybe McClellan held it in reserve. He's a nervous man about contingencies."

"They have reserves stacked up almost all the way back to Boonsboro. No, General French has that division and was all lined up behind Sedgwick's this morning. Where the hell has he gone?"

"This is not a battlefield that's easy to get lost on."

"It surely is not."

They took seats atop the mound now, observing Sumner's advancing column much like spectators at a sporting event.

Moving without hesitation, virtually unopposed by enemy fire, the lines of blue reached the Union position by the white church, passing it on the right and proceeding on into the woods where Harry had seen Rebels filing in among the trees.

Harry cursed himself. Why hadn't he run up to this Sumner or Sedgwick and told them what he had seen? Of course, in the midst of an advance, they might well have simply ignored him—a stranger in civilian clothes. He might not have gotten close to either.

But he could have told Knapp. He could have sent Knapp.

Harry started to speak to the sergeant but was cut short by an explosion of noise from the woods. It did not abate.

"My God," said Knapp, his spy glass fixed on the woods.

Again, all that was detectable at the distance was pyrotechnics and confusion. But the fire being laid down on Sumner's force seemed to be coming from three directions, all concentrated on the center.

"There's more Rebels in those woods than I've seen all morning," Knapp said. "It's a goddam ambush."

Harry swallowed. He had nothing to say, except to himself.

The fighting continued another twenty minutes, then little groups of men in blue began emerging from the woods, followed soon by what remained of the full body. They had no trees or rocks for cover, but they had the guns massed in the cornfield. As the Rebels came out of the trees behind them, hell bent for slaughter of their routed foe, the Federal cannons ripped into them, joined by other Union artillery units elsewhere along the line. The Federals must have had fifty guns, all firing grape and canister. Again the Confederates fell like a mown crop. Their line staggered. As Sumner's survivors ran, walked, and limped toward salvation, the Rebels ran back into their woods.

The Union artillerymen turned and followed their comrades in Sedgwick's division off the battlefield. The now hopelessly exposed Union force by the white church, assaulted again by Confederate reinforcements, fell back and began an unhappy retreat. Soon, no one possessed the cornfield but the dead and dying of both sides.

"Lee must have brought half his army up to this end of the line," Knapp said.

"If we had thrown everything in at once, that wouldn't have mattered," Harry replied. Eyes downcast, he held his face in his hands.

"Well, that didn't happen."

He looked up, gazing again at the landscape of bodies. "This is now a poor place to be," he said. He took out his whiskey flask, offering it to his new friend, who accepted it with a polite nod. "If at all possible, I should be happy to take dinner with you tonight, sir."

"Could be hardtack. Could be mighty late."

"I'd be honored whenever," Harry said. "I'll be at McClellan's headquarters, though I'm not sure where it will be."

"The way events are unfolding, Mister Raines, I don't think it's going to move much."

Knapp returned the flask and returned it to Harry, who was very much in need of the gulp he took from it.

"I'd best report to whoever took over from Mansfield. I expect that'll be General Alpheus Williams."

They started back toward their horses. Except for the moaning of the wounded and the distant rattle of traffic on the road, all was eerily quiet where there had been utter din. "Intermission," Harry said.

"A tragedy," said Knapp. "I wonder how many acts it has."


Harry spurred the roan toward Pry's Ford, where he had crossed Antietam Creek hours and so much bloodshed earlier. He looked very much forward to returning to the peaceful comfort of headquarters, but, glancing over his right shoulder as he descended the low ridge to the creek, he saw that this would have to be postponed.

Another Union division—presumably French's lost one—was marching off across the fields toward a house and barn in the distance. In a moment, Federal artillery from the left began firing shot and shell toward it, walking them forward along the ground in advance of the troops. In a moment, they found their mark at the top of a long rise just beyond the farm and began pounding it. The Federal column spread out, maneuvering into a wide front. When they reached the bottom of the rise, they began running at the double quick—an uphill charge.

Harry dared not return to Pinkerton without learning the outcome of this unexpected engagement. A single division charging the Rebel line, unsupported and with flanks exposed? Madness had spread to this part of the battlefield as well.

Driven more by curiosity than duty, Harry trotted the roan up the slope after the Union column, emboldened by the failure of any Rebel bullet to find him during all the morning's fighting and intent on learning the result of this new round of competition.

There were Confederates in the farmhouse just ahead, but, in the face of the parade-ground style of advance of French's relentless division, they leapt up and ran yipping back to a position at the top of the slope, a number of them firing as they withdrew.

As soon as French's column was past the place, Harry cantered up to the farmhouse, tying the roan to a porch post in the rear. Taking his field glasses, but leaving his Spencer rifle in the saddle, he moved to the front of the house, hearing more scattered gunfire ahead.

It became continuous. Though some of French's troops had spread off to either side, the main body was climbing the slope through a shallow ravine. If the Union commander thought that would provide protection, he had erred. A large-sized Rebel unit had gotten to the side of the ravine at a place where its men could fire into the Union column's flanks, and they did so with deadly effect.

General French or someone ordered a charge, one aimed not so much at dislodging the Confederates harassing them on the flank but at getting the division up to the main Rebel line. The mass of blue uniforms began to move. Within minutes, they were spread out all along the top of the rise, facing and returning murderous fire.

Harry felt guilty hanging back by the farmhouse.

Running at a lope, he reached the ravine and leapt into it, stumbling and rolling, just as several bullets buzzed overhead. Continuing on, his nerves numbed by his excess of fear, he reached the top, flung himself over the side, and hugged the ground, raising only his head and not by very much.

He didn't need field glasses to take in what was happening. The Confederates were thick along the line, firing like blazes, but as though from a trench. Harry could see fence rails piled and stacked in front of the Rebel position, and here and there heads. But no men standing.

French's men would rush the enemy, falter at the fence rails, fall back a few paces, cling to the ground, and then charge the line again. Neither side could rid the ridge of the other, but after much more of this, French would have damn few men left for the holding.

There was a hallooing and hurrahing from the rear. What looked to be a brigade—maybe French's reserve—was coming up the ravine. The fresh troops filled the gaps and restored order to the Union line, but failed to sufficiently alter the odds or the nature of the fight. There were more charges, each taking its toll of the Rebels, but each repulsed.

Harry had failed to bring a canteen. He lay in a now broiling sun, thinking of the cool waters of Antietam Creek so near behind him, yet not near enough to be convenient.

Ahead and to the right lay a dead man not thirty feet away. Hugging the earth, Harry crawled in painful fashion to his side. It took a great deal of pulling and tugging to get his canteen free, but Harry at last succeeded. He rolled over onto his back, pulled the plug, and poured the warm, gushing water into his mouth.

He hadn't taken but two swallows when a Rebel bullet struck the canteen and rudely ripped it from his hands, sending it sailing into the air and rolling several times over the ground.

Not knowing where the shooter was located, Harry rolled himself to his right, edging away from the spot as quickly as he could manage without further exposing himself. A moment

151

later, a Union private, a man as old as Sergeant Knapp had been young, dropped beside him, the mangled canteen in hand.

"Better drink it fast, son. It's been wounded sore." He flinched as a bullet struck the ground beside them, scattering dirt.

Harry gulped down what water he could, then put the ruined canteen aside and returned his attention to the combat. "You come up with the reserve brigade?" he asked the private, speaking in a near shout to be heard above the gunfire.

"Rear guard," the man shouted back.

Harry was about to remark that the private was still in the rear, but then, so was he. "There are no more reserves?"

"Supposed to be a whole corps or more behind us. Don't know where they are now."

Artillery shells were exploding overhead, flinging hot metal like rain. An officer on the ground ahead looked back, saw the private, and waved him forward. Reluctantly, the enlisted man rose on hands and knees. "Might as well be anywhere. Good luck to you, son."

He made it to the officer unscathed. A moment later, a shell struck the ground in front of them, throwing them both asunder. Harry started toward them, but neither man was moving.

Hunching down once more, he surveyed the Union line again with his field glasses. All was unchanged, except for the ratio of living to dead. Judging by the volume of enemy fire, the Rebels were being reinforced. McClellan had to do something here fast, or he could find his own line broken on the rock of the Confederates' entrenched position.

That last thought had not been formulated as a prayer but it may well have been perceived as one. Looking back, Harry saw to the rear and right another large body in blue coming up the slope in rapid fashion. As they drew near, it became clear that the angry, shouting, profane figure leading the entire division was a general—quite probably their commanding general.

He and his troops swept by in a Biblical fury, heading obliquely up the ridge to higher ground, moving faster as they approached the top. There were bursts of fire all along that section of line, but the division, moving now as three separate units, kept going, sweeping over the crest.

But they left many behind.

Curiously, the firing directly in front of Harry began to subside. Here and there he saw Union officers rise and wave their men on. Reluctant at first, they began to respond to these orders with increasing enthusiasm. In the lull of gunfire, he heard someone shout: "They're running!"

Harry rose as well. He had twisted his ankle somehow and had to limp, but he followed the others. Reaching the top of the slope, amazed that he could do so now without attracting a storm of minié balls, he walked slowly toward the stacked fence rails that had seemed so impregnable.

Reaching them, looking off toward Sharpsburg, he could see the fleeing Confederates, the Union division that had just come up now in pursuit, the mad general waving his sword.

Then Harry looked down, and wished he had not.

The Rebels had not entrenched. They had taken advantage of a long sunken road that cut between two farms, using it as a natural fortification that they'd improved with the stacked fence rails.

But they'd stayed in it too long. Union flanking fire had been catastrophic. The blood-soaked lane was filled with bodies, and thickly so. You could walk from one end to the other on them without touching ground.

He studied the bloodied face of a young dead boy who seemed to be looking at him—not reproachfully but with a slight smile. Turning away, Harry walked back a few steps and then threw up what remained in his stomach. He stood a long moment, breathing deeply and recapturing his equilibrium.

As had been said earlier in the day, there was opportunity here. McClellan had to be informed of it. There were doubtless dispatch riders heading hot along the roads to Pry House, but Pinkerton had made this Harry's job. He would see to it.

At all events, he wanted away from this place.

Untying the roan, he got wearily into the saddle and gathered up the reins. The Rebels were directing artillery fire onto

153

the Union position again to provide cover for their retreating troops. It was indeed time to leave.

He trotted the horse back up the slope briefly to make certain of the situation before he left it, then turned and headed down the grade for Pry's Ford and headquarters. He'd not progressed fifty yards when he heard a sort of shuddering shriek in the air behind him and then a great concussive roar as all at once he and his mount were lifted into the air, parting company as Harry found himself turning upside down. In the peculiar slowness of the moment, and the sudden silence that overcame all, he found himself wondering how much of him would be left when he once again returned to earth.

# Sixteen

There was no pain, no sound, no sense of impact at all, as Harry came back to the ground. Lying there, face upward, he felt as much to be floating as he had been in the air after the shell had exploded. His mind and eye were on the lovely little clouds that the heated earth had produced in the heavens. With the muggy air so still it seemed remarkable that they could actually be moving across the sky, but they were—heading east, away from the madness of the battlefield, on to a blissful, peaceful place, where they would completely evaporate, and die.

A sound hearkened, battering at his numbed consciousness. It was piercing, high in pitch, a sort of bleating. All of a sudden, it became quite loud.

Harry looked to his right. The roan was on its back, front legs and hooves pawing fecklessly at the air as it tried to right itself. The animal's rear barely moved, the legs lying limp. Harry ran a hand over his eyes and then attempted to stand himself, finding he could do so, that he could take steps.

He should have taken them in the other direction, walking away from this horrid scene. Instead, he did the right but dreadful thing, circling to the other side of the suffering animal and noting the huge hole in the roan's belly. He stared, bleakly, then circled further until he reached a point where he was behind the horse's thrashing head, where he could not see the bulging eyes. He wished he had a heavier caliber pistol than his Navy Colt.

Despite all, he ended the roan's suffering forever with just two shots.

He stood sighing for the longest time, then holstered the

revolver and went to the animal's side, removing the saddle bags and the Spencer rifle. It would be a long trudge to headquarters.

Instead of going back by way of Pry's Ford, he cut southeast across a field toward the middle bridge that took the Sharpsburg-Boonsboro road across Antietam Creek. It was being defended by no less than an entire corps.

"And who are you, sir?" said a long-bearded sergeant, standing at a stone wall at the west end of the bridge.

"I'm a scout. I was with General French's division on that ridge there. Had my horse killed by a shell."

The sergeant studied him, scratching at his scraggly whiskers. "Come with me."

He led him to a nearby tent fly, beneath which was seated a captain with an unhappy face. The colors identified the unit as the 16th Michigan.

Harry repeated his identity and explanation. "If I were a Confederate infiltrator, sir, I would not have been able to stroll as I did to the bridge. The fighting has been fierce up on that ridge. I have never encountered anything like it."

"Scout, you say?"

"Yes, sir. Reporting directly to Allan Pinkerton."

"And you're headed for McClellan's headquarters?"

"Yes, sir. Fast as I can get there without a horse."

The captain looked about the area. His men were mostly standing, their attention fixed on the slope Harry had just descended. He turned back. "How goes it up there?"

Harry sighed. He needed to tell all this to General McClellan; not some company commander.

"We've thrown the Rebels off the summit," Harry said. "I think they've run all the way back to Sharpsburg. If there was reinforcement, we could bust through that line and push all the way to the Packhorse Ford. We could capture the whole army."

The captain nodded, slowly and sadly. "We're being held in reserve. This is Fitz-John Porter's Fifth Corps. We've got all the reserve artillery just behind us and General Pleasonton's

156

cavalry division behind that. But they won't let us budge. They say we're all that keeps the Rebels from sweeping up the Boonsboro Pike."

"The Rebel army just now is about as likely to sweep up the Boonsboro Pike as you and I are to fly."

"Orders. Orders is orders."

"If you will allow me to continue on my way, perhaps we might alter that."

"Yes. Yes, of course." He took out a pencil and notebook. "Pleasonton has more spare mounts than the Rebs have cavalry." He scribbled out something and handed it to Harry. "We haven't many animals to spare but if you give this to one of Pleasonton's sergeants, you're likely to be accommodated."

"I'm obliged to you, sir."

The man looked closely at Harry's face. "You look like you barely survived."

"Yes, sir."

"And you're not just heading east to desert?"

"I have no interest in any other place than General McClellan's headquarters at the Pry House."

"Then let me delay you no longer." He did not rise but just nodded his farewell.


As it turned out, no one provided him with a horse. He trudged up to the porch of the Pry House well after noon.

Pinkerton was not present and no one among the several staff officers seemed to know where he had gone. Harry had no great inclination toward a conversation with McClellan, but he didn't want his day's work—such as it was—to be wasted. He entered the house, moving through a small crowd to an open doorway on the left. McClellan's voice was distinct in the clutter of others. The general was describing a maneuver of Marshal Ney's at Austerlitz.

Harry stepped forward. Though he carried the rank of captain, he didn't know if he should represent himself in military or civilian fashion. He decided on the latter.

"Excuse me, sir," he said. A silence abruptly fell. McClellan, seated at a table, looked both offended and curious.

157

Harry took another step. "I'm Harrison Raines, Mister Pinkerton's scout. I've just returned from the center of the line."

McClellan looked to a colonel on his right. "Have we not had dispatches from that position?"

"Yes, sir," replied the colonel. "From General French and General Richardson."

"And they report success?"

"Yes, sir. General French has occupied the enemy position at the top of the ridge. General Richardson is down. The wound is mortal."

McClellan returned his attention to Harry. "Do you confirm this, Raines?"

"The position has been taken, General. It was a bloody fight. When I left, the enemy was moving back rapidly on Sharpsburg."

"You're certain?"

"Yes, sir. I watched them go."

"So we are holding fast on the right and we have vanquished them in the center."

"Yes, sir."

"Do you think they are preparing for a counterattack?"

"General, I don't think they have force enough to fight a five-minute delaying action. They are badly shot up, sir. I'm not certain, but I think Lee has committed all his reserves."

"That's nonsense, Raines. General Lee must have a hundred thousand men out there."

"Sir, you have an entire corps in reserve, plus artillery and cavalry, all within an easy march of the ridge top. A concentrated attack ought to break them easy. You could take the town."

"I could march right into a trap. An attack like that would have both flanks exposed. I gather you are not a military man, Raines."

"No, sir."

"Well, leave such thinking to those of us who are."

"Yes, sir." He was quit of his duties. He was free now to go find Miss Barton and Caitlin. He turned to go.

"A moment, Raines. I have a job for you. I've ordered General Burnside to attack on the left. He complains he cannot get his people across a small stone bridge because they're opposed by a few riflemen on a little hill just beyond. This makes no sense. I'd like you to ride over there and tell me what's really going on."

This was where he'd picnicked with Louise Devereux upon their return from the West. "General McClellan, sir. He doesn't need to take that bridge. Around a bend of the creek there, sir, is a ford. Snavely's Ford. He could move across it easy."

McClellan whisked at the air as though at a fly. "Just go there, please, and come back and tell me what you see. We cannot conclude this day without engaging our forces on the left."

Harry hesitated. "Sir . . ."

"Damn it, Raines. Be off! We have other business here."

"Sir, I need another horse. Mine was hit by a shell on the ridge."

McClellan peered more closely, looking at Harry's dusty, dirty, blood-stained clothes and face. He turned to the colonel on his right. "Have someone get this man a fresh mount." McClellan leaned back in his chair. "Make haste, Raines. There is no time to waste."

Daftly, Harry came hold of the idea that the horse they'd give him would be his own, dear, steadfast Rocket. But of course nothing of the sort occurred. He was provided with a chestnut mare with white nose and stockings who had the look of the plod about her. That was all right. Despite McClellan's admonition, Harry was of no mind to make haste anywhere. He'd conclude this pointless duty and then find a place to sleep. He had no interest in any other accomplishment this day.

Proceeding down the road that paralleled Antietam Creek, Harry was surprised to find masses of troops sitting idly, their faces turned toward the sound of musketry and small-bore artillery to the south. He'd been told General Ambrose

159

Burnside had four divisions in his IX Corps, but expected them to be spread out in line of combat. Instead, they were inclined as though to the wide end of a funnel, at least three of the huge Union columns converging together at a point where the road turned toward the creek and crossed it over the little stone bridge.

But they were not moving.

Harry found Burnside nervously observing that point of convergence from a command post atop the hill nearest the bridge. It took a lot of explaining, and not a little pushing, for Harry to make his way through the thickly gathered staff officers and reach Burnside's side, but he had learned the ways of the army.

"General McClellan's compliments, sir," he said, quickly. "I am Raines, one of Allan Pinkerton's scouts. The general has sent me to ascertain whether your corps is now engaged."

Burnside, with his remarkable side whiskers, seemed amiable, if slightly mad. He lowered his field glasses, gracing Harry with a weird smile.

"Do you not hear the musket fire, Mister Raines? I've been engaged for hours. But we cannot make our way across that damned bridge."

"The stone bridge, sir?"

"Yes. That one down there. The only one in my section of the line. General McClellan ordered me to take the Confederate flank here as soon as convenient, but that bridge . . . I can't get but a company on it at a time."

"Sir?"

"I have four divisions, but I might as well have a platoon. There's massed Rebel infantry on that hill at the other end of the bridge. It's all target practice for them, except they hardly have to aim."

A major approached. "Captain Simonds' battery is moving in range of bridge area as ordered, General."

Burnside lifted his glasses again. "That'll help. Could use another."

Harry thought of the huge artillery reserve sitting idle at the center of the line. "Sir, there's a ford."

The general looked at him, blinking. Harry might as well have told him that General Lee had been captured and the Rebel army was in flight.

"What?"

"I live in this country, sir. I have a farm just outside Shepherdstown. I know this creek. There's a ford around the deep bend of the creek. Snavely's Ford."

"You're certain?"

"As certain as I am of my name."

"I was told there was no ford."

"Well, there is."

Burnside swore, gently, then shook his head. "What are your orders, Raines—besides coming here to nettle me with questions from headquarters?"

Harry decided to spare the general McClellan's instruction for him to scout Burnside rather than the Confederates. "I'm at your disposal, sir."

"I've started moving General Rodman's division to the left. Catch up with him and tell him about this ford."

"Yes, sir." Harry wished Burnside had sent him packing back to headquarters.

To reach the trail that led to Snavely's Ford, Harry had to take the road to the stone bridge. The masses of troops made the way almost impassable. They were standing and sitting idly, almost as in camp, as he started on his journey. But those near the bridge were hunched down, and even hugging the ground.

The Rebels on the hill beyond were holding their fire, probably to conserve ammunition, waiting for the next assault across the narrow span. Harry came as close as he dared—perhaps too close. Glancing to the right, he could see the heads of a few Confederate riflemen watching from the slope. With a shiver, it occurred to him one or more of them might have a weapon trained on him that very moment.

He steered the mare carefully through the huddled troops, urging her into a trot when he was finally clear of them. He was only halfway around the deep bend when he heard the first burst of gunfire, which quickly rose to a crescendo.

Another pointless attack had been ordered across the bridge. He slapped the mare hard with the reins, propelling her into a pounding canter.

Harry came upon the rear guard of Rodman's division at the end of the bend, and was almost shot for his trouble. Two bullets missed him. A soldier was about to fire a third when halted by a sergeant. Harry pulled the mare to a stop.

"I come from General Burnside," he said. "I have a message for General Rodman."

"Can you prove that?" the sergeant asked.

"I'm a Pinkerton man. Captain Harrison Raines. Take me to the general. Victory and many lives could depend on it."

The word "captain" worked more magic with the sergeant than the appeal of victory and lives. He turned abruptly and led Harry through the length of the column to the commander, who sat on horseback, studying a map.

The sergeant tried to pass Harry up through the chain of command, stopping first before a lieutenant. Harry ignored them and proceeded directly to the general.

"Sir," he said. "I've come from McClellan. I've knowledge of a crossing further up the creek. A ford, sir."

"Ford?" The general's attention seemed still on the battle noise back by the bridge.

"Yes, sir. Snavely's Ford. The creek makes a right-angle turn ahead a ways and it's about a quarter mile after that."

The general rubbed his cheek, frowning. "Had an Indian around here come by and say that. Long-haired devil. Claimed he was a scout. Didn't know whether to believe him."

"That would be Jack Tantou."

"Something like that."

If the general had acted on that word he would have turned the Rebels' right flank and made all those bridge assaults unnecessary. "You could have believed him, sir. He's a Pinkerton man like me. I have a farm in this area. I know the ground. The ford is there. If you use it, you'll come upon that hill overlooking the bridge from the rear."

"Who are you?"

"Harrison Raines, sir. A captain, as we have such ranks in

Allan Pinkerton's Secret Service. Reporting to General McClellan."

Rodman looked greatly disturbed, then finally decisive. "Very well. I'll march on your word, Raines. But if there is no ford where you say, I'll have you arrested."

"I will be with you, sir."

"Just stay out of the way." He looked to an aide.

"Excuse me, sir," Harry said. "Where is Tantou?"

The general seemed annoyed to have to deal with more such trivialities. "Don't know."

"Got him tied to a tree, General," said a nearby major. "Up there by the little run."

"May I see to his release, please?" Harry asked, as obsequiously as possible.

"Major," said the general. "See to it."

"These generals of yours, Harry Raines. They are idiots."

Tantou and Harry were walking their horses just behind Rodman's advance guard as they proceeded up the creek.

"Not all," said Harry. "You'll remember General Grant."

"They could use him here."

"I'm not arguing with you."

The ground was grassy, between rocks and large old trees. The Union soldiers around them were moving ahead without speaking, heads down, thoughts likely concentrated on the important role they had now to play. Harry's turned to the ford. The Rebels surely had a local like him with them, someone who knew the ground. They might well by now have the ford defended. Harry could be sending these men into a trap.

Even so, it would be a far more practicable enterprise than the mindless, repeated attempts to cross the little bridge.

Amazingly, the ford was undefended. Birds explosively abandoned the high trees with snapping wings at the approach of the Union troops. The Confederates had left them in peace.

Anxious to display his commitment and resolve, Harry moved ahead, wading the stream with the Federal skirmishers. Once ashore, he mounted his horse, and began the climb up the slope ahead of everyone. Tantou quickly joined him, his long rifle in hand.

"Bear to the right, Harry Raines," he said. "Into the trees. You don't want to come upon the graybacks in the open."

"If I go into those trees, our Federal friends might think I'm trying to join the Rebels. We could get shot in the back."

Tantou frowned, though it was hard to tell this from his normal expression. "Choose then. Between being shot in the front or the back."

"Let's just do our duty, Jack."

"If we did our duty, we would drop this McClellan into a well."

"Let's be shot in the front." Harry snapped his horse's reins and moved up the hill at a trot.

The plateau was as he had long remembered, relatively flat but sloping upward slightly as it extended to the ridge line overlooking the stone bridge. There were two wagons moving across it—one toward the Confederate position, the other away from it. They passed each other without slowing. Each driver was intent on his journey, neither noticing Harry and Tantou.

They were joined by a cavalry lieutenant, who seemed astonished at what he beheld. "That's the hill there?" he asked. "The one above the bridge?"

"Yes."

His horse was nervous, and skittered to the side. The officer pulled hard on the reins in quick discipline. "Where are all the Rebels?"

Harry scanned the field with his glasses, looking west toward the Potomac and then slowly around to the right, where sporadic gunfire was continuing at the overlook. "I think I see cavalry to the left. And there's infantry just beyond that tree line opposite."

The lieutenant confirmed this with a look through his own field glasses, then found something more. "I see more behind them. Maybe a brigade."

"General Rodman has a division."

The lieutenant looked behind them. "Well, here it comes."

164

The Union force was moving up the slope in highly disorganized manner, but in great numbers. Small parties of riflemen moved past without leaders.

"I must report," the lieutenant said to Harry. He nodded to Tantou and then turned his horse smartly.

More Union troops reached the plateau, platoons and companies and regiments, many officers among them. Gunfire erupted from the opposite tree line. A skirmish line of Rebels fanned out into the field and began shooting at the Federals, though they were out of musket range. At last Harry saw a Union general move forward, shouting commands to other officers. One large mob of blue-coated troops began forming up in coherent formation and set off toward the Rebel skirmishers and the tree line. Another, larger contingent, to Harry's immense satisfaction, set off for the ridge line overlooking the stone bridge.

"Now let us move into the trees," he said to Tantou.

They did so swiftly, dismounting and seating themselves, watching the ensuing battles as spectators.

"They cannot help but win here," Tantou said.

"I'm sorry Rodman didn't listen to you."

"I am sorry General McClellan did not listen to anyone, Harry Raines."

"When you scouted for General Kearny out West, did he listen to you?"

"Yes, he did. And he killed many Rebels. Chased them out of California."

Harry sighed, then took out his flask, sipping as a cavalry platoon jangled by heading for the ridge line. The gunfire across the field was increasing now. "I wish General Grant were here."

Tantou leaned forward, watching the progress of the Union advance. "They won't need General Grant."

Rodman's entire division was now up, so thick upon the field it had become more blue than green. Musket fire was now constant, and seemingly everywhere. A battery of Union artillery was brought up and quickly unlimbered. The noise of the first cannon to fire hurt Harry's head.

"The Rebels are running, Harry Raines," said Tantou.

A thin stream of gray and butternut could be seen emerging from the overlook by the bridge, heading for the tree line and their more numerous comrades beyond it. Not long after, blue coats appeared in the position. The stone bridge had finally been stormed.

And General Lee's right flank had been turned.

Rodman's division took nearly an hour to clear the Confederates from the field. Harry expected there'd be a pursuit, but once again there was none. Harry rose and stepped out into the open meadow. Troops were now sitting down themselves. Others milled about. More came up the slope behind him. Still more swept over the overlook from the bridge. Burnside was moving his whole corps up here.

But he moved no farther. Officers and sergeants began barking commands. Unit by unit, the Union soldiers began assembling as though on a parade ground, forming ranks, then mass formations. It was three o'clock before Burnside appeared satisfied. It had been one o'clock when the bridge had been crossed.

At long last, the order was given to advance. IX Corps moved on toward Sharpsburg, banners aloft, musket barrels and swords glittering in the hazy sunshine, the forward skirmishers moving at a trot in a double line.

"We'd best follow," Harry said.

Another one of Tantou's rare grins crept onto his face. "We'd best go home."

Harry looked to the west. "My home is the other side of the Rebels." They stood quietly a long moment. "I have to see this all the way through," Harry said. "I need to get across the Potomac."

"You will have to wait, Harry Raines. The Rebels don't leave yet."

Tantou proved correct. The remnants of the Confederate right hunkered down on the outskirts of the town, and, with the help of artillery, slowed the Union progress—in some places bringing it to a halt.

Harry trotted his horse back and forth along the rear of the line, trying to find a place where he might be useful, but finding none. The Federal artillery was late in coming, because it had been positioned across the creek to shell the overlook by the bridge, and had to be hauled to new emplacements up on the plateau. When finally ready, the batteries quickly opened fire, sending a heavy rain of lead and steel shot overhead.

Harry feared that it would not fly far enough ahead, that it might fall on the Union troops as it sought the rebels. Oddly, he had a sudden apprehension that a ball might falter in its trajectory and drop straight down, hitting him squarely. There were bullets whizzing in criss-cross fashion as well—some low, some high.

He stopped his horse, content now just to sit and watch. A general had once told him that there was no safe place on a battlefield. Surely many a general had been struck down on them—not a few sitting their mounts just as Harry was. General Grant had almost been killed in that manner at Shiloh when a bullet struck his sword.

The musketry and cannon fire was again oppressively loud. Despite this din, new sounds reached to his ear—the familiar yips and warbling shrieks of Rebels on the charge. Harry twisted in the saddle. To his amazement, the Rebels were not coming from Sharpsburg but from the side, up the lane that led from Snavely's Ford.

Some of the Federals, caught in the flank, were turning and running. Harry remained where he was, puzzling out the extraordinary situation. These new Confederate troops were coming from the canal. Could they be some reserve force Lee had kept in hiding? It was clear to Harry that the Rebel commander must have thrown in every reserve he had hours before, moving them back and forth to stave off the piecemeal assaults of the Union. If he'd had more, he would have sent them up at the double quick through Sharpsburg to turn back Rodman. This new force, bursting onto the field, were likely reinforcements coming from somewhere else, coming from the canal, perhaps crossing the river at Packhorse Ford.

But they would not have known to come here unless directed

by Lee. Was the general back by the canal? Did that mean he was preparing a retreat? If so, the rest of the huge Union army should now be preparing for an advance all along the line. How could one communicate that to McClellan? How could one persuade him of the dire necessity of such a move?

The Union guns were limbering up. Rodman had turned his line to face the yipping newcomers, but the rest of his division was pulling back. Burnside must have ordered a retreat. It occurred to Harry that was actually sound. If Burnside could reorganize his corps at the high end of this field by the overlook, he would have these new Rebels at a disadvantage—strung out on open ground charging up a slope.

Harry looked to either side, and then behind, wondering where Rodman might be. He flinched as a Rebel bullet zinged near. He neither saw the shooter nor heard the specific sound of the next bullet, which hit him, causing a white flash before his eyes and cracking pain along the side of his skull. He seemed to spin from the saddle. Then there was nothing.

# Seventeen

Harry opened his eyes to a fuzzy, starry night sky. It seemed improbable that such a peaceful vision should be there. He was surely imagining it, dreaming it. Or perhaps he was capable of neither mental function, or any mental function. Perhaps something far more profound had happened to him—the most profound something there could be.

That notion was swiftly contradicted. He began to feel the pain. A bayonet driven through the top of his head could not have produced more. He was paralyzed by it, and yet driven to move. He found himself writhing, and tried to stop that, failing. He heard himself moaning, fearing that whimpering and crying would be next.

Then he felt the soft hand on his cheek, and the pain began to diminish. It was not an illusion. The hand, the delicate fingers, were very real. He realized his head was resting on something soft—and very real as well.

"Where am I?" he asked. He could barely hear his voice.

"You are safe. Do not discontent yourself."

He recognized the voice. All was well. All would always be well. "I fear I could not discontent myself any more than I already am."

"Then be still, Harry. Be still."

He did the opposite, raising his head perhaps half an inch and then letting it fall back again in retreat from the agony. Rather than try again, he slowly, slowly turned his head to the left, discovered his neck hurt as well.

Someone had taken his spectacles, but he could make out a house and, nearer, a barn, their walls flickering with the reflected light of numerous campfires. Exerting himself

169

further, he turned still more, discovering he was in a veritable sea of wounded men, lying on litters or blankets or the bare ground. Some were writhing as he had been. Others lay perfectly still.

It was difficult turning back again, but he managed it, knowing there was reward.

"Lean close so that I may look upon your face, Caitlin," he asked.

She did so. Were it Louise, he might be graced with a smile, but Caitlin only gazed at him intently, her warm eyes full of tender concern.

"Is the wound mortal?" he asked.

His friend and chess-playing partner, Army Surgeon Lt. Col. Phineas Gregg, had told him that easily half of all battle wounds were fatal, with the death rate increasing if they involved amputation.

Yet amputations seemed to be all that field surgeons ever did.

At all events, they had not amputated his head.

Caitlin had been hesitating. "You are conscious now," she said. "That is encouraging."

"You are encouraging," he said. She was stroking his cheek. Of a sudden she ceased, and placed her hand on his brow.

"The surgeon said the bone is intact," she said.

"The bone?"

"Your skull. The bullet cut across the side of your head and you bled a great deal, but there was no fracture. I'm afraid there is great swelling. The flesh is thick with evil humours."

He wanted to touch the place in question, but decided against it. Her remark sounded so medieval—as he supposed one must expect of the English, especially those of theatrical bent. "Where are we? In Sharpsburg?"

"No. The Confederates are still there."

"Still there?"

"The Confederate wounded. In the morning they're going to start moving them, the ones they've brought back from the battlefield. There are many still out there. From both sides."

"Moving where?"

"A few to Boonsboro. Most to Frederick. There are thousands and thousands of wounded, Harry."

"How did you find me?"

"Your friend Mister Tantou found you, and then found me and brought me to you."

"I owed him a lot, and now I owe him more."

He desired more than anything now to be kissed by her, but she remained steadfast in her saintly gaze. But for the warmth of her legs beneath his head and the coolness of her touch on his brow, she could have been one of those statues in a Catholic church.

"I have every hope you will survive this night," she said, softly. "I have seen much worse this day."

"I am so happy to see you. I am so fond of you, Caitlin."

"And I you, Harry." She withdrew her hand. He felt her body turn, her legs moving somewhat beneath him.

There was a rustle of clothing. "How is he?" A woman's voice. Harry recognized it, but no name came.

She knelt on his other side, and leaned to look at him. Now he remembered. "Good evening, Miss Barton," he said.

"It is a horrible evening, Mister Raines. It was a horrible day. There has been no more horrible day ever. But I am glad to find you alive. Your friend—Tantou?"

"Yes."

"He said you were on the field all day, from one end to the other. You're to be counted among the very brave."

"No, Miss Barton. You will find brave men in a sunken road on the ridge back there. I merely observed."

"Well . . ."

She turned slightly, the firelight bright on her face and dress. Without his spectacles, he could not be certain, but he thought he saw something shocking. "Miss Barton, there is a hole in your sleeve."

"Yes, it has been a hard day."

"A bullet made that," said Caitlin. "She was tending to a fallen soldier, and was nearly struck herself."

"He died, poor boy," said Miss Barton. "So many of them.

And so young." She rose, wearily. "Caitlin. I know Mister Raines is your friend, but we have many others."

"Yes, Miss Barton." With great gentleness, Caitlin lifted his head slightly and shifted her legs away from him, lowering his head then with even greater care. Leaning over him, she kissed his brow, then pushed back and got to her feet. "Good night, Harry. We will meet again. Soon."

He closed his eyes, listening to the rustle of their skirts as they walked away. Some poor devil not far away began sobbing.

The pain swiftly returned. He did not know what to do about it, but his body did. He began to slip into unconsciousness again, hoping it was simply sleep, hoping he would wake again.

He did awaken, to discover it was yet another day. The pain was dull now; his whole head felt swollen. He gingerly touched the bandage that had been wound around the top of his skull, smarting sharply and quickly withdrawing it. He wondered how he must look.

"Good morning, Harry Raines."

Wincing, Harry turned toward the voice. Tantou was sitting cross-legged on the grass some three feet away from him.

"Good morning, Jack. How long have you been here?"

"Longer than Mister Pinkerton likes, but that does not matter. He has no need of us today. Of any scout."

"What do you mean?"

"Neither army is moving. They are where they were yesterday when night came and ended the fighting."

"How can that be?"

Tantou looked over his shoulder at some horsemen trotting by. "McClellan says he has won a great victory and does not need to attack. I think Lee is still there because he would like to find a way to attack. He will not find one. McClellan is not moving his soldiers but he has many, many cannons. Lee would gain nothing from his attack but more dead men."

"If he were as wise as he is supposed to be he would get across that river."

"Then he fails, Harry Raines."

"Jack, as long as that general has an army in the field, he wins. The damned Confederacy lives on."

"I do not understand this war."

"Yes, you do. You want to start one in Canada—except you Metis won't be fighting for slavery."

"No. We are the slaves."

Someone was singing a hymn. Harry recalled it was one he often heard in the Reverend Ashby's church. It was hard to hear, though, over the moaning and coughing.

"What is that smell?" Harry asked. "It's horrible."

"Horses," said Tantou. "They are burning the dead horses. They make piles of them and pour kerosene on them. There are many dead horses. This will take a long time."

"What about the dead soldiers?"

"They're burying them where they lay." He sniffed the air as might a hunting dog. "It will be a hot day."

Harry tried to sit up, failing, but able at last to rise on one elbow. "Do you know where those Rebels came from? The ones who hit us at the end?"

"The ones who shot you. Some of them were captured. Their general is named Hill. A.P. Hill."

"Where did they come from?"

"A long way. They marched seventeen miles from Harper's Ferry, then crossed the river, then ran up the hill. As good as Indians, these men."

"But we stopped them."

"They stopped us, too."

A breeze was stirring. Instead of freshness, it brought more stink. "Would you help me sit up, Jack?"

"You should sleep."

"No. I fear I won't wake up. Have you seen my wound?"

"Yes. It is ugly. You will have to comb your hair careful."

"Do you know what they did for it?"

"They put cotton on it to stop the bleeding. Then they put on that bandage."

A shiver of fear ran down Harry's back. He had spent enough time with Surgeon Gregg to learn the risks of wounds. "Have you any whiskey, Jack?"

173

"Since I am with you, Harry Raines, I always have whiskey." He reached inside his jacket and took out a surprisingly large flask. Uncorking it, he extended it to Harry.

"No," said Harry. "I want you to pour it over my wound."

The Metis hesitated. "I do not think you will like that."

"Of course I won't. But I think it must be done. It stops the festering. I have seen this."

"Maybe the pain will kill you."

"Please, Jack. Do it. As I would do for you."

Tantou was almost correct. Harry did nearly die. At the least, it felt like that. And when the whiskey was pouring on the raw cut, he wished he would.

"How are you now, Harry Raines?"

Harry blinked, trying to judge the time by the light in the sky. The light was more than he could bear. He put a hand over his eye. "Is there whiskey left?"

"Yes. There is whiskey everywhere here."

"I would sit up then, and drink some."

"You are crazy."

"No. Please help me, Tantou. I need to sit up—because very soon I will need to stand."

"Why?"

"Because I need to walk—to a latrine, soon."

Tantou wasted no more time. Kneeling near, he put one hand at Harry's back and another around his shoulder. In an instant, Harry was sitting erect, though his head was reeling. "Thank you. Give me a moment, Jack."

Slowly, the whirling stopped. Harry moved his legs so that he, too, was sitting crosslegged. He rubbed his forehead a moment, then reached toward Tantou. "Please, Jack. The whiskey."

He took a long, deep pull, and then another. He was still a little giddy, but felt immensely better. "How stands the Union now? Has Lee withdrawn?"

"Nothing has changed. There have been telegraph messages. Lincoln may be coming."

"Now?"

174

"In a week or two—maybe more."

"But surely McClellan will have moved."

"No. And now he has an excuse not to."

Harry took one more generous swig of whiskey, then reached for Tantou's hand. "Now I will stand."

He would always wonder how he managed, but he did. While standing by the canvas fencing they had placed around the latrine, looking out upon the sea of damaged men, he saw a young woman moving among them, looking into each face, then walking on.

Staggering from the enclosure, he sat down hard on the ground, somehow managing not to sprawl backwards. "Jack," he said, pointing to the girl. "I know her. Her name is Harding. Would you ask her if she would mind coming to me?"

"I will do as you ask." The Metis moved swiftly, coming upon the girl from behind. She was startled, and jumped back. Tantou pointed to Harry. Her expression changed from alarm to concern. She rose and, lifting her skirts enough to make haste, she came to him.

"Mister Raines?" She knelt beside him. "My God, what has happened to you?"

"I am fine," he said. "Why are you here, Ann? How did you get here?"

"My brother Richard. He served in General Crook's brigade. They said he was wounded, and that he was here. Have you seen him?"

Harry could scarcely remember the fellow. "I'm sorry. I haven't. Did you come through the Rebel lines?"

She was an extraordinarily pretty girl, but much of her attraction had vanished in the circumstance. Her brown eyes were reddened; her complexion blotched. "Yes. This morning. They let us through to find our kin."

"Are they retreating?"

"No. I don't think so. Shepherdstown is filled with them. The wounded. Every house is a hospital."

"Is all else well?"

"In Shepherdstown?"

175

"Have the people there survived the battle? There's been no trouble?"

"There is every kind of trouble, Mister Raines."

"What do you mean?"

"The war's run through the town like a flood. There've been shootings—neighbor at neighbor. We pray for the Rebels to leave so that we may put an end to this. My daddy . . ." She looked down at the ground, then at Harry. "I must go. I must find my brother. I hope you will be well, Mister Raines. I hope we will see you again."

She took his hand. He feared his flesh was clammy despite the rising heat of the day. "Ann, don't go back to Shepherdstown until the Rebels leave," he said. "Soldiers on retreat can do desperate things."

"You think the Rebels'll go? Did we whip them?"

"Most of them."

"I won't go back until I find my brother. God bless."

Harry watched her go. "Jack," he said. "I cannot remain here much longer."

"You will not have to," Tantou said. "Mister Pinkerton has sent for an ambulance for you. Take you to the railroad, and then to Washington."

"That is not where I desire to go."

"No?" said Tantou.

"Do we still have horses?"

"Yes. I have placed them in safe-keeping. Officers are looking everywhere for fresh mounts."

"As soon as Lee's army moves—and I've no doubt they're going back across the river—I'm going to follow."

"You will fall off your horse, Harry Raines. I will go with you."

"Mister Pinkerton may think us deserters."

Tantou got to his feet. "The deserters will be going in the other direction."

Tantou brought him some food—army stew, which he ate with little relish—and some lemonade, which Harry consumed thirstily.

176

"Where in hell did you get that?" Harry asked.

"General McClellan's headquarters. I stole it. I went to see Mister Pinkerton, to tell him not to send an ambulance."

"Did you tell him I'm feeling better?"

"I told him you were worse, that you could not travel."

"Why did you do that?"

"So he would not bother us."

"He doesn't need you to scout?"

"Why? This army is not moving. I told him I would stay with you until you died."

"Thank you." Harry made a face at him.

Tantou picked up the mess tin he had brought and began finishing Harry's stew. "You see that barn behind us, Harry Raines?"

Harry turned his head as much as he could. "Yes."

"I have been watching what they do all day. When they bring the wounded here, a surgeon looks at them. Some go into the barn. Some are left out here. Like you."

"Soldiers who aren't so badly wounded?"

"No. Those they think will die." Tantou scraped up the last of the stew. "You are lucky, Harry Raines."

It was nearing dusk. "Right now, I'm just sleepy."

"Then sleep. If it looks like you are dying, I will wake you."

"Always in your debt, Jack." Harry gently eased himself back to the grass. The Indian remained where he was, eyes on the horizon.

When Harry awoke again, there was only a little light left in the western sky. He lay there, on his side, watching it fade. But it did not. The gray was growing brighter, and turning pink. He wasn't looking to the west but to the east.

He rolled over. The wounded soldier who had been lying near him was on his back, mouth open, no longer moaning. Harry realized he was dead.

Someone was standing behind him. Looking up as best he could, Harry saw that it was Tantou, rifle in hand.

"You think truly you can ride, Harry Raines?"

"Let me see if I can stand."

177

Tantou reached and helped him, pulling him to his feet. He held Harry there with one hand, then let go, waiting to see if Harry would fall. Somehow, he did not.

"The Rebels are leaving," Tantou said. "Most of them are now across the river."

# Eighteen

With Tantou leading the way, they rode their horses at a walk into Sharpsburg. Harry better knew the way, but Tantou was more alert and clear headed and had better vision. The bandage around Harry's head interfered with his use of spectacles.

Though the sun had not yet risen, there was adequate light from the piles of dead horses that were still burning. There was no way of avoiding them without straying too far from the road.

"At the Alamo, the Mexicans did that to the Americans they killed," Harry said.

"You Americans did worse than that to the Indians you killed."

"Have you seen what some Indians have done?"

"But you Americans are supposed to be civilized."

"Times like this, Jack, I don't think anybody's civilized."

Some Union cavalry pickets had preceded them into Sharpsburg, taking up positions along the high street at the western end of the town. One of them challenged Harry, ignoring Tantou.

"We're scouts for Allan Pinkerton," Harry said.

"Where're you going?"

"As far as we can, until we run into Rebels."

"There was a few of them here, but they skedaddled. Still some of their wounded here." He eyed Harry's bandage. "You all right?"

"Right enough." He clicked his horse forward. "Be back presently."

The road ahead curved down toward the Potomac through

179

low, rolling hills—the landscape littered with the detritus of war, including loaded supply wagons lacking teams to pull them. General Lee had departed swiftly.

There were a few dead and dying left behind as well, and more numerous stragglers. At the sight of Harry and Tantou, some hurried away from the road. Descending the final slope leading down to the canal and river, they took note of a Rebel cavalry patrol paused on the towpath. Harry and Tantou slipped into the trees, waiting and watching until the horsemen moved on.

When they did, it was to splash across the river, heading for the narrow shoreline just below the Shepherdstown bluffs.

"More soldiers over there," Tantou said.

"Rear guard; won't be there long," Harry opined, sounding more the military expert than he was.

"Then what?"

"Then I am going into Shepherdstown."

"Do you not want to tell General McClellan that the Confederates have escaped?"

"He would use the term 'retreated.' It was a glorious victory, remember. But if you want to go back and inform him that the enemy has abandoned the field, I wish you well."

"No, Harry Raines. I said I would come with you."

They waited for nearly half an hour, then went down to the canal. There was movement across the river but it did not seem military. Possibly looters from the town, scavenging.

"Do you think they have gone?" Harry asked.

"Yes," said Tantou, flatly.

Harry put heels to his animal's flanks and it plunged on into the water. The river had risen, but not enough to impede their horses. Tantou followed and pulled up alongside, his hand around his long rifle.

"You are all right still, Harry Raines?" he asked.

"I'm weary but I'm feeling better. The nearness of home, I think."

There were Confederates aplenty in town, but they were mostly either wounded or medical personnel. Those who were still bearing arms ignored Harry and Tantou, likely assuming from Harry's bandage that they were simply more of the injured.

With Tantou following, Harry walked his horse carefully down German Street, as some of the wounded were lying in it.

There were many crowded around Doctor Ricketts' office. Doubtless few Confederate army surgeons would want to be in Shepherdstown to greet the Yankees and would at all events be needed by Lee in the future. So the services of the local physicians were much in demand. When Harry and Tantou dismounted and tried to enter, they were pushed back.

"Wait your damned turn," snarled a Rebel soldier with a bloodied shirt and jacket.

"I am not here as a patient," Harry said. "I am a friend of Doctor Ricketts. I'm here to bring him news."

"If he stops for a lot of palaver, he'll never get around to us."

Carrying his long rifle, Tantou stepped up and imposed himself between the soldier and Harry, looking down and staring hard. "Move," he said.

The man stepped back, setting a welcome example, and Harry and the Metis entered. Wounded soldiers were lying all over the floor of the outer office. Stepping carefully over and around them, Harry went into the doctor's surgery just beyond, finding it just as crowded.

Ricketts looked up from where he was working on a man lying sprawled on his table, a bone saw in hand. His wife was assisting. "Harry!" he said, with amazement. "Where have you been? What happened to you?"

"Got caught in the middle of the battle. I've been treated. I wanted to tell you that the Federals should be here directly— now that General Lee has moved on."

"Will their surgeons help these people?"

"I would so presume, but they've had a busy time with their own."

"It has been a horror here. It was the worst day that ever dawned on this planet." He stopped a moment, an anxious

181

look coming into his eyes. "I've news for you, Harry. Your brother's here."

Harry looked around him. "Robert? Here?"

"He took a ball through the arm. I am hopeful he'll recover. You'll find him at the Reverend Ashby's church. They're using it as a hospital."

"Thank you, Doctor." He hurried as best he could from the room and the office, fighting dizziness as he moved up the street. The church, happily, was not far. Harry found himself having trouble on the brick sidewalk, his boots clipping the sharp edges of the bricks and twice almost causing him to trip and fall. Reaching the front entrance to the church, set off from the main road by some fifty feet, he discovered it blocked by another assemblage of wounded Confederates seeking admission. Others were lying on the grass. There was a smell to the place. He wondered if he could ever escape that smell.

"Is there another way?" Tantou asked.

"Yes."

There was a garden to the rear, just off a side street. Harry went to it, climbing over the picket fence with some difficulty, then proceeding to the church's back entrance.

They had left the pews in place, and every one of them had a wounded man lying or sitting on it. Stumbling over a too full chamber pot, Harry staggered further into the room, Tantou more carefully following. Harry looked back and forth, to the pulpit and to the rearmost row. All these wretched men looked strangely alike.

He took another step, still looking about him, perhaps seeming some wild man.

"Glory be to God, it's you. Alive and standing."

It was a woman's voice. Harry looked about some more, but his vision was getting blurry.

"Damn it to hell, Harry Raines. Don't you keep your back to me after all we been through."

He turned slowly, still trying to stay erect. He saw long blond hair, bright blue eyes, and tanned skin covered with blood. "Allie," he said, in a mumble. He took another step, fell into her arms.

But this time, Harry did not lose consciousness. Allie took hold of him and caught his fall, lowering him to the floor. Looking up at her moist, worried eyes, he fought the darkness coming over him and managed somehow to dispel it.

Her hair was loose and scraggly. She wore the same cotton dress she'd had on when last he'd seen her. Both the garment and much of her skin were stained with blood.

Kneeling, she reached and gently touched his bandage.

"Is it bad?" she asked.

"At times. It's a graze, they said, but I take little comfort from that."

She lifted the bandage with great care, then lowered it again. "Looks like a plowed furrow. Where'd it happen?"

"The last fighting of the day—over by Snavely's Ford."

"There was fighting way over there?"

"Rebel reinforcements came up in the late afternoon. It was a hard time." He tried to focus on her face. "How did you get here?"

"Got caught by Reb cavalry. They took me to a camp. After the horse soldiers took off I told the others I had to take a pee. Went into the woods and lit out again. Trouble was, no way of getting through their line—so many of them all bunched up and getting ready for the fight. So I crossed the river and came here. Thought it'd be safer."

"Do you know anyone here?"

"A few. Got a cousin with a farm on the Harper's Ferry Road, but he and his family must have run off when the Secesh come up. Anyways, I've been stayin' in their house." She raised her head to look about the crowded room. "When they started bringing these poor devils in—well, I couldn't just sit there."

"They're Rebels."

"Not any more, they ain't. They're just busted-up men and boys. We've been losin' them steady, but more keep comin' in. Don't know where they find them."

"I fear the field is still covered with them. In abundance. Men from both sides."

183

"You're the first Federal we've seen—if Federal you are." She spoke accusingly, but her hand was on his cheek.

"Federal I am."

"Wasn't sure. That Rebel cavalry patrol got onto me pretty quick."

"Had I been there, they'd have had a slower time of it. Should have been there. I'm sorry."

"You had your business. That was a monstrous battle."

"Allie, I came in here for a reason. Doctor Ricketts told me my brother was here."

"Your brother?"

"My brother Robert. A Confederate captain. Looks like me only he has darker hair and a beard."

"You rest here a moment. I'll go ask." She touched his brow, then rose. He turned his head to watch her go to the altar, where an actual Confederate surgeon was plying his trade. He directed her through a door to the rear. When she did not reappear within a few minutes, Harry turned back, for his head and neck were hurting.

He had almost drifted asleep when she came to his side again. "Harry. He is in the house to the rear, and he's in a bad way."

Harry stared at her, learning nothing. "How in a bad way?"

"He has lost an arm."

Phineas Gregg had told him that only about half of amputees survived, and that the odds were worse the closer the wound came to the body.

"How much of an arm? All?"

She seemed quite distressed, now. "I don't know. You'd best come with me. If you can manage it."

Tantou had remained back by the door, leaning against the wall beside it. It was a habit that allowed him to keep watch over everything while remaining relatively inconspicuous. Harry guessed he might have noticed Allie and was allowing Harry some privacy.

Harry got to his knees, then signaled to the Metis for help. Tantou was beside him in a moment.

"Having trouble with my balance, Jack."

"No trouble." Tantou took hold of Harry's hand and arm

and pulled him to his feet. Allie came to Harry's other side. Together, she and Tantou managed to get Harry through the rear door. He almost fell crossing the small garden behind the church, but took a deep breath and urged himself forward. His brother was only a few yards away—likely near death.

The brick house, built in the German style common in Shepherdstown, was narrow but tall. It was filled with wounded, all of them officers. Again, a Confederate army surgeon had stayed behind. He directed them to the next floor.

Robert was in a back bedroom, near an open window. Harry expected he'd be sleeping, but he was staring up at the ceiling. The arm that had been removed was his right, cut off now just above the elbow. The stump was wound with a thick bandage that had darkened with blood.

Harry knelt beside him. Allie and Tantou moved back. "Robert?"

The eyes didn't move, and then they did. His brother seemed perplexed, uncertain. "Harry?"

Harry took his brother's left hand with his right. "It's me, Robert."

"Where am I?" The words came slowly, and with a rasp.

"You're in Shepherdstown, Robert. You're safe. You're home. My farm is but two miles away."

"Your farm. Mother gave you the farm."

"It's your home whenever you wish it, as I've always said." He looked, reluctantly, at the mutilated arm. "How are you, Robert? How is your wound?"

"Minié ball. Shattered my elbow. The arm is gone but still it hurts like hell."

Harry had a flask. "Whiskey?"

Robert considered it. "Yes. Thank you." Harry lifted his brother's head to aid him in the drinking. It caused a bit of coughing but Robert asked for more. He lay back, seeming less in distress. His eyes closed, then opened.

"You're wounded, too, Harry. How fare you?"

"A graze. It hurts and I get dizzy. But I manage."

"How were you wounded? I let you escape. Were you shot trying to escape?"

185

"No. It was later in the day. At Snavely's Ford."

"Why were you there?"

"You know why I was there."

"My brother the Yankee."

"Your brother the Virginian—who would not own his best friend."

Robert's reply was silence. They had had this argument a hundred times.

"I'm going to get you out of here," Harry said. "I'm going to take you to the farm."

"I am well attended here."

"I'm sure of that, but there's nothing more the surgeons can do for you. The farm is the answer. I can provide you with every comfort. With a peaceful haven. And with a nurse." He turned to Allie, who came forward hesitantly.

"How is he?"

"Allie? Could you come with us? And help me care for him?"

"Come where?"

"My farm is near." He was giving her little choice, but she seemed willing.

"I am near dyin' of being tired," she said. "Give me a place to sleep and then I'll do what I can."

"Robert," Harry asked. "Do you think you can make the journey?"

His brother, a very deliberate man, thought upon this, through his weakness and pain. "I think I will have to. The stink here alone could kill a man."

Tantou took a step nearer them. "You will need a wagon, Harry Raines. The Rebel army will have taken all of them."

"Maybe not. I have friends here. I'll find one."

Robert closed his eyes. It seemed a sign of agreement. He was placing himself in his brother's hands.

"Will you stay with him?" Harry asked Allie.

"I surely will. But be careful. There are some bad men in this town now."

"The Federals will be here soon. And I have friends."

\*　　　\*　　　\*

186

Harry, for some strange reason clear-headed now, went directly to Jim O'Malley's blacksmith shop, expecting him to be gone and happy to find him improbably there. He was sitting on a small chair in a shadowy recess, a shotgun on his lap.

O'Malley looked at Harry in disbelief. "Raines. It's you? Good God, man, what happened to you?"

"A slight wound. I got caught in the battle."

"So did Shepherdstown. Are there Federals coming?"

"As soon as General McClellan decides it's safe. In the meantime, I need a wagon. My brother Robert's here. He lost an arm. I want to take him to my farm. He'll die in that hospital. I want to take him home."

O'Malley sighed. "Damned Rebels came through here like a hay rake—taking everything. This is Virginia—a Secesh state. You'd think they'd be more respectful. But there is a conveyance. A buggy. Only one I know of left in town."

"Where?"

"The widow Ashby's. The Rebels were respectful of her loss."

"Jim. I need that buggy."

"She was a friend of your mother's. She has always respected your family."

"Damn it, I'm going to take it whether she agrees or not. I'll return it directly."

O'Malley rose. "Let me take care of it. Get your brother ready. We're all neighbors. You're a Shepherdstown man."

Harry was beginning to feel wobbly again. "I'll fetch Bob up. He's in the tall house behind the church."

O'Malley started for the door. Harry stayed him with a hand to the shoulder. "What of Caesar Augustus? Estelle? Evangeline?"

"The little girl is with Sally Thompson, as we agreed. She is well. Caesar Augustus and Estelle are safe in Pennsylvania. In Gettysburg. They'll be fine."

"Thank you, Jim."

"You've more to be grateful for. A Reb officer took your horse Rocket. He left him tied to a post at Klostermann's saloon. But then he was stolen."

"Stolen?"

187

"If you go to your farm, you will find him in the barn. He's in the loft. We took him round to the hillside door."

"Jim, ask me any favor for the rest of your life, and it surely will be granted."

"Everyone's safe, but we need the Federal army here."

"It will come. In the meantime, I must see to my family. When we get my brother home, I'll come back for Evangeline."

"A busy night."

"A busy, bloody day."

The widow Ashby offered no protest or complaint, content with Harry's promise to return the buggy. They lay Robert on the seat, with Tantou riding the horse that had been put into the traces. Allie rode in the buggy, holding Robert close against the bumps and ruts.

O'Malley stayed behind in Shepherdstown. He had much else to attend to. Harry wished they'd had more time for further conversation. He wished to know about many things.

They laid Robert on the big bed in the farmhouse's best bedroom. Allie pulled a chair up to it and stayed by his side. Harry shook his brother's weak hand, but said nothing, seeing that Robert wanted and needed sleep. As he thought upon it, so did he—but not yet.

He descended to the kitchen, inviting Tantou to follow him. He found jugs of corn whiskey still in the pantry.

"It's been the Devil's own day," he said, pouring two full glasses.

"You are a lucky man, Harry Raines."

"Yes, I am. Damned lucky. Robert lives. I live. Allie has survived. And here you are, Jack, safe as well."

They drank.

"And maybe the Union has won here," the Metis said.

"I think so. I sure as hell hope so."

Tantou yanked out a wooden chair from the kitchen table. "Sit, Harry Raines, before you fall."

Harry accepted without comment. He was so tired. "Louise went off with Wilkes Booth," he said.

"Yes. You told me."

"Caitlin Howard is still on the battlefield—with Miss Barton."

"It's a hard war."

"I don't want to go back to it."

"You did what they asked of you today. They are obliged to you."

"I hate this war, Jack. I hate what it's being fought for. In South Carolina they said this is the second war of American liberation—that they're fighting for their rights. The only right they've been willing to fight for is the right to own human beings as animals."

"These are your people, Harry Raines."

"No. Not my people."

There was a pounding on the front door. Harry looked up, dubiously. Tantou went to it. Jim O'Malley stood outside, his horse on the grass behind him.

"What's wrong?" Harry asked.

"Is your brother well enough for you to leave him?"

"I think so. Allie is with him. What's wrong?"

"If he is well, then saddle Rocket and come with me. There's terrible news."

"They've renewed the battle?"

"Harry. They found Ann Harding hanging from a tree."

# Nineteen

In a town full of the dead and dying, it was odd that one more fatality could prompt such excitement. Seemingly half or more of Shepherdstown's population had gone down to the river landing to see the grim scene—the many torches and lanterns giving the scene an oddly religious cast, like the rites the Spanish Catholics practiced down in the West Indies.

The girl's body had by now been cut down and laid upon the moist grass. Her eyes seemed to be staring at the starry sky. It was clear from the blood on her dress and arm and the untroubled nature of her expression that she had been killed beforehand, and then strung up—much like the Reverend Ashby.

Though the crowd was large, none drew too near. Harry made his way through the people and knelt down beside Miss Harding. It would be easier to tell in daylight, but it was clear to him she'd been shot.

Knowing nothing else to do, Harry took her arms and crossed them over her chest. He was about to close her staring eyes when he heard a stir among the onlookers and glanced back to see Mister Harding approach, swiftly and in high emotion.

Caring nothing for the bandage still wound around Harry's head, Samuel Harding thrust him aside and then stood over his daughter's body as if she were some object deposited there from another world. Disbelief was writ everywhere upon his face.

Then he returned to his old self. Harding owned an apothecary shop, a grocery, a hardware store, a bank, five houses on German Street, and three farms on the Harper's Ferry Road.

He was a man of much substance in Shepherdstown. He might have been mayor, had he not preferred to let that job be taken by a man he controlled completely.

He was a large man and stood very erect now, seeming to tower over everyone. The crowd fell silent. They looked like penitents.

"Can any of you sons of bitches tell me how this happened to my daughter?"

The silence became absolute. Harding took further note of Harry, who was now sitting up and about to get to his feet. "Raines, what do you know about this?"

"Very little, Mister Harding. It's my intention to attend to that lack."

"Why are you back in Shepherdstown?"

Harding was arrogant about his primacy in this town but secretive about his politics. He had, though, come out for the creation of a new, slavery-free state of West Virginia. An ad hoc assemblage of mountain counties run from a rump Virginia government based in Washington or Alexandria would give him a much freer hand as boss of his community than a Richmond dominated by the Tidewater aristocracy.

"I came with the Union Army, Mister Harding, but I'm going no farther with them."

"Raines. I'll talk to you when I have that need." With that, Harding picked up the limp body of his youngest child and walked off with her, out of the circle of lantern and torchlight and into the darkness.

Harry found O'Malley in Klostermann's tavern. It occurred to him that the blacksmith might have gone there in the expectation that Harry would likely turn up. It was the Shepherdstown establishment most friendly to their political views.

Indeed, O'Malley had a bottle of whiskey and an extra glass on the bar before him.

"You were down by the river?" Harry asked, moving beside him.

"No, sir." O'Malley slid the bottle to Harry. "It's bad

*Michael Kilian*

enough, the town turned into a Confederate Army mortuary. Seeing a sweet girl like Ann Harding in the same unfortunate way is more than I can bear just now."

"This was murder, Jim. She was shot and then strung up like the Reverend Ashby."

"Grimmer still."

They both drank. "I saw her—talked with her—shortly after the battle," Harry said. "She was on the field, wandering among the wounded like a lost angel who'd stumbled into Hell, looking for her brother Richard."

"Well, Hell it surely was." He paused. "Could she have been shot by some sentry or skirmisher?"

"I don't think so. All the fighting had stopped. As I think upon it, I haven't heard a gunshot since that time."

"Maybe we've just gotten so used to them we don't pay attention any more."

"There were so many guns going off in that battle it was all one enormous sound."

"We heard it."

They refilled their glasses. The barroom was strangely deserted, with only two drunken farmers and a sad-eyed wounded Confederate in the room. Klostermann had gone down to the river landing with the others. He returned now looking fretful, then gladdened by the sight of Harry and O'Malley.

"I don't know what worse thing can befall this town," he said, moving to the back of the bar. "We'd have a lynch mob on our hands if the people here had any idea who'd done this damn awful thing."

"There's an unfortunate thing to consider," Harry said. "Miss Harding had caught the Reverend's roving eye, and I do think there was some reciprocation."

"What are you suggesting?" Klostermann asked.

"At the funeral, there were several young ladies who mourned very deeply—indelicately deeply. Ann was among them."

"Many a good lady has become smitten by her pastor," said O'Malley. "You'd think they were actors."

192

"I'd have a care how you discuss the young miss," said the bartender. "And how loudly. Her father is a wrathful man."

"We are all wrathful men these days," Harry said.

A tall man entered the barroom—making no noise. Tantou. He walked just as quietly to the bar. Klostermann gave a glance to Harry, who nodded emphatically. The barkeep gave the Metis a glass, filling it.

"There are Federal troops now crossing the river. Cavalry. A brigade," Tantou said.

"They are sure as hell welcome," said O'Malley.

"What are we to do about Ann Harding?" Harry asked.

"Who is she?" Tantou asked, surveying the mostly empty room as he took another sip of whiskey.

"A young lady of this town. Just now found shot to death and hung from a tree down by the river landing."

"Like the church man."

"Yes. We had thought that a political act—an assassination. Ashby was secretly a Lincoln man and got found out. But this girl—she had nothing to do with any of that. But she had to do with the Reverend Ashby. Or so it strongly strikes me."

"Harry Raines. This is bad trouble you do not need," Tantou said, wisely enough.

Harry drank the rest of the whiskey in his glass. "These are my people, Jack, just as the Metis are yours."

"What about Pinkerton? He is your chief."

"I am wounded. I am caring for my brother, who is grievously wounded. He will have to understand that."

"And there is the child," O'Malley said.

Harry damned himself for letting that sweet creature slip from his mind. "Evangeline. I will come for her tomorrow, at the widow's house."

"With such a burden, you do not need this trouble, Harry Raines."

"I may not need it, but I'll deal with it." Harry stepped back from the bar, then turned to O'Malley. "Can you get word to Caesar Augustus?"

"Yes, though it will take some time." O'Malley sighed. "But I doubt he'll be wanting to come back to you."

"We're going to be a free state, Jim. The state of West Virginia. No more Old Dominion. No more slavery."

"I'll speak plain. You have more faith in that than Caesar Augustus does."

Harry poured another drink, consumed it quickly, set down some money, and nodded his thanks to Klostermann. "I shall see you gentlemen tomorrow."

Allie was waiting for him on the porch—one of Harry's rifles on her lap.

"You won't need that now," he said, sitting down beside her. "Union Army's come across the river. Some of it, anyway. The Confederates in town are now prisoners."

"Maybe I should go back there. Back to my tendin'."

He took her hand. "I badly need you here, if you could oblige me. How is Robert?"

"He is at rest. Sleeping deeply. That's all you can wish for. That he rest a lot and take nourishment. And that the arm doesn't fester."

"I'm so very grateful to you." He took her hand and kissed it, and a silence fell between them. His thoughts went to Caitlin and Miss Barton, doubtless still laboring on the battlefield, distributing their tender mercies as though from a basket.

He could still smell the piles of burning horseflesh.

"I stopped by your house," he said. "I found that your hired man had taken over and was causing your cousin Elspeth much discomfort. I apologize for taking such a liberty but I thrashed him harshly and sent him on his way. It was he who informed the Rebels about us. I do believe he went back to them and the tide of battle carried him off. Hope so, anyway."

"You need not apologize," she said. "I'd have thrashed him myself a number of times were that not seen as unseemly for a woman."

He hesitated. "I've sent for my man Caesar Augustus."

She removed her hand. "Your man? You speak as he was still a slave."

"He was my slave for less than a day. When my father gave him to me as a present I took him directly into Richmond to

194

write out manumission papers. That is why there is hatred in my family today—that I would turn a valuable piece of 'property' bestowed with my father's generosity into a human being no one can give or take."

She looked down the lane as though there was something there that would soon demand her presence. "Your brother Robert shares this hatred?"

"As you should have noted, he does not. But he fights to defend my father's rights."

"His fighting days are gone."

A bird in a nearby tree twittered, and then flew away in a swooping flutter.

"Allie, I've sent for Caesar Augustus and his—his lady. Estelle. I think they shall return, now that the Federal army's here and we're about to become a free state. But . . ."

"I'll stay with you, Harry. Leastwise till we know whether your brother lives or dies."

He looked down at her dress, much as he could see it in the night shadows. He was sure it was the one she'd been in all this while.

"My mother's clothes are still here. Her summer clothes. None of us could bear to remove them. You're taller than she, but as trim. I think they will fit, though they might display a bit of ankle."

"I'm hankering to display more than that," she said, rising. "I do deeply desire a bath. And if I may say so, plantation man, you are sorely in need of one yourself."

# Twenty

Harry awoke to the sound of Allie's gentle breathing and birds greeting the day just outside the open window. His head still hurt, though less so. She had bathed his wound and given him a fresh dressing along with the news that he seemed to be healing. There were men in this war with wounds that never healed.

She lay turned away from him—her blond hair spilling over the pillow, her left arm lying outside the sheet. She had very fair skin, but from just above the elbow on down her arm was as tan as her face. A worker, this woman—nothing at all like the self-styled "ladies" who feared that the slightest freckle might give people the idea they passed their days out in the fields chopping cotton.

He kissed her bare shoulder and then sat up, rubbing his eyes. The early sun was unusually bright, foretelling the heat to come. For now, it was pleasant. He fought an impulse to lie back down and spend the morning idly, happy in the comfort of Allie's nearness. With all his stock sold off, he had no duties to perform. With McClellan in no hurry to move his army much beyond Shepherdstown, Pinkerton would likely have no tasks for him—certainly not in his supposed condition as one of the wounded of Antietam.

But there was the dead Ann Harding—as clearly tied to the Reverend Ashby's murder as if they'd been hanged together. Harry had revealed to no one the overriding reason for his interest in these grisly crimes. His late mother had been very fond of the reverend. Her ghost would never forgive him were he to ride off and abandon the matter.

Harry stood up, going to the window.

"Goin' somewheres, plantation man?"

He raised his eyes to the hills across the river. There were smudges of smoke against the low sky. "I need to go into town. See Jim O'Malley about some unfinished business."

"Concerning that murdered girl?"

"The Reverend Ashby as well."

She threw the sheet back and stood up, moving immediately to where she had dropped her nightgown. "You're not going anywhere until you've had some breakfast," she said, as she pulled it on. "And you'll get none of that until I check on your brother."

Robert's face was as pale as the day before but he awakened quickly, his eyes darting from Allie to Harry and back again. "Good morning."

"And a good morning it is to see you this perky," Allie said.

"I am obliged to you, ma'am." The words seemed to take some effort.

"Rest easy, Captain," Allie said. "I'm going to be getting up some breakfast and I hope you will try to take some. Nourishment's essential. If you need encouragement, I can tell you that I think you're past the worst of it. You're not home yet, but if you've got this far and are still livin', you're well on the way."

Robert's eyes were still upon her, his thoughts kept to himself. Then he turned to look at his missing arm, as Harry guessed he must do frequently.

"Don't worry," said Harry. "That's a wound that'll get you promoted general. No need of a sword arm when you get to that rank." He smiled, though Robert did not.

"How goes the war?" Robert asked.

"I imagine General Lee is well into Virginia," Harry said. "The Union Army's here. No more battles for a while. You just rest and get well. You've nothing to worry about."

"Until I'm well enough to be shipped off to Camp Douglas—and a Chicago winter."

Harry put his hand on Robert's good arm. "They're still making prisoner exchanges. Certainly a wounded officer . . ."

Robert gave him a weak smile. "You presume, sir, that I want to go back."

Harry decided this was not a good time to pursue the possibilities raised by that unexpected remark. "I'm going into town," he said. "Much to attend to. Ann Harding's been murdered."

His brother's face went blank. "I do not know the lady." On his infrequent visits to this farm before the war, Robert had stayed clear of the townspeople. It had long been clear to Harry that his brother thought them his social inferiors.

"Well, I won't be gone long."

Robert couldn't remember Ann Harding, but he could remember some things. He was staring hard at Allie. "Your nightgown," he said. "That's my mother's." The garment had little flowers around the neck.

"Your brother loaned it to me. I came here on kinda short notice, as you may remember."

"Where're you from, ma'am?"

Perhaps his brother would live. Harry sensed the snobbery of yore coming to the surface. "She's from Boonsboro, Robert. She owns a large farm there."

"I would not begrudge you the garment, ma'am," his brother said. "I was just curious. As I say, I am obliged to you."

Harry left Allie less happy than when she had awakened. He wondered if she had patience for this, and worried she hadn't. An impetuous woman, not a long-suffering one.

"What are we going to do today, Harry Raines?" Tantou asked.

"Visit some people. Ask some questions. Introduce you to a friend who has been a great help to us. And retrieve a little girl."

"Your daughter."

Harry snapped back on Rocket's reins, turning his head as they abruptly stopped. "Who told you that?"

"The African man, Caesar Augustus."

"That is his surmise." Harry put Rocket into a walk.

"Surmise?"

"A guess. A guess based on evidence, but a guess nonetheless."

"Caesar Augustus, I think, is a smart man. And he knows you very well. Better than I know you."

"Her mother was a woman named Arabella Mills, a friend of mine since childhood. Arabella is dead now. The father abandoned her. She has no one. So I have provided a home for her."

"So then you are a kind man, Harry Raines."

"I am a Virginia gentleman, Jack."

"You have told me that. I do not understand what that means, except maybe you belong to a special tribe. But I am glad you are making a home for this girl."

"Her name is Evangeline."

"Yes. *Un beau nom*, like her."

"Let's be about our business, Jack." He moved Rocket into a trot.

Harry rode straight down German Street to the other end of town, and led the way down the lane to the river landing. Pausing to put on his spectacles, he dismounted and looked around at the trees, spotting finally the one he sought. The severed rope end still hung from its branch. The other end was tied fast to the tree trunk itself. He went to it and struggled with the knot, to little avail.

Moving swiftly, Tantou came up and sliced the rope in twain with his oversized Bowie knife, narrowly missing Harry's hand.

"You and Alexander the Great," Harry said.

"Who is that, Harry Raines?"

"A great chief from ancient Greece. There was a huge knot at the city of Gordium that no one could untie. He was challenged to do so and he cut it fully apart with one stroke of his sword."

"This is why they called him 'the Great?'"

"They called him 'the Great' because he conquered the world."

"Did he conquer Canada?"

"No. He never got to Canada."

199

"Then how can he be 'the Great?'"

Harry grimaced, then took a close look at the rope. "This is new," he said. "Very new."

"What does that matter to the dead girl?"

"It matters to me. It indicates to me that her killer may have bought the rope after deciding to murder her, and that this was a very recent decision. Perhaps I can find the storekeep who sold it to him."

Tantou grunted. Harry ignored him, looking about at the still soft ground at the base of the tree. There were several hoof prints.

"Whoever it was, they hung her from horseback. With so many people about the town, they could get away quick if someone saw them."

"Not them. Just one horse." Tantou eyed the ground closely. "The killer used the horse to haul her up, then dismounted to tie the rope to the tree." He squinted. "Maybe not a he. Maybe a she. A strong man would not have needed a horse."

Harry hadn't thought of that. He pulled out his handkerchief—a clean one he had taken from a dresser drawer that morning. "I'm going to take an impression of one of these hoof prints."

"A horse did not kill her, Harry Raines."

Ignoring this, Harry took the handkerchief carefully in hand and placed it over the hoof mark, then pressed it firmly against the earth. When he lifted it, a clear outline was evident.

"Wait," said Tantou. The Metis took out a handkerchief of his own and went to another print in the ground. "Shoe sole here. Very small." He followed Harry's example, producing a muddy stain on the cloth. Then he likewise folded it. Both were put in Harry's saddlebag.

"The nearest cobbler is in Boonsboro, though there is a store here that sells shoes," Harry said.

"Who sells rope?"

"The same store. And another one in Martinsburg. Another in Sharpsburg. Another in Keedysville."

"Where is the rope that hanged the churchman?" Tantou was looking downright menacing.

"I suppose it's still at Doc Ricketts'."

"Then we should go there and look at them together," Tantou said. "Maybe they came from the same place."

Mister Harding had taken his daughter to Ricketts', where she'd been put in the cellar until an embalmer could be produced. There were dozens of them working both sides of the river, but in the trade of dead soldiers. Harry supposed Harding was out trying to hire one as quickly as possible.

The doctor was working hard at his trade, too—sawing off yet another limb with the aid of a Confederate medical orderly.

"I want to look at Ann Harding's body," Harry said.

Ricketts gave him a hard look. "What's this about, Harry?"

"She was murdered."

"We all know that. The sheriff's been sent for, if he can get through from Charles Town. Still some Rebels down there." The doctor's patient had been given ether, and paid no mind as the last sinews of his arm parted and the limb fell to the floor.

"It's connected to the Reverend Ashby's demise, I'm sure of it. Just give me a few minutes with her."

Ricketts' attention returned to his dreadful task. "A few minutes is all I'll give you. If her old man comes back and finds you with her, I'm going to have another patient, possibly with mortal wounds."

"I'll be brief."

It was cool in the cellar but her body was beginning to swell in the abdomen. Harry wished Mister Harding swift success in finding an undertaker. In the meantime, with Tantou's help, he worked quickly—unbuttoning the top of her dress and pulling it and her camisole down to her waist.

He had assumed the night before that she had been shot in the chest, confronted by her killer. He saw now that it was quite the other way around. The entry wound was at her back—a small opening, the bullet perhaps no more than .32 caliber. The exit wound was much larger, and messy. She'd been

201

caught by surprise, and doubtless died with no knowledge of her murderer's name or purpose.

Harry wanted that spent bullet. It could now be at the bottom of the Potomac, for all he knew.

He began to redress her, fumbling with buttons, trying to avoid her still staring eyes. He'd seen the photographer Matthew Brady wandering about the battlefield. He wished he could fetch the man now, to capture this poor girl and her beauty before it was gone, so that she might be remembered well.

Returning her to the position in which he had found her, he rose, sadly.

"All right. Let us go, Jack."

"Go where?"

"I'm not sure. Maybe the blacksmith's."

"He, at least, is not a stupid man." As Harry headed for the stairs, Tantou lingered, muttering something over the girl's body. Then he followed.

"What did you say over her?" Harry asked, when they were out on the street.

"I told her I was sad she is not alive," Tantou said.

O'Malley was shoeing a horse, without much cooperation from the animal. Harry took the reins in hand and held him still.

"Thanks, Harry. Careful. He's a kicker."

Harry stroked the animal's nose. "Learned that lesson a long time ago. What's the news this morning?"

"No news. A lot of gossip. Much of it salacious. Some worse."

"Suggesting the Reverend Ashby and Ann and adultery?"

The blacksmith gave a horseshoe nail three well-aimed whacks with his hammer. "That's a leading theory, prompting others even less savory. Nice town we have here."

"These aren't nice times," Harry said, watching as Tantou went to a box of horseshoes, taking up two of them. "I examined her body this morning. She was shot in the back."

"If her father finds out you were examining her body, the

202

same fate may not elude you." Another nail went in. The horse was getting fidgety.

"I don't understand the adultery talk," Harry said, gripping the reins more firmly. "I don't doubt that there was infidelity here. But are they saying Martha Ashby did this in revenge? That little woman couldn't hurt a mouse."

Another nail. O'Malley was working more quickly now. "You hear that. Some say it might be Lemuel Krause. That fellow from Keedysville who used to be sweet on Ann. He wanted to marry her. She spurned him. Maybe she preferred the Reverend's company." He finished the shoe—apparently the final one—and let the hoof drop. Harry released the reins.

"I know that boy. He does work for Mister Harding. He was with Mrs. Ashby at the funeral."

"Then he may have a problem," O'Malley said.

Tantou came over with the two horseshoes. "You make these?" he asked the blacksmith.

The blacksmith was amused. "Every one that's in the box. That's my trade."

"They are very different. Different size, different marks."

"Horses come in different sizes, just like human beings."

"I know that," Tantou said. "You make them by hand. But can you tell each one from the others?"

"Tell?"

"Recognize. Know which is which."

O'Malley reflected upon this. The question had probably never been asked him before. He shrugged.

Harry realized what Tantou was thinking. "We were down at the river landing. Saw a lot of hoof prints close to the tree where they found Ann. I figured that the killer used his horse to pull the rope."

"His horse," said O'Malley. "Or her horse."

"At all events," said Harry, "do you think you could identify the horseshoes?"

O'Malley shook his head, as though astonished at such a notion. "I might identify a horseshoe as one of mine. But a print—in muddy ground—that's impossible."

"Could you give it a try?" Harry said. "Go down to the

landing and take a look?" Another shake of the head. "Please, Jim. Won't take long."

O'Malley took off his heavy gloves and dropped them at the side of his forge. "OK. As a favor, Harry."

"I'll buy you a drink at Klostermann's later."

Returning to the battlefield was a sorrowful journey. The wounded had finally been removed but there were still dead upon the ground and the piles of dead horses still smoldered. There was little breeze and the sickly smoke hung in the air.

"Let us not stay long in this place," Tantou said. "It is evil here."

"'Glorious victory,'" Harry said.

"Lee has gone back into Virginia. He could have done that without firing a shot or losing a man."

"His business is war," said Harry, gesturing at the littered field. "He must have thought it worth all this to take a chance at beating McClellan."

"If he had kept his main force on South Mountain, he might have done it."

"Didn't work out that way. And let us be grateful."

A number of people were moving about the open meadow—Union Army grave diggers, embalmers loading up new customers, civilians looking for kin. On a knoll, a photographer was busy at his peculiar work. Harry recognized him as Matthew Brady's assistant, Alexander Gardner.

He was taking a picture of a dead horse—unique in that the animal was not lying on his side but sitting on the ground with his legs under him—his head stiffly high, his eyes surveying the horrible scene with somber implacability. The horse could have been one of the gods of antiquity. It was no wonder that they'd not yet put him on one of the kerosene piles.

"Mister Gardner," said Harry, halting Rocket with a gentle pull of the reins. "You've unpleasant work today."

"Mister Brady wants pictures to take to his gallery in New York. Share the war with the folks who don't have to fight it."

"There are many of those," Harry said.

"This dead horse—it makes for a fascinating picture."

"Looking at him, it's like looking into eternity."

"A lesson for us all, Mister Raines."

"I wish you well, Mister Gardner. I hope many will see your pictures."

"Thank you, sir."

"Thank you. Have you seen Miss Clara Barton this morning—and an assistant, the actress, Caitlin Howard?"

"There were a number of women on the field—nurses. Most of them went with all the wounded to Frederick. But I think Miss Barton is where she's been for two days—on the Pofferberger farm."

"Where is that? I've forgotten."

"On the north end of the line. Just beyond the cornfield."

A wagon pulling out of the farmyard was laden with severed legs, feet, and arms, which the teamsters had neglected to cover with canvas. A cloud of buzzing flies rode escort.

Harry pulled Rocket aside to let the wagon pass and gain some distance away from them.

"She is there, Harry Raines." Tantou nodded toward a group of soldiers and civilians standing outside the barn.

Pulling on his spectacles, Harry recognized Miss Barton talking to an officer at the fence gate. He trotted Rocket up to them, but waited until she had concluded her conversation with the officer, who was a lieutenant colonel and looked to be a surgeon. He then approached, bowing from the saddle. She looked as though she had had no sleep whatsoever since they had last spoken.

She smiled upon seeing him. "You are alive, Captain Raines. And much better, it would appear. I am happy. Have you news?"

"No. I'm looking for anyone who may have knowledge of a young woman who was on the battlefield when I was at the aid station. Her name is Ann Harding. She's from Shepherdstown. She was looking for her brother."

"Did she find him?"

"I don't know. I was hoping you might tell me. She's been

murdered. It happened that night or the next day. She was found hanging from a tree by the Potomac the next evening."

Miss Barton shook her head sadly. "Women, too, now. You heap yet more melancholy upon me, Harry. It is hard to bear much more, and yet there seems no end of it in this war."

"I'm not sure Ann's death had anything to do with the war. I'm trying to find out as much as I can about her last hours. Her brother's name is Richard—Richard Harding. You're sure you did not encounter him?"

"Harry. I daresay I have encountered by now more than a thousand soldiers. I've not had time to ask all their names. Do you know his unit?"

"I think it was the 7th Virginia—a Federal outfit raised here in western Virginia. A lot of Shepherdstown men joined it early in the war."

"The records are poor. And I'm told more than twenty thousand men were killed or wounded in the battle. There's a registrar of casualties down by Pry House. Have you checked with his regiment? You're a poor scout, Harry, if you haven't."

He responded with a look of chagrin. "I am not thinking too straight."

"With your injury, it's a wonder you're thinking at all." She touched his arm. "Caitlin is down at the Methodist Church in Sharpsburg. She could do with a visit from a friend."

He found her in a rear alcove of the church, sleeping on the floor and using a soldier's haversack for a pillow. He was reluctant to disturb her, and so sat down beside her, leaning back against the wall and waiting for her to show signs of stirring.

It took a while. He was in fact asleep himself when she wakened, and touched his face to bring him back to consciousness.

"Harry?" She studied him with weary eyes. She seemed to have aged ten years.

He put his arm around her. "My God, Caitlin, look at us, look at where we are."

"We are where we must be, Harry. But it is good to see you

wherever we are." She rubbed at her eye. "This has become almost more than I can bear. But, God knows, it's nothing to what you men endure."

There was a scream from the main chamber of the church, but it abruptly ceased.

"You need rest, Caitlin. Can I take you to a hotel? Do you want to go back to Washington?"

"There isn't a hotel here that isn't occupied every inch by a wounded soldier," she said. "I can't go back to the city. Not while Miss Barton's here. No. I'll stay and soldier on."

"When you're done, would you like to come stay a while at my place outside Shepherdstown?"

"You're kind, but I will go with Miss Barton wherever she goes—I think back to Washington. Then I will rest."

"Caitlin. Shortly after you visited me on the battlefield, when I was wounded, a young woman from Shepherdstown came by, looking for her brother. She was a dark-haired, very beautiful girl named Ann Harding. Did you by any chance encounter her?"

"I saw such a young woman. I asked about her. She seemed almost a Shakespearean character, moving through the night so mysteriously."

"Was she with anyone?"

"Yes. She passed by once alone and then returned with a man—quite tall."

"Was he in uniform?"

"Yes. I believe he was. I think he was wounded."

"About what time?"

"I don't know. I've lost all track of time. Why do you ask this?"

"She was found murdered."

Caitlin shuddered, then rubbed both eyes. "Damn this war."

He touched her cheek. "I'm sorry. I shouldn't bother you with this."

She lifted her face to his and kissed him warmly. "Thank you for coming to me, old friend. Go now. I need to sleep."

He leaned away as she lay back on her crude bed. "I will come see you again when I can."

"No, Harry. I comprehend that you have very serious business. You attend to it. With Miss Barton, I will be well."

He kissed her hand. By the time he released it, she was
again asleep.

The Union Army provost marshal's office in Sharpsburg had
been established in a large house in the center of town. It was
doing a brisk business in what Harry assumed were deserters,
malingerers, looters, suspected Confederate spies, irate townspeople seeking compensation for damages, and fugitive slaves
who'd come across the river.

Harry and Tantou were compelled to wait their turn. After
a while, it occurred to Harry they might receive faster treatment if they were in leg irons bound for a court-martial. Those
who actually were so constrained were processed and rushed
out the back of the house quite swiftly.

Eventually, he and Tantou were brought before a weary
captain, an older, gray-haired man with a large moustache and
no beard. He had a pasty, splotchy face. Unlike the numerous
line officers about, he appeared even in the army to be spending most of his time indoors.

"I'm Harrison Raines and this is Jack Tantou," Harry said
before the captain could ask him. "We're scouts with Pinkerton."

The captain's eyes went quickly from one to the other, then
to Harry's head bandage. "Heard of you. I think you're the
fellows who found the ford on the left flank."

"Didn't 'find' it. Knew it was there. Our contribution was
finding a general who'd believe it existed."

The captain pondered this, then seemed to remind himself
of the numerous matters still before him. "What's your business, gentlemen?"

"Murder," Harry said.

The officer looked at Harry as if he were a madman.
"Murder? Sir, there've been thousands of murders all over this
battlefield."

"I don't mean combat, sir. A young woman was found shot
to death and hung to a tree across the river at Shepherdstown."

"When?"

"Last night. Not two weeks ago, the pastor of a church in Shepherdstown was found slain and displayed in much the same manner—only it was on this side of the river."

The captain seemed puzzled—and then exasperated. "Were Federal soldiers involved?"

"I don't know, sir."

The officer's large moustache twitched. "Well, Mister Raines . . ."

"Captain Raines, sir. The rank General McClellan has provided me—through Mister Pinkerton." Harry wasn't being pompous. He hoped this suggestion of equality between the two of them might help.

"Very well, *Captain* Raines. If you can provide me with any kind of evidence of U.S. Army involvement, I shall do anything I can for you . . ."

"But sir. Both were Union sympathizers. The pastor was aiding our cause."

"Raines. My job is crimes by the military and crimes against the military. And my jurisdiction stops at the river. Shepherdstown, you said."

"The girl's name was Ann Harding," Harry said. "She was uncommonly attractive. She was on the battlefield the night after the fight, looking for her brother, who's a Federal soldier with a western Virginia outfit—the Seventh. All I would have you do is to ask about if anyone might have seen her. Some harm might have come to him as well—and he is your jurisdiction."

The captain contemplated the numerous papers on his desk. "And if I should come upon such information, how should I communicate it to you? Where are you to be found, sir?"

"Send word to Mister Pinkerton. He will get it to me. And I'm sure General McClellan will appreciate your assistance in this matter. The girl's father is a very important man in these parts."

The officer returned to his paperwork. "I will do what I can. Meantime, tend to that wound of yours. We're beginning to have people dying from what were mere scratches."

\* \* \*

"Where are you going now, Harry Raines?" Tantou asked, as they walked to their horses.

"I thought I'd ride up to Keedysville and talk to Lemuel Krause. He was sweet on her but may have turned sour. Especially if he got some notion about Ann and the Reverend."

"What about your brother?" Tantou asked when they reached their horses. He was in his saddle as though with no effort at all.

"He is in very good hands, Jack. Lovely hands." Harry stroked Rocket's neck, then mounted also.

"The provost guard may come for him."

"They have a lot of other wounded to deal with first."

The Krause homestead was just south of Keedysville and something of a shambles. The barn roof was missing shingles and panes of glass were gone from the house windows. The horse grazing among the weeds in the front yard was sway-backed and its ribs were showing. It was fair surmise that Ann's motivation for spurning Lemuel's attentions had to do with her father's low opinion of poverty.

His knock was answered by a gray-haired woman in a greasy homespun dress. She stared at Harry vaguely. He'd never met her before.

"Harrison Raines," he said, giving her a slight bow. "I'm with the Federal army. I would like to speak with your son Lemuel if I could."

She was very short and had to twist her neck slightly to look up at him. "You're not takin' him?"

"Taking him?"

"Into the army."

"No, ma'am. The Union Army doesn't do that." He could have added the word, "Yet."

"What for you then?"

"Ma'am?"

"What you want with my boy?"

Harry hesitated, not wanting to make her any more wary. "I have a farm outside Shepherdstown. I wanted to talk to him about a job. I need an extra hand."

"Lem's already got a job. And it's in Shepherdstown. That's where he is now."

"With who?"

"With the widow of that preacher who got himself murdered—Mrs. Ashby."

They moved along the Sharpsburg Road at a trot. "You want to go lay hands on this Lemuel?" Tantou asked.

"Yes." Harry thought upon this. "No. Not yet." He pulled back on Rocket's reins, slowing to a walk as he thought further. "No. I want to go to the battlefield, to McClellan's headquarters."

"Harry Raines. You do that and they'll put you back to work."

"I'm not going there to look up Pinkerton or the general. I only want to find out where Richard Harding's regiment is situated."

"Why?"

"To find out if he was the man who was seen with Ann Harding the night before her murder."

"Well, I do not wish to go with you, Harry Raines. I do not want to scout any more for this stupid general."

"I do understand that."

"Then I will see you later." With that, he pressed heels to his horse's flanks and was soon lost to view in a cloud of dust.

Western Virginia's 7th Infantry Regiment had been badly shot up and was now commanded by a mere major who had himself suffered a wound to his arm. He received Harry in the remains of a tent that had been not a little shot up itself.

"Richard Harding?" he said. He scratched his head. "Yes, yes. A woman came through here looking for him." The officer pulled forth a sheaf of papers that Harry presumed was a muster roll. "Yes, here he is. C Company. Private Richard Harding."

"Where might I find him?"

"Out on the battlefield."

Harry looked out the tent opening in that direction. "Anywhere in particular?"

"There's a filled in trench up near what was the initial Confederate position. It's where they buried most of our dead. It's temporary. Until the families come for 'em—or send for 'em."

"Dead?"

The major rechecked the muster roll, which Harry saw had lines drawn through many of the names. "Private Harding was killed in our first assault on the Rebs. About midday."

Harry contemplated this. "Wasn't the family notified?"

The major pondered the muster. "Should have been." He shrugged. "Not so many of us left. A lot to attend to."

"I'll attend to it."

He went first to the Harding house—a large place on the bluff overlooking the river. A maid answered the door.

"Is Mister Harding in? I'm Captain Raines, from the Army."

"No, sir."

"I, I'm afraid I have bad news for him. His son Richard was killed in the big battle across the river. I wasn't certain he was informed."

"Yes, sir. He was informed. Late this morning. That's where he went. With Mister Prosper, the undertaker. To fetch back his son's body."

Harry bowed to her, as though to the Harding household. "Very well. Please extend my condolences."

"Yes, sir." She closed the door quickly behind her.

He was riding up German Street when he heard his name called, just as he passed Klostermann's tavern. "Harry Raines. Over here."

Tantou was standing on the high stoop at the entrance to the brick building, leaning against the wall. Harry turned Rocket toward him. O'Malley appeared in the doorway.

"Let's go to my place," he said.

Harry nodded and dismounted, walking Rocket as they moved on to the blacksmith shop.

212

"We've learned a few things," O'Malley said. He went to the bins of horseshoes, pulling forth one. He then produced one of the mud-stained handkerchiefs. "It matches. A very large shoe for a very large horse. I don't make too many of them. It's larger than the shoes I've made for Rocket."

Harry examined it. "Do you recall who you made them for?"

"Presuming the shoe that made those hoof prints was one of mine, I do indeed." He went inside his little office, returning with a small ledger book. "Only four. One of 'em was the Reverend Ashby. Very large man with a very large horse."

Harry sat down on an upended box, as he felt a bit of dizziness return. "Where is this horse?"

"I guess it'd be in his stable."

Tantou took the other handkerchief from his pocket. "We learned something else, Harry Raines."

"We couldn't find a match at the cobblers here, but we went back to Doc Ricketts' and compared it to Miss Harding's shoe. She was a tall girl. Her foot's too big for that print by the tree."

"It was made by a small woman," Tantou said.

Harry rubbed his chin. "I guess I know where to go next."

There was no answer when he knocked several times at the widow Ashby's door. He went around to the rear, achieving the same result. Turning to the stable, he unlatched the door and stepped inside.

All the stalls were empty.

# Twenty-One

Harry had expected Allie to be on the porch waiting for him, but his only greeting came from his two farm dogs, who after a round of barking at Rocket, ran up to have their heads patted and scratched.

Mounting the steps, he dropped his saddlebags and weapons on the hall table and proceeded into the kitchen, where he expected he might find her.

The room was empty. Fully oppressed now by a fatigue that far exceeded the debilitating effects of his wound, he slumped into a chair, staring blankly at the sink and hand pump, for want of any more pleasing object.

But he was soon provided with one. Allie came into the room, wearing a thin cotton frock and no shoes.

"Your brother is doing poorly," she said. "I do not believe the wound has gone septic, but he is running a fever. I have wrapped his head in cold cloths, but I don't know what else to do."

Harry raised his head. "You have already done so much, Allie."

She pulled up a chair and sat beside him, lifting his bandage. "Your wound improves. In fact, I am going to take this damn thing off for good."

Gently, she removed the bandage from his head. He felt a sudden cooling, though the wound itself began to throb.

"Thank you, ma'am," he said.

Allie took his hand. "Sweet thing, I have got to get back to Boonsboro and see to Elspeth and the return of our stock."

"Yes. Of course."

"Got no choice, Harry. My responsibility. You know that."

214

He kissed her hand. "I do."

"I've had a happy time here."

"That's amazing, considering."

"That Ricketts is a good doctor. Send for him if things get worse with your brother. Not to speak of yourself. But I have to go back."

She rose, letting go of his hand. "Are you hungry?"

"No."

"Do you want whiskey?"

"No."

"We should look in on Robert."

"Yes." Harry rose.


His brother seemed not to have moved an inch since Harry had last looked upon him. The candle Allie had lit illuminated his sunken face with a golden glow, but the pallor shone through like some metaphysical light. Harry knew he was in a bad way.

"Robert," Harry said, softly.

The eyes opened, nothing else stirred. "Who are you, sir?"

"I'm your brother Harry. We're in my house. Our house. Do you remember?"

The voice subsided in volume, but a clarity came into it. "Yes, yes I do. You have been most kind to me, Harry. Your lady—she has been very kind."

Allie stepped forward from the shadows and put a hand on his brow beneath the sodden cloth. The rag was as hot as his flesh. "We must wrap him in blankets. We must make him sweat."

Harry produced his flask. "This will help him do that."

They attended to the stricken brother as best they could— Harry finding yet more whiskey and more blankets in the house. It was a good three hours before the fever finally broke. Robert's labored breathing eased, and became something akin to normal.

Tantou had entered the room without their noticing. "You go now. I will watch him."

"Jack," said Harry. "You know so many things, but nursing . . ."

215

"We Metis survive because we take care of each other, no matter what. Go away, Harry Raines. You and Miss Allie. If things go bad, I will find you."

"I will leave in the morning," Allie said, in the hall.

"Yes."

"Harry, I've got no passion left. I've damn near got no feelings left. But I want you to be with me tonight. I want to sleep with you holding me."

"Allie, we want the same thing."

Once again he awoke to sunshine and the pleasant sounds of morning. Life seemed so slow in such a moment, worthy of contemplation.

But it didn't last. There was a rustling sound. He looked to see Allie stuffing clothing into saddlebags. The dress he'd given her that had been his mother's was folded on a chest. She had returned to trousers—and boots.

"No, Allie. You're to keep that frock. Anything you want."

"Got no room for it. Not much use for it, either, bringin' in our beef." She came over and sat on the bed. "Maybe I'll wear it when I come back." She leaned close. "I will come back, if you've no mind."

"No mind. Should I send someone with you? All those soldiers."

"Yankee soldiers. Anyway, I think I'll hook up with a wagon train. They've got a constant stream of them taking wounded through Boonsboro to the hospitals in Frederick." She patted his shoulder. "How's your head?"

"I'm fine, quite fine."

Allie looked closely to make sure, then rose and picked up her saddlebags, tossing them over one shoulder. "You got a rifle or shotgun I can borrow?"

He nodded. "Over the fireplace in the sitting room."

"Thanks. I looked in on Robert. He seems no worse than last night, which I guess is a good sign. I'd have that Doctor Ricketts look at him, though."

"I will."

She paused at the bedroom door. "Not my business to be interfering in yours, plantation man, but it seems to me that you're sure taking your own good time bringing that little girl of yours back here to home."

He sat up, carefully prodding his wound. He felt only crust and matted hair. "She's not my little girl. She's an old friend's little girl."

Allie pulled open the door. "I ain't arguing paternity. I'm just reminding you of your responsibility here." She hesitated. "I'll be back in three or four days—if you're of like mind."

"Very like mind."


Harry had never met the widow Sally Thompson but knew well her house on the hill. He let Rocket plod his way up the steep lane that led to it, forming in his mind the words he hoped would persuade the lady to indulge him with a few days more custody of little Evangeline.

Tying his horse to the porch railing, he ascended the high steps, turning to appreciate the view of town and river. A single artillery piece positioned in Mrs. Thompson's yard could command both.

He shook his head, amused but displeased with himself. It was a beautiful prospect, the view from this house. Yet here he was thinking of it in military terms. He had been in this war too long.

Knocking, he stepped back. When the door opened, a tall, somewhat fearful-looking woman with dark hair graying at the sides stood in the opening, Evangeline clinging to her dark brown dress.

But not for long. "Mister Harry!" she cried, and bolted toward him, leaping high. He caught her in his arms just in time.

She giggled. "Hello."

"Hello." He had forgotten how green her eyes were. He supposed she might grow up to be a very beautiful young woman, dusky hue or no.

He abandoned his plan to ask Mrs. Thompson to keep the girl a few days more.

217

"I heard you were hurt, Mister Raines. In the battle and all. Are you well?" Mrs. Thompson's voice was as fearful as her countenance. "So many killed in that battle. And now these murders."

She had agreed to take in Evangeline without compensation. Shifting Evangeline's weight to his right, he fished a five dollar gold piece out of his coat pocket with his left, handing it to her. "Thank you for your kindness, Mrs. Thompson."

The woman clasped both hands over the big coin as though she were afraid he might take it back. "Thank you, Mister Raines."

Harry paused. "What have you heard about the murders?"

Her voice grew faint. "They say that he—the Reverend Ashby—and Ann Harding, that they were . . ."

"Yes. I've heard the same thing." He started down the steps, careful of Evangeline, then halted once more. "Did you know Ashby?"

"I've attended services. I think he was a good man. Better than they're saying."

"Do you know his wife?"

She shook her head. She was withdrawing back into the house as he spoke his last "thank you."

It was much against custom to bring a woman or a child into a saloon. But Harry had been told O'Malley was in Klostermann's and he needed to speak to him.

The blacksmith was eating lunch at the bar. They moved to a table so that Evangeline might sit and Harry procured a boiled egg and some jelly biscuits for her and took an egg and a glass of beer for himself.

"Have you heard from Caesar Augustus?"

O'Malley nodded as he chewed another bite. "Yes. But you won't like what I heard. He doesn't want to come back from Pennsylvania."

Harry looked down at the table top. Klostermann kept his place very clean. "I expected as much. That leaves me encumbered." He ran his hand over Evangeline's curly hair. "Delightfully encumbered, but encumbered nonetheless, when I can ill afford to be."

"There's no one at your farm?"

"My wounded brother. Tantou's watching over him but I need Jack. Mrs. Robertson has gone back to Boonsboro. I thought of paying Mrs. Thompson to keep her a while longer, but I don't think she was happy there. At all events, the farm's her home now. She should be in it."

"Caesar Augustus doesn't want to come back to where there's slavery."

"There's no slavery on my farm. He's legally a free man."

"Estelle . . ."

"Dred Scott doesn't apply here—not with the Federal army camped all around. No paddy-rollers are going to turn up hot after runaways. They'd likely be locked up as enemy agents."

"Caesar Augustus got himself a job in a shoe factory in Gettysburg. They've a little house. This is what we hope for all our passengers on the railroad."

Evangeline had finished her egg. She smiled at Harry.

"Maybe I could send her to Gettysburg."

"Harry. You took her from Richmond. She's your responsibility."

The little girl now had jam spread over much of her face. Harry took out his handkerchief and wiped it away, then realized more would be coming. He grinned at her. "But I can't deal with these murders with her on my shoulders."

O'Malley finished his meal. "Why don't you hire someone else to take care of her? Lot of unfortunate women in this town who wouldn't mind some of your money."

"Give me the name of one?"

"Selma Keady. She lost her beau in the Peninsula campaign. Lucinda Weverton."

"If I had Lucinda Weverton resident in my house, the gossip could be heard in Boston. And half the Union Army would be lined up at my porch in hopes of her company."

"She's good with children. She could use the money."

"I'll think upon it. Did the sheriff ever get here?"

"Not yet. I'm not sure he's much interested. All these Federals around. He's not much of an abolitionist."

Evangeline came over and climbed up on Harry's knee.

When she was settled, he took a drink of his beer. "There's something we need to do," he said.

"We?"

"If you're of a mind to help me. I need to get into Martha Ashby's place. I want to compare our handkerchief print with one of her shoes. Same goes for her horse."

"I thought you said you wanted to find the Reverend's murderer because you felt you owed it to the widow."

"I do. And my mother would never forgive me if I walked away from this. But we've got to clear up these questions before we do anything else. The sheriff's going to get here sometime. If Martha Ashby's an innocent in this affair, we'd best be establishing that quick."

"And if she's not?"

"Let's not think upon that now. What do you know of this Lemuel Krause?"

"There are a hundred boys like him in this valley. Foolish fellows. Crazy with love for girls they can't have."

"Could he have murdered Ann Harding alone?"

"Sure enough. But why would he be involved in the Reverend Ashby's passing?"

"He's gone to work for the widow Ashby."

"We keep thinking in circles like this, Harry, we're going to bump into ourselves." He stood up. "Got to go back to my labors. Got to find some help myself. I'm getting a lot of trade from the army. These are good times for some people."

"When's the funeral for Ann Harding?"

O'Malley shrugged. "I heard her father wants to find her brother's remains first. He wants to bury them together. His only children."

"Is he a vengeful man?"

"You bet."

Harry stood. "When they have that funeral, that's when I'm going into Martha Ashby's house."

"You think she'll attend?"

"She'll have no choice. Her absence would prove every shred of gossip."

"You should talk to her first."

220

"The more I think upon that prospect, the more I think I should wait."

He stopped by Susan Hodges' house, but she had gone to Frederick to help with the wounded. Selma Keedy had no interest in moving to another house to attend to someone else's child, no matter what the pay. Rachel Fairbrother declined as well, suggesting he advertise for a governess in Baltimore or Washington.

It was enough frustration for this day. With Evangeline riding in front of him on his saddle, he returned to his farm, finding Tantou sitting cross-legged on the porch.

"Your brother lives," he said. "He sleeps."

"I've brought back Evangeline," Harry said, dismounting, and reaching to lower her to the ground as well.

Tantou said nothing, but rose and turned to reenter the house.

"I'm going to sleep a while," Harry said. "Then I'll make supper."

"I have already done this," Tantou said, and went inside after Harry.

# Twenty-Two

Harry slept badly, waking twice in the darkness. In the last instance, he sat up on the edge of the bed and stared out the open window for a very long time. He'd been dreaming, and his dreams had been about Allie. He missed her beside him in the bed. He wished he knew much more about her—and wished more that she'd come back sooner than she had said.

He listened to the night sounds, contemplating the mysteries that lurked in the further darkness. The simple life he'd hoped for here had vanished—perhaps for good. He touched his wound. There was pain, then a tingling. Then oncoming sleep, as he lay back upon the bed.

When he awoke again, it was to find Evangeline tugging at his arm.

"Mister Harry. I'm hungry."

He squinted at the window. The sun was only just up. He'd given no thought to breakfast—had no idea what might or might not be in the larder.

"Give me a few minutes, Evangeline."

"Minutes?"

"Wait for me in the kitchen. I'll be there soon."

He came down in shirt, trousers, and stocking feet. He found little in the pantry, but there was a jar of sugared peaches and he set those before her before doing anything else.

His farm had always been self-sustaining, possessing a sprawling vegetable garden, a chicken house whose inhabitants had somehow survived the passage of armies, and a few dairy cattle, currently in the barn. Pulling on an old pair of farmer's boots that were standing by the rear door, he went first to the chicken house, wincing at the odor but procuring an abundance of fresh eggs. The cows required milking, but he was not quite up to that yet.

Hearing the hoofbeats of a visitor, he returned to the house. As he stepped through the back door into the hall, he saw Tantou come in the front entrance, bearing a small sack. Entering the kitchen, the half-breed spread its contents on the table—a freshly cut and large slice of beef, another of pork, a loaf of cornbread, and a jar of butter.

Harry added his eggs. "A veritable feast," he said to Evangeline.

"Feast," she repeated.

"I bring something else, Harry Raines." Tantou set down the Shepherdstown newspaper, which benefited from the telegraph line that ran along the road to Harper's Ferry. "It is important news, I think. Good news, maybe. But maybe bad, too. You tell me."

Harry could scarcely believe the multiple headlines. He read over them twice, and paid particularly close attention to the article that followed.

He sat down, stunned. "He's freeing the slaves," he said. "Lincoln is freeing the slaves."

Tantou folded his arms. "Harry Raines, I speak French, Iroquois, Mingo and Sioux. I know English, but not as well as you. Still, I understand what this says. You should read again, with care."

Harry did so. "He's freeing the slaves in the South."

"In the states that are still in open rebellion on January 1, it says. The slaves in Maryland, Delaware, Kentucky, Missouri—the slaves in Kansas, other places—they stay slaves."

Harry sat back. He felt an onrushing joy he couldn't possibly explain to Tantou. "It's a big start forward," he said. "Especially for us. Virginia remains in open rebellion."

Tantou grunted.

"I despaired on that battlefield, Jack," Harry said. "All that death and mayhem—for nothing. It was a useless, stupid battle that neither side really won. But Lincoln has made something noble of it. Don't you understand?"

223

"He is a politician, this Lincoln. That much I understand."

Harry decided to abandon this debate. "Have you any other news?"

Tantou nodded. "There is a funeral today. The brother and sister Harding."

"At the Reverend Ashby's Presbyterian Church?"

Another nod. "Harding brought back his son's body from the battlefield last night. They are to lie side by side in the churchyard."

"We shall attend," said Harry, "though we may excuse ourselves halfway through."

Before leaving, he went upstairs to visit his brother, taking the newspaper with him. Robert still was very pale, but sitting up against his pillows.

"There's news," said Harry. "Are you feeling well enough to look at a newspaper?"

"Yes. Haven't read one—it's been more than a week."

Harry handed him the paper, pointing to the story. Robert read it very slowly, as Harry had done. Then he set the paper aside, gazing at Harry bleakly.

"How can he do this?"

"He's President of the United States," said Harry. "This is a wartime measure. Diminish the Confederacy's ability to support the war."

"It will only reinvigorate the Southern desire to fight the war," Robert said. "We stand to lose everything. If the Federal army comes up the Peninsula again and frees the slaves at Belle Haven, we're done for. You can't run that place without them. Father could be ruined."

"He could pay them wages."

Robert shook his head sadly. "Never would he do that."

A heavy silence fell between them.

"Let us put the matter aside for the moment," Harry said. "Ann Harding's funeral is this morning and I want to go to it. Would you mind if I left Evangeline with you?"

Robert gave a slight shrug. "I cannot be chasing after her, Harry."

"No need. I'll see she remains indoors."

He found her playing on the front porch with one of the dogs, and knelt beside her. "Evangeline. You know that my brother upstairs there is very sick and must keep to his bed."

"Yes. He is sick. Someone has taken his arm."

"I have to go into town for a while. Would you do me a favor and watch over him for me?"

"Watch over him?"

"Bring him anything he might need. Help him if he's in a bad way."

She nodded solemnly. "I will, Mister Harry."

"This means you'll have to stay inside the house—so you'll hear him if he cries out."

"I will."

He kissed her forehead then rose. It was too pretty a day for a funeral.

Selma Keedy, Rachel Fairbrother, and Susan Hodges had been friends of Ann Harding's, and were present for the brief services. Lucinda Weverton and Peggy Singleton were not, but they had no reason to be. Jim O'Malley and Hugo Klostermann were in attendance, as were most of the Union men in the town, wanting to honor Richard Harding's sacrifice for the Federal cause. The pastor who presided was from the Lutheran church, but that didn't matter. He was a Union man, too.

Martha Ashby was there, and appropriately so. Lemuel Krause was absent, but that was to be expected. Ann Harding's father, who sat through the service on the brink of great anger, might have made the occasion very unpleasant for the youth.

They filed into the churchyard with the others, hanging back to stand at the rear of the crowd. Harry moved very close to Tantou.

"You go first," he said. "I'll follow directly."

They were both in place at the widow Ashby's house within five minutes. Taking the handkerchief with the hoof print, Tantou went to the stable, slipping quickly inside. Harry had the more difficult task—opening one of the rear windows of the house, some five feet off the ground, and somehow manag-

225

ing to haul himself over the sill and into what proved to be a small bedroom.

They hadn't much time, but he poked into all the rooms of the house, settling finally on the large chamber on the second floor he took to be the Reverend's and Martha's bedroom.

She had a remarkable number of shoes—a dozen pair, two of them quite fancy. None of them matched the exact imprint of the mud-stained sole on the handkerchief Harry had carried with him.

But they were of the same small size.

Descending to the main floor, he returned to the room that had served as the Reverend's study. There was a roll-top desk against the wall—unfortunately locked. Harry pondered his next move, deciding finally on expediency. Taking the sheath knife from his boot, he tried picking the lock at first, but without success. Finally, again like Alexander the Great at Gordium, he broke the lock open. The widow would be upset, of course, but her public response to this break-in would be interesting to see—especially if there was none at all.

There were a number of letters, one in a woman's hand but without signature, professing much affection; several others from a Pennsylvania anti-slavery society. Nearly all the rest of Ashby's papers were normal business correspondence, dealing with repairs to the church roof, a complaint of an unpaid bill, communications from other Presbyterian clergy in the area, and similarly innocent matters.

One letter, however, folded over many times and hidden at the back of one of a multiplicity of small drawers in the desk, proved to be precisely the sort of thing Harry had hoped to find.

*Warn the general*, it said. *Assassins are afoot.*

There was no signature, but there was a drawing of an American flag in the lower right hand corner, and with it, the single letter "G."

As he slipped this in his pocket, Harry heard Tantou at the door.

"Someone comes, Harry Raines. We must go."

\*      \*      \*

226

Klostermann had been absent from the burial. Harry presumed he had gone to reopen his tavern, which happily proved to be the case. O'Malley was standing outside the establishment, reading the town newspaper, as though waiting for them.

"Emancipation," said Harry, with a broad grin.

"We should go inside," said O'Malley.

"I have been drinking too much in this war," Harry said. "And it is too early in the day."

"If we are inside, at the bar, it is an excuse for our conversation," O'Malley said. "And if we stay outside, we are most noticeable."

"He makes sense," said Tantou.

They took places at the far end of the bar, and Harry bought a round of good whiskey.

"This is on me," said Klostermann. "Such glorious news. I was having my doubts about this Lincoln, but now . . . he is the greatest President."

"To Lincoln," said Harry. He raised his glass and the others followed suit. "May he live long."

When they had all drunk, he pushed his money further forward. "Hugo. This is for the next round."

Klostermann lingered. "The hoof prints at the tree where Ann Harding was found—they match the shoes of the big draft horse the widow Ashby uses for her buggy," Harry said. "And the human foot prints there—those of a small woman's shoe—they are the same size as the widow Ashby's shoes."

"I won't be asking how you came to find out that," said O'Malley.

"The how and why don't matter," Harry said. "The result is what's of consequence. This is damning evidence."

"But what will you do with it?" Klostermann asked. "The sheriff, he won't come up here. I think he's afraid of being arrested as Secesh, which I do believe he is. Does the Army care about these murders?"

"No," admitted Harry.

"So what's to be done?"

"We'll get more evidence. And if I can get Mister Pinkerton to state plainly that the Reverend Ashby was an active Union agent, then the provost marshal's office will have jurisdiction. He'll have no choice to become involved."

"We've not much other choice," said O'Malley.

"I'll go try to find Pinkerton right now," Harry said, draining his glass.

"Harry Raines. You forget something." The Metis was staring hard at him over the rim of his whiskey glass.

"Evangeline."

"Yes. You leave her with your sick brother."

"I will find someone to help," Harry said, with a sigh.

"Good."

Selma Keedy did not wish to speak to him. Sarah Fairbrother brought Harry into her house to speak with her mother, who would have none of it.

"Mister Raines, I appreciate your predicament," said the mother. "But I cannot have Sarah staying in a house with so many unattached young men about. You know how this town is."

He did indeed.

Harry went next to the small, wretched farmhouse that had become the abode of Peggy Singleton and her two brothers. Peggy came to the door. Harry would rather have faced Jackson and his entire division.

"What the hell you want with us, you Yankee bastard?" she said, holding the door almost closed.

"I need someone to watch over my—the little girl in my house. I have much business to attend to, and there's no one else there except my brother, who was badly injured in the battle."

"Your brother the Confederate?"

"Yes. He is recovering. I'll pay you a dollar a day."

It was a generous sum, considering everything.

"My brothers'd kill me, I do this for you, Harry Raines. You go find someone else."

"I guess I'll have to."

"I wouldn't mind," she said. "But I can't."

*       *       *

The last girl on his list was Lucinda Weverton, who lived on the bluffs overlooking the river. His rapping on the door produced no response. He tried it one time more, and then again, without result.

Shaking his head, he abandoned the porch and went around the side of the house to the large back yard. There was clothing drying on several lines strung between the trees. He almost didn't notice the bare feet protruding from beneath a hanging sheet.

He flung the sheet back. There, hanging from a tree branch, her chest covered with blood, was Lucinda, swaying in the breeze.

# Twenty-Three

"All this seems a wrathful passage from the Bible," said O'Malley.

Harry had cut down Lucinda and lain her body upon the sheet that had nearly masked the crime.

"I am uncertain what to do," said Harry. "The sheriff won't come with the Union Army here, so there is no law. There used to be a town constable in Shepherdstown but he was swept away by the war."

"The widow Ashby couldn't have been involved," said O'Malley. "She was at the funeral."

"Lemuel," said Harry.

Tantou was gazing down at the dead girl. "I will find him—and bring him back to you."

"We've no idea where he may be," Harry observed.

"I will find him, Harry Raines." In a moment, Tantou had mounted his horse and ridden off.

"I'll take her body to Doc Ricketts," Harry said to O'Malley. "In the meantime, you find a way to alert the townspeople to this without provoking a riot or setting off a lynch mob."

"And how am I to manage that?"

"You're a resourceful man, Jim. If you can't think of anything else, call a meeting at Klostermann's. Hugo will appreciate the extra business." He looked down sadly at the body, then began to wrap the sheet over and around her. "I'll join you there presently."

Ricketts came reluctantly out of the rear of his house, a piece of jam-covered bread in hand. He munched on it thoughtfully as he contemplated the burden on Harry's horse.

230

"The same as the others?" he asked.

"I'm afraid so."

The doctor lifted the sheet, his head snapping back at the sight of Lucinda's face. "You haven't removed the rope."

"Evidence. If we had any kind of law at hand to concern itself with such niceties. That damned sheriff seems to think we're not part of Jefferson County."

"What about the provost marshal's office? This is no trifling matter."

"It's not a military matter. Until it is, they're not interested."

"Harry, this can't go on. We've got to stop it."

"I don't know how to stop it. These girls, Doc, they have something in common. Shall we call it a close friendship with the Reverend Ashby? We need somehow to persuade the rest of them to get the hell out of here before they're murdered, too."

"But that invites scandal. Their parents . . ."

"Better scandal than more gravestones." Harry sadly contemplated Lucinda's body, remembering her alive, walking so prettily down German Street, attracting the affectionate stares of every male. "Perhaps, Doctor, it would help if you would accompany me in my missionary work with them."

"Harry. There are still wounded. Many, many wounded. I came home only for a brief rest."

"I need someone whose opinion they will respect."

"I am judged a Union man, Harry, just as you are. Our opinions are not universally respected."

Harry turned away from Lucinda's body, scratching his head and regretting it as a wave of pain swept over him. He put a hand on to the doctor's shoulder to steady himself.

"Let me look at that," Ricketts said. He examined the wound carefully, bringing on more pain as he prodded its length with a finger. "You're improving, but there's still too much swelling."

"I hope you're not going to recommend amputating my head."

"Grim joke, Harry. You should get some rest."

"Can't. I'm going back to Sharpsburg."

"Why?" Ricketts asked.

"We need help with this." The doctor looked like one of his wounded, he was so weary. "In the meantime, I'd appreciate your help. If you can manage it, could you look in on my brother?"

"Certainly."

"And the little girl in my house, Evangeline. I need someone to keep an eye on her. I've tried, but . . ."

"I'll find someone."

"I shall pay generously."

"Just come back soon."


Pinkerton was not at McClellan's Pry House headquarters. Harry eventually found him in a tavern on Sharpsburg's main street—eating roast beef and potatoes and drinking lemonade.

"Raines! Are you returning to duty?"

"In a manner of speaking. We're beset with a terrible trouble in Shepherdstown. Murders."

Pinkerton frowned, then gestured to Harry to take a seat. "We are not police, Harry."

"The provost marshal is," Harry said, lowering himself into the chair. His dizziness was returning with the heat. "I need for him to take jurisdiction. This involves a Federal operative, Mr. Pinkerton. The Reverend Ashby. A Presbyterian minister. He was murdered just before the battle. Shot and hanged."

"I am not acquainted with this gentleman. We have no ministers in General McClellan's secret service."

"I'm aware of that. He was a conductor on the Underground Railroad. He passed messages to the North with the escaped slaves he sent along from Virginia. I have one with me."

Pinkerton chewed for a long moment. "Commendable. But this does not make him a member of the U.S. military."

Harry spoke more urgently. "Young women are now being killed—in the same dreadful fashion. The sheriff down in Charlestown is Secesh, and won't come to Shepherdstown while the army's there. Probably wouldn't come anyway, given the Union loyalties there. We have no law, Mister Pinkerton."

The detective dabbed carefully at his lips with his napkin. "Raines, there's a war on. These civil matters cannot be allowed to interfere with the Army and its mission."

"What mission? It's just sitting. Lee could be in Alabama by now. Or New York."

Pinkerton pushed back in his chair. Harry wasn't sure whether he'd had enough of his meal or enough of this conversation. "Captain Raines," the detective said with great solemnity, "your service to this army and the Federal government has been invaluable. You've been resourceful, even intrepid. And now you've been wounded—almost killed—performing your duty. Because of this, I've been happy to indulge you with a few days of leisure on your farm. But I cannot allow you to be distracted by these crimes, odious as they may be."

Harry sighed. "You won't help?"

"I cannot, sir. General McClellan will be remaining here only a few days more. Then we will take the offensive again. Every man of us will be needed."

Harry contemplated Pinkerton's words. "Would you object if I went to General McClellan?"

"He is very busy, Harry."

"Do you think he would be interested in reading this?" He handed Pinkerton the brief message he had found in Ashby's desk.

Pinkerton squinted as he read it. He then repeated the words aloud. "'Warn the general. Assassins are afoot.'" His eyes lifted. "What general?"

"I don't know. But this came from Ashby. I found it in his desk."

"Is it from him or to him?"

"I don't know. There's only that letter 'G.'"

"You think there are assassins who intend to kill General McClellan?"

"I think that is a possibility."

Pinkerton rose, dabbing at his lips again. "I wish you had told me that right off, Harry. I must go and warn the general, as the message instructs."

"You'll help me with the provost marshal, then?"

233

"No time for that now," Pinkerton said, moving past Harry.

"Mr Pinkerton!"

The detective halted, looking impatient.

"Am I a member of the United States military?"

"Yes. Of course. You're an army scout—on the Federal payroll."

"Good. Thank you. My respects to the general."

He left Rocket with a livery stable he knew and trusted, then walked to the provost marshal's office. Still beset with paperwork, the old captain appeared not to have budged an inch since Harry had last seen him.

His upward glance was hard. "I thought we had concluded our business, sir."

"There is something you should know."

The officer pushed at the stack of papers. "I know too much."

"You are aware of my status as a Union Army scout—on General McClellan's payroll."

"Yes, yes. What of it?"

"That I carry the rank of captain?"

"Yes. What do you want?"

"You accept that I am under your jurisdiction—subject to U.S. Army rules and regulations."

"Yes. And if you continue to take up my time this way I may enforce one or two of them in your regard."

"There is a regulation against military personnel murdering civilians."

"Most definitely, sir."

"Well, then. I am here to place myself in your custody. I confess to the murders of the Reverend Ashby and Misses Ann Harding and Lucinda Weverton."

# Twenty-Four

They took him to a barn off the Boonsboro Road that the provost was using as a prison. It had already acquired a sizable contingent of inmates, most in Union blue but a few in Confederate uniforms. There were two civilians—sharpers by the looks of them—and a woman, who had been accorded quarters of her own in a padlocked stall.

Four Union soldiers stood guard, unhappily. A number of prisoners were drunk, and the barn smelled of things far worse than livestock.

Taking a seat on a bale of hay, Harry was surprised, pleased, and then disturbed to find himself joined by a young sergeant with a friendly smile—Christopher Knapp. "Good to see you're still breathing," the young man said. "Why're you here?"

Harry lighted one of his small cigars. "To be perfectly honest, murder."

The sergeant was unfazed. "So's that fat private snoring off his carouse in the corner there. Only he's in irons. You're unfettered."

"I have friends in high places," Harry said, with a grin. He took out his flask and offered the youth a swig. It was accepted, enjoyed, and thanked for. Harry had a sip himself. "What misfortune has put you in here?"

"They have me for desertion," the sergeant said. "But it's a lie. A lieutenant I'm not so friendly with claimed I was absent from the battlefield and put me on charges after the fight."

"But that's not true."

"Maybe Little Mac will spare me. He's in high regard for the tender mercies he shows his troops."

"I'll testify on your behalf."

235

The sergeant's grin was rueful. "That might be more helpful if you weren't under arrest for murder."

"Why is that woman here?" Harry asked, nodding toward the stall. He could see the back of her head through the barred door.

"Prostitute."

"There are no prostitutes in Sharpsburg."

"Came with the army. A lot of them. Always do."

"Who'd she kill?"

"Some poor trooper who'd declined to pay her."

Harry imagined the altercation. "Well, at least he died at Antietam. His family won't have to know how."

The young sergeant reached for Harry's flask. "Who'd you kill?"

"I have confessed to killing a minister and two young ladies." What he wanted now was to sleep.

The woman in the stall began coughing, and had trouble stopping.

"So when is it you killed all these people?"

"I never said I did."


The day passed slowly, marked by the worsening of the smell, the addition of several new prisoners, and the removal of two others, both Union soldiers, one of whom was sobbing. Knapp eventually went back to his fellows, and Harry reclined against the hay bale, happy enough to have sleep.

In the early evening, they were served an unsavory meal—a swill made of beans and greasy salt pork—which Harry consumed and digested gingerly. It began to nag at him that he may have acted too impetuously. Locked away in this barn, he had completely lost control of the situation in Shepherdstown—and deprived himself of any means of keeping informed of developments. But worry at last succumbed to weariness.

When he awoke, it was to the sound of a rooster crowing. He could not imagine a live chicken in the midst of so many soldiers.

Not long after, the barn door swung open, admitting two soldiers with muskets and, trudging angrily after them, Allan Pinkerton.

"Have you gone mad, Raines?"

Harry sat up, yawning. "No, sir, though I've certainly had sufficient reason."

The detective stood over him, hands on hips, looking a trifle silly in his checked suit and bowler hat. He gestured at the other inmates of the barn. "Something like this—it brings dishonor on our service."

"That was not my intention, Mr. Pinkerton." Harry pulled himself up onto the hay bale. "I'm sorry if I have caused you embarrassment or inconvenience."

"You may well have caused me more than that, Captain Raines. Now, please, on your feet. We're leaving."

Harry did not feel like getting up for any reason. "I've confessed to three murders."

"You've not been charged with any crime. The provost marshal sent word to me and a rider to Shepherdstown to determine what the truth of the matter might be. The truth, sir, is that no one in that town suspects you of anything. You were lying wounded on the battlefield when the first of those girls was killed. Now I want an end to this nonsense. What is it you want, Raines?"

Harry stood up, in wobbly fashion. "I want a military judge to come to Shepherdstown, armed with the Federal writ. There's a building I know of we can use for a jail."

"Your request will be considered." Pinkerton looked to the soldier in charge and motioned toward the door. "We should go now."

"Something else, Mister Pinkerton. That young sergeant over there." Pinkerton looked, impatiently. "His name is Knapp and he is charged with desertion. It's an error. I know for a fact that he was on the battlefield. I was there with him. I would like him released."

Pinkerton took off his bowler hat and wiped his brow. "I have not the authority to do that, Harry."

"No, but General McClellan certainly does."

Pinkerton grunted. "Come outside."

They went to a shady place beneath some trees out of the way of the soldiery.

237

"The note you gave me about assassins," Pinkerton said, quietly. "General McClellan is much distressed. He has asked me to assign scouts to investigate. That means you, the Indian Tantou, and whoever else you want."

"You understand that to investigate this threat I must continue to investigate the Reverend Ashby's murder. They are inextricably linked."

"Just do not become distracted by local matters, Harry. General McClellan is the most valuable man in the Union cause. He must be spared."

Harry had no response to that. "I want Sergeant Knapp."

"Why?"

"I need a man in uniform available to me to enforce the Federal writ. I think he's intelligent, certainly cool of head, and no coward. He is innocent of the charges against him. If I am responsible for his release, he will be grateful and, I hope, loyal. Mister Pinkerton, in this war, men like Knapp cannot be spared either."

Pinkerton pursed his lips. "Very well. But you must leave immediately for Shepherdstown."

"I will leave directly upon Sergeant Knapp's release."

"Yes. Done. Send Tantou to headquarters when you need to communicate with me."

"He's an independent fellow. But I will send someone."

They had a view of a wide portion of the battlefield. Pinkerton contemplated it sadly. "If anything happens to General McClellan, Harry, we will lose this war."

Harry and Knapp clattered into town to find a crowd gathered outside Doc Ricketts' office. Harry moved Rocket toward them down German Street at a brisk trot, reining him in at the last moment. A friend, who ran the local bakery, turned to him excitedly. "More bad news, Harry. Peggy Singleton's been shot."

"Peggy Singleton?"

"Aye."

"She's dead?"

"Nearly dead. And almost hanged. But the killer was interrupted, so she survives."

"Where is she?"

"Doc Ricketts is attending to her."

With Knapp and his Spencer repeating rifle leading the way, Harry moved quickly through the crowd and into the office's foyer. "Doctor? It's Harry Raines!"

"Be right with you!" Ricketts called out from his surgery. "Don't come in! The lady is disrobed."

A high-pitched voice spoke after him, punctuating every other word with profanities. He'd heard her before.

Moving to the door, Harry opened it one or two inches, squinting as he peered through the opening. Peggy lay on the doctor's table, naked to the waist, squirming as he used some sort of metal instrument upon her.

Harry considered the situation, then pulled the door fully open and entered. The doctor looked to him with astonished and then angry eyes, and reached to pull a sheet over the girl. Harry took note of profuse bleeding.

"I'm here as a representative of the Federal government," Harry said. "I have military with me and a military judge is on the way. This is an investigation."

"Be quick about it, Harry. She is in pain."

Peggy glared at him, then winced and fell back. Harry put on his spectacles, the better to see her neck. It was roughened and flushed beneath the chin.

"Is the wound mortal?" Harry asked.

The doctor's glower indicated how indiscreet and bumbling he thought the question. "No," he said. "As I have told her. She is shot through the flesh of her right breast with a small caliber weapon—from the side, so it barely penetrated. Her assailant acted in great haste."

"May I see the wound?" Harry asked.

"Harrison Raines," Ricketts said. "You call yourself a gentleman."

"This is a Federal investigation, Doctor. Please indulge me."

Peggy gave vent to more profanity, then lay back, quiet, her eyes flicking back and forth, but avoiding his.

Ricketts held back the bloodstained cloth. Harry stepped forward, putting on his spectacles. Whatever the weapon, it had been relatively kind to her, striking the upper part of her right breast and emerging at an angle, missing the other breast and any vital organ. There were no powder burns, indicating the weapon had been fired at some distance, which may have accounted for the inaccuracy.

Harry stepped back. "Could the shock of the injury have rendered her insensible?"

The doctor nodded. "Yes. Certainly. Otherwise they'd have had a difficult time proceeding with the hanging."

"Yet they failed at that."

"Yes. Thank God. The miller's wife came upon them and they fled."

"This was down by the mill?"

"Not far from where that poor Harding girl was found."

"You said 'They?'"

"I think more than one."

Harry approached the Singleton girl again, hesitating, then taking her hand. To his surprise, she did not resist. "Peggy, I wish you no ill. My purpose is to apprehend whoever did this to you. Did you see him? Them?"

"No. They shot me from the bushes and then one of them took me from behind," she said, pausing to take a deep breath. It made her wince once more. "Next thing I knew, they had a rope around my neck and was trying to haul me up."

"You're sure you didn't see them?"

"Well, one of them maybe. From the back. He was riding a big dark horse. And wore a yellow shirt."

"Hat?"

"Don't remember."

"What color his hair?"

"I don't know. Maybe yellow, too. Damn it all, Mister Raines, I was fighting to breathe." She closed her eyes, her face turning into one large, anguished frown. Her fingernails dug into the flesh of his palm. He waited for this to cease, then withdrew his hand.

Harry turned to Ricketts, who was still cleaning the wound. "What can you do about the pain?"

"Laudanum. Whiskey."

"She's but eighteen."

"Pain's pain."

True enough. "Where were her brothers?"

Ricketts stood straight. "Don't know."

Harry sought Peggy's attention. "Where were your brothers? Where are they now?"

"Headed south—for the Southern army. Days ago. Left me on my own."

"Is there a way to send word to them?"

"Don't think so. Don't care to do so." She was an extremely pretty girl, even in these straits.

Ricketts had fetched a dark brown bottle. He poured an inch or so of it into a glass, then gently put it to Peggy's lips, raising her head.

"Did you find someone for Evangeline?" Harry asked.

"Yes."

"Who?"

"You're looking at her."

"But she refused me when I asked her."

"With her brothers gone, she is in need of money."

"I'll be back," Harry said.

After a search, he found O'Malley at the town apothecary's, buying horse medicine. He introduced Knapp as a friend to the cause. The blacksmith shook the sergeant's hand with great firmness.

"We'll have Federal law here," Harry said. "Soon. No need for Secesh sheriffs."

"That's a blessing," O'Malley said.

"I need quarters for a military judge. His name's Thorne. Colonel Thorne."

"Entler Hotel," said O'Malley, paying for his purchase. "They had some wounded in there, but most of them's gone."

The building was right across German Street from Klostermann's tavern.

"That will do nicely. Have you heard about Peggy Singleton?"

"The whole town has." O'Malley picked up his parcel and

241

nodded toward the door. "She lives?" he said, when they were outside on the wooden sidewalk.

"Yes. It's a peculiar wound. Messy, but in no way dangerous. One would almost think it self-inflicted, but there are no powder burns."

"Let us continue in good Herr Klostermann's tavern."

While the three of them waited for Klostermann to pour their beers, Harry asked O'Malley if Tantou had returned.

"No, sir. Not a sign of him."

"We need to talk to this Lemuel," Harry said, as the glasses were set down.

"We need to stop these killings," O'Malley said. "The other girls—Susan Hodges, Rachel Fairbrother, Selma Keedy—we must persuade them to leave Shepherdstown as soon as possible."

"But how?" Harry asked. "What they probably have in common is sin with the Reverend. They won't listen to us—surely their parents will not long abide us—if we broach the subject in that vein."

Knapp was following all this with interest—and some puzzlement—but Harry didn't want to stop to explain.

"Then we should seek another vein," said O'Malley. He put his mind to this. "Maybe we should go to all the families with daughters that age in the town. There aren't that many."

"There are enough to be days persuading them," Harry said, glumly. "And where would we send them?"

"The Army could help," Knapp said. "We've got a lot of empty ambulances now. Send 'em to Frederick to help in the hospitals."

Harry shook his head. "Susan's people are Secesh. Selma's are Quakers. We can't be dragooning young women for the Federal service. It's not come to that."

Klostermann had been hovering nearby, and came forward to refill their glasses. "You any closer to finding out who's doing this?"

"Not now, but we hope to be soon," Harry said.

"You still think it's political, or vengeful wrath on account of their sins?"

"I was thinking the latter," said Harry, after taking a sip of beer. "But it's since occurred to me that all the victims were Union folk."

"Not Peggy Singleton," Klostermann said.

"She still lives," Harry said.

"Someone shot her," said the tavern keeper.

"True enough." Harry stood, emptying his glass.

"She still at Doc Ricketts'?" O'Malley asked.

Harry nodded. "Maybe she should be watched over."

"Colonel Thorne, the Judge Advocate man, will be bringing a provost guard with him," Knapp said. "Dozen men or more, probably. Maybe we can borrow some to watch over the ladies."

"If you could arrange it," said Harry, "I'd be obliged."

"Where are you going?" O'Malley asked.

"Going to call on the Singleton family."

"But there's no one there."

"More hospitable that way."


The Singletons' place was a mile or more up the Martinsburg Road from Harry's farm—a dilapidated wreck of an establishment with several outbuildings near collapse and a house in only slightly better repair. Clearly, the two brothers and Peggy had moved here for shelter, not livelihood.

How then were they supporting themselves?

Harry rode past the holding, noting a front gate half off its posts, and guiding Rocket through it.

There were two cows, standing in the water of a small pond just inside the snake-rail fence that bordered the property. Supremely content, they stood without a hint of movement or wish for it. Nothing else on this run-down farm moved either—just buzzing insects and a bird or two.

He was fired upon almost immediately, the round coming close but striking the leather and wood of Harry's saddle rather than human or animal flesh.

Rocket jerked forward and broke into a gallop away from the house. Keeping low, Harry steered him to the property's snake-rail fence, jumped it, and hurried into the trees. Tying the animal fast to a low hanging branch, he moved on through the little woods toward the rear of the house.

There was a lean-to there, under which was tethered a scrawny roan horse. Beside it stood a large dark one, with the feet of a dray.

Entering the house, Harry paused at the foot of the stairs leading to the second floor, where he suspected the shot had come from. He could not decide whether to take a fuller reconnaissance of the ground floor, ascend the stairs, and confront the intruder, or take a chair and wait for the intruder to descend. He chose the latter course. He'd know exactly what to expect—a man coming down the stairs—whereas he'd no idea what he might encounter if he went up to the second floor himself. He chose a place where he had a clear view of the stairs and also the front door. If another party were to arrive unannounced, he'd have ample time to prepare an appropriate greeting.

Harry pulled back the hammer on his Colt with his thumb and rested the long barrel on his knee.

His assailant came thumping down the stairs a moment later. He had long hair somewhere between light brown and blond in color and wore boots and denims but no shirt.

"Lemuel!"

The youth looked to Harry but, seeing the pistol, kept on going, slamming the front door back against the house. Harry fired his pistol, seconds too late, more in frustration and anger at his own foolishness than any desire to kill or maim.

Disentangling himself from the chair—knocking it over in the process—he lunged through the door after the fugitive, finding the front yard empty and hearing no untoward sound.

Of a sudden, there was one—a crack like that in the game of baseball when the bat struck a ball.

It was immediately followed by a wailing yell. Harry hurried in its direction, around the side of the house. There, holding his long Buffalo gun, stood Tantou. Lemuel lay on the ground, clutching his head.

The Metis was examining the stock of his weapon, as if worrying it had been damaged.

"Where have you been?" Harry demanded.

"Here," Tantou said. "Waiting for him to come out."

"Did you not see me go in?"

"Yes, I did, Harry Raines."

"Did you not wonder what might happen?"

"Yes. I was curious."

"Why didn't you help me?"

"I had decided to when he came out of the house. I had to hit him with the rifle because he looked to be a very fast runner."

Lemuel was paying no attention to them, occupied as he was with his pain.

"You said you would bring him in."

"No, Harry Raines. I said I would find him. And so I did."

"Where?"

"On the river road. Near the mill."

"Well, why didn't you bring him in?"

"I thought it would be interesting to see where he would go."

"And where did he go?"

"Here."

Harry shook his head. Tantou turned away and looked about the yard. There were folded pieces of paper littering the ground near Lemuel, who had stopped his writhing and was watching them, though groggily. Tantou picked up the papers and brought them to Harry. "Letters," he said.

Examining one of them, and then another, and then a third, Harry came swiftly to a conclusion. They were addressed to Peggy, they expressed both ardor for her and for the Southern cause, and they were signed "G.," as was the warning about assassins.

The Reverend Ashby's first name was George.

Harry went and stood over Lemuel. "I'm placing you under arrest," he said. "Under Federal custody."

"Why?" The boy's voice was weak.

"Murders."

"I didn't kill nobody."

"You just tried to kill me."

"I didn't kill nobody." With that, Lemuel lapsed into unconsciousness.

# Twenty-Five

Slinging Lemuel over the big dray horse, they took him back to Shepherdstown. He didn't regain consciousness, and for a moment Harry considered taking him to Doc Ricketts'. He decided instead to install the boy at Entler's and send the physician over to him later.

With Lemuel safely locked in an upstairs room of the hotel, Harry took Tantou, O'Malley, and Sergeant Knapp in tow as escort and rode out to the Harding place—a sprawling establishment noted for the handsomeness of the galleried, three-story-high brick house and the tall oaks that surrounded it. The mansion was as close to the Potomac as Harry's farm and had a dock with a small sailing skiff and a long rowing boat moored to it.

Mr. Harding was at home, in the midst of a midday meal. He was less than happy to receive Harry and his party, but did so, taking a few more bites of his stew and then ushering the four of them into his study, which served as office for his many enterprises.

He seated himself behind his immense desk, inviting the others to do as they pleased. Harry took a large leather chair directly opposite the man.

"Well, Mister Raines, why don't you explain this intrusion," said Harding, displeasure expressed as much by his huge, black eyebrows as with his tone.

"We have taken a young man into custody—Lemuel Krause."

Harding slammed his fist down on the desk top, causing a glass ink stand to rattle.

"Lemuel Krause. Lemuel Krause. Should have known."

246

"There is at this point only suspicion," Harry hastened to say. "But enough to hold him."

"Based on what?"

"We caught him at the Singleton place, after he fired a shot at me. He'd been going through Peggy Singleton's things. He took some letters."

"Letters? You mean those bumpkin Singletons can read?"

"Mr. Harding, Peggy's been shot—could have been killed. She's the latest victim. The letters were to her from the Reverend Ashby."

Harding leaned closer, eyebrows down, face darkening. "Signifying what?"

Harry realized the trail he'd started down here led directly off a cliff. He needed a lie—and in a hurry. "In the church, the Reverend had a sort of club, for young ladies. He offered them moral guidance at critical points in their young lives. Sometimes he wrote letters to them—apparently."

"And Ann was in this 'club?'"

"I believe so, sir. So were the other girls who were attacked."

"You are saying that Lucinda Weverton had turned to the Reverend for moral guidance? Lucinda, who's been tramping out with soldiers? And that Secesh trash Peggy Singleton? Are you saying, Raines, that they and my sweet Ann were in the same church group dedicated to virtue? Have you lost all your senses? You were shot in the head. Is this the result?"

"Mr. Harding, I am in no way equating the virtue of your daughter with that of Lucinda Weverton. The Reverend Ashby, apparently, ministered to each in his own way. It may be that the Reverend offered Ann advice and solace after she spurned the attentions of Lemuel Krause."

"You say the Army has taken him into custody on suspicion. Suspicion of what?"

"As of this moment, the attack upon Peggy Singleton. But I feel strongly that the murders and the attack on Peggy Singleton are all connected. Which is why I have come to you."

"To tell me you think Lemuel Krause did all these killings?"

"No, sir. To ask your help. There are three other girls the

247

Reverend was ministering to. Selma Keedy, Susan Hodges, and Rachel Fairbrother. I would have them flee this place until the matter is resolved. I lack the stature to persuade them to leave—or persuade their parents to allow it. Especially those of Southern sentiment. You are a man respected throughout the community."

"You expect me to go to these people and tell them to remove their daughters from this town, lest they suffer the same fate as Ann?"

"It would be a most useful thing to do."

Harding was struggling, not with his thoughts but with his emotions. His grief was still writ large on his hard face—as though it were now a permanent condition. He rose and, head down, took two paces across the room. Then he stopped, staring at Harry as if he truly did think him a madman. "But Raines, you said you have locked up Lemuel Krause in the Entler Hotel. And under guard, yes?"

"Yes."

"Then the danger to these ladies must be past."

"Harding's only being logical," O'Malley said, as they all trooped into Klostermann's tavern, taking places at the near corner of the bar. "If your theorizing about a wronged woman's vengeance is correct, and Lemuel has indeed been her instrument, then his confinement spares the young ladies."

Hugo Klostermann brought whiskey and beer, and lingered.

"Theories are not certainty," Harry said, lowering his voice, as the tavern was quite full despite the early hour. "Until we are certain, I fear for them."

"What about this warning sent to Ashby?" O'Malley asked. "Assassination. Generals. There's more murder to be looked for in that than in adultery."

"Which general is supposed to be assassinated?" Sergeant Knapp asked. "I can't believe the Secesh government would want to have any of them removed—especially McClellan."

"Why is that?" Hugo asked.

"He's the South's best weapon," Harry responded. "Having

him in command of the Eastern armies is as good as having an extra half million men added to the Rebel cause. He could have pinned Lee against the river and taken the army of Northern Virginia in detail if he had moved. But he didn't budge. He still sits at Pry House. Remove McClellan and replace him with one of the generals out West, then the South would find itself in real trouble."

"Lincoln will replace him," Tantou said.

"One would have hoped," Harry said. "But I certainly wouldn't look to Richmond to want to hasten the process with an assassin's bullet. It's far more logical that Ashby and those poor girls died for their sins. Yet . . ."

"Those who were murdered were from Union families," said Tantou, knocking back his whiskey. "All from the same tribe. The Southern girl—she was not hurt. Not badly."

O'Malley nodded. "If this is vengeance, it does seem to have a political point of view."

Harry lighted one of his small cigars, focusing on the smoke from his first puff. "Where does the family of Selma Keedy stand?"

"There's only her father, but he's with Lincoln," O'Malley said. "Got two boys in the war. With a regiment at Fortress Monroe."

Harry knew the Fairbrothers to be anti-slavery—Rachel especially. She had taken a considerable liking to Caesar Augustus—just as Evangeline's white mother had. "And Susan Hodges?"

"Secesh," said O'Malley. "And firmly so."

Harry thought upon this, as Klostermann refreshed all their glasses. "We have to protect them," Harry said.

"It is none of my business, Harry," said Hugo. "But how can you be so certain about this? You said you could tell by the looks on their faces at the Reverend's funeral. Many women were saddened by the Reverend's death. Many loved to hear him preach."

"But not all found such favor," Harry said. "These girls— they're the prettiest in town."

"I think we ought to investigate the possibility it was an

outraged father," O'Malley said. "Mr. Harding's right enough capable of killing the Reverend for such a reason."

"But not his own daughter," Harry said.

"Maybe the Reverend's death isn't related to the others, much as it seems otherwise," O'Malley responded.

This colloquy was advancing nothing. Harry emptied his glass. "I'm going to talk to those girls. I'd appreciate it if you'd accompany me, Sergeant Knapp. Anyone else who feels like coming, I'd be obliged."

"Got to get back to my forge," said O'Malley. "The Army'll string me up if I don't deliver as promised." He nodded his thanks to the tavernkeeper.

Tantou stood even straighter than usual. "I will go now to the Hodges', Harry Raines, if you will tell me where that is."

"Why there?"

"She is in the most danger." Tantou put on his wide-brimmed hat and walked out of the tavern, prompting others to move out of his way.

Klostermann waved farewell, and moved on down the bar to attend to another customer.

"All right, Knapp, let's do our best," Harry said.

Happily, Rachel Fairbrother had been sent to her sister in Chambersburg, Pennsylvania, when it appeared there might be a battle. Her mother did not expect her back until the middle of the next month at the earliest.

"Her sister has given birth to her second child," she said, as they stood on her front porch. "Rachel is helping out." She looked worriedly at Knapp, who smiled amiably in response. "Is something wrong, Mr. Raines?"

"The Army is investigating the unfortunate occurrences in Shepherdstown," Harry said, offering his own smile of reassurance. "I understand Rachel was a friend of Ann Harding's. I hoped to ask her a few questions—about people Ann may have been friendly with."

"Oh dear."

"I can wait until she returns."

"I could send for her."

"No, Mrs. Fairbrother, please don't do that. The new child should come first." It was pleasant to think of a new life, rather than the latest death.

"Yes. You are right."

"No need for haste. She should stay in Chambersburg as long as she likes."

"Yes. Yes. Good day to you then, Mr. Raines. We remember your mother with much affection."

"As do I, Mrs. Fairbrother."

Selma Keedy lived down river, on a farm near the Harper's Ferry Road. Selma was in the back yard of the place, helping her mother with the washing. Mrs. Keedy greeted them and their interruption with small welcome.

"What brings you to our farm, Harrison Raines? I do not recollect that you have visited it before."

"I wish a word with Selma, if I might," said Harry, dismounting Rocket. "About Ann Harding."

"We've had little truck with the almighty Hardings. Nor they with us." The woman, who had a bent back and was partially lame, threw a patchy sheet over the line. "No more than we ever had with the almighty Raineses."

Selma, who had hair nearly as dark as Ann Harding, and was just as pretty, looked from Harry to Knapp, her eyes lingering on the latter. Then she turned to assist her mother with the clothespins.

"We were all members of the church together," Harry said.

"It was not a church or pastor I favored," Mrs. Keedy said, gruffly. "We went because we're Presbyterian and it was near, and because Selma had friends there."

"Including Ann Harding?" Harry asked.

"I knew her from the church fellowship," Selma said. "But that's all. What do you want to know, Mr. Raines?" She gave Knapp a quick but friendly glance.

"Can you think of anyone who would want to take her life? Or Lucinda Weverton's?" Harry said.

"No, sir. I just figured it was someone doing the work of the Devil." Another sheet went over the line, this one in better condition. "I was more the friend of poor Lucinda.

251

She went the Devil's way, but the wages of sin were too harshly paid."

Harry surveyed the unkempt yard. He suspected much of the work about the place had been long neglected. "Where is Mr. Keedy this day?"

"He's upstairs," said Mrs. Keedy. "The ague's on him. Third time since spring and the worst."

"You've no one else to work the farm?"

"Hired men for the harvest—when you can find 'em. And a damn poor harvest it is. We had our wheat field trampled, cattle taken, pigs and chickens, too. They stripped our apple trees in a day."

"They?"

"Soldiers. Both sides."

Rocket stepped nervously to the side. Harry took a tighter grip on the reins. "Have you changed your views?"

"Do that now?" said Mrs. Keedy. "After all these battles? So many dead? I want the war to end, Mr. Raines. But not by givin' those damn Rebels their way. They're the worst people in Shepherdstown. When we get our own state, we ought to run 'em all off—as far into Virginia as we can get 'em."

These were good people. Harry remembered that now. "Mrs. Keedy, I've come for another reason." He nodded toward Knapp. "The Army's taking a hand in trying to stop these murders." He paused. "We've done some investigating. We don't know why, but the killers have been following a pattern. The girls were faithful followers of the Reverend Ashby's ministry." Selma turned away, blushing. "They were also uncommonly pretty. As Selma is. Mrs. Keedy, we believe your daughter is in danger. I've come to urge you to send her away as soon as possible. If you've no kin or friends to take her, my friend Clara Barton, I'm sure, could find her work as a nurse in the many hospitals in Frederick."

"What kind of danger?"

"I regret to say, in danger of precisely what befell Ann Harding and Lucinda Weverton."

Selma appeared finally to comprehend what he had been saying. She stepped back from her work, stricken.

"Why did you not say this when you rode up?" Mrs. Keedy said. "We have kin in Buckeystown. I will send her there. Might she have an escort?"

Knapp nodded. "I'll spare a trooper."

The Hodges' farm was off the Charlestown Road, some five miles southeast of Shepherdstown. Asa Hodges had owned two slaves, but sold them off after John Brown's raid on Harper's Ferry.

They were at least a mile from the place when they heard the gunshots.

253

# Twenty-Six

Arriving at a gallop, Harry and Knapp flung themselves from their saddles and hurried up the steps to the Hodges' porch. The front door was standing open. Pistol drawn, with Knapp following, Harry stepped inside, only to be immediately confronted by a tall figure with a long rifle in his hands.

"Tantou! Why are you here?"

The Metis stepped back, lowering his rifle butt to the floor. "I told you I would be here."

He had. "What happened?"

"A man fired a shot at the girl, the one named Susan. Rifle shot. Long range."

"Is she all right? Where is she?"

Tantou nodded to a hallway behind him. "In a bedroom with all her family. You should talk to them, please, because they think I did it."

"Was she hit?"

"No. But she is very scared."

"Did you get a good look at the shooter?"

"Good enough to hit him."

"Hit him? Did you kill him?" Harry took a step back to the door.

"I don't think so. He rode away."

"Which way?"

"North. Into the trees. Could have gone to Shepherdstown. Could have gone to Harper's Ferry."

"You didn't pursue him?"

"May have been more of them. Wanted to protect Susan Hodges. Wait for you."

Harry swore. They might have ended the matter right then and there. "Did he have yellow hair, this shooter?"

"Don't know. Wore a hat."

Harry swore again—at himself. He was thinking it might be Lemuel. But Lemuel was locked up in Shepherdstown.

Mister Hodges was coming down the hall. The old man's face darkened at the sight of Sergeant Knapp.

"So you are a Yankee agent, like they say," said the father.

"I'm an Army scout, Mister Hodges. I'm here on official business. We came to warn you—about what just happened."

"Arriving too late."

"Tantou was here," Harry said, gesturing to the Metis.

"He's with you?"

"Another Army scout. General McClellan will vouch for him."

The father moved closer. "I don't doubt that he would, Raines," said Mr. Hodges. "Where I think you're lying is about coming here to warn us. I think you came here to run us off—just like you Yankee bastards ran off the Singletons."

"The Singletons have a new place—down by mine." It was a pointless thing to say.

Hodges was nowhere near Tantou's height, or even Harry's, but he thrust his head forward intimidatingly. "Old man Singleton and his wife had to flee to kin down in the Shenandoah Valley after you Federals fired their house. You ran the boys out of the county and probably into the Confederate army."

"Peggy Singleton's still here."

"And she got shot for her troubles—nearly killed. Well, we ain't going to budge a step. We built this place ourselves. Every plank and brick. This is the sovereign state of Virginia—late of the United States. Your army got no writ here. You're the invaders."

"I am a Virginian, sir," Harry said. "My family's been in Virginia since long before yours wandered in." Another stupid thing to say.

"Your pappy and brother are with Lee, where you should be!"

255

"Mr. Hodges," Harry said. "I came here to say one thing, and I'll say it again. Susan's life is in danger. If you won't send her away, keep her in the house at all times. Keep a guard on your place. Be vigilant. That shooter might have killed her if Tantou hadn't intervened."

Harry knew Hodges at heart to be a fair and rational man, however wayward on the issues of secession and slavery.

"You're telling me, Raines—on your mother's grave—that he wasn't one of your men?"

"Yes. I don't know who he was. I'd like to try to find out, but instead I'm standing here arguing with you about the safety of your daughter."

There was a rider coming up outside, fast. Harry stepped back, opening the door wider, to see Jim O'Malley gallop into the front yard, pulling up sharply at the porch steps. He remained in the saddle.

"Big trouble, Harry. Old man Harding's got half the town stirred up and they're fixing to make a move on the Entler Hotel to give Lemuel what Harding says he's got coming."

"What're you doing here, then?" Harry asked. "People'll listen to you. You should be back in town trying to calm them."

"Calming them is going to take every man we can lay hands on, including you."

Harry looked back at Mr. Hodges, who shouted, "Go on! Get off my property now!"

The sun had set by the time the four of them trotted into Shepherdstown, their progress down German Street halted abruptly by the crowd gathered outside the Entler.

Sergeant Knapp moved to the fore, calling out, "U.S. Army! Make way!"

To Harry's surprise, people began to step aside, but sullenly. One large man who recognized Harry grabbed his stirrup. "We want Krause!" he complained. "The Army won't let us near him."

"He's in their custody. Harm one of those soldiers and we'll have a full division in town." Knapp, Tantou, and O'Malley were moving on ahead of him.

256

"How's it their business?" the complainer said. "Ann Harding was a civilian."

"Army's only law we've got at the moment. Where's Harding?"

"Down by the hotel."

"You should go home," Harry said, kicking his stirrup loose from the man's grip and urging his horse forward. There were women in this assemblage. He looked to Klostermann's tavern and saw people spilling out from the doorway.

At the hotel, the crowd was so thick there was no parting them. Harry dismounted and handed his reins to Tantou. Instead of toward the hotel entrance, he moved obliquely to the right, approaching Harding from the side.

"You've got to call a halt to this, Mr. Harding."

"I only want to talk to the boy. These soldiers won't let me."

"This mob . . ."

"They're quiet. But numerous enough to make our feelings known to that colonel."

"Did you stir up all these folks yourself?"

"Tend to your own business, Raines."

"I am. I've just come from the Hodges' place. There was another shooting this afternoon. Susan Hodges escaped injury, but—"

Harding turned and gripped him hard by both shoulders. "Another shooting. You see? We've got to put an end to this."

Harry took hold of the man's wrist, trying to push him back. "You're not thinking straight, Mr. Harding. This happened in late afternoon, long after Lemuel was locked up."

There was the sound of breaking glass, coming from around the side of the Entler. People began shouting, and surging that way. Harding turned to follow and Harry let himself be carried along.

A soldier with fixed bayonet stood at the bottom of the stairs but quickly began to back away, raising his weapon toward the ceiling. Harry found himself pushed against the railing as they ascended to the second floor, and for a moment

257

thought the wood might give way and send him tumbling to the floor.

The man to his right, apparently recently arrived from Klostermann's judging by the smell of him, stumbled and fell flat against the stairs, easing the pressure against Harry. He stepped over the man's head and plunged on, hurrying along just behind the leaders of this procession.

There were of course no cells in the Entler—just individual rooms that could be locked from either side. The invaders, not knowing which was Krause's abode, began knocking open every one of them.

"He's in the back!" someone shouted. "On the right—at the end of the hall!"

They were about to kick it in when a large figure pushed past Harry and went to the door. It was Harding, and he had a large revolver in his hand.

"Now!" he said.

It took three kicks, but the door gave way, slamming against the wall.

Harding and three or four others rushed in. Then came the cry, "He's gone!"

# Twenty-Seven

H arding organized several search parties, dispatching them
in directions of his own choosing. Knapp rightly called
them "lynch" parties, but there was no stopping them, and the
military simply stood aside.

Disgusted, Harry went directly across the street to Klostermann's tavern. There was no room at the crowded bar, and then
suddenly there was, as customers took note of Tantou, Knapp,
and O'Malley following behind Harry, and still heavily armed.

"A bottle of whiskey, Hugo," Harry said. "We're in a thirsty
mood. If you haven't Old Overholt, your best will do."

"You seem in a bad mood."

"Yes. Indeed I am. Have you Old Overholt?"

"Best I got is some Tennessee sour mash a Rebel officer
left behind."

"That'll do nicely," Harry said.

Klostermann returned quickly with two bottles, putting one
under the bar. He filled four glasses quickly.

"What happened?" the bartender asked.

"Can't believe you haven't heard. Lemuel Krause escaped
from Entler's."

"I brought food over there 'round noon time. He seemed
locked up pretty well tight then."

"'Pretty well' wasn't quite good enough." Harry drank, but
not so quickly as Knapp, who had emptied his glass.

"Better get back and help the colonel sort this out," he said.
"Where'll you be? Here?"

"Yes." Harry reconsidered this, then finished his drink,
poured another, and downed that. "Maybe, later."

"Where're you going?" Klostermann asked.

259

"Going to where I should have in the first place," Harry said. "Would you join me, Tantou?" He looked to O'Malley. "Could you stay here and keep an eye on things? Matters may well get out of hand—especially if they catch him."

"Where'll you be?" O'Malley asked.

"Not far."

They went out the back of Klostermann's, crossing the yard and turning right at the next street. Tantou slung his long rifle over his shoulder, then took out his long-barreled .44 caliber revolver.

"We are looking for Lemuel Krause?" he asked.

"We are looking for the truth. I'm going to visit someone in a house just up the street. I'd appreciate it if you would station yourself outside in case someone has followed us and intends to interrupt my conversation."

"Yes. I will do that, Harry Raines."

They reached the Presbyterian Church. "Here," Harry said.

Harry rapped gently on the door. He'd left his Colt revolver in his belt, though he wondered if this wasn't a mistake. Lemuel had fired at him first that morning.

Martha Ashby opened the door slowly, but evidenced no hostility.

"Is Lemuel here?" he asked.

"Is he why you came?" she asked, quietly.

"Part of the reason."

There was uncertainty in her eyes, but she stepped back, allowing him to enter. "In truth, Harrison, I am surprised that you haven't called upon me sooner."

"I've been in no hurry to do this, Mrs. Ashby. Not under the present circumstances."

"Harrison, your mother and I were very good friends—the times when she was here."

"That has been on my mind for some time."

"Come into the parlor, Harrison. I'll bring refreshment."

"Is Lemuel here?"

"No. Of course not."

Harry had not eaten since breakfast. This reminder of that made him a little dizzy. He seated himself on her horsehair sofa, leaving the rocker with its comfortable cushions for her.

She returned with biscuits and jam—and tea. Setting this on a small table, she poured him a cup and put butter and cherry preserves on two biscuits. He ate them quickly, took a sip of tea, then leaned back, folding his arms, uncertain how to begin.

"Where is Lemuel then?" he asked, finally.

"I was told soldiers were keeping him in the Entler House— that he's accused of those murders."

"Not by the Army, Mrs. Ashby. Only in the case of your husband. Harding believes Lemuel killed his daughter. Harding stirred up a small mob down on German Street. I think a lynching is intended."

The widow blanched. "Lynching? Lemuel?"

"He escaped, Mrs. Ashby. I don't know how. He must have had help."

"And you thought he'd come here?"

"He's been working for you."

"I needed someone, with George gone. There's so much to tend to."

Harry drank more tea. "Mrs. Ashby. There'll be a new preacher here soon. You'll have to move."

"I know that very well," she said. "Lemuel was helping me pack things. Move them out to my little farm."

"Is that where you're going?" Harry asked. "You plan to work that farm?"

She smiled sweetly. "That was my intention. Lemuel was going to help me work it. Maybe another hired man. It was an agreeable prospect." She shrugged. "I've nothing else."

Harry studied her face for any sign of deceit—anything not normal. If she had loved her husband as much as Harry had assumed, her anger and sorrow ought not to have much diminished. But she was serving him tea as cheerily as she might on any neighborly occasion.

He took a deep breath. "Mrs. Ashby, your relationship with Lemuel has occasioned some talk in the town."

Her expression remained unchanged. "I am aware of that,

261

Harrison. This is a small community, even with so much soldiery about. Gossip poisons it quickly. But I assure you, such talk is calumny. I like the boy. He had been a help to me and I hope I have been that to him. But it has been an innocent friendship. He loved Ann Harding. Still does. They were going to run off together."

"Can that be so? She spurned him."

"Her father spurned him."

"But he had no prospects. I can't imagine her settling down with a penniless farmhand."

"He is not well educated, Harrison, but he is very smart— and hardworking, and ambitious. I was going to take them in on my farm. Provide them with a beginning."

"He took a shot at me, you know. Why is that?"

She shrugged. "I cannot say. He has been much picked upon. Were you armed? Were you pursuing him?"

"I had gone to the Singleton place. What would he be doing there—this swain so smitten with Ann?"

"I cannot say."

Harry shifted on the couch, which he was beginning to find uncomfortable. "I hesitate to say this, Mrs. Ashby. There are people who are of the mind—who think it credible—that you and Lemuel might be capable of dark deeds, occasioned by your husband's——"

"Dark deeds, Harrison? Do you mean these murders?" She refilled his teacup. "You've known me since childhood. Do you seriously think me capable of that?"

"I am making no accusations, Mrs. Ashby. I am merely acquainting you with the nature of the talk. But there is damning evidence. Hoof prints at more than one of the murder sites that might have been made by Lemuel's big farm horse. Women's foot prints as small as your own. Lemuel had reason to be out of his temper, given the humiliating way he was treated by Ann Harding's father. And all the girls who died had something in common, and it wasn't just that they were young and very pretty. They had a strong affection for the Reverend Ashby. You would not be the first wife provoked by such shameful conduct."

262

There was a muffled report, sounding more like a child's popgun than a lethal weapon. But Harry supposed that could be a function of distance. Two more such pops followed.

"Should we be alarmed?" she asked.

"We are in a sea of armed men, Mrs. Ashby. It's surprising we have not heard more."

She began to rock back and forth, slightly at first, then more vigorously. "Harrison, I have long been aware of my husband's indiscretions. How could I not have been? He brought one girl into the house when I was off at the farm. But murder him, and all those lovely young girls? You're suggesting that I wanted revenge and Lemuel was my instrument. Merciful heavens. As I told you, Ann and Lem were in love."

"Mrs. Ashby, there is talk of lynching. Lemuel is the object of this maniacal pursuit. You may be in jeopardy as well. If the truth is on your side, we must bring it to bear."

She set down her tea cup. He caught himself wondering if she might have a pistol. He knew the Reverend had owned a Remington revolver.

"As I say, Harrison, I've known about the Reverend's sinful proclivity for some years. If I had wished to send him to his just reward, I would have done it years ago—when I first learned."

She rose, going over to a small desk in the corner. Opening it, she pulled forth one drawer, removing from it a small journal book with a red leather cover. Then she reached beneath the desk, struggling a moment, then producing a similarly diminutive volume, but bound in gray.

Both she handed to Harry. "The one on top, as best I could keep it, contains my record of my late husband's female friendships, commencing in 1854. I doubt there's a libertine in New Orleans so prolific in his indiscretions, yet in our little town, no one—few, anyway—ever knew."

Harry opened the book, but closed it again with no more than a glance at the first page. His eyes met hers.

"The second, Harrison, was kept by the Reverend. It is a compilation of the identities and activities of people he knew or suspected were operatives in the cause of the Confederacy.

You are, are you not, of similar service in Father Abraham's crusade."

"You know I am that."

"I would expect nothing less from a son of your mother."

"Thank you."

"Please put it to good use. I didn't know what to do with it. This town is so divided. I feared it might bring me harm if found."

Harry didn't want to deal with that now. He slipped the book into his coat pocket, but kept the journal of indiscretions in his hand.

Mrs. Ashby did not return to her seat. She stepped back, leaning against the desk. "Go ahead and read it, Harrison. You will find that he did not only favor attractive young women. There are attractive women of all sorts abundant in this valley. One of the names you will find surprising and shocking."

He glanced through some of the pages, stopping abruptly at one. He studied the entry there with something akin to horror. "I do not believe this."

"I forgave her. She was my friend."

"It cannot be. No." He continued on through the book, as though there might be some mitigation to be found in the later pages. There was not.

He closed the journal and stared at the cover but it began to blur.

"That was how it was with the Reverend, Harrison. No woman was immune to his attentions and attractions. I'm sorry."

"You are not bringing her with us?" Tantou asked, as Harry came up to him.

"No."

"You believe she was no part of this?"

"I will not know what to think until I can talk to Lemuel, but she has filled my mind with doubts."

"I heard gunshots from over by the river."

"I heard them. Couldn't tell where they were from."

264

Tantou stopped and looked back at the Ashby house. "Harry Raines, something is wrong."

The light had gone from the parlor windows. All was still. "What do you mean?" Harry asked.

"We are the only ones here."

Harry looked up and down the street. "Yes. Very perceptive of you."

"Parties of armed, angry men have gone out looking for Lemuel Krause."

"Yes."

"None have come here, where he worked. Where he enjoys friendship with Mrs. Ashby. We come. No one else."

"Perhaps it was thought she's been bothered enough."

"I don't think so, Harry Raines."

They continued on to German Street in silence. There were a few people still about, and several soldiers outside of the Entler Hotel, but, with so many on the road, the town otherwise appeared as it might have at this hour before the war.

Klostermann's tavern still had customers. Among them was Jim O'Malley.

"Where did you go?" he asked, as Hugo quickly filled their glasses.

"The widow Ashby's."

"Learn anything?"

"Nothing useful."

"Half the town is out looking for Krause," Klostermann said.

"Have you seen Sergeant Knapp?"

"He's out looking for Lemuel as well," Hugo said. "A troop of Union cavalry came in to reinforce those at the Entler and he took some of them with him."

"I heard gunshots."

"They came from across the river. Don't know what they meant."

"Where's Mr. Harding?"

"With all the others—out looking for the boy."

"With so many searching, why have none gone to the widow Ashby's? She is his friend. He works for her."

Klostermann grinned. "Word was you had gone there."

"Where would that word have come from? I told no one."

"This is a small town, Harry," Klostermann said. He set another bottle on the bar top. "Here. This whiskey is on the house."

"You're very generous, Hugo," O'Malley remarked.

"Always for friends."

Tantou stiffened—his head cocked to one side.

"What is it?" Harry asked.

"Some of them now come back," said the Metis.

They took their whiskey out onto the sidewalk. Down German Street hill came an odd procession: Union cavalry at the fore, then some townspeople running along on foot, then a group of mounted civilians.

Knapp, seeing Harry, turned his horse to the side of the street and dismounted. "They've killed him. Nothing I could do to stop them."

Harry looked to the civilians on horseback, their faces fiendish in the light of the torches they carried. Mr. Harding, riding a huge bay horse, led this group. As they passed, Harry noted that one of the mounts bore its rider lengthwise across the saddle, bound hand and foot to it—long yellow hair aflutter with the trot.

"Mr. Harding!" Harry shouted. "What have you done?"

"We have done justice, Raines," Harding said, as the column moved past. "There will be no more of these murders."

After these people had gone by, Harry moved close to Knapp. "How did this happen?" he asked.

"Don't know. We came upon 'em as they were returning on the Charles Town Road. He was headed south, Harry."

"Was he armed?"

"Harding says so."

Harry turned to O'Malley. "How could he have gotten a gun?"

"There're quite a few at hand, Harry. The Confederate wounded brought in piles of them."

"The gunshots came from across the river. Yet they caught Lemuel heading south."

O'Malley shrugged. "It's a curious night."

Harry gulped down the rest of the whiskey and set his glass by the door. "I can take no more of it. I'm going home." As he swung into the saddle, a great weight of fatigue came over him. He had neglected his brother Robert too long.

"What about Lemuel Krause?" Tantou asked, going to his own horse.

"In the morning."

Rocket moved into an easy trot.

Reaching his farm, Harry and Tantou went to the stables, unsaddling their mounts and putting them in stalls with fresh straw, feed, and water. Rocket needed a rubdown, but that, too, could wait until morning.

There was another horse in the stable that did not belong to him. He walked very quickly to the house.

Robert was sleeping, but quickly waked at the touch of Harry's hand upon his shoulder. "Are you well, Bob?"

"I have slept most of this day."

"And the child?"

"She has been much with me. Brought me supper. Bread and beef. And lemonade."

"You have fared better than I today."

Robert gripped his forearm in friendly fashion. "We should go home, brother."

"One day soon you will. But this is my home."

Robert relented in his hold on Harry's arm. "That was Mother's wish."

"There's a strange horse in the stable. Where's it from?"

"Don't know. Been sleeping."

Harry stood straight. "Sleep some more."

He found Evangeline in her own bedchamber, her slumber one of gentle breathing. He was fortunate that no misfortune had visited his house in his absence. He should not neglect them again.

Tantou had remained outside, deciding he would sleep well armed upon the porch. Harry went wearily to his own bedchamber.

The naked woman he encountered beneath his sheet stirred as he settled at her side.

"I've come back, plantation man."

She put a hand on his chest. He reached to touch it, then lifted his head to look upon her face. "I am pleased to see you, Allie."

"Where have you been?"

"Let us talk in the morning."

He kissed her, then rolled back on his side. There had been two entries in Martha Ashby's journal that had shocked him.

# Twenty-Eight

Harry knew the sounds of this house better even than he had come to know the flesh of the woman who lay sleeping beside him. There was someone coming up the stairs, but walking slowly, with pauses. The light outside the window was still a dim gray.

He had put his Colt in his boot. He brought it to hand and quietly rose from the bed. Allie shifted her position slightly, but showed no other sign of wakefulness. Going to the door, which he had left partially open, he stepped into the hall, closing the door behind him just as his brother Robert reached the top of the stairs. Harry lowered his pistol.

"Lazarus rises," Harry said.

"My thanks to you for that, Harry."

"Why have you risen?"

"Because I thought I could. I've been to the necessary." Robert grinned, celebrating a triumph.

Harry looked sheepishly at his revolver. He had no place to put it. Robert took note of the state of his undress. "Mrs. Robertson is here," Harry said, only compounding his embarrassment.

"I am grateful to her as well, as you know." Robert came forward along the railing, but with slowing step. "This is more tiring than I had thought."

Harry moved to help him, but his brother raised his one hand to forestall this assistance. "I can make it, Harry. I can do it on my own. I think now I will live."

"Will you sleep?"

"Oh yes."

"Then a good day to you, sir."

269

Returning to his room, Harry commenced to wash and shave from his basin. Allie made some grumbling noises, then sat up. "I wasn't dreaming," she said. "You have returned."

"You, too."

"Ain't I welcome?"

"You are very welcome."

"But you seem troubled."

Harry lowered the razor. "It was a bad night. They killed Lemuel Krause. He'd been arrested by the Army, but escaped. Some of the townspeople organized themselves into vigilante groups and hunted him down."

"No trial?"

"He wasn't charged. Just locked up. Martial law."

"Who brought him in?"

He resumed shaving. "I did. Yesterday morning. He took a shot at me over at the Singleton place. I turned him over to the Army and they locked him up in the Entler Hotel. He escaped from there a few hours later. How he managed this I cannot imagine." He set down his razor and wiped the remaining shaving soap off his face. "How did your sojourn in Boonsboro go?"

"Well enough. Didn't lose much. Still haven't found a new hired man to replace Bannister, though."

Harry began to dress. "Allie. You told me you didn't know the Rev. Ashby. That you went to his church only once, just to hear him preach."

"That I did. A fine sermon." She was eyeing him curiously.

"Mrs. Ashby believes you knew him better than that."

"I've never even talked to that woman. I don't believe I've ever set eyes on her."

Harry finished buttoning his shirt, then pulled on some clean trousers. "Mrs. Ashby kept a journal of her observations. I have it. There are many entries. One of them relates to you."

She swung her legs over the side of the bed, sitting there a long moment, staring down at her pretty feet. "Why are you doing this, Harry?" she asked.

He spoke before thinking—at least before thinking about the hurt he might cause. "I'm curious," he said. "As what

270

you told me isn't the truth, I'm curious what the truth might be."

Allie stood, reaching for her camisole. "Well, God damn you to Hell, sir. My private life is no business of yours."

"I'm not interested in your private life, Allie. I'm interested in the Reverend Ashby's."

"I can tell you our friendship was pretty brief. It was also kinda interesting. It had absolutely nothing to do with what you're worrying about now."

"Your husband died only a year ago."

"Something I should have thought about when I made your acquaintance, Mr. Virginia Gentleman."

Her words stung as much as they were intended to do. "I'm sorry, Allie."

"You are?"

"Yes. It's just that I'm at a desperate pass. A great confusion has descended upon all of this. In the meantime people keep dying. It's all the same as the battle we just went through: Confusion, death, and nothing really decided."

She began pulling her dress over her head. "If this Lemuel was the murderer of these people, then you have nothing more to worry about. If there's more killings, at least you'll know for certain that he wasn't the one."

"I despair of ever having certainty again."

She put her bare feet into slippers and brushed by him, going out into the hall and down the stairs. When he descended himself, he heard her moving about the kitchen.

"Do you want breakfast?" she asked, fussing with the wood stove.

"I want to go into town before it gets to stirring."

She handed him an apple. "Take this, then. You can't think smart on an empty stomach."

"Thank you."

She returned to her labors, keeping her eyes from his. "I'm not sure I'm going to be here when you get back."

"That's up to you. I apologize if I have given offense." He waited for her to turn to face him, but she did not. "This excuses nothing," he said. "But there's something I'd have you know."

271

She sighed. "I hope you're not going to tell me that you love me."

"There's another entry in that journal that disturbed me as much as yours. It accounts for my disposition this morning."

"Anyone I know?"

"I do not think so."

"Then I should not be concerned."

"I am. She was my mother."

Stretched out on the porch, Tantou awakened the moment Harry stepped across the threshold. He did not rise, however.

"I'm going into the town," Harry said. "Will you come with me?"

"No, Harry Raines. There is roast pig in your smokehouse and eggs and butter in your pantry. There's fruit, too. I will breakfast well, and then join you later." He closed his eyes.

"I mean to accomplish something this day."

"I will help you do that—after I eat."

The town's resident undertaker was still full up with commerce in war dead, as were the several transient practitioners of the grisly trade who'd descended upon Shepherdstown in the wake of the Union Army. Lemuel had consequently been taken to Doctor Ricketts' basement, where Harry, joined by Sergeant Knapp, examined him.

Lemuel hadn't stood much of a chance.

"He's been shot through the chest, the back, and the side of the neck," Harry said. "He wasn't gunned down trying to flee. He was either bushwhacked or surrounded in his place of hiding. The vigilantes knew where he was."

"I know it was on the Charles Town Road," said Knapp. "If he'd kept going, he'd soon have been in Rebel territory, beyond the reach of Federal law."

Ricketts came down the stairs. "I've sent word to the boy's kin across the river," he said. "Haven't had any response, but it's early yet. If they don't come, we may have to bury him here."

"In the Presbyterian cemetery, next to Ann Harding," said Harry.

The doctor removed his spectacles and wiped them clean with a handkerchief. "Don't think Mr. Harding would like that."

"I have ceased worrying about what Mr. Harding would or would not like," Harry said. "It's the Union Army running this town now; not Mr. Harding."

"Until the Union Army leaves," said Ricketts. "I tell you, Harry, if I never see another soldier, in blue or gray, I'll be joyful."

"It's the soldiers who are settling this question, Doctor, and in favor of our cause. We have a great chance here—creating a new state, free of slavery—but we shall waste it if we can't stop local quarrels like this one. We must put an end to this thing and bring the perpetrators to justice—Federal justice. Here in Shepherdstown."

"I'm not arguing with you on that, Harry. But the town is so much divided. There are days when I fear we'll have a civil war of our own."

Harry looked to Knapp. "Who brought Lemuel's body here?"

"Harding's party. They came back with him pretty quick."

There had been a young man riding close to Harding the previous night. His name was Scruggs. Nathaniel Scruggs. He worked at Harding's grocery.

"If Krause's folks do not come for him," Harry said to Ricketts, "send for me. I will see to his burial."

"And where will I find you?"

"I'm going to Harding's grocery, and then the Entler. I'll be findable."

"Grocery?" said Knapp. "You hungry?"

Harry had eaten the apple Allie had given him, but it hadn't sufficed. "Hungry for food; hungry for knowledge. I'd appreciate your company."

Scruggs was behind the counter, totaling up a woman's bill. When he was done, Harry ordered hard-boiled eggs, slices of ham, and two warm beers for Knapp and himself.

"That was neat work last night, the way you people ran

273

down Lemuel Krause," Harry said. "You ought to join the Army scouts."

"Wasn't me," said Scruggs, a tall and lanky young man with overlong hair. "Mr. Harding skunked him out. Woulda thought he was a hunting dog."

"Where'd you corner him?"

"He was holed up in the Mastersons' barn. Up in the loft."

"And he fired on you?"

"Was about to. Charlie Harding saw him with a pistol in his hand, his head sticking out the hayloft door. Charlie let off a shot. He said it missed, but Lemuel was dead when the rest of us got there."

"Dead. And shot three times," Harry said, munching the last of his ham.

Scruggs shook his head. "Don't know about that. I don't even own a gun, Mr. Raines."

"Then what were you doing out with that search party?"

"Mr. Harding wanted every able man."

So did the Union Army, to end the war, yet here stood Scruggs behind a grocery counter. "The Masterson farm's only a mile out of town. Why would Lemuel stop there?"

"Don't know, Mr. Raines."

"Did Harding go directly to that barn?"

"No, sir. We stopped at two other places first."

"Search 'em good?"

"No. We moved on pretty quick."

"Until you got to the Mastersons'?"

"Yes."

"The Mastersons left town because of the war. They were the only ones on the Charles Town Road to do so."

"I guess." He turned to the shelf behind him, and began pointlessly rearranging tins and boxes.

"Did Lemuel really have a gun?"

"Sure. Must have."

"Well, who has it?"

Scruggs continued with his pointless rearrangement. "I don't know. Maybe Mr. Harding." One of the tins fell from Scruggs' hand with a clatter.

"Was it a pistol or a long gun?"

"I don't know." He retrieved the tin, dropping it again in the process. "Mr. Raines, I don't know I should be talking to you any more about this." He returned the tin to the shelf, and then just stood there, his back still to Harry.

"Why not, Nathaniel? Everyone in town is talking about this matter."

"I just don't think I should. And anyway, I don't know anything more. I went out there with Mr. Harding, and I come back with him."

"Very well," Harry said, as he finished his beer. "You've told me enough."

"What do you mean?"

Harry paid for their meal and walked out without another word.

"You left him in the dark," Knapp said, as they walked on toward the Entler. "Me, too."

"Harding knew where Lemuel was hiding. He knew somehow that Lemuel wouldn't leave that barn. He saw to it that Lemuel was killed as quickly as possible. What I need to know now is who told Lemuel to go to that barn and stay there."

"Maybe the same person who helped him escape," Knapp said.

"Whoever that is."

Another platoon of provost marshal's guard had been sent from across the river to reinforce the men who'd been on duty at the Entler. A major was in command. Harry identified himself and presented his bonafides.

"Yes, I know about you, Raines," said the major, a gray-haired man with short-cut beard who looked the lawyer he doubtless once was. "You're the scout who captured that Krause boy."

"And brought him here," said Harry. "Where he did not remain long enough."

"I suppose not."

The major looked at Knapp with some curiosity. The sergeant had failed to salute and was following the conversation with barely concealed amusement.

"I would like to see the soldier who was posted guard here outside Krause's room," Harry said. "Mr. Pinkerton, I'm sure, would appreciate it."

The guard, a private as gray as the major, was eventually located at a small encampment down by the river landing and summoned to the Entler.

"Have they explained to you who I am?" Harry asked.

"Yes, sir."

"You're in no trouble, friend. But I need information. Who visited the prisoner Krause aside from Mr. Klostermann the tavern keeper?"

"Only him, sir. While I was on duty. And that was pretty much all day."

"Did you search the food basket he brought?"

"Yes, sir. Didn't find anything you couldn't eat. And I went into the room with him."

"And Mr. Klostermann?"

"He had no weapons."

"Did the key to the room leave your possession?"

The private looked to Knapp, as though seeking an explanation for this inquisition by a strange civilian. None was forthcoming. "No, sir. In my pocket all the time, except when I opened the door for Mr. Klostermann."

Harry thought a moment. "I want to have a look at this room."

The chamber was small, containing only a narrow bed, wooden chair, chest of drawers, and a washstand. The sole window was near a corner of the room. It was small as well. Harry was able to open it with ease.

Poking out his head, he surveyed a fenced yard with two soldiers standing in it, smoking their pipes. There were houses beyond the fence.

The drop to the ground was perhaps a dozen feet. Hanging from the sill, he could have managed it with ease.

"Were there soldiers posted down there?" Harry asked, after withdrawing his head back into the room.

"During the day, that's where we stay—except for mess call," said the private.

"What time were you relieved?"

"Few minutes after six."

"I'd like to talk to the man who relieved you."

"You can't, sir. They took him over to Sharpsburg for court martial."

"As a witness?"

"On charges. He reported for duty drunk."

"Reported here?"

"Yes, sir."

"At what time?"

"Don't know. When he didn't turn up, the corporal of the guard let me go to mess call. We heard later about my relief being drunk."

Harry pondered the still open window, then nodded. "Very well, private. I thank you."


There was a farm wagon drawn up in front of Doc Ricketts' office. Harry realized to whom it must belong and quickened his pace. By the time they reached it, an older man Harry took to be Lemuel's father emerged from the front door of the small brick building, his son's body slung over his shoulder. His wife tottered behind, rubbing at her eyes.

Harry waited until Mr. Krause had laid the boy's body on the wagon bed, and then stepped forward. "I'm sorry to bother you at such a time, Mr. Krause, but I must ask your indulgence."

"*Vas?* What do you want?"

Harry hadn't realized how German the Krauses were—though, as he thought upon it, the few words Lemuel had spoken to him were with a slight accent.

"I am a Federal officer," Harry said. "I need to examine your son."

"Examine?"

"It won't take but a moment. If you will allow me." Mrs. Krause was contemplating him bitterly.

The father slammed the rear gate of the wagon back into

place and fastened it quickly. "*Nein.* You will not disturb him."
He started toward the wagon seat, his wife following.

"Sergeant Knapp, draw your revolver on this man."

Knapp considered this for a few seconds, finally raising his
pistol just as Krause had climbed into the seat. "I'm afraid
I'll have to ask you to oblige Captain Raines, sir. Or I'll have
to place you under arrest."

"You Goddamn sons of bitches! You leave my boy alone."

It took more courage than Harry had needed on the battlefield to climb aboard that wagon, but he did so. The father
turned in the seat and seemed about to club Harry with the
nearest heavy object at hand. Hoping Knapp would not have
to shoot, Harry steeled himself and went about his business,
going quickly through the pockets of Lemuel's overalls.

"What, now you rob him?"

"No, sir. Only of this." Harry held up a folded piece of
paper.

The old man squinted. "What is that?"

"Something that belongs to me." Harry got off the wagon
with great haste, landing hard on his left ankle and twisting
it. Another pain to add to the lingering list of others. "You
may go, Mr. Krause. Thank you for your cooperation."

Krause swung his wife up on the seat beside him and
snapped the reins, commencing to assail Harry and Knapp
with a stream of German profanity. Knapp watched the noisy
departure, then turned to Harry.

"What did you find?"

Harry handed him the folded paper. The sergeant read it,
or tried to, frowning. He returned it.

"What's it mean?"

"Let's go get a drink."

There were only a few in the barroom, all men of the town.
Harry and Knapp went down to the far end. Klostermann
moved quickly to serve them.

"Any news?" the tavern keeper asked.

"How could there be news?" Harry replied. "Lemuel's dead.
His family has just now taken the body away."

Klostermann filled their glasses. "You think that's the end of the murders?"

"Don't you, Hugo?"

"*Sicher*. That's what everyone says."

"Well, let us all hope so." Harry took a sip of the whiskey and then reached into his pocket. "You are just the man I need to see."

"Why is this?"

"Because you speak German." He handed the tavern keeper the folded paper. "What does that say?"

Klostermann studied the paper, looking puzzled.

"What's wrong, Hugo? Don't you know German?"

"Yes. *Ich spreche Deutsch schön*. It says, 'Go to the farm. Wait. Help will come.'"

"I believe there's a word in English." Harry took another sip. Knapp hadn't touched his.

"You asked about the German words. You know the English one."

Harry took back the note. "It says, 'Go to the Masterson farm. Wait. Help will come.' Yes?"

"Yes."

"Curious," Harry said. "I found it in Lemuel's pocket. I didn't know he could read German. Wasn't sure he could read at all, at first. But apparently he had a fair amount of book learning."

"The Krauses are German," Klostermann said. "The old man comes from Hesse."

"Did you know Lemuel well?"

"Sometimes he come in for beer—when he was working for Mrs. Ashby."

Harry finished his drink. "We have to go, Hugo." He put a coin on the bar top.

Klostermann pushed it back. "Stay, I'll buy you another."

Harry left the coin where it was. "No thank you, Hugo. We have things to do."

"About the murders?"

"Yes. Much to do."

"You said there was no news."

*Michael Kilian*

"But there may be."

Knapp knocked down his whiskey in a gulp, then followed Harry out of the bar.

"Where're we going?" the sergeant asked, as they walked toward the bottom of German Street.

"Around the next corner," Harry said. "We'll head toward O'Malley's, but when we get to the next block around the corner, we'll double back to the stable behind Klostermann's tavern. Then we'll wait."

"For what?"

"That I am not sure yet."

There were openings between the slats of the stable door, giving an ample view of the rear yards behind the buildings along German Street. The back door of Klostermann's tavern opened no more than a minute after Harry and Knapp had entered their hiding place. It was not Hugo who emerged, however, but the old black man who worked for him.

"Is he what we're waiting for?"

"I hope so."

When the old man was three buildings ahead of them, Harry opened the stable door and followed—Knapp just behind. They had to clamber over fences, crouching down finally behind one of them as the object of their interest reached his destination, disappearing inside.

"What place is that?" Knapp asked.

"Mr. Harding's bank," Harry said.

# Twenty-Nine

"What do we do now?" Knapp asked.

"I wish I knew," said Harry.

They were sitting upon a stone wall atop the slope that overlooked the town from the west, hoping they'd not be noticed. Harry offered Knapp one of his small cigars, then lighted one himself.

"You want to arrest your friend Klostermann? I expect he knows a hell of a lot about this."

"Maybe. Maybe not." Harry blew a plume of smoke into the clear air. "But if we grab him, we'll be showing our cards to one and all."

"And a piss poor hand it is."

"No. The cards are good. There just aren't enough of them."

"You're trying to fill an inside straight."

When he was a professional gambler, Harry had never done that. "Guess I am."

They puffed on their cigars. Except for the occasional military traffic, everything seemed normal. A gang of laborers were working on the trestle of the ruined bridge over the Potomac leading to Maryland. Smoke was rising from O'Malley's blacksmith shop. The bells of both the Lutheran and the Rev. Ashby's Presbyterian Church began to ring. It was noon.

"We've established that all the victims were slain with a pistol—smaller caliber than a rifle or musket," Harry said, thinking aloud.

"Guess so. I didn't look at any of them."

"Lemuel's rifle was large bore—maybe fifty caliber."

"Maybe he had a revolver as well."

281

"What would a farm boy be doing with a revolver? He'd have a hunting weapon."

"Maybe someone loaned him one."

The church bells had stopped. "If you'll oblige me further, Sergeant Knapp, I'm going to call on the widow woman again." He stood up.

"Why's that?" Knapp rose, brushing off his trousers.

"At the moment, I can't think of anything else to do."

There was no response when Harry rapped on the door, but in a short time Martha Ashby emerged from the church. She was as gracious as always, but much subdued.

"How may I assist you today, Harrison?" Her eyes were reddened. It had not been twenty-four hours since Lemuel had been killed.

"I need to consult your journal again, Martha."

"And why is that?"

"I've forgotten something. I think something important."

Despite her outer calm, Harry sensed she was hating every second of this encounter. Her eyes went to Knapp. "I presume this is an official call, then?"

"Yes, ma'am."

"Very well. I was about to burn it." She led them into her parlor, going again to her husband's desk.

"I would prefer that you do not burn it," Harry said, as she with obvious reluctance handed it to him. "In fact, I'm afraid I shall have to keep it."

"You should have said that at the outset."

"If I did, you'd not have let me have it."

She stepped back, arms folded. "Are you so willing to embarrass all those families? To embarrass me?"

"I will do everything I can to spare you that. But this could prove vital when I present my case."

"Your case? Present it to whom?"

"To Colonel Thorne, the military judge now residing in Shepherdstown. As I told you, Martha, because the Reverend was working for us, his murder is a Federal crime—and the Army has jurisdiction."

282

She seated herself on her rocker, folding her hands and looking downcast, defeated. "What do you want to know, Harry?"

"The women you name in this journal—are they listed in chronological order?"

"Mostly."

"How were you able to be that precise?"

She dabbed at her right eye with her apron. "I was aware of every one. I learned where he took them."

"And where was that?"

"Into the church. There's a loft."

Harry looked down the list of names. "Was Ann Harding the first?"

"No. Your mother . . ."

He cut her short. "Of the girls who were murdered. Or almost murdered. Was Ann Harding the first?"

"I told you, Harry. I do not believe there was anything more than friendship between them. She loved Lemuel."

"But Mr. Harding might have thought there was more."

"Then he was grievously misinformed."

Harry's head was hurting once more. The entries in the journal were becoming blurry. "Do you think Harding was capable of murdering the Reverend?"

"I think that man is capable of anything."

"But not of killing his own daughter. Maybe Lemuel. But not her."

"I should hate to think our community the abode of anyone who could do that."

Harry rubbed his forehead, then his eyes. "Of all these girls, these women. Who was the last?"

"The last?"

"The last into the loft."

"That I cannot say for certain. It might have been Lucinda Weverton, or Peggy Singleton. Or that Robertson woman. All the town's talking about you and her, Harry. Your mother would——"

"From what you've told me, I suspect my mother would have little to say on the subject."

As if chastised, she folded her hands primly in her lap again. "Is there anything else you want? I'm preparing to leave Shepherdstown. I'm going to our farm."

"Just one thing. Did the Reverend keep any weapons?"

"No."

"Not even a shotgun for hunting?"

"He was much opposed to hunting. All God's creatures, he used to say."

Harry closed the journal. "Very well . . ."

She smiled. "But I have a revolver."

"A Remington?"

"George bought it for me when the war started—after that battle at Romney. He was often gone, preaching at other churches, smuggling Negroes across the Potomac up to Pennsylvania. He wanted me to have it for my own protection."

"May I see it, please, Martha."

"Why?"

"Please." He nodded toward Knapp. "This is a Federal matter. I don't want to cause you any more difficulty than you've already endured."

She rose, with a sigh. "Very well, Harry. I'm putting my trust in you—though, Lord knows, I've no real reason to."

She went upstairs, her small feet moving up the steps quietly. Harry heard a drawer being opened. A moment later, she descended, entering the parlor with the pistol barrel first, as though aiming at him.

It occurred to him that she was aiming at him. She could get off a shot before he'd even reach the Navy Colt in his belt.

"Martha?"

She lowered the barrel and brought the revolver to him. It was a .44 caliber Remington, too large to have made the wounds the young ladies had suffered.

He examined it carefully. It was well oiled and there were no powder stains on it anywhere. If it had been fired recently, there was now no way of telling.

He turned the cylinder. The weapon was fully loaded,

complete to percussion caps. Using his penknife, he pried forth one of the cartridges. This he placed in his coat pocket. Then he spun the cylinder so that the hammer would strike a full chamber when the pistol was fired.

"You keep it," Harry said, handing it back. "I fear that you may need it. When will you leave for your farm?"

"Tomorrow. Maybe the next day."

"Good. I'll send you word of what transpires."

She reached into a pocket of her skirt. "I found this. I think you should read it, Harry."

He accepted the paper and unfolded it. The pencil printing was the same as the earlier note about a general and an assassin. "'Harding is for Secession,'" he read, aloud. "Where did you find this?"

"In a pocket of one of my husband's jackets."

"Did you look through the other pockets? Other jackets?"

"There was nothing. Only this."

The paper looked fresh. "Secession became an issue for Virginia a year and a half ago. This seems new."

"Harrison, I can only tell you the truth. I was going through his things a few days ago and I came upon it. When he placed it in his pocket I do not know. But you are welcome to keep it."

In wobbly fashion, Harry got to his feet. He pocketed the note.

"I wish you well, Martha."

"We shall see."

Doctor Ricketts was not in his office. Frustrated after repeated knockings on the door, Harry led Knapp to the rear of the little building, where he used his small penknife to open the lock there.

"How did you manage that?" Knapp asked.

"One of my fellow agents—scouts—was once a Boston police detective. He taught me how to do this. Doesn't always work, but it did now."

"I guess crime's a matter of who's doing it."

"And why," said Harry. "Come along."

They went down to Ricketts' cellar, where he had kept the dead bodies that came his way and stored whatever artifacts he'd taken from them. There was a glass jar with bullets covering the bottom. Taking a seat next to a long table, Harry poured them out. Then, one by one, he held them up next to the cartridge he'd taken from Martha Ashby's revolver.

He'd learned something of the rudimentary principles of the French science of ballistics from his Army surgeon friend Phineas Gregg back in Washington, but this knowledge was of small use now. The spent rounds were so misshapen they defied comparison with the clean, fresh bullet. He was barely able to tell their caliber.

"Christopher, would you look at these and tell me if you find any similarities."

The sergeant came forward and commenced a one-by-one examination of his own, ultimately setting two of the fired rounds aside. "These two match, I think," he said. "Thirty-sixes. Can't tell about the others. They're all too small to have come from that woman's pistol."

"What about this one?" Harry picked up a larger piece of metal.

Knapp leaned near, squinting. "Not sure it's a forty-four. Are you sure these are the rounds that killed those people?"

Harry sat back, glancing at the shelves along the wall. "No, but they're the only ones I see."

"Maybe we should get out of here."

Harry thought a moment, then rose. "You're right."

"Where next?"

"Go see Jim O'Malley. Get the news of the day."

"If you want the news of the day, you should go to the tavern."

"That, too."

Klostermann was away on an errand and the old black man was tending bar. He was not so generous with free drinks nor so interested in their conversation. Still, Harry waited until he had moved away before speaking.

"What do you make of this?" he said, handing the black-smith the folded note.

O'Malley studied it. "Depends on who wrote it."

"Don't know that. It was among the Reverend Ashby's things."

"Like that note about assassins?"

"Intelligence that Ashby was passing on," Harry said. He thought upon this. Pinkerton said he had never received any messages from Ashby. But then, Pinkerton worked for McClellan. Perhaps Ashby had been reporting to some local commander—maybe at the brigade or regimental level.

"Harding has always kept his politics in his pocket," O'Malley said. "Makes good business sense—the town being divided like it is. I wouldn't have thought him Secesh, though. You'd expect him to side with the winner."

"We're a long way from becoming the winner."

"That note could be a fake," said Knapp. "You don't know who wrote it, or when."

"True enough," Harry said. "But if it's a fake, so's the other one."

"Confusion abides and abounds," said O'Malley. He sipped his beer.

"What news have you?" Harry asked.

"Not much. They say Lee's now south of the Rappahannock. People are wondering why the Federal army's still here."

"General McClellan is unfond of movement."

"The railroad's open again."

That was good news, though Harry had no interest in going to Washington.

O'Malley took another sip of beer. "And people are saying that a lady from Boonsboro may have taken up permanent residence here."

Harry grumbled to himself. There were times when this lovely little town was too small. "That question has not been decided."

"How about you? Still going to settle down here?"

"The war permitting," Harry said.

"Doesn't permit much."

287

Harry finished his whiskey. "When does your colonel get back?"

"I think tonight."

"Would you tell him I'd like to see him in the morning?"

"I do believe he is at your disposal."

"I'd also like a guard posted at Mrs. Ashby's."

"I can attend to that myself."

Klostermann entered the tavern. "Let's go," said Harry.

The tavern keeper smiled to see Harry and his companions at the bar, but his happy countenance soured as he realized that they were departing.

"Stay," he said, coming up to them. "Drinks on me."

"No, thank you," Harry said. "Maybe later."

Outside, he climbed wearily onto his horse's saddle. The sun was getting low in the sky, turning the leaves of the trees along German Street a golden hue. In a month, they'd be that color on their own.

"My thanks to you, gentlemen," he said.

"You think we're getting anywhere with this?" Knapp asked.

"I don't know, Christopher. I just don't know."

Knowing his mount would get him home if he were dead asleep, Harry let the reins fall slack and rode with arms folded and head down, deep in thought. As they neared his farm, he took them back up again, proceeding past his gate and moving on down the road until he came to the Singleton place.

Trying to recall exactly where Lemuel had been when he'd fired his shot at him, Harry decided on the right corner of the decrepit farm house and headed up to it. Turning the horse, wishing there was more light in the sky, he took out his own rifle and aimed it at the spot along the fence where he had been.

The distance was too great to be sure of a killing shot or even to be certain of the identity of one's target. If Lemuel was not an imbecile, as Martha Ashby insisted, he must have been acting out of great desperation—desperate to kill his victim or desperately fearful the victim would kill him.

But Harry had meant Lemuel no harm and he could think of

no reason why Lemuel would want to shoot him—unless it was the fact that he was leading the investigation into the murders.

Or trying to.

A sound behind him caused him to yank his horse around again and raise his rifle toward the house. But it was not repeated. There was no light in the house. As he prodded the animal back toward the road, he caught a moving shape to the side of his eye. Looking to it, he found himself witness to the silent, early evening flight of a large owl, which quickly disappeared into the trees.

He urged his horse into a trot.

His small, peculiar family was gathered in the kitchen—Allie stirring something on the stove, Evangeline playing with one of the dogs, brother Robert restored to enough strength to sit in a rocker Allie must have hauled in from the front parlor.

"You are still here," he said to her.

"Someone has to feed these poor people."

"Where is Tantou?" Harry asked.

"Been gone since this morning—just like you."

Harry took off his hat and slumped into a straight-backed wooden chair. He sighed. "I might as well have stayed here."

"Didn't accomplish much?"

"Just added to my confusion."

She went to the table with her pot and poured its contents, which looked to be stew, into a blue and white china bowl. "You could just drop the whole damn thing, you know," she said. "We could get back to a peaceful life."

"And when did anyone in this town last have that?"

She had boiled some vegetables and put those in a bowl as well. He noted she was barefoot and wearing a thin dress against the kitchen heat. "You're sure a grumpy cuss tonight," she said.

"Sorry. At all events, I think Mr. Pinkerton would like me to see this through—given the trouble he's gone to on my behalf. We have a colonel and a platoon of soldiers down there at the Entler, waiting for me to bring the culprit to the bar of military justice."

"I'd be just as happy if they all packed up." She began putting the food on the table.

"What is the news of the war?" Robert asked.

"There isn't much. Lee's gone south. McClellan sits here."

"Is the road to the South still open?"

"You mean to Charles Town? I suppose so—except for cavalry patrols and brigands." He realized why Robert was asking. "Bob. It is one thing to climb aboard a rocking chair in your state of health. Quite another to sit a horse."

His brother fell silent. Harry sat staring at the remarkably clean floor a moment, then rose and went down the hallway to his office, where he poured himself a large whiskey. He was still at his desk, sipping it, when Allie appeared in the doorway.

"You saw I was serving supper," she said.

"Yes. I'm sorry. I'm not so hungry tonight."

"Well, plantation man, you'd better be—because I'm not going to go to such bother again if you won't eat."

He sighed again and rose, following her meekly.

Harry had several more whiskies after dinner. Allie joined him for a time, but could not long bear his silence. Slapping her hands on her thighs, she stood up. "I'm going to bed," she said.

"I'll be along presently."

"You needn't bother."

He finished his last whiskey, then put out the oil lamp and wearily mounted the stairs. He looked in on his brother and Evangeline, then went to his own room, surprised to find the bed empty. There were two more bedrooms in the house and he supposed she had gone to one of them. He considered going to her, but decided he was not up to the kind of conversation that would likely ensue.

He took a long time finding sleep and it was fitful at best. He was wakeful enough to be aware of his door opening slowly some time after. Thinking it must be Allie, he flung open the counterpane, but quickly realized the figure in the doorway was too tall to be her.

Yet another gunshot. Harry hit the floor hard.

# Thirty

Harry rolled from his bed, landing hard on his elbow. His Navy Colt was on the dresser—a long scramble in full view of the figure in the doorway.

But the intruder was no longer there. Reaching for his spectacles on his nightstand, Harry moved a few feet forward and put them on. He was mistaken. The intruder had not vanished. He now lay in a heap on the floor. Moving yet closer, Harry looked up to see another dark figure standing just to the side of the other—a very tall man, with long hair.

"He is dead, Harry Raines."

Harry stood up, his elbow still stinging. "Where have you been all this time, Jack?"

"With you. I followed you all day."

"I didn't see you."

"No. If you had, the bad men would have, too."

"What bad men?"

"Here is one here. He has a revolver."

Harry knelt and felt for it. He touched still warm flesh, and then cold steel. As he rose again, the door across the hall opened a crack, and then all the way. Allie emerged, holding a candlestick.

"What in hell's going on?" she said. She sniffed. "Was that a gunshot?"

"Yes," is all Harry said.

She came closer, her candle illuminating the stranger, who lay face down. Blood was seeping onto the wooden floor.

"He had this pistol," Harry said, still holding the weapon by the barrel. He took it in both hands and examined the cylinder, finding it fully loaded. The hammer was cocked.

291

Harry was surprised it hadn't gone off. "Where were you, Jack?"

"Sleeping on the porch. He woke me."

"How did he get up here?"

"He got ahead of me. I didn't want to shoot until I know *bien sûr* what was his intent."

"Well, that we know sure enough." Harry set the dead man's pistol on the dresser. "Let's see who he is."

Allie stepped back, diminishing the light in the process. Tantou stuck the toe of his boot under the man's chest and heaved him over.

"Bannister," said Harry. He looked to Allie. "Your hired man."

She retreated further, hand over her mouth, horrified. "Son of a bitch."

Robert appeared at his door. He must have taken a long time getting from his bed.

"It's all right, Bob. A man with a grudge. Tantou stopped him."

"You are not injured?"

"No. Go back to bed. You, too, Mrs. Robertson. Jack and I will take care of this."

Harry went to the bedroom Evangeline used, finding the child sleeping quietly. He left her undisturbed.

He and Tantou carried the body downstairs and out to the barn. "We'll take him to Doc Ricketts in the morning."

"Too many of his patients come dead, Harry Raines."

Harry returned to the house surprised to find Allie still there, once again in the kitchen, but fully dressed. A packed carpet-bag had been left in the hall. Harry was still so furious with her—and with himself for becoming so smitten he'd failed to see what she was about—that he could not speak. When she put a fresh cup of coffee on the table before him, he did not say "Thank you"—the first time in his life he'd ever been so ungentlemanly.

"You really think I tried to have you murdered, plantation man?"

He took a sip of coffee, but made no reply.

"Well," she said, "you're the biggest damn fool I've met in this war. You should be a Union general." She returned to the stove.

"You may stay as long as you need to, Mrs. Robertson. If your horse is still lame, you may take one of mine. If you take it South, you may return it after the war."

"What the hell're you talking about?"

Harry stood up and drank down the coffee, though it was still very hot. "Good day to you, madam."

The air was cool this morning. Harry had taken along Bannister's horse to bear his body into town, holding its reins with his right hand. He had to fight the impulse to release them and let the animal bear its unpleasant burden off into the hills.

"What do you think, Jack?" Harry asked.

"Think of what?"

"Think about Alice—Mrs. Robertson."

"I think I am happy to have killed a man who was about to kill you. I think Mrs. Robertson is the best woman you know."

"But . . ."

"That is all I think, Harry Raines."

They left Bannister's body with the doctor, who had just opened his office and was looking forward more to his coffee than to another cadaver.

"You'll have to explain this to someone," he said, in parting.

"I'll likely spend the whole day doing that."

Colonel Thorne was at breakfast. "You're here early, Raines."

"With a reason. I think we may be able to conclude this matter today."

Thorne took a bit of egg, and then a sip of coffee. "We have to follow military procedure. All I can do just now is hold a preliminary hearing."

"That may suffice."

"I hope so. I have a dispatch from Mr. Pinkerton. He would appreciate your presence at headquarters as soon as convenient."

"I'll attend to his wishes as soon as we conclude."

"That's your concern. All I can do is pass on messages. But there's another matter that does come under my jurisdiction. Your brother."

"My brother is seriously wounded and has lost his arm."

"He is in your house."

"As an invalid."

"I'm just giving you fair warning, Raines. The time is coming soon when he'll have to take an oath of loyalty to the United States of America or be sent to the prison hospital at Fort McHenry."

With the addition of wooden barracks, the famous Baltimore fort had been turned into a sprawling prisoner-of-war camp.

"I'll make him aware of the situation. I would be very pleased if he took the oath."

"The goddamned Confederacy just has to be the stupidest idea in the history of this country." Thorne took another bite. "How do you plan to proceed with things today?"

"I'll present my findings, and you determine where things should go after that."

"Sounds agreeable."

"Here's the disagreeable part." He handed the colonel a sheet of paper. "These are people I want arrested."

Thorne tilted back his head, squinting at the list. "You know where we can locate all these people?"

"Yes. Most I should think are known to you by now."

"This Mr. Harding. You mean the Mr. Harding who owns this town?"

"Not all of it. A small but significant part. But that's irrelevant. Yes. That Mr. Harding. I do believe he is in town."

"And his grocery clerk?"

"Yes."

"And his two sons?"

Harry nodded.

"And Mrs. Ashby? The widow of the Federal agent whose murder brought the Army into this mess?"

"Yes, sir."

"Good Lord."

"I have good reason, Colonel."

"Whatever your reason, I'm ordered to indulge you." He read again. "Klostermann, the tavern keeper."

"Yes. Him, too."

There was one name left on the list. "Is this in error?"

"No, sir."

"Mrs. Alice Robertson?"

"Yes, sir."

"I'm given to understand that this woman now abides with you."

"She may yet be found at my farm. If your people hurry." Harry lighted one of his small cigars, mostly to stem his nervousness. "I told her she could linger as long as she liked. She has a fondness for the little girl in my care. I don't think she will dash. If she does, it may well be into the Confederacy, which is all the same to me."

"You want them brought here? The rooms are small."

Harry thought upon this. "Perhaps the Presbyterian church."

"And what do you hope to accomplish by detaining these people, uh, Captain Raines."

He couldn't give the honest answer, which was that he had no firm idea. His hope was that, by gathering them together in a group in the presence of Federal muskets, he might provoke some illuminating discourse or revelation. "I will bring evidence of a conspiracy."

"Against the United States government?"

"Against its interests, embodied by the good Reverend."

Rice folded the paper and put it in a pocket of his officer's tunic. "This will take some time."

"I'll be in the tavern."

"But you have Klostermann on the list."

"Arrest him last."

\*       \*       \*

295

Harry tried to drink very slowly, but the Federal soldiers were taking a considerable time in carrying out his request. Standing at the bar, he kept his back to the tavern's front door and window. The sight of Allie being taken under arms like St. Joan to the stake was more than he could bear. He wondered how he'd found the nerve to order this done.

But it had to be. It all had to be if he was to get this dreadful business behind him.

His glass was empty. For the fourth time, he ordered another whiskey from the old black man behind the bar. Klostermann was again absent.

And then he wasn't. Bustling through the door, Hugo saw Harry and came to his side.

"Harry. They're arresting people! They have even brought in your woman friend, Mrs. Robertson!"

"Calm yourself, Hugo. This is merely a hearing. There'll be no hanging today."

"But why is this happening?"

Harry took a gulp of his drink. They were going down faster. "The Federal government disapproves of the Reverend Ashby's murder. And of Lemuel Krause's murder. I am sure they also heartily disapprove of the murders of those poor young women, but those incidents do not fall within the reach of the Federal writ."

"But why Mrs. Robertson?"

"Her hired man, Bannister, tried to kill me last night. He now lies in Doc Ricketts' cellar, in no need of hanging." Harry drank again, wondering how to judge the point between not enough and too much whiskey before attending to the day's odious chore.

"Bannister?"

"You don't know him, Hugo? You seem to know everything about everything that occurs in Shepherdstown these days."

Klostermann went behind the bar, then returned to Harry's end, facing him. "Would you like schnapps, Harry? I have schnapps."

It seemed the most inappropriate time imaginable for that

sweet German liqueur, but Harry shrugged, and then nodded. "Thank you."

"*Bitte schön.*"

"Do you have relations in the South, Hugo?" Harry asked, as he sipped the clear liquid.

"This is the South, Harry. We are on the southern side of the Potomac."

"I mean on the Rebel side of the fighting."

"Sure. I have people who have been in the Shenandoah Valley more than one hundred twenty years. Many Germans in the Valley."

"Stonewall Jackson is active in the Valley. Sometimes Mosby. Guerrillas, spies, and Confederate Home Guard. Many nasty folk."

Klostermann stepped back from the bar. "None of them bother us here."

"I don't know how you can say that."

Hugo managed to get a weak smile onto his broad face. He poured Harry another schnapps. "I have news," Hugo said. "The Singleton brothers have been killed. They ran into Union cavalry down in Ranson. Tried to shoot it out with them and lost."

"Ranson?" It was a village just outside of Charles Town.

"That's what I heard. They were stupid men. More fight in them than brains."

"I do not lament their passing." Harry sipped the schnapps.

"What are you doing in here, Harry?" Hugo said. "Don't you want to look after your woman? The Federals are in a harsh mood after that battle. So many dead and wounded. They could hang her for a spy."

Before Harry could reply, the front door opened, admitting Sergeant Knapp and a squad of Union soldiers. "They're ready for you, Captain Raines," Knapp pronounced.

Harry took out his Navy Colt and aimed it unhesitatingly at the tavern keeper. "Hugo, you're under arrest."

Tantou had been waiting outside, sitting on the steps with his long rifle. When Harry emerged from the tavern, the Metis fell in beside him. There were many people now out on the street.

"You have made some of them very angry," Tantou said.

"That doesn't matter. This is Federal business. There are eighty some thousand troops just across the river." Harry looked behind him. Hugo, unbound, was walking meekly between the file of Union soldiers led by Knapp. "Did they bring in Harding?" Harry asked.

"Yes. And his two sons. But not until he has called for his lawyer."

"Lawyer?"

"Yes. A lawyer named Grieves. From this town."

Harry's father had once said that, if Lawyer Grieves had practiced his trade in Charles City County in the Tidewater— instead of up in the barbarian western mountain counties of Virginia—he would have been shot dead in the street within a week. Lawyer Grieves was a land transaction man, ever for the main chance, and had grown quickly rich from the practice. Harding would not have owned a third of what he did had it not been for this attorney, who had studied law at Thomas Jefferson's University of Virginia.

How he could help Harding in a criminal matter was not clear, unless it was by dint of his extremely clever mind.

As they entered the church, Harry kept his eyes averted from Allie and Mrs. Ashby, but was able to take note of perhaps two dozen townspeople in the pews—friends or relations of the accused. All others were being barred at the door.

Two tables had been set up before the altar. Colonel Thorne was seated at a small, third table set beside the altar on the dias, a notebook before him.

"Are you ready to commence, Captain Raines?"

"Yes, sir."

"And you, Mr. Grieves?"

The lawyer, a flamboyantly well-dressed man with carefully trimmed moustache and goatee, rose. "If it please the court——"

"It would please the court to note that this is not the court," said Thorne. "I merely represent the Judge Advocate. I'm here solely to determine if criminal charges should be brought against any of those accused under the statutes of military justice—in the case of the murder of the Rev. George Ashby, who was engaged in the Federal service, and Lemuel Krause, who was murdered while a witness in a Federal investigation."

Harry's dizziness was returning. It was all he could do to stand at his little table.

Thorne consulted a small book, which Harry took to be a legal manual. "As you are doubtless aware, this town has been placed under martial law—solely because of the absence of any civil legal authority," he said. "The army is empowered to arrest or detain civilians without warrant, or even reasonable grounds, in the belief that they are engaged, or if not detained might engage, in insurrection or disorder. We can limit the right of assembly, impose curfews, forbid the sale of alcohol, and search for and seize weapons without warrant." He closed the book. "As I said, I intend no trial here. But if there is sufficient evidence of infractions here, I will order those involved held under arrest until civil authority is restored. But in the case of the murder of the Reverend Ashby, if there is sufficient evidence, that person or persons will be subject to trial by military tribunal."

Harry stole a look at Allie. Her eyes were trained on him like cannons.

"So are you ready to proceed, Captain Raines?"

"Yes, sir." Harry sat down, pulling forth his notes from a pocket. He was surprised to find Tantou taking a seat beside him, then realized his friend meant to intervene in the event Harry did something awkward—like fall down.

But he managed to rise. There was no witness chair. He would have to turn and face his suspects where they sat. This was very informal, but not enough. He had counted on heated conversation and provocative exchanges, not so much legal procedure.

He turned first to Mr. Harding, who sat facing him like a statue of some stern pagan god. "Sir," Harry said, "can you tell me how it was that you led your unlawful lynch mob directly to the farm where Lemuel Krause was hiding?"

299

Harding said nothing. Lawyer Grieves rose instead. "I object, sir, to the characterization of the good citizens of this community as a lawless lynch mob."

"You will refrain from such reference, Captain Raines," said Thorne.

"I am also, sir," said Grieves, "surprised that testimony is not being taken under oath."

Colonel Thorne grimaced. "Has anyone a Bible?"

They were, of course, in a church. Knapp stepped forward, plucked a Bible from the back of a pew and brought it to Harding. He swore his oath as though cursing.

Approaching Harding, Harry commenced his presentation with as decorous as possible a revelation of the Reverend Ashby's romantic proclivities and citation of the ladies involved—leaving out his own mother. Thorne sat up straight, his eyes now wide and attentive.

When Harry mentioned Ann Harding, her father's complexion darkened almost to the color of plums. He began coughing and wheezing.

"You, you scoundrel!" Harding sputtered.

Harry waited until the man had regained control of himself.

"I do not believe that Miss Harding was romantically involved with Reverend Ashby," Harry said, "and did not mean to imply that. She admired him greatly, but her true love, I believe, was the unfortunate Lemuel Krause." He turned to address Harding directly. "Which is why I believe Mr. Harding killed him or had him killed."

"Our main concern here, Captain Raines," said Thorne, "is the demise of the Reverend."

"Yes, sir. I'll get to that."

"To begin with, please."

Reordering his thoughts, Harry laid out his essential premise. "The Reverend Ashby was killed for the reasons stated on the note that was pinned to his body. He was indeed a Lincolnite—a Federal agent, working in the cause of suppressing the Southern rebellion and restoring the Union. The other murders were intended to distract from the true reason for Ashby's."

"You're saying they're all by the same hand?" Thorne asked.

"Hands, sir. It was a conspiracy—a conspiracy involving at least one very strong man and a small woman."

Harry proceeded to lay out the connections. Mr. Harding owned the building that housed Klostermann's tavern. Klostermann had brought the German language message to Krause, directing him to the Masterson farm where he was killed. Harding had led his group to the farm before going anywhere else. Mr. Harding was a Secessionist who was working secretly against the Union cause on the eve of the Antietam battle.

Further, Mrs. Ashby, who was from Roanoke, Virginia, far down in the very Confederate Shenandoah Valley and still had a plentitude of relatives there, had ample motive in wanting her husband dead. She had befriended Lemuel, who was more than willing to do her bidding. Klostermann, whose family also were longtime settlers in the Valley, had regularly sent messages to Harding and spied upon the conversations of Unionist customers at his bar.

Harry came reluctantly to the subject of Mrs. Robertson. He said their relationship had begun with her trying to shoot him and ended with her hired man trying to do the same. Without being too indelicate, he noted that Allie had made a point of physically distancing herself from him for the night during which Bannister had attacked. He also noted that he had seen Bannister working for the Confederates in Sharpsburg just before the battle. He concluded by saying that Allie had been on friendly terms with the Reverend Ashby earlier in the year.

"They're all connected," he said. "All these people."

Avoiding what he was sure was Allie's fierce glare, he deposited before Thorne Mrs. Ashby's journal, Klostermann's note directing Lemuel to the farm, the notes Mrs. Ashby had given him warning generals of assassins and declaring Harding a secessionist, and one of the spent, fatal bullets.

The colonel squinted unhappily at the bullet, then turned to Harry, motioning him close. "Is this all you have?" he asked.

"I might have more. This is what I want to begin with."

"This is not enough."

"Let's see how they respond."

Lawyer Grieves spoke for Harding, addressing first the question of his loyalty. "You have this note describing Mr. Harding as a Secessionist, Captain Raines. Did you take the time, sir, to inquire as to which secessionist movement this might refer?"

"What do you mean?"

"It may have escaped your notice, Captain—given your travels and long residence in the Tidewater and the Federal City—but the western counties of Virginia are in the process of seceding from the Confederate portions of the state and joining the United States as a free state. Petitions have been filed and votes taken. All that remains to establish a new state of West Virginia is formal annexation by the United States government. The third name signed to the petitions from Jefferson County, sir, is that of Mr. Harding. He is a Unionist who would happily bring the western counties into the Federal union as a non-slave state. If Confederate conspiracy there is, as you allege, Mr. Harding certainly had no part of it." He turned and bowed slightly to Colonel Thorne. "If you wish, your honor, I can obtain a copy of the secession petition. I had little time to prepare for this hearing."

"Is that necessary, Captain Raines?"

This revelation had struck Harry like a blow. "No, sir."

Lawyer Grieves turned to his client. "Mr. Harding, what led you and your search party to the farm the night Mr. Krause was killed?"

"We were on the Charles Town Road. We heard gun shots. We rode in that direction. We found Lemuel in the barn— dead. We brought his body back to Shepherdstown. That is all there is to it."

"You have witnesses to testify to the truth of this?"

"Yes. My clerk there. My two sons. Mr. Crim, the barber. We had nearly twenty in my party. They'll all tell you what happened."

Grieves turned to face Thorne. "And why had Lemuel Krause been taken under arrest in the first place?"

"He had tried to kill Raines, there."

Grieves abruptly addressed Harry. "Can you offer any proof of this? The boy was brought here unconscious from a blow to the head, apparently struck with a pistol barrel. Seems more likely you tried to kill him, rather than the other way around."

"He fired a shot at me. One of my fellow scouts struck that blow to keep him from firing another."

"The Indian."

"He's a French Canadian, sir—a scout in the service of General McClellan, just as he served General Grant and General Kearny out West."

The lawyer stepped before Klostermann. "Did you write the note that Captain Raines has given the colonel—advising him to go to the farm?"

Hugo was sweating. "Yes. I give it to him. I wrote it."

"Lemuel Krause was in the custody of the U.S. Army," Grieves said. "You are aware that by aiding him in his escape, you have committed a serious infraction?"

"I didn't aid him in escape. He climbed out the window all by himself. It was the Army that left the window unlocked."

"Nevertheless, you are in jeopardy. Why did you put yourself at risk to help him?"

"He was a good boy. I was afraid for him."

"Why? He was in Federal custody—under the protection of the Army."

"Harry Raines. I was afraid for what he would do. He and his friend almost broke Lemuel's head open."

"Why then would you want Lemuel on the outside—where Captain Raines could get at him?"

"I thought he would be safer away from this town."

Harry's head was reeling and he was having difficulty following the colloquy. He couldn't understand why Lawyer Grieves was being so hard on Hugo. The tavern keeper had been working for Harding. That much was painfully clear. Harry had been talking his head off in front of Klostermann, assured by O'Malley that he was a strong Union man who had helped when he could with the Underground Railroad. Harding, it had just been shown, was also a Union man—a supporter of a slave-free state of West Virginia.

"Colonel Thorne," said Harry, putting a hand to the back of a pew to steady himself. "May I interject with a few questions?"

"As I understand my instructions from headquarters, you can do fairly much as you please, Captain Raines," Thorne said. "Certainly you can't make this proceeding any more irregular than it's become."

Harry ignored this, focusing entirely on Klostermann. Waiting for his head to clear, he walked across the floor to stand directly in front of the man.

"Hugo, you have been spying on your customers ever since you opened your establishment, haven't you?"

"There is gossip. That's what you hear in barrooms. Gossip. Sure, I gossip. Just like you and your friends."

"You don't just gossip, Hugo. You send messages to Mr. Harding."

"I don't know what it is you are saying."

"Yesterday you eavesdropped on a conversation I was having with my associates. You sent your man out back to run down to Mr. Harding and relate whatever you heard us say that you felt important."

"I sent him to tell Mr. Harding I would be late with the rent. I lost a lot of business because of the fighting."

"Why didn't you tell him yourself?"

"Because I was afraid he would be angry."

Harry moved to Harding. "Is Klostermann's story true?"

Before the man could respond, there was a commotion at the front of the church. A cavalry captain strode in, smacking his dusty gantlets across his thigh as he advanced. "Which one is Harrison Raines?"

The colonel nodded toward Harry. The captain handed him a folded dispatch, began a salute, thought better of it, then strode out again.

The message was brief:

*The President is here. Come at once.*
*Maj. A. E. Allen*

The name was the sobriquet Pinkerton used in his operational correspondence.

The President. Small wonder Pinkerton had been trying to reach him.

Harry pondered the matter, standing silent with all eyes upon him. "Assassins," the message to Reverend Ashby had said. Not "murderers." Not "killers."

Going to the colonel, Harry showed him the dispatch. Thorne's eyebrows shot up. "The President?"

Harry placed his finger to his lips. "I must go. We cannot proceed with this."

"Surely not, but what do I with these people?"

Thinking upon this, Harry rubbed his chin, giving the assemblage a quick glance. "Let them go."

"Sir?"

"I've been an idiot. Let them go. All of them." He surveyed the group one more time. "No. Keep Klostermann. Under guard."

His head was clear now. He strode out of the church even more rapidly than the cavalry captain—Tantou and Sergeant Knapp following quickly behind.

He thought he heard Allie call his name, but there was no time for that.

# Thirty-One

They reached McClellan's headquarters a little before noon, finding it bristling with soldiery but without the general or his enormous staff. With the President in the camp, the troops seemed excited—and not a little nervous.

"I'm one of Mr. Pinkerton's scouts!" Harry shouted to a corporal. "I need to find him, quick!"

The soldier looked them over, taking apparent comfort in Sergeant Knapp's presence. "He's up along that ridge there, above the main camp," the corporal said. "It's a big white headquarters tent, above all the others. You see all those soldiers around it? That's because the President's there."

"Thank you," Harry said, turning his horse with a sharp pull of rein.

"Wait a minute. Hold on there. Your name, sir?"

"Captain Raines. Harrison Raines. With Pinkerton for a year now. So's he." He nodded toward Tantou.

The corporal scribbled this down on a piece of paper he took from his pocket. "All right. You can go now. They may not let you near him."

Indeed, the perimeter guard established for the presidential meeting took a dim view of armed civilians thundering up the slope toward the commander-in-chief. Two of the soldiers leveled muskets at Harry's chest.

Luckily, he was wearing spectacles, and able to spot Pinkerton lounging against a tree a few yards from the big tent. The great detective's eyes were on the open tent flap, not searching for dangers that might lie elsewhere.

"I've come to see him," Harry said, pointing. "The man in

the derby. Pinkerton. I'm one of his scouts! Damn it, man! This is urgent!"

Pinkerton remained oblivious to his presence. A lieutenant came up to Harry and demanded to know the meaning of the ruckus. Calming himself, Harry repeated his request to see Pinkerton, again stressing the urgency of his need. Warily, the young officer considered this, then with some obvious reluctance turned and trudged up the rise toward the Secret Service chief. Harry wished he had sent a runner.

Tantou brought his horse up beside Harry's. Knapp followed. "We are looking for two men only?" Tantou asked.

"Two tall men," Harry replied. "The Singletons are six feet and four inches the both of them." He looked to a clump of trees just above and to the left of the headquarters tent; then another below and to the right. Turning in his saddle, he surveyed the city of tents below. They could harbor a thousand assassins.

"If they're here, I imagine they'll be in Federal uniforms," said Knapp. "Lord knows they had ample pickings on the battlefield."

He was right. Any civilian bearing arms would be challenged, as Harry and his party had been. Nothing needed less explaining than a man in blue with a musket.

They would not be using muskets, whose accurate range was no more than a hundred yards. Rifles would be required. But from what firing point?

Harry pointed to the nearest clump of trees. "Jack, Christopher. While I'm talking to Pinkerton, scout that tree line—all the way around to the right."

"But they're mostly behind where the President is," Knapp said. "Not much of a clear shot."

"They only need one. I just want to be sure of things."

Tantou prodded his horse forward, saying nothing. Knapp shrugged and moved on up the rise also. Harry turned again, pleased to see Pinkerton coming down the slope.

"At last you arrive, Raines," Pinkerton said. He removed his hat and wiped his balding head. "I need every man. Have you concluded that business in Shepherdstown?"

"Not satisfactorily, sir. I detained the wrong people. The right ones, I fear, are here. Assassins, Mr. Pinkerton. The Reverend Ashby was going to warn us."

"Assassins here now?" Pinkerton looked over the ground as frantically as Harry had done—and needed still to do.

"They're named Singleton. The worst men in town and Secesh to the marrow. I am certain they are here and mean harm to Mr. Lincoln."

"How so?"

"There's not time to explain, Mr. Pinkerton. You must get the President away from this place."

"That's impossible, Raines. He's meeting with General McClellan. They're deciding the fate of the Republic—of the Union Army. And most certainly deciding the fate of General McClellan. Though I do not understand how there can be complaint about so decided a victory."

Harry was prepared to argue against that assertion all that day. But there was indeed no time—not another minute. "Mr. Pinkerton, I do believe these men are here. I would urge you to organize search parties to go through the camp—all the ground within rifle range. All the tents. Please."

There was some stirring among the many officers about the tent. A moment later, the President and McClellan came out into the sunlight.

"Harry, I cannot disturb this event."

The officers were organizing themselves into a group—much like a squad of ordinary soldiers falling into a formation. Lincoln, towering over them all—especially General McClellan—took his own place just to the right of the commanding general. Harry's strong admiration for the President had increased tenfold with the news of the Emancipation Proclamation, but he had to concede that Lincoln in his inelegant frock coat struck a preposterous figure among the brilliantly uniformed officers. His absurdly high top hat added an almost comic touch. He seemed much the figure depicted in the vitriolic cartoons of the opposition Democratic newspapers.

He suddenly realized the reason for this peculiar assemblage. A photograph was being taken. The artist was not Harry's friend and drinking companion Matthew Brady, whose long, pointed nose with beard to match made him unmistakable at almost any distance. Harry knew not who the photographer was, but the situation was dangerous. Lincoln standing there, unmoving, recognizable from half or a mile away, was the best target presented any adversary gathered at this bloody battlefield.

"This is madness, Mr. Pinkerton. You must get the President to a safe place at once."

"But Harry, if your assassins are the threat you say, why have they not yet attacked? Mr. Lincoln has been here all morning."

Tantou and Knapp had reconnoitered the trees to the left of and behind the tent and were rounding the small woods to the right.

"Mr. Pinkerton, I am begging you to trust me. I wish only the president's safety."

"He wouldn't leave if I put a pistol to his breast to demand it, Harry. But I will scratch up some soldiers for you, if you will wait."

"Thank you."

Pinkerton walked too slowly to the captain of the guard. While they negotiated the deployment, Harry impatiently turned again toward the vastness of tents stretching down the slope.

Tantou came cantering up beside him—Knapp not far behind. "No one is in the trees, Harry Raines."

Harry scanned the camp again. "If you were to do such a thing, Jack, where would you position yourself?"

Tantou looked to the President and the general, then back down the slope. "From inside one of those tents."

"Which tent?"

"Any of those in front. One or two rows back, maybe—if there is a clear shot."

"How can there not be a clear shot? He stands up there like a flag pole. I don't think Pinkerton believes me. Though a day ago he was in panic."

"What do you want to do, Harry Raines?"

"What I want to do is run up there and shout, 'Get down, you damn fool!' But I'd probably get shot myself by these troopers." He studied the trees behind them for a moment, then dismounted and pulled his field glasses from his saddle-bag. "Can you get up that tree. Jack? The big elm?"

Tantou needed only a quick glance. "Yes."

Harry handed him the field glasses. "Take these—and that long gun of yours. Get up in that tree and if you see one of the Singletons—anybody you think might be one of them, taking a mark on the President—shoot him."

"Maybe I shoot an innocent soldier."

"Take care not to. And take care not to shoot me. I'm going down there."

Tantou nodded, then swung his mount into a trot back up the ridge. Pinkerton finally concluded his discussion with the officer and headed back toward Harry—only three soldiers following him.

"You are perspiring, Raines," Pinkerton said. "Are you ill?"

"I am fretful, Mr. Pinkerton. Is there no way you can persuade him to show more sense?"

"He feels that it would be an insult to General McClellan. If he cannot be safe here—in the midst of the army—where then?"

"You don't believe me."

"Harry, we have been through half this day without harm." He gave Harry a reassuring pat.

Too much time was passing. "You may well be right, Mr. Pinkerton, and I wrong. But as I could be right, let me have my way."

Pinkerton backed away a step. "Yes, yes, Harry." He gestured. "I've brought you these men."

A boy with foraging cap askew, an overweight man in spectacles, and a dark-bearded man with angry eyes—all privates.

"Mr. Pinkerton, we should search the whole camp."

"Yes, yes. Be at it."

Harry drew his small force aside, urging them close. "We're after killers, Secesh assassins. Two of them. Very tall young men, and likely dressed in Union blue. I know them. Sergeant Knapp knows enough about them to spot them. You know what's at stake."

"You mean Lincoln?" said the angry-eyed fellow.

"Yes. Mr. Lincoln." He sighed. "We believe they may use one of these tents for cover. What I want to do is go through all the tents—starting with the row immediately before us. We'll split up and start at both ends." He nodded to the angry-eyed man. "You come with me. You two go with Sergeant Knapp."

The angry-eyed man eyed Harry's Navy Colt. "This'll be close work. Muskets'll get in the way. We need pistols."

Harry considered this. "No time. Fix bayonets. They'll do for close work."

The soldiers they encountered did not take kindly to Harry's unannounced intrusion. One corporal with a pronounced Irish accent tried to bar Harry's way into his tent, relenting only at the prodding of the angry-eyed private's bayonet.

There was a woman in there. A mere girl from the looks of her. But no one else.

"She's my sister," said the corporal.

"It doesn't matter," Harry said. "We're not looking for a woman."

He was struck by the abundance of females in the camp—washing women, cooks, prostitutes like the lass in the corporal's abode, wives accompanying their husbands, nurses like Miss Barton and Caitlin Howard.

The two of them moved on down the line, interrupting a card game, rousing a drunken soldier from his slumbers, disturbing a solemn setting in which a soldier was reading the Bible to two others, finding several tents completely empty.

Harry went to the back of one, spreading the opening an inch or two. He could see Lincoln, still posing for photographs with McClellan. It took such a long time to complete a single plate.

He stepped back. Tantou had excellent eyesight.

Knapp and his men entered. "Nothing," the sergeant said.

"Next row," Harry said.

They went four rows more, with the same negligible result. A fifth row beckoned, and many more after that. He was reluctant to go too much farther down the slope. It would be a hard pull getting back up the hill if anything happened.

"One more row," he said to Knapp.

The sergeant viewed him skeptically, then shrugged. In his time, Knapp must have obeyed a hundred orders he found less than sensible.

They started in the middle this time, each team working its way toward the end. But the result was the same. The tents either contained innocent soldiers or were empty. Harry was turning back when he thought he heard his name called.

Looking sharply down the lane between the tents, he saw Knapp pointing up the hill. Not comprehending, Harry broke into the double quick to join him.

"I saw a tall soldier go into a tent up there," Knapp said.

Harry caught his breath. His wooziness was returning. "Which tent?"

"Fifth from the left," said Knapp. "As I recollect."

"He was carrying a weapon?"

"Yes, indeed."

"Then let's go."

As they moved up the rise, they devised a sort of plan, though not much of one. Harry would lead the way into the tent. Knapp would follow, providing cover. The three soldiers would watch for escape by another exit.

One row away, Harry paused to check the load of his Navy Colt. He was ill-prepared for the gunshot that seemed to shatter the entire world.

Knapp was still standing. So were the three soldiers. Up at the top of the rise, Lincoln was not to be seen, but there was not the commotion that would have attended upon a presidential injury.

"We go!" Harry said. "Hurry!"

They went to either side of the next tent. As they came to the following lane, there was another shot. A moment later, a tall soldier Harry was sure was Samuel Singleton stumbled forth from the tent Knapp had indicated, dropped the rifle he was carrying, and then dropped to the ground himself like a felled tree.

Lunging on, Harry tripped over a taut rope and slammed down against the hard earth, his pistol discharging into the dirt. He took a breath and then thrust himself back onto his feet.

Knapp had stopped, watching him. Up by the tent, soldiers who had pressed forward from either end of the camp now retreated a few yards. There were civilians among them as well, including women—frightened but drawn to the excitement.

The angry-eyed private came to Harry's side. "Two of 'em?"

"Yes," said Harry. He cocked his revolver again, more cautious now, and walked the rest of the way to Samuel.

The boy had a horrible wound in the abdomen, carved by a large bore weapon. He was alive, his pale blue eyes staring at a sky of the same color, but motionless. His injury was so profound he could not even moan. Harry still could hear the cries of the Antietam wounded when he tried to go to sleep at night.

Two brothers.

Harry moved to the side of the tent opening, thinking himself an idiot to seek protection from a thin piece of canvas. Pulling the flap aside no more than an inch, he saw the splayed legs of Eben Singleton.

Just beyond were small, black shoes just beneath a woman's skirt. Harry pulled the tent flap further to the side, just as Peggy Singleton turned from her position at the tent's rear opening to aim a long rifle at him.

The blast of the discharge that followed deafened him utterly.

# Thirty-Two

The President's soulful face looked more lined and weary than Harry had ever seen it, but the eyes, at least, reflected some happiness. Certainly some humor.

"This puts me in mind of a story," he said. "Once, back in Illinois, a woman was riding horseback through the woods. As I stopped to let her pass, she also stopped and, looking at me intently, said, 'I do believe you are the ugliest man I ever saw.' Said I, 'Madam, you are probably right, but I can't help it.' 'No,' she said, 'you can't help it, but you might stay at home.'"

Harry had heard this story before, so only smiled. Lincoln, who must have told it a hundred times that year alone, guffawed and slapped his knee, causing the small camp chair he was seated on to teeter. Behind him, General McClellan made a point of ignoring the repartee, staring out the opening of the tent.

"So, Raines, if this old face of mine is so ugly people want to shoot at it, I guess I'd better stay at home."

No laughter this time. Harry didn't know what to say.

"But none of us can do that," Lincoln said. He waved his long arm toward the tent opening and all it revealed. "Not while all these brave men are away from their homes." He leaned back. "Pinkerton has told me of your enterprise and exploits. I am once again much obliged to you. And I am grateful for what you've done for the army, irrespective of my own situation here."

"Thank you, sir."

"You should have a reward. If you were in uniform, I suppose I could make you a general. But I think we have far too many of those."

314

McClellan moved closer to the tent opening.

"There is something I would appreciate, Mr. Lincoln," Harry said. "A pass. To move between the lines."

"I thought you'd been given one."

"Yes, sir, and it has proved most useful and necessary. But this is for someone else. A woman who lives in Boonsboro but has business on the other side of the river. A woman who has been of considerable assistance to us. Certainly to me."

"A woman?"

"She has performed a great service. It was she who shot the last of the assassins."

Lincoln turned to Pinkerton, who with amazing swiftness produced a blank pass.

"Then she has surely earned it," the President said, putting the blank form on his knee. "Her name?"

"Mrs. Alice Robertson."

Lincoln wrote this out carefully, then signed the pass at the bottom. "I'm not sure my passes are respected," he said. "In the last year and a half, I have given passes to two hundred and fifty thousand men to go to Richmond, and not one has got there yet."

Harry laughed as he accepted the little document, as much now in amusement as gratitude.

McClellan walked out of the tent.

"Thank you, Mr. President," Harry said, rising. "And thank you for the proclamation. Now we truly have a cause."

Lincoln's eyes darkened slightly. He had held this cause sacred for three decades, no matter how much he disguised his zeal with carefully worded moderation. "Pinkerton tells me you were under fire in the battle."

"I charged no Rebel line, sir."

"You were of great service, Raines. So it is you and all those thousands like you who should be thanked for the proclamation."

Lincoln shook his hand. Harry stumbled out of the tent in something of a daze. He realized he had just experienced the most important moment of his life.

\*    \*    \*

The bodies of the Singletons had been laid out in a row outside the shack-like establishment of one of the military undertakers who were still doing business dealing with the wounded who were expiring daily. The embalmer was hovering just behind the soldiers who were standing guard over the three dead siblings, as though he feared some rival would snatch the bodies away.

Harry wondered at the man's relish for the job. Tantou had hit the belly of one of the brothers and the chest of the other with his large bore bullets, making a bloody mess of both. Allie's scatter gun had sent Peggy Singleton off to her reward no longer pretty.

Allie, Tantou, and Knapp stood off to the side, waiting for Harry to complete his examination. He did not take long.

"Will there be some kind of inquiry?" Allie asked.

"No," said Harry, flatly. Pinkerton and the President had assured him of that.

Tantou was holding his arm, which hung a bit askew. Harry had never seen him show pain before.

"What's wrong with your arm?" Harry asked.

"One of McClellan's guards shot at me. I think he thought I was one of these people."

"Did he hit you?"

"No. I jumped out of the tree so he would not have another chance to hit me. But I did not jump well."

"Can you ride?" Harry asked. As he thought upon it, Tantou could probably ride with every limb injured.

"Yes, Harry Raines. I can ride."

"Then let's ride."

"Where are you going?" asked Allie.

"Back to Shepherdstown. I'll stand you all to whiskey. You, too, Christopher. Mr. Pinkerton is arranging a month's furlough for you. You're free to go where you will."

"That's worth the lifting of a glass."

"I hope you will join us, Alice," Harry said, softly.

"A woman? In a saloon."

"After today, ma'am. I can think of no objection."

"Well, I can. I'm going back to Boonsboro—after I pick up my things."

"Allie . . ."

"Glad I could be of service to you, Harry. That Secesh vixen
would have killed you in another second. Did you acquire my
pass?"

Harry presented it to her as he might some valuable jewel.
"As requested."

She quickly put it in a pocket of her skirt. "I will put it to
use."

"I don't understand your need of it. Do you fear the Union
Army is going to skedaddle north again? Or do you have business down deep in Virginia?"

"I have business." She mounted her horse, spreading her
skirts carefully to either side of the saddle. "There'll be a
surprise waiting for you when you get home, sir."

"Surprise?"

"You go have your drinks. And do take your time. So that
the surprise will be waiting for you."

"Better I go home first."

"No. Do not do that. You'll ruin everything."

"You will not wait for me?"

"It's going to be a long war, Harry. We shall see each other
again." She moved on out at a fast trot.

As the rest of them went to their horses, one of a small mob
of newspaper reporters who had come out for the President's
meeting with the general broke away from the others and came
up to Harry.

"I know you," he said. "You're a regular at the Palace of
Fortune—least you were. What're you doing out here?"

"I have a farm out here."

"You were in the President's tent."

"We are acquainted."

"Those civilians who were killed—you know what that's
about?"

Pinkerton and Mr. Lincoln were firm on the point that they
wanted nothing said about an assassination attempt. "It'll only
encourage 'em," Lincoln had said.

"They're people from over in Virginia—Confederate spies,"

Harry told the newspaperman. "That's what I'm told, anyway. Some soldiers cornered them and they made a fight of it."

"Do you know who killed them?"

"I believe it was an Army scout." Harry pointed. "He was over by that tree."

"Thank you, Raines. Obliged." The reporter took off hurriedly in the direction of the tree from which Tantou had fallen.

They took O'Malley from his work and started toward a saloon near the river landing, assuming Klostermann's was closed.

But it wasn't. They found the old black man tending bar and one of Harding's sons over at a corner table—from the look of it, going over accounts.

"Whiskey, please," said Harry. "A bottle. Old Overholt, if you have it."

"Yessir, I do. Some came in today from Pennsylvania."

"A moment. Where is Klostermann?"

"Mr. Klostermann, they done take him to jail."

"At the Hotel Entler?"

"No, sir, they take him up to Hagerstown."

"But why is the saloon open?"

"Mr. Harding, he own the building. He say he wants the bar open, so open up I do."

"Thank you."

"When you going to tell us?" O'Malley said, when the whiskey had been served.

"Tell you what?" asked Harry, after taking a healthy sip. The events of the day were wreaking havoc on his nerves.

"How you came to decide to let all those people go. How you figured it was the Singletons after all."

"I didn't figure out much at all, truth to tell," Harry replied. "Mostly I figured out that the things I had figured out were wrong."

"Such as Mrs. Robertson," said Knapp.

"Most especially Mrs. Robertson. But I got a lot more wrong than that. I should have stuck to what I thought at the

318

beginning—that the Reverend Ashby had been murdered because he was working for the Union—that they hung him to that tree as an example, as kings did in the Dark Ages." He drank again. "But when those poor young women were treated the same brutal way, I half believed it had to be widow Ashby who was taking revenge—with Lemuel's help. Who else could hold such a grievance against them?"

"But you let her go."

"As I thought upon it, it made no sense. She had reason to take revenge on my mother, to be frank about it. But she didn't. They remained good friends. She could have gone after Mrs. Robertson with equal reason, but she did nothing. Such barbarism wasn't in her nature. And surely she couldn't have persuaded Lemuel to kill Ann Harding, the love of his life. Just wouldn't have. It was ridiculous. The Singletons made a big mistake when they picked Ann for a victim."

"But then you thought Harding was behind it all?" said O'Malley.

Knapp was following all this closely, but Tantou seemed little interested.

"It had to be Rebs—fanatics. The girls' murders were just to distract us from their main intent, which was the assassination Ashby was going to warn us about. I couldn't believe they'd want to eliminate McClellan from command, but there are other generals who'd be a real loss. When the President turned up, that clinched it."

"But Harding?" O'Malley asked. "His own daughter?"

"I always took him for Secesh. He has a cousin in the Reb army. Hugo Klostermann was working for him—spying for him—or so I thought. And I knew for a fact Hugo was lying to me—in most particular about the Singleton brothers being killed by a Federal cavalry patrol down at Ranson outside Charles Town. McClellan hasn't allowed a single blue coat more than five miles beyond Shepherdstown, on either the Harper's Ferry or the Charles Town roads. He's afraid of starting another battle. The general orders for today were to avoid hostilities at all cost."

"Those could be the general's orders for the rest of the war," said Knapp.

"Which is why it's taking so long," Harry said.

"When you found out Harding was for the Union, for an independent state of West Virginia—that's what turned you around?" O'Malley asked.

"It gave my brain a push. Which it needed. I stopped to think about Lemuel's going to the Singleton place. Why did he do that? Why did he take a shot at the first person to come riding up the lane? Lemuel was after the Singletons because he'd figured out they'd killed Ashby and Ann Harding. He took a shot at me because he presumed it would be a Singleton riding up the trail to the Singleton house. Who else would want to go there? Thank God he wasn't a better shot—or was too impatient to wait for the range to close."

"Maybe just too afraid to let the Singletons near him. Those two could shoot the legs off a flea," O'Malley observed.

"Which is another reason I doubt they'd let themselves get killed by a Union cavalry patrol," Harry said.

A group of civilians entered the barroom—men from the town. Harry half expected Harding to be among them, but he was not. One of the men, Tobias Johnson, operated the town print shop and published a newspaper that came out irregularly. Harry hoped he would not come around to ask questions. Johnson nodded to Harry, but proceeded to the bar with the others. Harry replied with a wave, but then quickly turned away.

"How did you know the Singletons were about to try to kill the President?" Knapp asked.

"I didn't. But I thought that if there was a chance of that happening, we ought to make sure it didn't."

"'Damned close run thing,'" said Knapp. "Isn't that what Wellington said after Waterloo?"

"You have far too much education for a sergeant," Harry replied. "I'm going to make you a lieutenant."

"What?"

"Actually, it's President Lincoln who is going to make you a lieutenant—part of your reward. Soon you'll outrank that

320

officer who tried to have you shot." Harry turned to his friend the Metis. "As for you, Jack, you need no longer worry about our government sending you back to Canada to answer for that trouble with the RCMP. They want you to stay with the Army."

"As this army never leaves here, that is very fine with me, Harry Raines."

"What about you, Raines?" Knapp asked.

He pondered the question. He realized that, with this business done, his war was over. Pinkerton wouldn't dare coerce him into service after what they'd managed to accomplish for Lincoln's sake. His future, now, lay just two miles down the road.

"I am content," he said, draining his glass. "But I think I am going to get drunk." He waved to the black man for another bottle.

His horse got him home by sunset, needing no guidance. As they came up the lane, he recalled suddenly that Allie had promised him a surprise. When he neared the porch, he saw precisely what it was—and was overjoyed.

"Caesar Augustus!" he cried.

The man who was once briefly his slave and always his best friend stood just outside the door, joined in a moment by Estelle and Evangeline.

"Marse Harry!" he called back, with a wide grin.

Harry hated it when Caesar Augustus addressed him so, but let the matter pass. He dismounted, clumsily, but managed to keep his feet. When he had mounted the steps to the porch, the two men embraced, then stepped back.

"You tired of the land of the free?" Harry asked.

"With the Proclamation, this here's gonna be the land of the free."

"That's not until January."

"It's good enough for me. There were good people in Pennsylvania, but this is home."

"It's going to be a new state in the Union," Harry said. "The State of West Virginia. No slavery—with or without the Proclamation."

"Then you must be a happy man."

"You've no idea." The three of them could go back into the horse business—himself, Caesar Augustus, and his brother. Robert wouldn't have to switch sides and join the Union Army. All he needed to do was swear an oath of loyalty to the United States of America and become civilian. The war would end for all of them.

"Excuse me," he said. "I must talk to Robert." He went through the door and started up the stairs.

"Wait!" said Caesar Augustus.

Harry kept going. "Be right back."

"Marse Harry. Stop! He's gone!"

Harry froze. "Gone? You mean, dead?"

"No, sir. I mean gone from this place. Gone back South."

Harry came back down the stairs slowly. "But how? He could barely walk. And there're Union pickets and cavalry patrols out there."

"The lady took him."

"What lady?"

"Lady with long yellow hair. Said she was your friend. Said she had a pass through the lines. She got Robert dressed in some of your clothes. Got him on a horse. And off they went."

A falling tree couldn't have stunned him as much as he was now. Harry went over to his black horsehair sofa. His head reeling, he dropped onto it, searching for belief. Robert hated this war as much as he did. By going back into Confederate service, he'd be once again at risk.

"You want supper, Mr. Harry?" Estelle asked.

Harry shook his head, muttered "Thank you," and then stretched out on the sofa, boots and all, closing his eyes.

When he awoke, it was to the dim red glow of firelight. Someone had pulled off his boots and put a blanket over him. That person was still in the room.

"Caesar Augustus?"

There was no response, but then the person sat on the sofa beside him, running cool fingers over his cheek.

"Mrs. Robertson," he said.

"The name is Allie."

"I thought you'd gone off with my brother."

"I did, but not for long. I got him through the Federal line, got him to some Rebel cavalry."

"You've no idea how much I wish you hadn't."

"He wouldn't have sworn the oath you wanted him to. He just wouldn't do it. And if the Federals took him, he'd end up in a prison camp. He'd die there, Harry. You know that. Specially if it was one of those places like Camp Douglas up in Chicago. He'd never survive the winter."

He looked up into her large blue eyes, which had dancing glints of firelight reflected in them. "I'm sorry I subjected you to such disagreeable inconvenience today."

"That's all right. I'll find a way to make you pay." Her grin looked slightly maniacal in the firelight.

"This is going to be a very long war, Allie."

She kissed him. "'Bout time you figured that out, plantation man."

# Thirty-Three

They had not made Harry a general, but he had with amazing swiftness received a government contract to acquire, break, and train a thousand new cavalry mounts, delivering as many as possible for the Army of the Potomac's next campaign. Harry, Caesar Augustus, and O'Malley had traveled upriver to Ohio and brought in the first one hundred—animals of mixed quality but sufficient to the need. It saddened Harry to think how many were going to end up like the poor beasts slaughtered at Antietam. Only a question of time.

Harry prided himself on being one of the very best riders in the state of Virginia, but when it came to breaking and training, Caesar Augustus was his superior, just as O'Malley was the better at treating an animal's ailments. It occurred to Harry that the blacksmith could just as well have been a horse doctor as a tradesman, though people doubtless trusted him more in the latter capacity.

Caesar Augustus had a fine bay gelding in the fenced-in pasture behind the main barn, and was working him on a long lead, drawing it ever closer as the horse made his circle. He worked in shirt-sleeves, despite the cold. A wind coming down the river was stiffening. Harry pulled his coat tighter around him and put on his gloves.

His name was called; the voice feminine.

"There's a carriage coming up the lane—a barrouche."

Harry could not imagine anything so elegant turning up in this country. Perhaps Harding, as he had come clean on the true nature of his political sentiments, was now revealing to his fellow citizens of Shepherdstown the true extent of his wealth.

Coming around the side of the house, Harry saw that the callers were a short man in a derby hat and checked suit and a dark-haired woman wearing no millinery at all. The carriage was being driven by a coachman in blue military uniform. An armed soldier sat to his right.

The man in the derby descended from the vehicle but the woman remained where she was. Harry put on his spectacles. He'd already recognized Pinkerton. The woman was Louise Devereux, and she was not, he gathered, returning to the farm.

Harry continued across the yard. As he passed, he took note of Allie, Estelle and little Evangeline observing from the porch.

"Mr. Pinkerton," Harry said.

They shook hands. "Terrible news," said Pinkerton. "Terrible news."

Harry could only wait. Had they lost another battle?

"General McClellan has been relieved of command," Pinkerton said. "Can you imagine? After the great victory here? It was the President's own decision. He complained we let Lee's army escape and then failed to pursue him. The Rebs are back between Washington and Richmond and Mr. Lincoln has rashly given command of General McClellan's army to General Burnside."

Here was good news and very bad. If the Rebel army could not yet be destroyed, outside Richmond was the best place for it to be. General Lee pinned down defending his capital was infinitely to be preferred to a General Lee marauding about the countryside—especially in the countryside of the Upper Potomac Valley.

The Rebel army would never be so much as inconvenienced if McClellan remained in command of the Union forces. Lincoln had seen to the general's request for more horses to replace so many that McClellan complained were fatigued, doing so with a tersely written note in his own presidential hand asking what the general's horses had done that could possibly have fatigued them.

So the Union Army would at long last be on the move again—but in the hands of Ambrose Burnside. His chief contribution to the great battle in September had been to pointlessly send assault column after assault column across the stone bridge on the Army's left flank instead of seeking another crossing over Antietam Creek. Until General Rodman had gotten some regiments across Snavely's Ford, a few hundred Georgia troops had held Burnside's entire corps at bay.

"Burnside is a poor choice," Harry said.

"Yes, but the Congress likes him. I fear our general has fallen out of favor with that den of iniquity. Otherwise, the President would not have dared do what he did."

"Will you work for Burnside?" Harry asked.

"No. I will serve our sacred cause, but in my fashion. I was hired by General McClellan to organize our secret service and I will depart with him. He is going back into the railroad business and will become my client."

"Client?"

"I am going back to Chicago and form a detective agency, Harry. It will be the greatest detective agency there is in the world. An army of keen-minded operatives using the most up-to-date techniques of police science. I will specialize in railroads—for without our railroads, the cause is lost—but will provide agents for the government as practicable and as needed."

Harry knew what was coming next.

"I'd like you to join us, Harry."

"I don't want to move to Chicago. I was there once in a January."

"I'll assign you wherever you wish. I need you, Raines. I could use Mr. Tantou as well. Joseph Leahy is coming with me. At least I have his promise. And the pay, sir, will be most generous. The railroads provide much better than the U.S. government."

"The U.S. government is providing nicely, thank you."

Pinkerton removed his hat, wiping the bald top of his head in nervous habit despite the cold. "You intend to stay here, Harry?"

"The war's passed on."

"The war isn't over."

Harry sighed, glancing over his shoulder to the porch. Allie's eyes were no longer on him, but on the lady in the carriage. "That is Louise Devereux in the barrouche, Mr. Pinkerton? Your erstwhile prisoner?"

"An able woman. She is coming to Chicago with us."

"You're not saying that just to entice me."

"She is abler than you, Harry."

Shaking his head, Harry walked over to the carriage. Louise, dressed very grandly, produced her gloved hand to be kissed. He shook it instead. "Miss Devereux, it is good to see you after so long an interval. It is good to see you well."

She gave him one of her dazzling curtain call smiles. "How nice to see you, Harry—in one piece after that horrible battle."

"You're going to Chicago? A lady of New Orleans."

"They have much in common. And Chicago has money."

"I shall be very happy for you."

"And I for you, Harry," she said with a quick glance at the women on the porch. "You must be quite content in all this, this domesticity."

"I find it most agreeable."

"So I recall."

Pinkerton was standing beside them, rapidly becoming uncomfortable with the direction of this conversation. "We must be off, Harry," he said, climbing aboard the carriage and taking a seat opposite Louise. "We're taking the noon train. Just stopped off to see you on the way."

"Won't you stop longer? Take some refreshment with us?"

"No, time, Harry. No time." Pinkerton paused. "You should know that Hugo Klostermann was shot yesterday by a firing squad, having been found guilty by a military tribunal of espionage."

"Espionage? He was just passing on barroom gossip."

"To ill effect, Harry. To very ill effect." He closed the carriage door. "We have patrols looking for the Hardings."

"What are you saying? John Harding, the banker?"

"And his sons. Klostermann, at his trial, sought leniency

327

by informing us of Mr. Harding's true involvement in the whole bloody business. Klostermann was working for Harding after all, and so were the Singletons."

"But he's one of us. He signed the statehood position."

"A useful thing for him to do, under the circumstances. But he did not want the Union in this part of Virginia. For whatever reason, he wished to maintain the status quo."

"This means he killed his own daughter, and I cannot believe that."

"According to Klostermann, the Singletons did that, but by accident. They were trying for Lemuel Krause, because of his connection to the Ashbys and their service to the Union."

"Then I was powerfully wrong," Harry said.

"You were right enough to save the President's life. That won't be forgotten."

Pinkerton looked to his driver, but Harry stayed him. "How soon does Burnside march?"

"He has begun already. It is already late in the year for campaigning. He heads directly south." Pinkerton leaned forward. "I leave you with a word of warning, Harry. Do not go to Washington. Lafayette Baker will be heading the Federal security service now. He is not only a corrupt and dangerous man, but he hates you."

Pinkerton tried once again to signal the driver, but this time it was Louise who stopped him. "I have not yet bid Harry a proper farewell," she said.

She motioned Harry near, then lifted herself in the seat to kiss him warmly and lengthily on the lips. "A fig for domesticity," she said, and with flashing eyes and a return of the dazzling smile, called to the driver herself to get underway. A crack of the whip, and they were off.

"And when will those two be returning?" Allie asked, when Harry finally mounted the porch steps.

"I should think not soon," he said.

"Not soon is soon enough," she said. "Come in now and have some dinner."

*  *  *

It was cold that night but they slept naked, clinging close to each other beneath a warm sheet, several blankets, and a thick counterpane. She seemed happy, but Harry was not so content. The reason had not to do with dissatisfaction, but rather too much of it.

She slept, and he did not. There was moonlight, and it touched the details of this familiar room, bringing hints of ghosts and many memories. When he was a very small child, but old enough to make the summer journeys to this place, he sometimes crept into this room and his mother's bed, seeking the reassurance of her presence.

Allie gave him that now. He would be so unhappy to leave her.

He rolled over, facing the window. The trees were bare of leaves and he could see a line of hills to the east, marking the divide in the mountains where the Potomac flowed through on its way to Washington.

She began rubbing his back. "You are restless tonight, plantation man."

"I cannot sleep."

"What ails you?"

"Nothing at all."

"What agitates you?"

He took in a deep breath, noting that her hand had ceased its comforting motions. "Allie, will you become my wife?"

She took her hand away and turned onto her back. When he did the same, he saw that she was staring up at the ceiling.

"I have thought upon this very question—much of this day and on other occasions," she said, quietly.

"And?"

"And I cannot. It was a hard thing, losing my husband, losing him the way I did. It was hard being without a man. You were a happy discovery, but I figured it as a passing encounter—like so much in these times. Now you are more than that. Much more. But I cannot marry you now. I do not wish to lose another husband, not like that. Marriage speaks to a future, and we none of us in this country have that."

329

"Marriage speaks of more."

She put her hand now on his chest. "Well, that we already have, Harry."

They lay still like that a long time, then he said the words he'd been holding back. "I'm going to ride in the morning for Burnside."

"I knew that the instant I saw that fancy carriage come up the lane."

"You saw my brother off to his army. It's the same with me. I can't stay here while all those men are marching south. Burnside's a fool. He'll need all the help he can get. I know that country as well as I know this. I know the Rappahannock River crossings. I can be of some value. I have to go."

"Who was that woman in the carriage?"

"Her name is Louise Devereux. She is one of Pinkerton's agents—an actress of considerable talent and an actual French countess, though Louisiana raised. No one's sure what she is besides."

"Why did she kiss you that way?"

"She saved my life once, and takes liberties. Pinkerton brought her along as bait in his hopes to beguile me into joining his enterprise in Chicago. But I think she came merely to mock me."

"You are not going in that direction?"

"No. Jack Tantou's coming by in the morning to say goodbye. I will ride with him to Burnside."

"Well, I cannot marry you, Harry. But I will wait. I must spend time with my people in Boonsboro, but if I am not here, you will know where to find me."

"I haven't even a *carte de visite* photograph of you to take with me."

"That you shall have—and more." She came close to him and kissed him. "Let us take our happiness where this war provides."